In spite of trayal, he'd allo..... for a favor.

Suspecting her affair with Carlos, he had surveillance equipment installed all over the mansion. Once he showed her the very graphic video of her and his uncle going at it in the satin-lined coffin, he'd used it to his advantage.

Michael suspected his uncle knew more about his parents' accident than he'd let on, but couldn't prove a thing. Desperate to uncover the truth, Michael blackmailed Candace into getting Carlos to confess on tape. If she failed, she'd be killed. Stuck between a rock and a hard spot, Candace had done things to the old coot that disgusted even her. But those things had made the old man sing like a canary and the taped confession had saved her life. After her mission was a done deal, Michael kicked her out of Vegas and told her if she ever returned, he would rip her lungs out.

Reaching Carlos DeVeccio's bedroom, she got a little thrill as old memories surfaced. Just a few more seconds and she'd fall into the arms of her lover. She smiled to herself. She had returned to Vegas for a reason. She was flat broke. But after tonight, Michael would be her ticket back into the world of luxury. Then she'd be mistress of the manor once more. And more to the point, she'd have access to his billion dollar bank roll.

With a devious smile, she pushed her way through the heavy mahogany door. Crossing the threshold, she entered the house of horrors. Carlos DeVeccio had been a real nut, one straight out of the books. But with her fetish for face masks, she loved his collection and had often come into his wing just to admire them. What a thrill it had been to have sex in the coffin, howling along with the werewolf. Some might think it a bit kinky, but they didn't know what they were missing. Calling out to her lover, her pulse quickened a beat. "Michael? Are you here yet, darling?"

That's when she heard it, manic laughter from the final circle of hell. A slither of fear trickled down her spine, releasing a wild rush of adrenaline. Carlos?

She thought about the death of Lacy Diamond. Two Ninja assassinations were no coincidence. Sensing danger, she felt for her sword. It was gone. Panic soared through her. Where the hell was it?

The laughter got louder and louder, moving in closer and closer. It seemed to be bouncing off the walls. She couldn't tell from which direction it was coming. Just then, the bell in the tower gonged, thundering off the walls like canon balls. Instinctively, she covered her ears with her hands. Where the hell was Michael?

Evil eyes from the face masks followed her every move. She had to escape this hell before it was too late. She couldn't think over the gonging of the bell. Every few seconds, the werewolf howled at the moon. She screamed, even though she knew no one would ever hear her. Floundering in wild disarray, disoriented by the darkness and relentless gonging, she searched in vain for the door. Her arms swam in mid-air, like a person drowning, desperate for an anchor, something to hold onto. She reached out and grabbed at nothing. She had to find a way out of this mausoleum of the living dead before it was too late. Where the hell was Michael?

The laughter got closer. Perspiration drenched her skin. The chilling laughter echoed in her ears, louder and louder, closer and closer. The bell in the bell tower broke through the thin filament of sanity she had left. The werewolf open his mouth and howled at the moon. Where was Michael? He'd know what to do. He was a master swordsman. His fencing skills were extraordinary. He could wield a Ninja star with his eyes closed and hit the mark. Where was he?

Blood thundered in her ears, but not loud enough to block out the manic laughter. It was close but she couldn't see a thing. She wished she had her sword. She turned to run; it was too late. She heard a distinct click. The killer had just depressed the button on her Zorro sword, releasing the thirty-seven inch blade. His psychotic laughter reached an ear-splitting crescendo just as the bell in the tower gonged out its last chime. From the dark shadows, Valentino pounced, her Zorro sword gleaming in the moonlight.

"Surprise!" he thrust the sword into her heart. "I promised to make you scream, darling Candace. Let me hear you scream."

MASK OF THE BETRAYER

Sharon Donovan

Whimsical Publications, LLC

Florida

Mask of the Betrayer is a work of fiction. Names, characters, and incidents are the products of the author's imagination and are either fictitious or are used fictitiously. Any resemblance to actual events or persons, living or dead, is entirely coincidental.

To purchase the authorized electronic edition of *Mask of the Betrayer*, visit www.whimsicalpublications.com

Cover art by Anastasia Rabiyah
Editing by Krystal Cranfield

Published in the United States by
Whimsical Publications, LLC
Florida

ISBN-13: 978-1-936167-06-7

Printed in the United States of America

ACKNOWLEDGEMENTS

To the staff at Whimsical Publications, LLC:
With special thanks to Janet Durbin for making this dream a reality. Krystal Cranfield for editing this book. Anastasia Rabiyah for the artwork.

Special note of thanks to:
Cold Case Homicide Detective Scott Evans of the Pittsburgh Police who supplied information about guns, obtaining a confession and getting into the mind of a killer.

My critique groups, partners and proof readers. And last but not least, to the readers. The mind has always fascinated me. It can bend. It can break. It can snap. Mask of the Betrayer is a chilling tale of mind manipulation and control. I hope you enjoy reading it as much as I enjoyed writing it.
Happy reading!

PROLOGUE

RED ROCK CANYON, NEVADA
TEN YEARS EARLIER

Deep in the underbrush of the Red Rock Mountains, The Hunter crept through the rugged terrain, a landscape of sharp twists and turns, toward the mansion nestled in the foothills. A moon hung low in the dark, desert sky. His eyesight as keen as the surrounding night predators, he slipped through the thicket, focused on his mission. The fragrant yellow flowers of the creosote bushes filled his senses. Power surged through him as he stalked through the dry carpet of the forest, pinecones crunching in his wake. A slight breeze stirred through the ponderosa pines, sounding like the wise, old whispers of the Paiute Indians buried thousands of feet below in the windblown sand.

He fingered the weapon in his hooded dark jacket, a *shuriken*, a Ninja star, a throwing death star laced with poison. His heart jackhammered in his chest, adrenaline pumping at a wild rhythm. He licked his lips in eager anticipation. From deep in the woods, a coyote howled, barely discernible over the wild beat of his heart.

He spotted the mansion in the distance, torch-lit lanterns casting willowy shadows on stained-glass windows. A bell tower loomed in eerie silence. Smooth marble lions with their mouths open in silent roars guarded the entrance gate. He scoffed to himself. As if they could keep him out. It would be poetic justice to wield the death sword into the old man's throat, watch his face twist into an ugly grimace as the poison seeped into his jugular vein and into his system, just the way he'd taught him to do when he'd trained him to be his number one assassin.

Adrenaline surged through him, filling him with a sense of power as potent as a deadly panther. How his fingers itched to hurl the death star into the betrayer's throat. *Easy now*, he warned himself as he emerged from the thicket and into the sagebrush-lined trail, crouching low in the shadows of the undulating pine branches. *Don't blow it, keep your cool.*

Despite the cold night air of the Mohave Desert, sweat trickled down his spine. But his insides remained cool. Blending into the shadows of the mansion, he shimmied along the red bricks of the estate, camouflaging himself in the swaying branches of the towering pines. From deep in the thicket, the throaty call of a raven screeched, foreboding an eerie warning. *How befitting*, The Hunter thought. And just like the poem, soon he'd be rapping at his chamber door, and DeVeccio would be nevermore.

Keeping low to the ground, the sounds of the night predators at his back, he crept up the stone steps leading to the mansion, sheathed his hands in latex gloves, and inserted a key in the heavy, mahogany door. He stood in the foyer of the two-story mansion, contemplating his moves. He glanced at his watch. Quarter to midnight. And when the clock strikes twelve, the death star will hit the mark. Bull's eye.

Water gushed from the gaping mouth of a lion head fountain, giving the foyer the look of a Greco sanctuary. A grand sweeping staircase led to upper wings. From upstairs, the sultry vocals of Patsy Cline drifted down, the bittersweet lyrics laced with heart-wrenching pain. A lamp in the parlor cast an amber glow on tiger skin sofas. A large screen television and wet bar took up an entire wall.

Creeping along the marble floors to the sleek mahogany bar, The Hunter liberated a bottle of finely-aged bourbon from the shelf, wishing he had time to indulge in a premium cigar from the walk-in humidor. He raised the jug in a silent toast and slugged some back.

Cocktails over, he strutted down the hallway, the lyrics of his favorite song playing in his head. *A hunting we will go, a hunting we will go. Heigh ho the dairy-o, a hunting we will go. We'll catch a fox and put him in a box. Heigh ho the dairy-o, a hunting we will go.*

Reaching the great room, his majesty's private domain, he stalked across the threshold and entered the hall, giving a mock salute with his middle finger. The roiling presence of Carlos DeVeccio filled the room, making his nerve endings twitch. His fingers tightened around the death star as vivid memories flashed through his head.

The Hunter sneered at the twelve leather chairs surrounding the large ebony table where the big man presided over meetings every Saturday. Then he looked up at the wall where a pair of sabre swords gleamed in the moonlight. Directly above the king's throne, presenting a daunting aura, a fleshless face mask hung. The Hunter scoffed, envisioning the big man ruling the world with his big shot fist from behind his masquerade. He thought about the coming attractions and smiled. In three easy strides, he reached the wall. With lightning speed, his jack-be-nimble fingers removed the skull mask from its hook and fastened it around his face.

Sneaking up the staircase, focused on his mission, The Hunter blended into the shadows of the dark wood paneling, concentrating on every sight, scent, and sound, just as the old man had taught him. From the bathroom, pellets of water hit the glass shower door as steady as a hard rain. The old man was singing, his low voice echoing through the corridor. From behind his mask, The Hunter grinned.

Entering the master bath, The Hunter silhouetted himself behind the doorjamb, crouched down low, and waited, fingering his Ninja weapon. The water stopped with a jarring screech. The Hunter's heart danced a wild rhythm, his fingers tightly coiled around the death star, ready to wield it at a second's notice. *Hurry up,* he silently urged. *Come on, come on out.*

Just as Carlos DeVeccio stepped out of the shower, the bell in the tower gonged out twelve piercing chimes. Programmed to execute the betrayer at midnight, The Hunter's heartbeat accelerated. His fingers tightened and released, tightened and released. *Come on, you bastard. You deserve to die for what you did. Turn around.*

Still singing, Carlos DeVeccio did an about face when he caught sight of the Ninja star whizzing through the air, the deadly blade aimed straight for his throat. With a hissing zing, it hit its mark.

Stunned, he fell to the floor with a heavy thud, his face twisting in pain as the poison seeped into his jugular vein and into his system. Lying on the cold, tile floor, belly up and dying, his eyes grew wide with shock when The Hunter removed his mask and grinned at him.

Still smiling, The Hunter shrouded the corpse, whistling the tune to his favorite song.

CHAPTER ONE

Present Day Las Vegas

Pouring himself two fingers of finely-aged bourbon, billionaire business tycoon Michael DeVeccio walked onto the verandah of his mansion and gazed into the foothills. The raw beauty of the Red Rock Mountains encompassed him with miles of open valleys, rugged terrain where rock formation changed from a startling white limestone to an iron-rich red, and lush forests full of petrified logs and wildlife. What a rush to climb to the top of the mountain and survey the dazzling Vegas Strip like king of the jungle.

Fishing a Marlboro from the pack, he tapped it three times on the parapet before lighting it. He inhaled deeply, allowing the nicotine to filter into his brain.

Under The Hunter's moon, night predators slithered out of the underbrush, just on the periphery of the jagged twists and turns of the canyon. A coyote howled from deep in the woods, its keening wail slicing through the quiet. Michael loved the call of the wild. The primitive cries got under his skin, arousing him. Dominant and defiant, animals fought to protect what belong to them. He especially admired the sleek moves of the panther. With its keen eyesight, acute hearing, and uncanny ability to sneak up on its prey unnoticed, it pounced on its victim in one slick move. Michael understood the moves of the night predators. He was one of them.

Michael DeVeccio had it all. A billion dollar construction company that built luxury resorts all over the world, a twenty-four room mansion with servants at his beck and call, the most dazzling club on the Vegas Strip, a fleet of outlandishly expensive sports cars, a private jet, and more money than he could use in ten life times. He had it all with the exception of one thing: a son, an heir to his vast domain. And once he found the perfect woman to carry the heir to his dynasty, the DeVeccio Empire would rule the universe.

He envisioned the ideal woman as being flawless in every way. She'd have an inner beauty that would shine as much as her outward appearance, she'd have proper etiquette with impeccable manners, and she'd be cultured in fine arts. His perfect woman would be well educated on current events when hosting parties and galas for his business associates. She would be honest and sincere and loyal to him and only him. And she would not be a woman beguiled by his wealth and fortune. Yes, he mused, taking a final drag of his cigarette. This perfect woman would be angelic and worthy of producing the heir to his kingdom.

The time had come to find that woman.

And it would happen.

He ruled it so.

Ж◇Ж◇Ж

Drawing on her extensive experience as head curator to one of Chicago's most prestigious art museums, Margot Montgomery prepared for an exhibition with the meticulous precision of an automaton. Everything had to be perfect. If the focal point of a show was murals, she would negotiate for the ideal portraits from a limited collection, using the skills that had earned her a reputation as a sharp buyer. For the rare and exotic, she'd travel to Europe and Mexico, recruiting paintings that had never been displayed on this continent.

Exhibits featuring the unusual and impressive captivated people, drawing them in with their mysterious and enchanting aura. By combining existing collections with innovative outreach, the audience interaction was vastly increased, keeping the museum doors open to newcomers as well as those who frequented the gallery.

Using her most cunning assets, Margot prepared for an exhibit by selecting an appropriate theme, placing the focus on viewer interpretation. This could not be achieved without first understanding the artist. There was a myriad of ways in which to expand on this particular gala, and Margot's goal for the Frida Kahlo show was to bring the artist to life by exposing her broken spirit and bleeding heart.

The display room in the east wing of the museum was the chosen site for the upcoming exhibit. Large and spacious, it was simultaneously inviting. Muted light from the windows mingled with gilded light from the candelabras, illuminating the paintings in foreboding, shadowy figures. Depending on the featured artist, dismal days added to the theatrical atmosphere.

Margot stood back and observed while her crew prepared for the exhibit. Her curatorial staff had gone far and beyond the call of duty, working overtime until all was done to perfection. As prior to every show, she looked at the paintings through the speculative eyes of a viewer, surveying them systematically from the doorway.

The east wing of the museum was enshrined with self-portraits of Frida Kahlo. Characteristic of her self-murals, her penetrating eyes seem to consciously and directly meet with the gaze of the viewer. The paintings illustrated an unflattering glimpse of her broken spirit, sense of hopelessness, and the hand-wringing anxiety with which she lived her life.

From across the room, Sophia Andretti didn't miss a trick. Assistant curator for the past two years, she was developing excellent interpersonal skills under the tutelage of Margot, her mentor and friend.

Margot's eye for detail and sharp focus had served her well in the art world. Between her amazing ability to meet challenging deadlines and her savvy sense of fashion, she was a woman to be admired and respected. Not a thread of her strawberry-blonde hair was out of place, each tress secured in a neat chignon at the nape of her neck. Beneath the burgundy wool skirt of her stylish Gucci suit, her Prada pumps clicked with authority as she undulated through the gallery. Cool and professional, Neiman Marcus personified.

Clipboard in hand, Sophia joined Margot. "This will be the best exhibit, very moving. I can't even imagine what Frida Kahlo must have gone through."

Before responding, Margot scanned each portrait, her sharp green eyes raking every corner. "That's her claim to fame. Frida Kahlo was notorious for expressing her pain through her self-murals. It all started after the bus accident that resulted in her broken spine, collarbone, and countless other injuries. But the worst was the steel handrail which pierced her body, skewered her womb, and came out through her vagina, leaving her unable to have children."

"Ouch," Sophia cringed. "That must have been horrible! And to think she began painting while in the hospital, lying on her back recuperating. I can't believe that she had a mirror bolted to the ceiling, studied her reflection, and painted herself. The courage it must have taken to reveal her physical torment and anguish that way."

"She was preoccupied with mortality and the fragility of her body," Margot stated. "A lot of her murals focused on funerary imagery. And in other murals, she painted herself bleeding, injured, wounded, or victimized."

Sophia sighed sympathetically. "I guess she was looking for refuge. And if her physical pain wasn't bad enough, she had a husband who couldn't keep his pants on. All those affairs, even with her own sister. It must have rocked her world!"

Margot shrugged. "They supposedly had quite a tempestuous love life. Her husband was renowned for his worldly philandering. But even after a divorce, Frida never stopped loving him, wanting him."

Passing the "Two Fridas", the most symbolic of the artist's self-murals, Sophia and Margot stood in front of it, transfixed by the mirrored image.

Totally lost in the double self-portrait, Margot said, "Frida painted this shortly after her divorce from Diego Rivera. He asked her for the divorce after he had the affair with her sister, ripping Frida's heart in half."

Sophia didn't hold back. "I'd castrate my Tony if he did that; put an end to his messing around."

Margot laughed. "Before you become the next Lorena Bobbitt, let's stick to business. The significance behind the double image is a split identity. It's a true portrayal of Mexican surrealism. The Frida in the wedding dress represents the woman Diego loved; and the other Frida, the woman betrayed, was in jeopardy of bleeding to death. Diego's affair with Frida's sister was the ultimate betrayal. It broke her in half. The blood seeping out of her heart clearly signifies that she is slowly bleeding to death emotionally; the mirrored image reflects her soul. This portrait fascinates people because it conjures up different images in different people about their own lives. I think this will be our best show yet. And after I get the final mural in the collection tomorrow at the art auction in Vegas, everything will be complete."

On her way to her office, Margot was so enmeshed in her own thoughts she nearly passed her door. The haunting self murals of Frida Kahlo were embedded in her head, all those fragmented glimpses of dual imagery. With a Master's degree in art from the University of Chicago, Margot's minor in psychology complemented it nicely. The complexity of the mind fascinated her. Because the various interpretations of Frida Kahlo's state of mind were revealed through her self-murals, the exhibit would be a real show stopper. And after her trip to the art auction in Vegas the following day, the gala would come full circle. As an added bonus, she'd also get an up close and personal look at the art sculptures and paintings at DeVeccio Plaza.

ЖЖЖ

Flaming copper finials bordered the entrance of DeVeccio Plaza, drawing guests in with its regal appeal. Standing tall and mighty in a sky of midnight blue velvet, the flaming torches gleamed like shooting stars with tails. The interior of the grandest resort on the Vegas Strip gave chase to marble staircases with elaborately turned balustrades and high end sculptures behind beveled glass enclosures. Rushing down the corridor after snagging the mural she bid on, Margot fought the urge to kick off her high heels and walk barefoot down the plush, red carpeting.

The beckoning wail of sax drifted out of the piano bar; the bluesy sound of jazz getting into her skin. After spending the better part of the afternoon negotiating at an art auction, unwinding over a chilled martini sounded like utter bliss. Seduced by the sound, she sauntered up the three steps leading to the mezzanine and ordered a Pomegranate martini.

"You got it, doll," the bartender winked.

"Whatever the pretty lady wants is on the house," the

man approaching the bar said in a buttery soft voice. "And give me a bourbon on the rocks, Jazz."

Margot turned around and came face to face with the billionaire tycoon of DeVeccio Plaza. His shocking blue eyes left her breathless. With his sharply defined features, full sensual lips, and all that black wavy hair, he reminded her of a Greek god.

"Allow me to introduce myself," he said. "I'm Michael De-Veccio. Welcome to my palace."

Every pulse in her body was as charged as an electrical current. Michael DeVeccio, legendary for building luxury resorts in every continent, exuded strength and power from every pore. His world renowned success preceded him. And here he stood in front of her in all his glory, one hundred and eighty pounds of raw, sexual energy. Mesmerized by his hypnotic blue eyes, she met his gaze. "I'm Margot Montgomery. It's a pleasure to meet you. Your resort is everything it's rumored to be, simply breathtaking."

"Thank you." he edged a bit closer. "I've always fancied it to be the jewel of the Strip. I didn't think anything could outshine DeVeccio Plaza. But I was wrong. Nothing could possibly compare to the sparkle I see in your eyes."

Margot felt the heat all the way to her toes. The intensity of his gaze left her feeling wild and reckless. She'd known this business mogul for less than a minute, and was totally beguiled by his charismatic personality. She traveled abroad at least once a month to galas and exhibitions. She had been wined and dined by movie stars, celebrities, and sheiks. But not one of them had the illuminating presence of Michael DeVeccio. An energetic force seemed to radiate from him, making her feel as if she had been drinking champagne.

"You're very beautiful," he said. "So, is the woman with the intriguing green eyes married?"

Captivated by him, Margot answered a bit breathless. "Ah...single. I came here for an art auction, the one in your ballroom. I'm a curator for an art museum in Chicago, and came to bid on a mural for the exhibit I'm hosting."

His penetrating gaze locked into hers. "And I'd be willing to bet you walked away with the mural you had your sights set on. You strike me as a determined woman that sets her goals and achieves them. That's a trait I admire very much."

As the hot sound of jazz drifted through the piano bar, a

warm desert breeze blew in from open terrace doors, the seductive undertone thick and heavy. The sassy wail of sax and the sweet lilt of piano counterpointed, stirring the air with its sensual rhythm.

Michael checked her out as he sipped his bourbon, coolly assessing her. *An interesting woman,* he mused, *an ideal candidate.* He studied her, taking note of her natural beauty and clear, intelligent eyes. *And a genuine smile, a rare trait in today's society.* With his killer instinct for judging people, he summed her up. Strong-willed and dedicated to her cause. A woman who abides by rules and regulations. Indeed, yes. Margot Montgomery could be the woman befitting to carry his heir. He would have to definitely get to know her better. He smiled, displaying a set of perfect white teeth. "It would be my pleasure to take a walk out on the terrace with you, show you the view from up here. It's magnificent, you know, looking down on all those dazzling lights of the Vegas Strip. Come on, I'll show you."

ЖѺЖѺЖ

Shrouded by a sky of shimmering lights, an unparalleled view gave way to a sweeping view of the Las Vegas Strip. DeVeccio Plaza stretched out in front of them for miles and miles. A cascading waterfall graced the entrance, and a wax museum of whimsical figures filled an entire block.

Margot sighed. "This is like a castle in a fairy tale. You must be so proud. Do you live here?"

"I live in the DeVeccio ancestral home, about fifteen miles or so in Summerlin. It's a mansion tucked away deep in the Red Rock Mountains. It's not too far from Red Rock Canyon, which has some of the best hiking trails I've ever hiked on." He touched her face. "Do you have any idea how gorgeous you are? With all that golden hair, you remind me of an angel."

She felt his searing gaze. Giving him a shy smile, she said, "If you keep staring at me that way I fear I might melt. Your gaze is as penetrating as the artist I'm showcasing in my exhibit. I'm featuring the self-murals of Frida Kahlo, and thanks to the art auction held in your ballroom this afternoon, I have the entire collection to make it a smashing success."

"I admire a woman who has a fine appreciation for the arts," Michael said. "I especially admire a woman who pays particular attention to detail. It's an important asset, one overlooked by many employees. You are a fascinating woman and I'd like the chance to get to know you better. I hope you'll consider going out to dinner with me the next time I'm in Chicago on business." He paused, watching her expression. "It would be a pleasure to wine and dine such an intriguing woman."

"Are you building a resort in Chicago?"

He stared long and hard into her eyes. Finding the perfect woman to carry his heir was like searching for a needle in a haystack. His gut reaction told him he'd just found her. He sipped his bourbon, watching her over the rim of his glass. "I'm looking at property in the Lincoln Park area to build one of my resorts. So I have both an office and a condo in Chicago. I'll be tied up in Italy for the next few weeks with my newest enterprise off the coast of Tuscany. But when I come back, would you like to have dinner with me?"

"Depending on my schedule and whatever shows I'm hosting, I'd love to."

"Excellent." His gaze locked into hers. "Now, why don't you tell me all about yourself?"

Margot sipped her chilled martini, feeling the heat of his gaze run through her body. She lowered her eyes before looking at him. "I think those hypnotic blue eyes of yours are casting a spell on me. I'm finding it very difficult to concentrate."

"I like the direct way you have of telling me exactly what's on your mind," he said. "Honesty in today's society is so refreshing and very much appreciated. When I'm in Tuscany, I'll be counting the days until I come to Chicago. I do a lot of business there and hope to see quite a bit of you when I'm in town. Now why don't you tell me all about being a curator."

Margot's expressive green eyes sparkled. "It's my passion. I simply love hosting galas and shows for the museum. It's so fulfilling and keeps me on the cutting edge of culture in the art world. Being head curator has a lot of responsibilities, but I'm very dedicated and up for the challenge. Creating a theme for a show is so exciting, bringing artists to life through their work. Take my upcoming show for instance, the Frida Kahlo exhibit. My goal is to make my viewers feel her pain through her haunting self-murals. And in order for my job as head curator to be complete, I have to do everything in my power to get the entire collection. There was one I couldn't get, no matter how many galleries I searched. So when I heard about this hard to find painting being auctioned in your hotel this weekend, I knew I wouldn't stop until it was mine. Now I can rest easy."

"Just one look at your face tells me how passionate you are about your shows," Michael said. "You should see your eyes. They light up brighter than the neon lights on the Strip when you talk about them. Your love for the arts radiates from deep within. I understand. My passion is face masks. I have quite a handsome collection of them from all over the world. I love showing them off at my parties. Before my uncle died, he held a masquerade ball every New Year's Eve, and I've carried on with the tradition. The masquerade's a real social event; all the big players of Vegas dressed to the nines."

"Sounds impressive," Margot said. "Your rags to riches story is legendary. I remember reading about it a few years back in a magazine article. What a fascinating life you've led. You are an amazing man and you must be so proud of all your achievements."

Michael reached into his pocket and fished out a Marlboro, tapping it three times before lighting it. "I love living in Red Rock now, but that wasn't always the case. My heart was in the small inland harbor off the coast of Tuscany where I grew up. For a long time, that's where it stayed. I lived there until I was twelve, when my parents were killed in a car wreck. After their funeral, I came to live with my Uncle Carlos, my father's brother. That was the day my life did a complete one eighty. I went from living a simple life in a fishing port to one of absolute power.

In his day, my uncle was one of the most feared and revered icons on the Vegas Strip. He built the DeVeccio Dynasty from the ground up, starting with his first gambling casino, DeVeccio Plaza. After that, his resorts started shooting up all over the world like mirages, and within a decade, the DeVeccio Dynasty snowballed into one of the most powerful business conglomerates in the world. And since my uncle's no longer living, I'm the CEO of the entire DeVeccio

Empire."

"Did the police ever find your uncle's killer?" Margot asked, staring into pools of midnight blue. "I remember his death being broadcasted all over the media. It must have been so terrible for you, losing the man who raised you as his own son."

"It was one of the worst days of my life," Michael flicked the ash of his cigarette. "I thought of Uncle Carlos as my father. I did everything I could to help the police with their investigation, but nothing ever panned out. Carlos DeVeccio was a high profile figure at the time of his death. What a shock to everyone who knew him. He was bigger than life and twice as bold. He was in great shape and had the mind of a steel trap. To have his life end that way, murdered in his own home, in his own bathroom. I think one of his enemies got to him, one of his business competitors. I found him the next morning, all slumped over. He'd just gotten out of the shower and was still naked. I'll never forget that day as long as I live. As a matter of fact, two weeks from tonight marks the ten year anniversary of his death."

"How awful," Margot said. "Finding your uncle that way must have traumatized you. Didn't the police have any leads at all?"

"Unfortunately not. The crime was never solved and remains open to this day. Uncle Carlos was one of the old time gangsters running Vegas back then, and it was no doubt a personal vendetta. My uncle had his fair share of enemies, make no mistake. He was one shrewd businessman. He held meetings every Saturday in the great room of his mansion, his private domain. The hall vibrated with his presence the minute he entered the room, still does as a matter of fact. A life-size portrait remains in there, a tribute to the big man himself. That's where I learned what was expected of me to take over a major construction company. I can still hear the booming voice of my uncle, loud and sanctimonious, echoing off the walls, making grown men tremble in their boots. You can imagine what a shock it was to realize I was being trained to take over the entire DeVeccio Dynasty. Gambling casinos and all that money seemed wrong to me at first, against the morals my parents had instilled in me. But eventually, I was seduced by all that power."

"Your uncle didn't have children, no kids to carry on his

empire?"

"Just one son: Luciano. He was killed in an accident. After his funeral, no one was permitted to mention his name because it upset my aunt and uncle. Aunt Bella eventually died of a broken heart and Uncle Carlos threw himself into building his empire. So when I moved in, he treated me like his son and never made me feel like second best. I owe a lot to the old man; he made me what I am today. But enough about me. I'd much prefer talking about you. So why isn't an enticing woman like yourself married? You're so beautiful and have such a passion for life. What's wrong with those men in Chicago?"

Margot's heart skipped a beat. Something about this legendary magnate made her forget her own name. She'd never allowed a man to get to her before. Nothing had ever gotten in the way of an exhibit. But from the moment she looked into the brilliant blue eyes of Michael DeVeccio, his intense gaze unraveled her. Giving him a coy, come hither look, she said, "I guess I never met the right man."

"Good answer," he smiled. "Sometimes fate has a mind of its own. I'm a firm believer in destiny. And I think we were destined to meet tonight."

CHAPTER TWO

Looking very vogue in her emerald green wool gabardine suit, Margot hosted the Frida Kahlo exhibit as if it were the last show she would ever put her name to. Smiling as she led the tour, she provided guests with information pertaining to the featured artist.

"For many years, little was known about the life or paintings of Frida Kahlo. But after a retrospective exhibit in London, her modest range of paintings was resurrected from virtual obscurity to world-wide recognition. The artist suffered many hardships to become one of the world's most popular female painters, and her dozens of self-murals illustrate the pain she endured during her life. Tonight the theme of our show is *The Imagery of Tragedy.* You will see as we study each of her portraits that the pain and heartache she wished to portray through her paintings is palpable."

A woman in a black Armani suit cleared her throat. "Is it true Frida Kahlo began painting her self-murals while recuperating in the hospital from an accident?"

"My assistant will be happy to answer your question," Margot turned to Sophia.

In a long flowered skirt, blue silk camisole, and a lace shawl, Sophia stepped forward. "That's correct. Frida Kahlo survived the accident but underwent numerous surgeries. While she recuperated, she had a mirror bolted to her hospital ceiling, studied her reflection, and painted herself."

With emphasis on deeper layers of consciousness, the tour group focused on the dream-like quality and emotional intensity of the self murals which made them unforgettable.

A distinguished elderly man with snow-white hair stood before "The Wounded Deer". The portrait illustrated the artist depicting herself as a frightened animal, running away.

Walking over to him, Margot smiled. "This painting suggests that Frida is a timid creature of nature that has been wounded by fate or an unknown force. She compares herself to a deer that has been shot by arrows. The broken branch lying on the ground represents her broken spinal column—or perhaps her broken spirit."

"All of her paintings seem to combine fantasy with realism," a college student who mentioned studying art and history commented. "Especially in her 'Henry Ford Hospital' mural. Look how she connects internal organs and other meaningful objects outside her body with umbilical cords."

The "Henry Ford Hospital" painting illustrated Frida Kahlo lying in bed, a tear on her cheek as blood slowly seeped out of her internally. Among some of the things painted were a female torso, a male fetus, a snail, a sewing machine, and a pelvis.

Turning to the group, Margot spoke. "The general impression of the painting is the absolutely crushing psychological pain she endured during her miscarriage. The male fetus represents her hope for a boy, the snail suggests the slowness of the agony, the sewing machine may indicate piercing pain, and the pelvis indicates her inability to have children."

Finishing the tour where it had begun, Margot graciously thanked her entourage. "Ladies and gentlemen, that ends our exhibit for this evening. Thank you for supporting the arts. We invite you to join us in the west wing for wine and cheese as a tribute of our appreciation."

ЖҖҖҖ

Finishing a glass of Chardonnay as she slowly unwound after the show, Margot stood in front of the "Two Fridas" portrait, lost in her own thoughts. Fascinated by the mirrored image portrayed in the mural, she thought about all the artists over the centuries whose work depicted their tortured souls. Mesmerized by the inner demons of the mind, she didn't notice Sophia come up behind her.

"You sure are drawn to that mural," Sophia tapped her on the shoulder. "Why the obsession with it?"

"It stirs my curiosity," Margot turned around. "Psychology was my minor in college and what makes the mind tick has always fascinated me. The mind is such a powerful tool. Just think about it. When you feel good about yourself as a person, you glow from the inside and confidence oozes from every pore. But when someone makes you feel bad about yourself, it destroys your confidence and can lead to severe scarring of the psyche. I remember studying a case in psychology class about a child who was beaten down by his parents, both physically and mentally. He grew up with such a destroyed psyche he turned into a demented killer. It's been known to happen, time after time."

"I guess," Sophia shrugged, more interested in a person's outward appearance than inner demons haunting their psyche. "Hey, did you get a load of the rock that woman in the black Armani had on her hand? Betcha it was worth a cool quarter of a million. How about it?"

"I didn't notice," Margot laughed, amused by her assistant's quirky personality. "Since you are the material girl of our art gallery, I should have sent you to Vegas to bid on the portrait at the art auction held at DeVeccio Plaza. The resort is simply awesome. But then again, if I sent you, I wouldn't have had the pleasure of meeting the billionaire tycoon himself, close up and personal. And let me just say, pictures do not do Michael DeVeccio justice. He has these midnight blue eyes that are absolutely mesmerizing, the face of a fallen angel, and his body is one hundred and eighty pounds of raw sexual energy."

"Ah, man," Sophia drooled. "Some blondes have all the fun. So come on, what's he like? Is he all that and more?"

Margot gushed at the memory. "Words cannot possibly describe him. He has this daunting presence about him that makes him stand out in a crowd. It's like an aura that defines him: strong and bold, and a bit intimidating. It's no wonder he's one of the most powerful men in the world. He could make the strongest of men wither under his scrutiny. No kidding, Sophie. You'd have to meet him face to face to see what I mean. Let me just say, he certainly got my full attention. So much so that I've agreed to see him again. He's in Tuscany right now building his latest resort, but when he comes back tomorrow, we're going to dinner. He has a condo here in Lincoln Park because he has his sights set on some land in Chicago."

"How convenient, a lover's tryst. Maybe he has his sights set on you."

Margot raised a perfectly arched eyebrow. "Like I said, we're going to dinner—and that's all. Can you imagine how many women throw themselves at Michael DeVeccio? A billionaire with the jazziest club on the Strip? He could have his pick of a lot of different women, and I'm sure he does. Just because we're going to dinner is no reason to thrust us into a wild love affair. I'm sure the media does that as soon as they get wind of a story with someone as high profile as Michael DeVeccio."

"You never know," Sophia laughed. "I just want to see you happily married the way I am. It's high time you found something to do with your weekends other than plan exhibits. Maybe Michael DeVeccio is just the man to knock your socks off, or your stockings and Prada heels. How about it? But just in case I get tired of my Tony some day, does this billionaire have a twin?"

"No way," Margot laughed, locking up as they left the gallery and walked out into the crisp Chicago night. "There is one and only one Michael DeVeccio."

Ж◊Ж◊Ж

Pouring himself a bourbon on the rocks, Michael walked onto his balcony and gazed into the foothills. Fishing a Marlboro from the pack, he tapped it on the parapet three times before lighting it. His trip to Tuscany had gone well, he mused, blowing a smoke ring into the cool desert night. The DeVeccio Plaza being built off the coast of Tuscany would be one of his best resorts yet. And, he thought, a smile curving his lips, everything was moving along right on schedule for the grand opening. Absolute power was his.

Master at the game, Michael knew how to manipulate people into doing precisely what he wanted them to do. He had the uncanny ability of zeroing in on an adversary's Achilles heel and using it for his own gain. It was all about control and manipulation. All men had a weakness, even the strongest. And once a weakness was exposed, Michael DeVeccio moved in for the kill.

Flicking the ash of his cigarette, he stared into the darkness. Under The Hunter's moon, night predators slithered out of the underbrush, just on the periphery of the rugged terrain. In the distance, the eerie howl of a coyote keened, stirring his blood with the call of the wild. From the time he was a teenager, his uncle taught him to hunt and kill. Hunting and killing human predators had bothered him at first, going against the Christian beliefs and morals his parents had instilled in him. But as his uncle pointed out, animals killed to protect what was theirs. And people were no different. Killing to protect was necessary in a world of absolute power. And once he began thinking of himself as an action figure in an action movie, killing had gotten under his skin. He was The Hunter.

His mind drifted to Margot Montgomery, the perfect woman to carry his heir. Tomorrow night over dinner, he'd put her to the test to see if she was worthy of such a prominent role.

The time had come to propagate the DeVeccio dynasty. When his son was old enough to understand and appreciate the world of absolute power, he'd teach him the ways of running one of the most powerful business conglomerates in the world. One day he'd hand the reigns of the DeVeccio Dynasty over to his son. And his son in turn would do the same, thus the legacy would thrive for generations to come. Blowing a smoke ring into the woods surrounding the estate, he hoped Margot would pass the test. He wanted a beautiful woman who knew her place in his world. He thought of Lacy and frowned. She was becoming more of a noose around his neck every day and the time had come to cut her loose.

Lacy Diamond had been his obsession for the past ten years. How he'd lusted after her when she was his uncle's lover. As cold and calloused as Carlos DeVeccio was, Lacy had the old man wrapped around her little finger. His uncle had given her anything she desired: a stately manor in the Red Rock Mountains, expensive trinkets, fancy cars, and jewelry befitting of a queen. Whatever Lacy wanted Lacy got. With the exception of marriage.

Carlos DeVeccio had buried his wife Bella and had no intention of marrying again. When Lacy realized that, she started coming on to Michael, figuring if the old man wouldn't marry her, the young stud nephew surely would. And while Michael had given her an engagement ring, he had no intention of marrying a cheap Vegas showgirl any more than his uncle had.

Although Lacy's feminine wiles had kept him interested for the past decade, the wild lust and animal magnetism he'd once felt for her had run its course. Her selfishness had destroyed his lust for her, and her betrayal had been the ultimate sin. Lacy viewed men on their bank account and prestige, always demanding more. With her recent addictions to narcotics and gambling on top of heavy drinking, she couldn't be trusted. With all the secrets his uncle had spilled to her during their affair, the ones that could put an end to the DeVeccio Empire, she needed to be subdued with some heavy-duty tranquilizers. Permanently.

With her outstanding gambling debts, her insatiable appetite for luxury, and her constant bitching about setting a wedding date, Lacy Diamond appealed to Michael about as much as riding a burro through the Mojave Desert. He had given her the engagement ring before she'd become such a nuisance. Not that he ever had any intention of marrying her or permitting her to give birth to his son. Not likely. He'd given her the ring to test her fidelity. And she'd failed the test miserably.

Desperate for money one night to feed her gambling addiction, she had sold her body to one of his business associates. After that, he swore to never touch her again. She'd betrayed him and would pay for her deadly sin. Michael lived by the mantra his uncle had taught him: betray me and die by the sword.

Tonight, he would kill Lacy Diamond for her sin, just as he'd killed dear old Uncle Carlos ten years earlier.

ЖҢЖ

Getting into Ninja attack mode, Michael crossed the threshold of the great room whistling his favorite tune. *A hunting we will go. A hunting we will go. Heigh ho the dairy-o, a hunting we will go. We'll kill a fox and put her in a box.*

Heigh ho the dairy-o, a hunting we will go.

A large and imposing portrait of Carlos DeVeccio graced the wall. His daunting presence filled the room. With his fist held high in the air, the sense of his undeniable power reached out from every corner.

Michael studied the painting. Firm jawline, thin lips stretching over a mouth ready to belittle the largest of men into little piss ants, raven hair streaked with silver, and piercing black eyes that saw straight to the soul. His unblinking stare seemed to follow Michael wherever he went, silently beckoning him to honor and obey. Michael stood before that portrait and flipped him the bird.

"You trained me well, Uncle Carlos. Under your expert tutelage, I learned how to wield the death star into the throat of the betrayer and then cover the corpse with the death mask. And wasn't it poetic justice I should do to you what you taught me to do to others? You thought you were so clever, ruling the world with your big shot fist. The whole while you sat at the head of your table, deciding who had the right to live and die. All along, it turned out you were the biggest traitor of them all. The high and mighty Carlos DeVeccio presiding, judge and jury, calling all the shots from behind a masquerade. What a fake. But I discovered your dirty little secret and made sure you paid the price for committing the ultimate sin. And placing your skull mask on your corpse was indeed sweet revenge. But never fear, Uncle Carlos. All was not lost. Under your expert tutelage, I learned how to lie, cheat, and kill. All for the sake of absolute power."

Depressing a microchip on the gilded frame of his uncle's portrait, a secret passageway opened with a slight hiss. Strutting into the steel vaulted room, Michael tapped the encrypted code into a hidden keyboard. A small wall vault opened to reveal a drawer of shuriken, hand-held blades to kill betrayers. And in a container next to the weapons was a boundless supply of latex skull masks to place on the corpse. Snatching one of the Ninja stars, a four point blade the size of a coin, he concealed the weapon between his fingers. Then with great pleasure, he removed a mask, grabbed his black hooded jacket from the hook, and left the room. It was time to go hunting.

ЖҜЖҜ

Spotting the mansion in the distance, adrenaline surged through The Hunter's blood, filling him with a sense of power. The sounds of the Mojave surrounded him as he charged through the foothills of the Red Rock Mountains. As he neared the estate, his heart pumped with eager anticipation.

Fashioned with old-world charm, arches and columns made up the Mediterranean-inspired courtyard. Citronella flame lanterns graced the entrance. A barrel tile roof and copper gutters adorned the front of the manor, and wrought iron balconies bordered the stone mansion. Removing his cell phone from his hooded jacket, he called Lacy. "Listen, doll. Looks like I won't be over tonight after all. I flew straight to Chicago on my way back from Italy and am dead tired. I had some business to take care of and won't be in Vegas until morning. So you just enjoy your bubble bath and you'll see me sooner than you think." With a coy smile, he snapped the lid of his phone, sheathed his hands in latex gloves, and slid his key into the carved wooden door.

Stopping in the entryway, The Hunter listened. A cascading waterfall meandered over rocks of lavender and jade. Other than the sound of gurgling water, the classical sound of Baroque coming from hidden wall speakers, and the accelerated beat of his heart, all was quiet.

Descending the steps to the sunken living room, The Hunter came face to face with the grinning gargoyle. He grinned right back. Adrenaline pumping through his veins, he strolled down the long hallway leading to the library. Westminster chimes played the third quarter hour melody. In one fluid move, The Hunter entered the room. Under his weight, an old floorboard creaked. Totally unfazed, he strutted to the desk and turned on the computer, his nimble fingers typing in the password: DiamondEmpire. The screen illuminated and he deleted files, removed the hard drive, and pocketed the flash drive. He'd leave nothing to chance. Lacy stored everything on her computer. No doubt, somewhere on the hard drive, there would be enough scandal to wipe out the DeVeccio Dynasty.

With his blood thundering in his ears, he pulled out the latex skull mask and slipped it over his face to conceal his identity. Fingering his weapon, his heart danced a wild rhythm.

Tip-towing up the Alaskan marble stairway, his rubber heeled boots didn't make a sound. A fern-lined corridor painted willowy patterns on the wall. Camouflaged in the darkness, he scaled along the corridor. Preceded by his shadow, he blended into the wooden paneling. Shimmying into the bathroom, he slid behind the door and waited, his Ninja star ready to wield at a second's notice.

Silhouetted in candlelight, she soaked in a slipper-designed, clawfoot tub, her honey-blonde hair pinned on top of her head. She was singing, her smoky voice floating through the scented air. Closing her eyes, her long lashes swept over her cheeks like fans.

She sank deeper into the fragrant bubbles, circling the brass gooseneck spout with her big toe. A heavy candle burned on the pink pedestal sink; a cherub ceiling fan rotated rhythmically, stirring the heady scent of roses through the steamy mist.

From the library, the Westminster melody played sixteen notes, followed by twelve piercing chimes. The resounding peels sliced through the quiet. Sensing a presence, she bolted upright. She went to scream–but it was too late. With a hissing wiz, the spikes of the death star nailed into her jugular vein, blood gushing into the fragrant pool of bubbles. As the deadly blade sliced into her voice box, her face twisted into an ugly grimace, her lips forming a silent scream. Her head rolled back, hitting the lip of the tub with a muffled thud. Struggling for breath, her strength ebbing, her eyes grew wide with shock when The Hunter removed his death mask and grinned at her.

CHAPTER THREE

Twenty more minutes and he would be knocking at her door.

Standing in front of her full-length mirror, Margot checked her look. After spending the entire afternoon at a boutique on Oak Street getting her hair and nails done, she looked good. Her dress cost her an entire month's salary, but the sexy way it made her feel was worth it. She'd chosen a simple gold necklace and hoop earrings to go with the red silk gown. A shiver of anticipation raced up her spine as she sprayed Sachet of Roses on her throat and wrists. Just as she applied her lipstick, the doorbell rang. Her heart skipped a beat.

There he stood in a black silk shirt with thinly defined pinstripes, winter-white pleated trousers, and a camel leather jacket, looking like he'd just stepped off the pages of GQ. The subtle scent of his masculine cologne filled her senses. Under the glow of the moonlight, his dangerously hypnotic blue eyes caused the pulse in the hollow of her throat to flutter.

"Margot," he stepped into the foyer, handing her a bouquet of red roses. "For you." he perused her from head to toe. "You look simply gorgeous."

In a gesture as old as time, Margot brought the roses up to her nose and took in their sweet essence. She smiled demurely. "Red roses are my favorite flower."

He smiled. "Beautiful roses for a beautiful woman." Brushing her lips with a feathery kiss, he added, "And you, Darling Margot, are simply flawless."

An explosion on the Waterfront could not have moved her more than his tender kiss. Between his lips touching hers and the sound of his husky voice, she felt warm and over-heated. Fussing with the cellophane wrap around the roses, she sniffed the flowers once more. "I'll just go put these in some water. Would you care for a drink before we leave?"

"No, thank you. We really ought to get going. I made reservations and it's about a thirty minute drive."

"Of course," she said, turning on a whisper of silk. "I'll be right out."

ЖХЖХЖ

"My chariot awaits." He held the door open as she sunk into the buttery soft leather seat of his cherry red Ferrari. Leaning over, he fastened her seat belt and whispered in her ear, "The way you look tonight, I'll be the envy of every guy in Chicago."

His warm breath tickled her ear. And when his masculine scent invaded her senses, Margot nearly swooned. She looked into his eyes and sucked in her breath. "My favorite flowers and all this flattery? You certainly know the way to a woman's heart."

The door closed with a gentle swoosh, mingling the smell of expensive leather with his cologne. Margot sunk deeper into the luxurious cushioning, running her finger along the smooth interior. She watched him cross the street in front of her, his tall lean form silhouetted under the street light. He moved with ease, sure-footed and confident.

"All right," he said, sliding into his seat. He reached over and put in a CD of soft instrumentals. The engine softly purred as it glided down the icy bricks of the cobblestone street.

"I love your car," Margot said, enjoying the novelty of be-ing swept away for once in my life. "I've always had a secret desire to own a fancy sports car, but as practical as I am, I know it will never be more than a fantasy."

"She runs like a dream," Michael said. "And since I do so

much business here in Chicago, I keep my Ferrari in the garage of my Lincoln Park penthouse." he looked over, his blue eyes sparkling in the glow of the streetlight. "I made reservations at Crystal's, the best restaurant in Chicago as far as I'm concerned. Have you ever eaten there?"

Butterflies danced in the pit of her stomach every time he looked at her with those amazing eyes. They were as hot as lasers and just as deadly. She cleared her throat. "I've never had the pleasure, but I've heard about it. We were supposed to have our Christmas party there this year, but the gallery owner decided to host it at his home."

Michael's eyes gleamed with satisfaction. "Good. It will be my pleasure to take you there for your first dining experience. You're in for quite a treat."

As they neared the loop of Chicago, the magnificent skyline came into view. The Sears Tower and the futuristic-looking Marina City Corncobs dominated the sky. The downtown section shimmered with its dazzling array of Christmas lights. The shops and boutiques bordering the elevated train track of the city looked as picturesque as a Norman Rockwell painting. When they pulled into the parking lot on the dock, Christmas music echoed on the waterfront.

Located in Navy Pier, Crystal's stood out as a true Chicago landmark. A must see for visitors and a standing hot spot for Chicagoans; it bustled with excitement. Walking down the dock of the pier hand in hand, Margot and Michael enjoyed the myriad of attractions. Boutique doors jingled as shoppers scurried in and out, arms burdened with packages, getting an early start on gifts. Shrouded by the magnificent skyline of Chicago, the seats of the Ferris wheel idled back and forth one hundred and fifty feet in the air.

ЖЖЖ

"Welcome to Crystal's, Mr. DeVeccio," the hostess greeted him. "The private dining room is ready for you. If you will please follow me right this way."

Reaching the top floor, the elevator doors soundlessly parted and the hostess escorted them down the plush carpeting. She unlocked the door; the heady scent of pine drifted out, fresh and fragrant. A Douglas fir stood tall and mighty in the far corner, beautifully decorated with one of a kind blown glass ornaments. A crackling log in the fireplace added a warm glow of hearth and home. A man grinning from ear to ear tapped out a jaunty deliverance of Lady in Red on the keys of a Baby Grand.

Michael's gaze swept the room, making sure all was to his satisfaction. "Thank you, Pamela. Everything looks perfect."

"Of course, Mr. DeVeccio," the hostess turned to leave. "I'll tell Pierre you're ready for drinks."

"Michael," Margot gushed. "This is awesome. I had no idea you were bringing me to the private dining room. I feel so honored, like a princess."

"Better get used to it," Michael helped her into her chair. "I intend to spend the rest of the evening showing you just how special you are to me."

A cranberry scented candle graced a table decorated with a pleated white tablecloth. The large picture window opened to the remarkable Chicago skyline, the Ferris wheel, and the Christmas lights on the dock and waterfront.

With a blast of horns and a regal entrance, a strolling violinist, chef, and a man pushing a vintage French flower cart swept into the room.

"Would you just look," Margot said on a gasp. "All my favorite things. Well, I must say when you do it up, you really do it up big. This is spectacular."

"I wanted to bring an evening in Paris to you," he kissed her hand. "This is only the beginning. Pierre?"

With the panache of a French chef, Pierre uncovered the platters of appetizers. Steam billowed out, sending the aroma of smoked salmon, toasted crab cakes, and shrimp bruschetta through the room. While he was dishing out the culinary delights, another server uncorked a nicely aged pinot. He poured a little in a glass and set it down.

With expert precision, Michael picked up the glass, twirled the wine in a swirling motion, held it up to the light, inhaled it, and brought it up to his lips for tasting. He nodded his approval and the server filled both glasses.

Over the wine and appetizers, Margot stared across the candlelit table at Michael. He stared right back, his hypnotic blue eyes searing into hers. It was the perfect setting—a snowy night, a cozy ambiance, and a man who knew how to romance a woman.

"So," Margot said in a voice she barely recognized as her own. "Tell me how things went in Italy with your latest resort."

Michael refilled their wine glasses, silently collecting his thoughts. He brought the goblet to his lips. Taking a sip, he met Margot's gaze. "Business went well. I'm using a new approach with my latest resort, combining late Gothic architecture with Romanesque. The results will be stunning, and the grand opening is right on schedule. As a matter of fact, things went so well I was able to come back a day earlier than expected. I got into Chicago late last night around midnight and stayed at my Lincoln Park condo. With the time change, I slept most of the day and feel well-rested for my date with you tonight."

Fascinated by the ever changing hues of his eyes, Margot barely heard a word he'd said. His eyes changed color with his moods, going from a hard steely gray when he talked about business to a shocking blue when he got fired up about his newest architectural wonder. And when he looked at her with such a searing gaze over the candlelight, his eyes turned a shade of midnight blue; she felt the heat all the way down to her ruby-red toenails. Snapping back to the present, she realized he was now talking about his past.

"So that's my life story in a nut shell. A poor fisherman's son strikes it rich when tycoon uncle hands over the reigns of his billion dollar dynasty. I had it all living with Uncle Carlos. A mansion built for a king, the best educations in Ivy League colleges, fancy sports cars and more money than I knew what to do with. But there was a price to pay. Uncle Carlos ran his ship with an iron fist, demanding family loyalty and respect. He held meetings every Saturday in the great room, and under his tutelage, I learned how to become master of the game."

"And you never married?" Margot sipped on her wine, wondering why someone hadn't snatched up this gorgeous hunk of man.

Michael tapped his Marlboro on the table three times before lighting it. He took a drag and slowly exhaled a ring of smoke, watching it curl into the air before answering the question. "I'm divorced, have been for well over ten years. Candace was one of the dancers at my club and we married shortly after we met. What a mistake. The world was hers for the asking, but nothing ever satisfied her. She had it all: the cars, the staff, the limo, and more money than an heiress. All I asked in return was a son to carry on the family name and business. But instead of giving me a son, she gave me nothing but trouble. While I broke my back making billions, showering her with gifts and fancy sports cars, she was out there cheating on me with half the men in Vegas."

"I'm sorry," Margot said with genuine sympathy. She felt for this man who had been taken by a heartless gold digger with the morals of an alley cat. "That must have been so hard on you. Whatever happened to her?"

"I kicked her out of Vegas and told her to never show her face in my town again. I had enough of her adulteress ways when I had the unfortunate mishap of being married to her. Believe me, Candace knows better than to ever return. She's been duly warned."

"You should be grateful a woman like that didn't have your child," Margot remarked, wondering how any woman in her right mind could cheat on Michael DeVeccio. She broke off a piece of garlic bread and nibbled on it, methodically putting her thoughts into words. "I've never been married, but I think once you take an oath in front of God and your family to be faithful for the rest of your life, it should be taken seriously. Those vows are sacred and should be honored."

She blushed, catching herself. "Listen to me go on and on. It's my moral upbringing. I have very definite ideas when it comes to fidelity in a marriage. Why get married if you don't intend to keep your wedding vows? I have a friend whose husband cheated on her from their honeymoon on until she finally had a complete breakdown. She takes antidepressants now and still isn't the same vivacious woman she once was. It's very sad. I feel a lot of people go into marriage with the nonchalant opinion that if it doesn't work out, just get a quick divorce. Not only is that a pathetic way of thinking, but what about all the time and money it took to plan the wedding. Some couples expect a luxurious spread from parents who can't afford it, only to toss it all away a year later. I guess that's why I never got married. When I say 'I do', it's going to be for keeps, and I wouldn't make a promise I had no intention of keeping."

Michael sipped the last of his wine, listening intently to every word Margot spoke. His infallible gut reaction had never let him down before, and his assessment of Margot Montgomery was right on the money. She was a dream come true and would be the perfect woman to carry his heir.

He reached across the table and took her hand in his. "You're an incredible woman. I would love to see you again. With the holidays coming, I intend to spend a lot more time in Chicago."

Margot's heart fluttered with excitement. Until now, only preparing an exhibit for a show had stirred this type of emotion in her. The thought of spending the holidays with Michael filled her with a sense of girlish giddiness that was totally new to her. She put her fork down and smiled. "I'd like that, too."

"You don't eat very much," Michael remarked, noticing how she'd dabbled with her food. "Was something wrong with your meal?"

"Absolutely not," Margot daintily dabbed at her mouth with the corner of her linen napkin. "Everything was superb. Those sea scallops were to die for. It's just that I battled my weight all through high school and college and am now very calorie conscious."

"I admire that," Michael said. "I govern my life on control and discipline. It keeps my focus sharp and keeps me well-balanced. I begin my day working out in my gym or with a run. When Uncle Carlos was alive, part of our nightly ritual before dinner was fencing in the great room with the swords. My uncle was the master swordsman and insisted I learn under his tutelage. Martial Arts is a great way of learning both defense and hand and eye coordination. That's the problem with kids today. They spend far too much time sitting in front of computers playing games instead of working out. There's no discipline. My son will be skilled in Martial Arts, and I look forward to teaching him. My cousins and I used to fence when I first moved to the Red Rock Mountains. We fancied ourselves the Four Musketeers."

"I'll bet you made quite an impression on the girls," Margot teased with a smile. "Do you still fence when you get together?"

A far away look clouded Michael's sparkling blue eyes for a second, turning them a dull steely gray. "No. We were as close as brothers when I first moved in with my uncle. You see, my Aunt Monica is my mother's sister and she and her three sons lived in the valley, close to my uncle's mansion. After my parents were killed in the car crash in Tuscany, my aunt took me under her wing, wanting me to spend time with her and her boys. So during my teenage years, I spent my summers hiking the trails of the canyon with Johnny, Ricky, and Jimmy O'Toole. We were so close we took an oath to be blood brothers one summer afternoon on one of the petrified logs in the forest. But as we grew older, we grew apart because of our family loyalties. You see, Margot, the O'Toole Dynasty is the DeVeccio's number one competitor."

"Family rivals?" Margot asked. "I bet that was really hard, going from close cousins and best friends to stiff business competitors."

"Indeed, yes," Michael fished a Marlboro from the pack and tapped it on the table three times before lighting it. "Truth be told, I took it as a sign of betrayal. And betrayal in my life is unforgivable, something I simply won't tolerate. That's what my uncle drilled into my head from the time I was twelve. But enough about the past. I much prefer the present. Now tell me some of your interests so I know what to plan for our next date. Is there a play or a symphony you'd like to see?" he winked over the candlelight. "Or a city anywhere in the world you'd like to dine in? Just name it and my private jet awaits. The world is yours for the asking. Don't be shy about letting me know your heart's desire. In the meantime, why don't we end the evening with a dance. I do believe they're playing our song, Always and Forever. I have a feeling we were put on this earth to make beautiful music together."

CHAPTER FOUR

A half dozen officers and plainclothes detectives gathered at the crime scene to investigate the homicide in the Red Rock estate. The victim, Lacy Diamond, a twenty-eight year old Caucasian female, had been stabbed to death in her bathtub. Las Vegas Metro PD Homicide Detective Diego Santiago was first to arrive at the scene, looking like a warrior about to do battle. He did the initial walk through, deep lines edging the corners of his mouth, his broody brown eyes scanning the scene for trace evidence. As he walked around, his long mahogany ponytail swayed from side to side. Part Spanish and part Navaho Indian, his voice had a steely edge. When he entered the crime scene in the master bath, he came to a dead halt. "Holy hell." his eyes hardened. "Damn."

The victim sat upright in her bathtub. Her head, lolled off to one side, rested on the coiled ledge of the pink tub. Her throat had been slashed, a throwing star with blades on all sides, wedged deeply into her jugular vein. The face of the corpse was covered with a latex skull mask. The victim's left arm hung over the side of the tub, stiff with rigor mortis, the fingers skimming the surface of a pink cell phone on the marble floor. A huge diamond ring on her left finger gleamed in the morning sun.

Santiago stared at the body. "Looks like a Ninja assassination. A master wielder with deadly intent. And whoever did it hit the mark. Bull's eye." He turned to his team. "Let's get on it. I want the killer nailed. Haven't seen anything like this in ten years, since the Carlos DeVeccio murder, my first homicide case, still unsolved to this day. The Ninja star that killed him was diced up with poison. We won't know if this victim was poisoned until we get the autopsy report." He noted the time for the record. "EMT responded to nine-one-one, arriving at 7 a.m., pronounced victim, identified as Diamond, Lacy, at 7:03 a.m."

During a second walk through, crime scene investigators took photographs, drew sketches, and documented the scene before gathering and bagging evidence for the lab. They searched the entire master suite with flashlights, using an oblique angle. Ten years on the force with an impressive record, Santiago saw things other cops missed. His uncanny ability to get inside the mind of a killer made him shine as one of the teams' brightest stars. The room snapped with electricity the moment he entered. His daunting presence filled the room. With just a hint of a Latin lilt, his voice vibrated. "Who found her?"

"The maid," one of the officers said, "got here this morning just before 7 a.m. Called it in when she stumbled into this nightmarish scene. Hell of a thing to find. The smell alone is enough to gag a maggot. This corpse's been laying around for a day and a half, easy."

"Where's the maid now?"

"Down in the kitchen with one of the female officers. She doesn't speak much English and is pretty shook up."

After forensics finished with what they needed, the skull mask and murder weapon were processed. The face of the corpse revealed green eyes wide with fright, her mouth twisted into a garish scream. One of the rookie cops backed up and choked, his hand covering his mouth. "Shit."

A window seat at the foot of the bathtub opened to a full spread of the Red Rock Mountains. To the left of the clawfoot tub, the thick, waxy remains of a candle burned on the pink pedestal sink. The ceiling fan oscillated in an eerie rhythm, stirring the smell of decomposing fluids with the funereal smell of roses.

The lingering scent of perfume filled the bedroom, expensive and very feminine. A brass canopy bed with a pink satin ensemble dominated the room. Cheerful bluebirds chirped in the wake of the newly dawning day, and from open terrace doors, a gentle breeze rustled, billowing the gossamer curtains out like angel wings. An empty glass of wine and a pack of Virginia Slims lay on an antique telephone seat in the far corner. Resting on the lip of a diamond-studded ashtray was a partially smoked cigarette marred with pink lipstick. The same shade of pink smudged the rim of the wine goblet. Several tubes sat upright in a holder on the vanity, neatly arranged according to color, the last one on the right labeled pink ice. Santiago gestured to all three. "Bag and tag those. And check the messages on the phone."

The art gallery in the suite displayed Mardi Gras masks of the Veiled Lady, a Crying Mime and the Joker. Santiago moved in for a closer look. "Seems the victim was a fan of masquerades. And look what else." He walked over to the Queen Anne desk and held up a letter opener. "The Ninja star on the handle is identical to the throwing star lodged in the victim's throat."

CSI dusted for prints, both latent and visible. Santiago studied the nude corpse. No sign of a struggle or rape, although results were pending. The victim's painted red fingernails made detection of skin or blood beneath them difficult. "Do a TOX and check the fingernails for any possible DNA. Swab the inside of the mouth and sweep the body for fibers and hair. Check for semen."

Santiago watched the medical examiner check the body for contusions or pinpoint hemorrhaging on the skin. "Find anything?"

The medical examiner documented his notes, then looked up. "Obvious cause of death is internal bleeding. The TOX report will show if there was any drugs, either prescription or street. The victim took a single laceration with a blade, penetrating into the left side of her neck, severing her carotid artery and internal jugular vein. Her laryngeal nerve was also cut, the nerve that goes up to the voice box, making screaming impossible. Death was almost instantaneous, some time around midnight, night before last, judging by the rigor mortis. No visible sign of rape."

Santiago's eyes hardened into narrow slits, pupils and irises merging into one. "Some small comfort." He studied the victim's face. She'd been a beautiful woman with long honey-blonde hair, green eyes, and a heart-shaped face. His gaze settled on the wound in her throat. "The Ninja star has many names. It's sometimes referred to as a throwing star or a death star. Originally, it was used to slow down an opponent by wielding it into the arm or hand to dislodge a weapon. But other throwing stars are meant to kill, and this was one of them. The killer used a shuriken, a death star. The same type a blade that did Carlos DeVeccio in. And his face was covered in a skull mask, too, the one he wore during meetings, according to the nephew. How about the vic's family? Anyone we gotta get in touch with?"

"Just her mother," a female officer said. "She's on her way. Two uniforms went to her home to give her the news."

Finishing up, CSI placed the corpse in a body bag and zipped it up. Santiago took a last look at the victim's left hand, stiff and bloodless and so garishly white he wanted to puke. By contrast, her long red fingernails gleamed like streaks of blood. The team bagged the diamond ring, a rock of at least three carats, surrounded by an explosion of emeralds. No mention of a boyfriend or husband. Whoever had placed that ice berg on her finger needed to be told. His penetrating gaze focused on the female officer. "Find out who she was engaged to."

"Already on that. Left a message on the vic's cell. Called to cancel a date at a quarter to midnight, night before last."

"Who is it?"

"Michael DeVeccio."

"You gotta be kiddin' me."

"Fraid not."

The hair on Santiago's neck bristled. Michael DeVeccio had been the number one suspect in his uncle's death ten years ago, but was never convicted.

Carlos DeVeccio had been one of the richest and most powerful men in the world, proprietor of a billion dollar dynasty. His nephew was the sole beneficiary. Santiago recalled the iciness in Michael DeVeccio's eyes when he questioned him, the same look he'd seen in the eyes of cold-blooded killers.

His instincts, honed from ten years on the street, sent a familiar chill skittering up his spine. His blood tingled the way it did when he was on to something big. The nephew might have gotten away with killing his rich uncle ten years ago, but no way in hell was he getting away with it again. This time Santiago would nail the son of a bitch, lock him up, and throw away the key.

He raced down the marble steps and out the door of the Red Rock estate, his ponytail swaying in the breeze. He yelled over his shoulder, "Let's go."

ЖХЖ

Santiago and Officer Stevenson tore down Charleston Boulevard toward the DeVeccio estate. Every nerve ending in Santiago tingled with excitement. Reaching into his shirt pocket, he unwrapped a piece of Juicy Fruit and stuffed it into his mouth.

Stevenson watched him, wondering how long it would be before he reached for a cigarette. He quit on a regular basis, at least once a month. She raised an eyebrow. "So what makes you think the rich boyfriend offed Lacy Diamond?"

"Gut instinct. Never lets me down. It's like a sixth sense."

"How so?"

"Can't explain it, so don't ask. I just know."

As the unmarked patrol car eased around the horseshoe bend in the road, the DeVeccio estate came into view. Fluted pilasters flanked the wrought iron entrance gate. Two lean and mean Dobermans slinked out of the shadows of the pinyon trees, snarling and growling as they hurled themselves against the gate. Santiago flashed his badge under the security camera, and within seconds, the heavy iron bars lifted with a jarring screech. As they eased through, the attack dogs eyed them, their ears erect, their canines fully exposed.

The patrol car careened its way up the long driveway leading to the mansion. Several sports cars gleamed in the early morning sun in front of the six-car garage, buffed and shined like vehicles lined up for a car show. A silver Porsche, a black Ferrari, a signature red Dodge Viper, and an emerald green Jaguar. Off to the side, a midnight blue Hummer and a chic black stretch limousine glowed. Santiago whistled, envying the dream machines. What he wouldn't give to own one. Pulling up along side of them, he turned to Stevenson and smirked. "Think we'll get towed?"

A quiet serenity surrounded the DeVeccio estate. Enclosed by a sweeping view of the Red Rock Mountains, the sprawling mansion overlooked a beautifully manicured lawn.

Marble lion statues guarded the courtyard, their mouths open in silent roars. Massive columns and a turned balustrade flanked the white stone porch, and a wrap-around verandah hugged the entire mansion.

The butler let them in, looking put upon by a visit from the police. He scowled, his thin lips perched into a pout. "If you'll follow me this way. Mr. DeVeccio is in the parlor."

The parlor resembled a museum. Blue silk drapes flowed from a bank of floor-to-ceiling windows, and a Venetian crystal chandelier suspended from a sixteen-foot vaulted ceiling. Plush leather sofas enclosed a wet bar, and a mammoth stone fireplace took up an entire wall. Polished heirlooms displayed on white marble tables gleamed in the muted sun pouring in from windows. At the far end of the living room, beveled glass doors opened to a terrace balcony leading to a patio with a geometric sunken pool.

Michael DeVeccio lolled on a Queen Anne chaise lounge, reading the Wall Street Journal. He sipped a cup of coffee, looking every bit the billionaire tycoon.

Santiago strutted toward him with purpose, his long legs eating up the floor. He flashed his identification. "We meet again after ten years."

Michael DeVeccio looked up and smiled. "Detective Santiago. And what brings you to my humble home? Am I remiss in paying my taxes? Or perhaps you're collecting for the Policeman's Ball?"

Santiago glared, his broody brown eyes filled with challenge. "Lacy Diamond is dead, slashed in the throat. Just dragged your girlfriend's corpse out of her bathtub, zipped her up in a body bag and sent her downtown where she'll be laid out on a slab in the county morgue. Got any ideas who might have killed her?"

Michael stood up and refilled his coffee, his expression stone cold. He sipped the gourmet blend and set it down, meeting the detective's gaze. "Lacy was killed? Someone murdered my girl? While she was taking a bath?"

"Yeah. Mind telling me where you were the night before last around midnight?"

Michael's eyes never changed expression. "In Chicago for a business meeting. My pilot flew me straight to Chicago on my way back from Tuscany. I spent the night in my Lincoln Park penthouse and then had dinner with a friend last night at Crystal's."

Santiago stared him down. "Still as slick with the lies as you were ten years ago, aren't you? When did you get back to Vegas?"

"This morning. At precisely 7 a.m."

"You can verify that?"

"Of course." Michael fished out a Marlboro and tapped it three times before lighting it. He walked to the window and stared at the sand stone cliffs of the canyon. "I can't believe Lacy's dead. Who would wanna kill my girl? Everyone adored her."

"Not everyone." Santiago watched the billionaire closely. How he'd love to wipe that smug expression off his face. He hadn't so much as flinched when told about the brutal slaying of his girlfriend, a woman he was engaged to. Santiago had gotten more of a reaction when he used to write up traffic tickets. "How long were you and Ms. Diamond engaged?"

"Six months. It's been an ongoing relationship for the past ten years. Last month, we set a date and were in the midst of planning an intimate Christmas wedding at my club. And just what are you doing to solve this case, detective? Surely you're not here to inform me the killer has slipped through your fingers, just like my uncle's?"

Santiago's pulse quickened a beat. "The killer didn't slip through our fingers. Quite the contrary. Now how about telling me when you last spoke to Lacy Diamond."

"The night before last, while she was taking a bubble bath. I called her on her cell phone."

"While she was taking a bubble bath?"

"That's right."

"And what time was that?"

"Precisely quarter to midnight. I called my girl to tell her I had to fly to Chicago and wouldn't be over as planned. I also called just to hear her sweet voice. She had the voice of an angel. I called to hear it one last time before she closed her eyes."

Santiago took a step closer. "One last time before she closed her eyes?"

Michael flicked his ash in the sterling silver ashtray and smiled. "That's right, detective. I call Lacy every night I'm not with her. I know she always takes a bubble bath between 11:30 and midnight to relax her before she goes to bed. If

I'd only known it was the last time I'd ever hear her sexy voice..."

If Santiago had any doubts the billionaire was the killer, he didn't any more. DeVeccio enjoyed the challenge, taunting, teasing, playing a game of cat and mouse. He was as crazy as a fox and just as sly. But Santiago was good at getting into the mind of a killer, and sooner or later, he'd trip up the smug billionaire. "So DeVeccio, did Lacy Diamond have any enemies you were aware of? Anyone that might want to hurt her?"

Michael shrugged. "Not as far as I know. Lacy was a dancer at my club. Men of all ages adored her. She had the face of an angel and the body of a hooker. She attracted men like magnets. Could be one of them developed a crush on her, a fetish for her affections. No one could tease men better than Lacy."

"So you think maybe she got the wrong guy hard? Teased the wrong cock? Rubbed up against someone who wanted a little more than she was willing to give?"

Michael yawned. "Could be, detective. Lacy was a beautiful woman and turning men on was what she did best. Getting guys hard kept them coming back to my club. It won't be easy, replacing Lacy Diamond. I doubt anyone can fill her shoes."

Santiago studied the billionaire. Women would be attracted to him. And with a fat bank roll to boot, no doubt he could get any woman he wanted. It was obvious he worked out on a regular basis, all those bulging biceps. Snappy dresser, too, all decked out in his billion dollar threads. And not a hair out of place, probably had a trim and a style at the same uptown salon where he had his nails buffed. The billionaire was far too cool for someone Santiago would bet his badge had killed his fiancé.

"And you didn't mind your girlfriend getting all those men hot at your club? That didn't bother you? Didn't it make you a little jealous? A little crazy? So crazy with jealousy you wedged a Ninja star down her pretty throat, and covered her corpse with a mask, a death mask, just the way you did your uncle ten years back?"

Michael met his gaze and smiled. "A Ninja star? And a death mask? Just like Uncle Carlos, the case you have yet to solve? Don't tell me there's a Ninja assassin on the loose?

Perhaps you'd better get going, put out an all point bulletin."

"Just one more thing. How are you in martial arts?"

"I'm the grand master. I've won awards in wielding a Ninja throwing star. I'm so good I could wield a death star with my eyes closed and hit the mark every time. Bull's eye."

CHAPTER FIVE

Nestled in the posh residential section of the Gold Coast, Margot's Chicago-style bungalow offered a rural respite from the bustling downtown loop. With its street facing gable, stained glass windows, and turret, it slumbered in a sleepy meadow of woodland pines and rolling hills. Just beyond her private enclave, the elevated track encircling the downtown section of the city thrived.

Her cat, Zeus, rubbed Margot's leg when she returned from her morning jog. She leaned over to scratch his ear. "Tough day?"

The plump orange tabby scampered through the light dusting of snow in hot pursuit of a yellow throat warbler. The bird swooped down just as the fat cat pounced, and then soared into the winter skies with a flutter of wings.

Fumbling for her key, Margot admired the autumn wreath of English roses, red dogwood, and rustic bittersweet on the door. Humming the song she and Michael had danced to the night before, she reached over and got the mail from the box, haphazardly sorting through it as she opened the door.

Splashes of late morning sun poured into her glass encased atrium. Spider plants and hearty ferns added a cheery atmosphere to her makeshift greenery. Between bamboo chairs, leafy canopies of wild flowers spilled from rustic wooden barrels. Zeus leaped onto the window seat, purring away.

Getting a mug of coffee, Margot turned on the television and joined the plump feline, giving him a gentle nudge. Hugging her knees to her chest, she watched flurries swirl from the sky. Her mood was as merry as the snowflakes. Outstretched pine branches captured the snow, flocking the bristly needles with a mist as finely spun as angel hair.

Christmas this year would be the best, she mused, lazily sipping on her hazelnut coffee. She'd invited Michael to spend Christmas at her parents' home, and he, in turn, had invited her to his annual New Year's Eve masquerade ball. She couldn't wait. Who should she portray? With her closet full of costumes, dressing up wasn't the problem. The problem was dressing up to impress Michael DeVeccio. Something classy, gorgeous, and sexy—all rolled up in one.

Sighing, she stroked Zeus's back as memories of the night before filtered through her head. Just then, the doorbell rang, snapping her out of her revelry. She peeked out the window, pleasantly surprised to see a florist's truck sitting curbside. The delivery man stood on her front stoop, holding a monstrosity of flowers. Racing to the door, she yanked it open.

"Delivery for Margot Montgomery," the disembodied voice muttered from behind the green cellophane. "Looks like you've got yourself quite an admirer."

Grabbing the arrangement with both hands, Margot thanked the man and brought the flowers into the atrium. Her hands trembled when she read the card. "Margot. To the perfect woman. Always and forever. Michael."

She must be dreaming. Three dozen of the most beautiful red roses she'd ever seen sat in a Waterford vase. Fussing over them like a school girl, she wondered how she'd managed to go thirty-two years without so much as a crush. The songbirds outdoors echoed the joy in her heart. Then, breaking news came on the television.

"Lacy Diamond, fiancé of billionaire tycoon Michael DeVeccio, dead. Ms. Diamond was found earlier this morning in her Red Rock estate, the victim of a brutal slaying. Lacy Diamond, beautiful and vivacious, dead at the age of twenty-eight. She and Michael DeVeccio had planned to marry on Christmas Day."

Margot watched in shock as a press conference got under

way. Channel 2 circled with their cameras, along with CNN and FOX, shooting questions at Michael with rapid fire.

"Mr. DeVeccio. What is your reaction to the brutal slaying of your fiancé? Any idea who might have slashed her throat while she was taking a bath? What are you planning to do about finding your lover's killer?"

Michael answered the questions, his charismatic voice transcending over the media. "Naturally I am devastated about my fiancé's death. She was a beautiful woman who I'd planned to marry on Christmas Day. We were planning to marry at my club, just a small intimate affair. I have no idea who could have committed such a heinous crime, but the police are investigating. I want her killer brought to justice."

"Mr. DeVeccio, wasn't yesterday the ten year anniversary of your uncle's death? Carlos DeVeccio, the Vegas icon who built the DeVeccio Dynasty from the ground up? Wasn't his throat slashed too? And weren't you the prime suspect in his death? Did you kill your fiancé the same way you killed your uncle? Did you kill Lacy Diamond before she could get her hands on your billion dollar fortune?"

"No comment."

Margot slumped down in the window seat in a heap, feeling like she'd been punched in the gut. Her stomach rolled, threatening to upheave her breakfast. How could she have been so stupid? Billionaires like Michael DeVeccio didn't fall for nobodies like her. She was just some idle trinket to toy with when he came to Chicago. She berated herself for falling for such a line of bull. She ought to know better, and she did.

The face of Michael's fiancé had been splashed all over the media, a face beautiful enough to be featured in a magazine. Margot's heart sank. That gorgeous woman had been engaged to Michael DeVeccio, her Michael, and they had planned to marry on Christmas Day, the day he'd promised to spend with her and her family.

Margot stared at her beautiful red roses, a bitter-sweet reminder of their enchanted evening the night before. Last night had been too perfect to be real, and that's just what it was. That old proverb popped into her head: Beware of false promises. Whoever thought that one up certainly knew a thing or two about falling for a line of bull.

But she had fallen for it and the truth hurt. Her heart wedged in her throat. Tears threatened; within seconds, they gushed out and trickled down her cheeks.

And what about Michael being accused of killing his uncle ten years ago? Could there be any truth to that? What was the story with this Lacy Diamond? Who killed her? Anxiety throbbed at her temples. Michael told her he'd gone straight from Tuscany to his Chicago condo and had slept the day away until their date. Why had he made such a point of giving her all that added information? At some point during that time frame, Lacy Diamond had been murdered. A sick feeling weighed her down, chipping away at her subconscious. Was she his alibi?

The phone rang, its piercing ring breaking through her turmoil. She let the machine pick up. It was Michael, sounding as sincere as he had the night before. "Margot, no doubt you've heard the news about Lacy by now. Let me explain. It's all a big misunderstanding, a big mistake. After meeting you, I planned to break off my engagement with Lacy. Honest I did. Come on, Margot, pick up. I know you're upset and you have every right to be. Just let me explain. You are the woman I've searched the world over for—and I won't let you go."

Tears rolled down her face as she listened to the message again and again. As it played for the umpteenth time, she uncorked a bottle of champagne she'd been saving for a special occasion. Slugging some back straight from the bottle, she figured if this wasn't a special occasion, she didn't know what was. After downing half the bottle, she poured the rest over the roses, her beautiful and flawless red roses. Almost instantly, they fell apart and wilted, just like her.

The phone rang again; this time it was Sophia. She picked up the receiver.

"Margot, you poor thing. How are you holding up? I couldn't believe my eyeballs when I turned on the screen. The louse was engaged. What a prick. Wanna fly to Vegas and kick him in the nuts so hard he'll be a soprano? I've done it before and I can do it again. And what's all this about him being a suspect in the murder of his uncle ten years ago? I'm doing an online search in the archives; it's true. Michael was a suspect in his uncle's death, but he was never convicted. Holy cow! And now his fiancé gets her throat slashed the same way? Stay clear of him. The dude's nothing but bad news. Hey, I got it, the perfect solution. You've been yakking about writing a best selling thriller, right? Why not start now? Come on, Margot. It will be good therapy. With your nose for a story, you can do it. What do you think?"

Margot's head spun, trying to keep up. Before she knew it, Sophia's quirky sense of humor got the best of her and she laughed out loud. "Listen, Sophie. How about coming over. Bring a couple bottles of wine and we'll knock 'em back while we solve the problems of the world."

"Give me twenty minute, half hour tops. And in spite of everything else, I'm dying to hear all about your date with the Casanova killer. We'll dish the day away. I'll stop for a pizza, too. So how about it? Double cheese and pepperoni?"

"Get the works."

ЖХЖҜ

Streaming sunshine poured through the windows of the bungalow the following morning. Zeus frantically meowed for his breakfast. Margot pried one eye open and quickly closed it. Her head pounded and the room rotated around her in circles. Zeus meowed all the louder, showing no sympathy whatsoever to the fact his mistress had one hell of a hang-over.

"All right," Margot groaned, rolling over on one elbow to discover she had fallen asleep in her atrium. Three empty bottles of wine appeared in her unfocused gaze, along with an open pizza box with nothing in it but a few crumbs, crumpled bags of chips, her laptop, several pieces of paper from the printer, and curled in a ball in front of it all, Sophia slept off her hangover.

Margot stood up, stretched her aching muscles, and slowly staggered into the kitchen. Zeus sat impatiently at his dish. She opened a can of food, the smell of the fishy blend gagging her. Groaning, she put on a pot of coffee and went to the bathroom in search of some aspirin. Catching sight of herself in the mirror, she gasped. Mascara streaked down her cheeks and her hair stood straight up in clumps like a punk rocker from a few decades back. Popping back the aspirin, she downed them with some water and went to get the coffee.

Scuffing down the hallway in her fluffy slippers, wrinkled jogging suit, and steaming mug of coffee, she couldn't remember ever feeling worse. Her bloodshot, bleary eyes refused to focus and her head felt like it was lopsided. Weaving, the coffee sloshed out of her cup, leaving a trail of zigzags on her newly burnished cherry wood floors.

From outside, the snow plow screeched and scraped, followed by the soothing lull of shovels digging and gliding as neighbors cleared their walks. She glanced out the window, amazed at how much snow had fallen. Her doorbell rang. Setting her coffee down, she opened the door and came face to face with Michael.

"Margot?" his eyes flickered with amusement. "May I come in?"

Margot just stood there, her mouth agape. Never in a million years did she expect to see Michael standing at her door. And of all mornings, when she looked like something the cat dragged in.

The picture of Lacy Diamond flashed through her mind, not because she was dead, not because she had been brutally murdered, but because she'd been engaged to Michael and was gorgeous enough to be a movie star. Margot felt frumpy and simple, like some lowly peasant. Much to her humiliation, tears filled her eyes and the flood gates broke.

Michael had her in his arms in two seconds flat, bringing in a gush of cold Chicago wind. "I'm so sorry, Margot. I never meant to hurt you, honest." He stroked her hair, kicking the door closed with his foot. "Don't you know how important you are to me, how much you mean to me?"

Just then, Zeus let out a ferocious hiss as he hurled through the air, wrapping himself around Michael's legs, claws fully extended. The sharp rip of material zinged off the glass encased atrium.

"Zeus!" Margot scolded the feline, but the fat cat made a beeline for the sofa, his claws clicking rhythmically on the hardwood floors as he ran for his life. She stared in astonishment at the bloody knee popping through the hole of Michael's tailor-made trousers. Sputtering, she said, "I'm sorry. My cat never acts like that. I don't know what got into him. I'll…"

"Forget about the pants," Michael brushed it off with a dismissive wave. "I have plenty of clothes. We need to discuss Lacy. I want you to believe me when I tell you it was over. I was going to break our engagement, honest. Just give me..."

A loud crack exploded as Sophia's fist met Michael's jaw line. "Take that you two timing son of a bitch. That will teach you to lie and cheat. By the way, I'm Sophia Andretti, Margot's best friend and assistant curator. So did you do it, Mr. Big Shot? Did you kill your lover? Men like you make me sick." She gave Margot a sidelong glance. "I still say we oughta kick him in the nuts so hard he'll be singing' like a soprano. It's not too late."

Sophia Andretti glared at Michael through puffy, blood-shot eyes. Dressed in an oversized Chicago Bears shirt, she looked mean enough to take on an entire team of burly line-backers.

Michael rubbed his chin. "So much for introductions. I always did say they're overrated. Since neither of you are at your best, why don't I fix breakfast for you. I think getting some food into your stomachs could only help. Margot, do you have anything in your refrigerator? If not, I'll run to the store and get some bacon and eggs."

Margot stood there, flabbergasted. Michael was at her door in the middle of a blizzard, begging her forgiveness for keeping his dead fiancé a secret, she looked like death warmed over, Zeus and Sophia attacked a billionaire tycoon, and his wanted to cook for them. She blinked several times, wanting nothing more than to roll up in a ball and die. She huffed out an exasperated breath and hurled her hands in the air. "I just went to the market yesterday when I heard the forecast. If you want to cook, knock yourself out."

Sitting in the atrium, Michael served goat cheese and mushroom omelets, bacon, flaky croissants, and fresh fruit cups. He poured the coffee and took a seat next to Margot. "So, by the looks of things, you two really tied one on last night. Dare I take credit, or do you make a habit of drinking heavy?"

"I rarely drink more than one glass of wine," Margot said. "And yes, you might say we toasted you plenty last night."

"We sure did," Sophia grinned, winking at Michael with one unfocused eye. "Weren't your ears burning? But, hey. I've decided anyone who comes here to the windy city in a blizzard to beg forgiveness, tolerates physical abuse, and has the culinary skills of a gourmet chef, can't be all bad. So come on, Margot, have a heart. At least give him a chance to tell his side of the story, otherwise, it will be your ass I'm kicking next." She stood up, brushing the crumbs from the jeans she had changed into while the food was cooking. "Looks like the roads are clear enough for me to head out of here. Think I'll just run along and leave you two love birds to work things out. My Tony's probably worried sick about me. It was a pleasure meeting you, Michael. I hope the next time we meet will be under better circumstances."

"Sophia," Michael stood up. "It's been interesting to say the least."

After Sophia left, Margot took the dishes into the kitchen. Michael settled into a bamboo chair next to the dead roses, reading the crumpled up papers he'd gathered from the floor.

"Well I'm ready to talk now, Michael." Margot joined him. "What are you reading?"

"About the Casanova killer of Red Rock Canyon. Interesting stuff. Tell me, Margot? Who is writing this bestselling thriller? You or Sophia?"

Margot's face turned a bright shade of crimson. She'd forgotten all about the story she'd started last night. With Sophia egging her on, the writing had gotten out of hand. They had the serial killer doing kinky things to his victims and Lord knows what else after so much wine. Embarrassed, she snatched them out of his hands. "We were just kidding around, two drunken fools. I've been kicking around the idea of writing a thriller, and, well, what can I say?"

"Margot," Michael's voice was barely more than a whisper. "I'm no killer. Look at these hands that have just cooked a gourmet breakfast for you and your body guard. Do they look like the hands of a cold blooded killer?" he traced the outline of her lips with the tip of his finger with such gentleness it made her tremble. "Believe me, Margot, I didn't kill Lacy, and I certainly didn't kill my uncle, the man who treated me like his own son. The media is always looking for gossip when it comes to the rich and famous."

"I don't think you're a killer, Michael. If I did, you wouldn't be in my home right now, alone with me in the middle of a blizzard. And as far as Lacy is concerned, it's going to take some time to get over that shock. I won't be lied to or cheated on. Above all else, I will not be made a fool of. I need to make that clear before we continue dating."

"Margot, these words come straight from my heart. The

minute I met you, I knew you were the perfect woman for me." He stared into her eyes. "I've searched the world over for a woman like you—and I have no intention of letting you go."

CHAPTER SIX

The meandering hills of Chicago Heights gave way to sleepy valleys surrounded by woodland pines, the lakefront, and miles of rolling meadows. Shrouded by the elevated track making up the inner circle of the Loop, the brightly decorated homes in rural Chicago were as magically alluring as a Santa village.

As Margot pulled up in front of her parents' home, several inches of snow blanketed the ground, adding to the holiday ambiance. Outstretched branches from huge spruce trees undulated in the wind, blowing heaps of snow all askew. With candles in the bay windows, a massive holly wreath on the white wooden door, and wood smoke billowing out of the red brick chimney, it was as decorative as a gingerbread house.

Margot loved Christmas when the world was born anew. Sharing the traditions of an old fashioned holiday with her family brought it all full circle. This year was all the more reason to celebrate because Michael was coming to Chicago to spend it with her.

Too bad Michael's pilot had delayed his flight, Margot mused. But with the blizzard hovering over Chicago, she understood. It was just that she'd wanted to spend the entire day with him. Better late than never, she figured, noticing the sudden onslaught of lights all over the neighborhood, as if set on a timer. The warm glow from the twinkling lights beneath the eaves filled her with a sense of inner peace. Although she'd wanted to wait for Michael, he'd insisted she go to her parents as planned.

Singing along to classic Christmas carols on the radio, Margot got a firm grip on the cat caddy and opened her car door. As the howling winds of Chicago whipped her scarf around her face, she took a skid that sent her skating along the slick pavement. Zeus meowed frantically as she walked up the candy cane lined walkway.

The minute she walked through the door, the mingled scents of bayberry and honey-baked ham filled her with the comforts of home. The headiness of the fragrant pine stirred nostalgic memories from Christmases past. Cherry wood logs blazed in the stone fireplace, giving the house a warm, ethereal glow.

From the foyer, Margot watched her father fiddle with the logs in the fireplace. Kneeling on the brick façade, Justin Montgomery adjusted the chimney flue, making sure the smoke and heat were properly channeled. Christmas carols played softly in the background, the perfect accompaniment to the cozy ambiance.

Standing up, he dusted his hands on his black corduroys and poked at the dwindling embers. Heaving a sigh, he thrust a log into the fire, the dry wood cracking as bright orange flames shot upward. Closing the screen, he lit his pipe. That's when he noticed his daughter, standing in the foyer, quietly watching. "Margot," he said, his cheeks flushed from the fire. "How long have you been standing there?"

"Long enough to see you haven't lost your touch," Margot smiled, releasing the traumatized Zeus from his caddy. The plump tabby made a beeline for the tree, batted the one-of-a kind Christopher Radko Mickey Mouse ornament onto the hardwood floor and gave chase.

"Margot," Sara Montgomery bustled out of the kitchen, her hands full of freshly baked cookies. "Where's Michael?"

"His flight was delayed because of the snow storm," Margot said. "But he'll be along shortly."

Holiday favorites gleamed on bookshelves and cozy alcoves. Walking across the hardwood floor to the coffee table, Margot picked up the ceramic carousel she had made one year. Winding it up, the horses pranced to a cheery medley of Jingle Bell Rock. A smile teased her lips as visions of Mi-

chael danced in her head. Then she sat before the fire with
her parents and indulged in a holiday toast while they waited
for the guest of honor to arrive.

Nibbling on stuffed mushrooms and crab dip, the Montgomery family carried on with yearly traditions. The scene
was warm and inviting. Icicles formed beneath the eaves of
the house while the indoors blazed with a cheery glow. The
peaceful serenity was broken by the sharp jingle of Margot's
cell phone. She got it on the first ring.

"That was Michael," she gushed, her cheeks all aglow.
"He's coming up the hill. Just wait until you meet him. And
talk about handsome, let me just say Hollywood actors have
nothing on him. His eyes are the bluest you've ever seen.
Just you wait."

"I say it's about time a man's gotten under your skin,"
Margot's mother preened. "I do believe my girl's in love. Out
of all the men you've dated over the years, none of them has
had this affect on you."

Just then the doorbell rang and Margot dashed to the
foyer, stars in her eyes as she flung the door open. The minute she saw him, butterflies fluttered in the pit of her stomach. Her blood ran hot when she gazed into his magnetic
blue eyes.

"Michael!" Margot pulled him in on a gust of wind. She
couldn't remember ever being so taken by a man in her life.
Michael DeVeccio stole her breath. "I'm so glad you made it
safe and sound. Come in out of the cold and warm up. I can't
wait to introduce you to my parents. They're looking forward
to meeting you, too. Come on, give me your coat. You must
be frozen."

Michael kissed Margot, his lips hot in spite of his icy skin.
His gaze swept appreciatively over her black silk slacks and
shimmering silver sweater. "You look like a beautifully
wrapped Christmas gift, one I'd love to find under my tree."

Feeling the heat after that slow perusal of her body,
Margot's blood turned to liquid heat. The tips of his long eyelashes were dusted with snow, making his blue eyes appear
all the bluer. She took his leather coat. "I'll just hang this
up."

While she draped it over a kitchen chair to dry, her
mother came into the foyer, grinning like a cheshire cat.

"Michael, it's a pleasure to meet you. I'm Margot's

mother, Sara. I must say my daughter wasn't exaggerating when she said you were movie star handsome. In my day, you are what we would have called a heart throb."

"You're too kind. And you look far too young to be Margot's mother. Let me just say good looks do indeed run in the Montgomery family. It's easy to see where Margot gets her beauty. Thank you for inviting me. There's nothing I enjoy more than the traditions of an old-fashioned Christmas. It means a lot to me. Truly."

Michael winked as he handed over a beautifully wrapped gift. "For the charming hostess. Just a small token of my appreciation for your warm hospitality."

"You didn't have to bring anything," Sara Montgomery gushed, touched by the gesture. "Thank you so much. I'll just put it under the tree with the rest of the presents."

Margot came into the living room to find Michael chatting companionably with her parents, bourbon in hand. No need for introductions, she mused. Everyone seemed to be getting along.

Justin Montgomery might appear to be hospitable, but looks could be deceiving. From behind the thick lenses of his semi-rimless bifocals, he studied Michael through speculative eyes. Scanning him from head to toe, something just didn't seem right. From his perfectly groomed hair and fingernails to his custom-designed clothes and Italian leather loafers, something just wasn't right.

As a professor at the University of Chicago for the past two decades, Justin Montgomery knew a thing or two about people. If something was too good to be true, then it usually was. He'd been keeping tabs on the murder investigation of Lacy Diamond. It was far too reminiscent of the Carlos DeVeccio murder to be an idle coincidence. As the family meandered into the dining room, Justin Montgomery decided to keep both eyes on the billionaire tycoon.

The candlelit table was beautifully set. A red satin runner with gold embroidered angels ran the length of the white linen tablecloth. A centerpiece of holly leaves spiraled around a hurricane lamp.

"Everything is delicious," Michael said, graciously accepting another slice of ham. "The best restaurants in the world can't compare to a home cooked meal. My compliments to the chef."

Sara beamed, noticing the understated interplay going on between her daughter and Michael. She'd never seen Margot's eyes shine quite so bright before. Sighing contentedly, she said, "Help yourself to more. We have plenty. There is no greater compliment to a cook than a clean plate."

Picking up on Justin's misgivings, Michael directed the conversation to Margot's father. "I understand you're an English professor at the university. That must be so rewarding, helping students reach their goals."

"It has its moments," Justin peered at Michael through his eyeglasses. "Margot tells me you've been in Italy building a new resort. Mind telling me a little about that?"

"Not at all. The DeVeccio family has been building luxury resorts and casinos for generations, both here and abroad. I'm in the process of building a huge conglomerate off the coast of Tuscany, but my construction crew ran into some problems. With architecture, there's always interference with the workers and the building codes."

"Michael," Margot urged, "Tell them about this latest De-Veccio Plaza, how truly awesome it will be when it's done. It sounds so magnificent – like one of our luxurious skyscrapers here in Chicago."

Michael's blue eyes blazed in the candlelight. "The style of this tower is a new approach, using aspects of late Gothic architecture with Romanesque elements along with modern amenities. The resort will feature an 80-foot vaulted ceiling in the lobby, marble floors, solid oak doors, mirrors with gold leaf edgings, rare paintings and sculptures, and a glass façade. When it's finished, the hotel will showcase my most eclectic design to date, blending glamour and grandeur in one."

Justin chomped on a stick of celery and grunted, "Hmm."

"Michael," Margot stood up, clearing the dinner plates from the table. "If we're going to go to Midnight Mass, we'd better get going. It gets really crowded and we don't want to stand."

Sara had just opened the gift he'd given her. "Michael, I've wanted to get a cappuccino maker for so long now. I love it."

Michael smiled. "Thank you both for your hospitality. The dinner was delicious. When I look back on this night, it will be with warm and fond memories of a loving family."

ЖЖЖ

From the bell tower of St. Ignatius Cathedral, twelve chimes rang through the star-lit night, calling the faithful to the Midnight Mass celebration. Peace and serenity transcended through the congregation as parishioners filed into candlelit pews. The mahogany seats gleamed under the glow of the pure white candles at the end of each row. To the accompaniment of trumpets, flutes, and harps, the choir broke out in glorious exultation.

"Aren't they beautiful?" Margot whispered. "Like a chorus of angels. I forgot to remind you to make a wish. If you make a wish when you walk into a church for the first time, your wish will always come true."

"One of my wishes has already come true," Michael leaned over and kissed her. "I feel so blessed to have found someone as flawless as you. As I've mentioned, I've searched the world over for you, the perfect woman to fulfill my dreams and make my life complete. But I'll be happy to make another wish."

The mass ended with an instrumental of Silent Night, and the world was born anew.

"Let's go say a prayer at the Nativity Set," Margot suggested. "We do indeed have a lot to be thankful for in our lives."

Shrouded by fragrant pines, the Nativity Set was illuminated in blue lights. Huge red and white poinsettias decorated the altar. And shining tall and bright, a star on the tallest pine led the way to the perfect sight.

Kneeling before the Nativity Set on the solid mahogany kneeler, Margot and Michael indulged in a moment of silence.

"About that wish," Michael whispered, reaching into his vest pocket, withdrawing a brilliant diamond ring in the shape of a rose. A spiraling array of Brazilian emeralds surrounded it, giving the illusion of dew dampened leaves. The ring sparkled under the lights. His penetrating gaze seared into hers. "I can't think of a wish I'd rather have granted than this one. You are the perfect woman for me. Marry me, Margot. Make my dreams come true."

Totally captivated by this man who had stolen her heart, Margot stared in astonishment at the rock glittering between his fingers. It had to be the most beautiful diamond she'd ever seen and he had just proposed to her, right at the altar. Biting her lip, she blinked to make sure she wasn't dreaming. Slowly, she looked into Michael's hypnotic blue eyes and knew he was the one.

Holding out her left hand, she said, "Yes. I'll marry you. I think I fell in love with you the moment I looked into your eyes. And from that moment, you had me under your spell. I love you, Michael. Always and forever."

Michael slipped the ring on the third finger of her left hand. "You've made me very happy, darling Margot. Never disappoint me or give me reason to doubt your innocence. That is my golden rule and a sin I will not forgive. You are the perfect woman, my angel."

CHAPTER SEVEN

As the DeVeccio corporate jet made its thrilling descent into Vegas on New Year's Eve, Margot stared out the window in awe. Since meeting Michael DeVeccio, her life had been a whirlwind of continuous change. Her diamond captured sunbeams coming in from the window, exploding into a kaleidoscope of colors on the plane's interior. Michael had given her the engagement ring a week ago, and looking at it still made her heart tap dance in her chest. Spending Christmas with Michael at her parents had been wonderful, and going to his masquerade ball filled her with sheer excitement.

She looked out the window and took a picture. The view of Red Rock Canyon was simply staggering. As the jet angled over the sloping terrain, the sun cast an amber glow on the roughly defined rock formation. She took a few more pictures with her digital camera—and then sat back in her seat as they circled the airport. Just a few more minutes and she would see her man. Yanking her compact from her purse, she checked her makeup and fussed with her hair. Then with a sudden jolt, the jet hit the ground and they landed.

Racing down the terminal, Margot spotted Michael instantly. He winked at her, looking dangerously seductive in a pair of khakis, a short-sleeved white shirt, and a silk tie with subtle splashes of aqua. Her heartbeat tripled as she hurried toward him.

"Michael," she was in his arms in seconds flat. His masculine scent filled her, making her weak in the knees.

"You look gorgeous," his gaze swept over her. "The tailored look suits your personality, perfect just like you. I can't wait to show you my mansion that will be our home once we're married." Picking up the bag at her feet, he said, "Come with me, my driver's out front."

As they exited the airport, a sleek black limousine pulled up to the curb. The driver held the door open and Margot sunk into a cushion of luxury.

Once they drove past the exit, the terrain became noticeably rougher, more uncultivated. With just an edge of danger, the pioneer spirit of the Wild West lived on in the foothills of Red Rock Canyon. Burros and wild horses galloped free on the landscape. Patches of tumbleweed and sagebrush weaved in and out of the road, and deep in the underbrush, coyotes, bobcats, and mountain lions roamed.

Margot's skin tingled as they delved deeper into the foothills. The temperature had dropped and she felt a slight chill. Then she thought about the brutal stabbing of Lacy Diamond—and she broke out in an icy shiver. The thought of a killer stalking the mountains so close to Michael's Red Rock estate caused a ripple of fear to skate down her spine. Was he still out there? Who had killed her? Wanting to rid the morbid images from her mind, she moved a little closer to Michael, her insecurities melting the minute he put a reassuring arm around her. "Do you think the killer will strike again?"

Michael smiled to himself. His voice was soft, barely more than a whisper. "Darling Margot. Hush now. Do you really think there's a boogie man out there? Allow me to set your mind at ease. Lacy probably messed with the wrong person. The way she'd been mixing booze and narcotics, who knows what she was into. And with her outstanding gambling debts, she might have owed someone a lot of money. I got her out of more than one jam. So quit your worrying. I'm sure it was an isolated incident. Besides, the safest place you can be is in my arms. Trust me."

"I've never felt safer," she said, snuggling closer. His muscular arms snaked around her small frame, easing away the last of her worries. How could she think about a murderer when she was with this man who made her feel so safe and secure? But all the same, she'd feel a lot better once the police caught the murderer. She turned her head upward. "I worry about you. This killer seems to be stalking people close to you. What if you're the next victim?"

"You're getting yourself all riled up for nothing," Michael said, gingerly stroking her throat with his fingers. "Just because my uncle and Lacy were stabbed with a Ninja star is no reason to think I'm next. Don't be ridiculous. Obviously, whoever killed them had some sort of personal vendetta, a score to settle. It happens all the time with rich people. The world's full of nuts. I'm not in the least concerned about some lunatic stalking me. Believe me, whoever killed Lacy and my uncle is not after me."

"I guess," Margot said, still not convinced. She peered into the foothills as if she might spy the killer in the deep underbrush of the forest. "You know, I've been wondering about something. You said your cousins are coming to the masquerade party tonight. Why would you invite them since you're no longer close? Didn't you say you and your cousins grew up together and were best friends until you had a falling out over business?"

"That's right," Michael confirmed. "I used to be very close with Johnny, Ricky, and Jimmy O'Toole. When I first moved to Vegas, They were like my brothers. We hiked the trails of Red Rock Canyon, fished on the lakes, and slept under the stars. But once we grew up and accepted our responsibilities as men in our respective companies, we grew apart. But the New Year's Eve masquerade ball is a tradition, an annual bash started decades ago by Uncle Carlos. It's attended by all the big shots of the Vegas Strip each year, even our competitors. Uncle Carlos lived for his masquerade and his suite still mirrors his passion for masks. Just wait until you see it. You'll love it. Speaking of masquerades, what beguiling character will you portray tonight?"

Margot smiled mysteriously. "I guess you'll have to wait and see. And you?"

"Don't you worry, Margot. You'll be the first to know."

As the sun disappeared behind the Red Rock Mountain, the desert sky was a striation of color, blending into a menagerie of pale peach, magenta, and deep indigo. A sultry breeze stirred through the cavernous mountainside, carrying with it the scent of a coming storm. As twilight settled over the desert, a vulture hovered over the canyon, foreboding an eerie screech as it circled high above the foothills.

Nearing the top of the mountainside, the road suddenly narrowed into a sloping ridge, and for the next few minutes, the only thing separating the limousine from a drop of several thousand feet was a mound of crumbled rock. Just as suddenly, the horseshoe curve fanned out into an unexpected oasis.

Margot started to say something, but lost it on a gasp when she spotted the DeVeccio estate in the distance. Fluted pilasters graced the entrance of the long driveway. Out of the shadows, two sleek Dobermans crept, assuming their positions on either side of the entrance. Silent and deadly, they watched the limousine career its way through the electric gate.

"They're so quiet," Margot commented, thinking they were as rigid as the stone statues surrounding the entrance. "Don't they bark or come up to greet you or anything?"

Michael stared at her as if she were stupid. "Simon and Jude aren't pets. They're attack dogs, trained to kill. Their job is to prowl the estate for intruders and go straight for the jugular vein."

Shrouded by the Red Rock Mountains, the estate fanned out into a well manicured lawn. Beautifully sculptured stone lions flanked a regal courtyard. Joshua trees, pinyons, and ponderosa pines towered over the two-story estate. Wrought iron balconies bordered the upper windows, and a wraparound verandah hugged the stone porch. Beneath it, a garden of roses bloomed within the confinements of a redwood arbor.

"Oh, Michael," Margot gushed. "This is beautiful. The picture you showed me didn't do this place justice. I can't wait to see the inside."

Michael liked her response. "It will be my pleasure to give you the grand tour. Welcome to my kingdom."

ЖЖЖ

A heavy mahogany door opened to a marble foyer, separating a parlor from the dining room. The parlor showcased priceless antiques, including a Victorian chaise lounge with carved claw legs. A log burned in the stone fireplace, permeating the room with the rustic scent of birch. Pleated blue silk drapes flowed from floor to ceiling windows, and a white Baby Grand graced the far corner.

As curator of an art museum, Margot recognized and appreciated fine art and antiques. Judging from what she could see, the family heirlooms in the parlor of the DeVeccio estate could be displayed in some of the most prestigious museums in the world. "What I wouldn't give to showcase some of these at one of my exhibits. Some must go back several centuries. That elephant with the ivory tusks over there is gorgeous. Where's it from?"

Michael picked it up and rubbed the glossy tusks between his fingers. "My uncle got this on one of his trips to India. It's worth a small fortune. Auctioneers are always trying to get me to sell, but I wouldn't dream of getting rid of it. You see, Margot, it has sentimental value to me. Uncle Carlos gave it to me for good luck. If the tusks are turned up, according to an old legend, they will protect its owner. Now let's move on. There are twenty-four rooms to see and if we don't hurry, the guests will be here before we're ready for them."

The dining room resembled Sherwood Forest. A solid oak table dominated the center of the room, and a bar of the same wood hugged the back wall. Robin Hood and his Band of Merry Men practicing their unparalleled archery through Sherwood Forest portrayed through life size oil paintings made for a surreal setting. Thriving ferns gave the illusion of oak trees in the deep underbrush.

"I feel like I'm really in Sherwood Forest," Margot stared at the photo of Little John. His unyielding gaze met hers as he arched his bow and arrow straight at her heart. Margot felt a little chill. "Your uncle must have been quite a character."

"Indeed, yes," Michael said. "Uncle Carlos loved to hunt, and he had an obsession with Robin Hood and his Merry Men. He took me into the deep underbrush to teach me how to hunt when I was a young teenager. He used to say being a hunter was like being an action figure in an action movie. Remember that nursery rhyme, *Heigh Ho the Dairy-O?* Well, dear old Uncle Carlos used to change the words to '*A hunting we will go, a hunting we will go. Heigh ho the dairy-o, a hunting we will go. We'll catch a fox and put him in a box. Heigh ho the dairy-o, a hunting we will go.*'"

ЖҖҖ

The west wing of the mansion featured rooms used for meetings and entertainment. Six pocket doors opened to an elegant ballroom with cherry hardwood floors. A crystal chandelier hung from a sixteen foot vaulted ceiling, and marble fireplaces with gold leafed accents added to the Victorian motif.

"This is where the masquerade ball will be tonight. How do you like it?"

"I love it," Margot did a semi circle. "This looks like a grand ballroom from the royal courts of England. I can't wait to dance the night away with you. And those fan masks on the wall are perfect accents for a masquerade. I love that Crying Mime with the jewel tears. And there's the Jolly Jester. Oh, and look at the sophisticated Lady with a black lace veil. I can't wait for the party. It will be so much fun."

"It will be a night to remember," Michael's eyes gleamed. "A night full of surprises. Now come with me to the great room where my uncle held his meetings."

The great room vibrated with a hushed undertone, mysterious and dark. The air seemed to stir with an intangible presence, daunting and foreboding. Even before Margot spotted the large and imposing portrait of Carlos DeVeccio, she felt his penetrating gaze. Something about the great room made her skin crawl with an uneasiness she couldn't quite put her finger on. Maybe the large black marble table and the twelve chairs surrounding it. Then she looked up and her blood ran cold. Directly above the black leather chair at the head of the table, a set of sabre swords gleamed in the muted sunlight.

Between the deadly weapons and the hushed undertone, she had seen enough. A large window boasted a panoramic view of the Red Rock Canyon. Chills prickled up and down her spine. She half expected the killer to wield a death star at her from some undisclosed part of the deep woods. Practically throwing herself into Michael's arms, she said, "I've seen enough."

Michael smiled. His arms coiled around her like a cobra as he whispered in her ear. "What's the matter, Margot? Do you think the killer is watching you?"

ЖОЖОЖ

A grand sweeping staircase led to the upper wings. As they walked through the barrel-shaped corridor leading to the master suite, their footsteps echoed. Margot gasped when she entered the master bedroom. "I love it. It resembles something straight out of an old Hollywood movie. I can't wait to move in once we're married. To think this will all be my home is like a fantasy come true." A ceiling fan oscillated, stirring the subtle scent of roses through the room. Just beyond, a terrace balcony overlooked the grounds of the estate.

The desert ambiance encompassed Margot, filling her blood with a slow sensual heat. Her eyes settled on the Casablanca bed. Under the amber rays of the setting sun, the brass finials shimmered. She sighed wistfully. "Casablanca has to be one of my favorite movies. It's so timeless."

"Play it again, Sam," Michael winked, giving an impressive imitation of Humphrey Bogart. "But you, darling Margot, are much more beautiful than Ingrid Bergman. She can't hold a candle to you. No one can. You are the perfect woman." Leading her onto the terrace, he expertly twirled her around in a semi circle before drawing her into his arms for a tight embrace. As if by magic, a bluesy instrumental of *As Time Goes By* wafted out of the hidden speakers of the rich mahogany paneling.

Seduced by the music, they moved as one, their bodies gliding together in a slow sensual rhythm. The sweet lilt of the piano keys drifted through the air, counterpointing with the sassy brass of sax.

Holding her gaze, Michael sang the words, his voice potently seductive. *"You must remember this...a kiss is just a kiss...a sigh is just a sigh...as time goes by..."*

Margot joined in, her sweet voice the perfect rhapsody. As they danced under the desert sky, the duet became a game of seduction, a mating ritual. The breeze stirred, causing the ponderosa pines to sway back and forth in tempo to the music. As the sun set behind the Nevada mountains, the sounds of the Mojave closed in around them. From deep in the woods, the mournful wail of a coyote echoed across the canyon.

The call of the wild aroused Michael. Yanking Margot into a tight embrace, he grazed her bottom lip with his teeth. His mouth swooped down on hers with a feverish rush, his tongue teasing and taunting, delving deeper and deeper, rough and demanding. Adrenaline and testosterone surged through his veins, causing his heartbeat to accelerate at an alarming rate. He felt like a wild animal, hungry and ready to attack. Silhouetted by the desert sky, his sinewy form looked dark and dangerous. Pulling her closer in one predatory sweep, he whispered the words, "You are mine."

His erotic kisses made her tremble and quake, just on the verge of eruption. Her breath came out in a ragged sigh, the need to be his sweeping through her with a wildness she'd never known. She was so close to him she could feel his erection, hard and rigid—and ready for her. She responded to his kisses, making his groans more primal, blatantly sexual. He tightened his grip, kneading her back with fingers far from tender. Their hips swayed together in a sensual rhythm, rocking back and forth on the slippery edge of no return.

"You are so beautiful," he whispered. "How I want you." The warm desert breeze rustled through her long coppery hair, fanning it out in wild disarray. His hands settled on her hips, pulling them closer, making her aware of his desire. "Do you have any idea what you do to me? How much I want you?"

She did. From the moment they'd met, she knew he was the one, her one true love. Every pulse in her body throbbed, every nerve ending twitched, and every beat of her heart pumped wildly. With his tall, sinewy body outlined against the mountains, his black wavy hair blowing in the breeze, she thought he had to be the sexiest man on the planet. His hypnotic blue eyes seared into hers like lasers, making unspoken promises of fulfillment. She knew, oh how she knew. Looking directly into his eyes, she said, "I surrender."

He branded her lips with predatory kisses that left her gasping for breath. The reckless beat of her heart matched the wild beat of his. The desert breeze heightened her senses. Every taste, every smell, every touch. How she wanted him. On a breathless moan, she whispered, "Michael, how I need you."

His eyes grew dark with raw sexuality. His hair rippled in the breeze, shading his face in partial shadow. His mouth came down hard and determined, his lips devouring hers. But suddenly his kisses came to a riveting stop and he shoved her away.

"Michael?" she stared at him, her lips still throbbing from his kisses. "What is it? Did I do something wrong?"

He caressed her cheek, in complete contrast to the invisible wall that had gone up between them. "Not at all. You did everything right, absolutely perfect. But we won't make love until we're married. We'll have a Valentine wedding, full of red roses and romance for my perfect woman."

CHAPTER EIGHT

Sitting in one of the guest rooms of the east wing, Margot dressed for the masquerade, her head in a haze. A Valentine wedding in six short weeks. Her entire body tingled with excitement. She could hardly believe she was actually going to be mistress of this mansion so soon. Swept off her feet in a bubble of bliss, she felt as if she'd been drinking champagne all night. She had so much to do and so many things to take care of she didn't know where to begin.

Smiling as she got ready, she sat on the vanity stool and brushed her hair. Using pins from a fluted jewelry dish, she clipped her hair on top of her head. With one of the pins in her mouth, she wondered what it would be like to live in this twenty-four room mansion. What would her responsibilities entail being married to one of the richest men in the world? She'd sure miss her job as head curator of the museum in Chicago, but with her extensive experience, she had no doubt she would get hired in one of the Vegas galleries.

But first things first. She had a wedding to plan and a bungalow to put on the market. Her heart soared with excitement. Then she glanced out the window at the Red Rock Mountains and thought about the killer—and her heart sank.

With a killer lurking about so close, how could she sleep, especially with all the traveling Michael did? A part of her wanted to forget all about it and focus on her wedding, but as disciplined as she was, she could not ignore the insecurities pecking at her subconscious. Why the bizarre similarity in the deaths of Uncle Carlos and Lacy Diamond? How strange for both of them to be assassinated with a Ninja death star. And in both murders, Michael had been questioned. The whole thing bothered Margot. With a history of anxiety attacks, she didn't need the stress of something so disturbing playing on her subconscious.

Another fact to consider was the location of the DeVeccio estate. Nestled deep in the Red Rock Mountains, it was fifteen miles from civilization. Peaceful and serene, maybe, but she had more than a few qualms about living so close to where a killer stalked. How was she supposed to just forget Michael's uncle had been killed in this very estate, just down the hall from their bedroom? And those eerie vultures hovering the canyon gave her the creeps. When she looked at the rock on her finger, all her insecurities slipped away. In the very near future, she'd be Mrs. Michael Alan DeVeccio. She laughed at his initials: MAD. Of all the blarney; Michael was the sanest person she knew.

Slipping on her diamond fishnet stockings, she took in the feminine essence of the guest room. Designed in a charming motif, the wall paper portrayed a king and queen dancing at a regal ball. The four-poster bed with a lace ensemble and oversized pillows seemed as if it were made for them. Above the vanity, a lovely Victorian photo depicted a woman sitting amidst a garden of roses, fanning herself, while a man in waiting played the flute. Margot envisioned Michael courting her from a bygone era.

Yes, she thought as she glued on her false eyelashes. Michael DeVeccio had to be a hopeless romantic, and she'd soon be his wife. And in a few minutes, she'd be introduced as his fiancé at his annual masquerade ball. She couldn't wait to dress as Madame de Sade. With the legendary charms of the lady in question, she would haunt the ballroom until the witching hour.

Her gown, a low-cut red satin with brocade detailing and thigh-high slits made her feel very naughty and very out of character. She put her wig on and secured it with a few pins. Then she slid into her heels, black spikes with rhinestone accents. The fingertip gloves complemented her ruby red fingernails and her diamond ring. Adding her favorite eau de parfum to her throat and wrists made her feel very feminine. The subtle scent of roses was fresh and lovely. After fastening the sequin half mask around her face, she gave herself the once over. Oh, yes, she would indeed be bell of the ball tonight. Right on time, Michael rapped on her door three times.

There he stood in all his glory, Valentino. Donned in black trousers, white shirt, black satin sash, and pleated flowing robe, he looked handsome enough to do all the things that had earned him the reputation of a lady killer. He would indeed make an entrance nobody would soon forget. A pair of black gloves that fit him like a second skin and a feathered top hat completed his masquerade. Removing his black mask, he kissed her, tipped his hat, and presented her with a single red rose. "For you, Darling Margot."

"Thank you, Valentino," she cooed theatrically, taking the rose between her teeth. "I might have known you'd be some romantic hero. Rudolph Valentino suits you so. You're every bit as handsome—and certainly a lady killer."

"And you," he eyed her admiringly. "Make a very sexy Madame de Sade. You will out dazzle everyone in the ballroom. Speaking of which, it's about that time to make our grand entrance." He put on his top hat and refastened his mask. Extending his arm, he said, "Shall we?"

ЖЖЖ

Margot and Michael descended the long and winding staircase leading to the marble foyer. From the west wing of the mansion, the jazzy deliverance of the Big Easy drifted out from the ballroom. The mingled aromas of grilled meats and seafood presented an insatiable aroma. As Margot and Michael made their entrance into the ballroom, they were received with laborious applause. Smiling at his guests, Michael blew them kisses.

"Valentino!" the women squealed. "We love you!"

The grand ballroom of the DeVeccio ancestral home offered a warm and inviting ambiance. A sultry desert breeze blew in through the open terrace doors, billowing the gold pleated drapes in careless disarray. Huge silver buckets of wild exotic orchids flanked either side of the stone fireplace, and the cherry hardwood floors gleamed under the brilliant light of the chandelier.

Platters of grilled meats, seafood, and hot wings rotated on Lazy Susans. Cinnamon-scented candelabras gave the ballroom a warm ethereal glow. An assortment of sinfully rich desserts featured lady fingers, chocolate truffles, and petite pink party cakes. Caterers bustled around with trays of chilled champagne, while bartenders busied themselves serving up libations of the house. Two guests from the Royal Court of England kicked up their feet on the dance floor, footloose and fancy free.

Dressed to the nines in plush velvet, King Henry twirled Ann Bolin in an impressive spin. The essence of style and grace, Lady Ann peeled back her layers of velvet skirt to reveal a metallic underskirt. The guests went wild. A real crowd pleaser, Lady Ann shot up her trumpeted sleeves and gave her audience the high five. Thunderous applause exploded on the floor.

"Michael," Margot shouted over the clapping. "Do you know who they are?"

"Of course I do," he whispered in her ear. "That's my cousin Jimmy and his wife Brooke. Come on, I'll introduce you."

"Hey, Jimmy," Michael slapped his cousin on the back. "You rascal, you. Some floor show. " He turned to Lady Ann Bolin and kissed her hand in true Valentino style. "Brooke, you look lovely. Pregnancy agrees with you. Allow me to introduce my fiancé. Margot Montgomery, this is my cousin Jimmy O'Toole and his wife Brooke."

"My pleasure," Jimmy kissed her. "I sure hope you know what you're getting into marrying my cousin."

"I know Michael's the best thing that ever happened to me," Margot batted her false eyelashes at Valentino. "He's a keeper. But truthfully, I'm still in the state of shock. We've only been engaged for a week and I don't think it's had time to sink in. We're planning a Valentine's Day wedding. You'll be there, of course?"

"We wouldn't miss it," a man portraying a sinister looking pirate joined them, winking at Margot. "I'm Ricky O'Toole, Michael's cousin. Pleased to meet you."

Michael fished out a Marlboro and tapped it three times before lighting it. "I was telling Margot how we fancied ourselves the Four Musketeers when we were growing up. Remember the year we dressed as them? We made an impression on all the guests at that masquerade."

"Damn straight," Jimmy lit up a cigar. "Thought we were tough shit. We were all decked out and looked pretty good. Those were the days, huh? Ricky has the only picture. I wouldn't mind having one, something to show my kids."

Michael scoffed to himself. The Four Musketeers indeed. His cousins were nothing but traitors, and their day was coming. Not tonight, but soon. Like the predators that stalked the canyon, he'd hunt them down, one by one. He grinned at his cousins. "Yeah, those were the days. Listen, I see a friend of my uncle's over there. Grab Johnny later and we'll toast one up for old times."

Margot and Brooke hit it off instantly, right from the start. They fell into easy conversation, like old friends catching up.

"Since I'm pregnant," Brooke bit into a pink party cake. "If I can't drink, I might as well eat. So where are you from?"

"The Gold Coast of Chicago. I have a bungalow there on Lake Michigan. It needed a lot of work when I bought it, but after all the renovations, I have no doubt it will sell. The Gold Coast is a hot ticket on the market, only minutes from the downtown Loop. So between my wedding plans and selling my home, I'll be busy."

"That's a gorgeous ring," Brooke commented. "A real eye catcher. So tell me all about your wedding. Will it be here or Chicago?"

"Nothing's definite yet. But we've decided on a date, Valentine's Day. And on the way from the airport earlier, we passed Colony House, a replica of the mansion from *Gone With the Wind*. That's one of my favorite movies, so we'll check it out."

"You'll love it. I've been there for showers and weddings and it really does resemble Tara. I wanted my wedding there, but Jimmy and I got married in Paris. I love your costume, by the way. Those diamond fishnets are so cool. Before these two baby whales took up residence in my belly, I had ankles."

"Well, you look great," Margot said. "And it isn't all pregnant women who can get out there and dance the night away like you did earlier. I can't even imagine having twins. Do you know what you're having?"

"Baby dolphins," Brooke laughed. "The way they're kicking and swimming in there. But seriously, Jimmy and I are having a boy and a girl."

"Margot," Michael interrupted. "Come with me. I want to introduce you to some of the other guests."

ЖХЖХЖ

Later on that evening, Margot met the oldest of Michael's cousins, a man dressed as The Phantom. Dark and mysterious, he presented an aura of suspense in plush velvet with an attachable cape, boot tops, and grand feathered hat. He wore a white mask. He brought her hand to his lips and kissed it. "Madame de Sade, you sexy thing you. May I have this dance? By the way, I'm Johnny O'Toole. And you must be Margot. Come on, let's show them how it's done."

And before Margot could stop him, he dragged her out to the dance floor, twirling her around until she was dizzy. His booming voice thundered over the crowd. "Hope you have your dancing shoes on." He spun her around Dracula and his Three Brides. "Because I'm in the mood to dance all night, you sexy thing, you."

Michael worked the room, mingling with several politicians and celebrities of the Vegas Strip. The charm rolled off his tongue in spades. Party or not, he never missed an opportunity to control and manipulate. Rolling out the red carpet for his competitors and associates kept him on the cutting edge of success. Whether it was feigning interest in a political race or a game of golf at Red Rock Country Club, he found their Achilles heel and used it for all it was worth. it never took long to find a person's weak spot—and use it for his own gain.

"May I have this dance?" Michael approached Eve Carlton, portraying Cleopatra in a shimmering bronze dress, raven-black wig, and impressive vulture headdress. "You do the Egyptian queen justice," Michael whispered in her ear. "But getting straight to the point, I wanted a moment alone with you to tell you how sorry I am about your club going bankrupt. The way I hear it, you have less than six weeks to come up with the money. That's most unfortunate."

"You have no idea how hard this is on me," Eve said, mortified word had gotten out about her financial woes. But she shouldn't be surprised. Nothing went on in Vegas that Michael DeVeccio wasn't aware of. Sighing heavily, she said, "If only there were something I could do to come up with the cash."

"Perhaps I can help," Michael expertly dipped her. "I'll be willing to lend you the money, with substantial interest, of course. And it goes without saying, should I ever need a favor, all interest fees would be dropped."

"Oh, Michael," Eve gushed. "I'd be forever grateful."

"Not at all," he kissed her cheek. "Thank you for the dance. Now if you'll excuse me, I need to rescue my fiancé from my cousin. Come and see me sometime next week and we'll arrange the finances. And Eve, don't worry about a thing. Just leave it all up to me."

ЖЖЖ

"All right, Johnny," Michael tapped The Phantom on the back. "That's enough dancing with my girl. I'm cutting in."

A real ladies' man, Johnny O'Toole kissed Margot before letting her go. "Thanks for the dance. I'm gonna go cut the rug with my mother over there. But I'll be back. Save another dance for me, you sexy thing."

With moves Valentino himself would envy, Michael glided Margot along the glossy cherry floors of the ballroom, holding her close in his arms. "You are the most beautiful woman here tonight. And I must say, you certainly made quite an impression on my cousins. I'll take you over to meet my Aunt Monica in a little bit. Right now, she's dancing with Johnny."

Margot glanced across the room at the woman portraying Mae West. Her hot pink satin dress was bathed in black lace, and she wore a fashionable hat, topped off with a side ostrich feather. "Your aunt certainly is built. Or is that dress deceiving? She must take care of herself."

Michael tipped his hat to his aunt. "That's all Aunt Monica. She takes very good care of herself. She has the best of spas to keep her young, trendy clothes, younger men, and all that O'Toole fortune at her disposal. Aunt Monica always did have a way of landing on her feet."

The dance floor vibrated with footsteps as guests glided, clomped, and stomped across it. The Joker hopped around, laughing like a fool. The Deranged Clown spun around the floor. Dressed in black and white checks and a black mask, An Evil Jester rubbed up against the Smoldering Temptress, whispering crude suggestions in her ear. Covered in voodoo pins from head to toe, the Voodoo Doll danced alone.

But it was Zorro who turned heads from the moment she'd sashayed into the ballroom. Drop dead gorgeous in a crimson body suit and long flowing cape, she had the attention of every male in the ballroom. Her long platinum hair billowed around her voluptuous body and red feather mask. Sheathed in a crimson scaled scabbard, her Zorro sword rested on her left thigh.

The men all stared. The Mysterious Stranger in a black cape swept Zorro away with the moves of a ballroom dancer, looking for all the world like her long lost lover. As soon as the song ended, another masked guest asked Zorro to dance, and before long, she'd danced with nearly every man at the party.

"Michael," Margot whispered in his ear. "Everyone is captivated by Zorro. Do you know who she is?"

Michael watched Zorro glide across the ballroom floor with Jack the Ripper. Chic and elegant with the legs of a dancer, she danced the night away, her patent leather heels never touching the ground. A crimson rose pendant graced her long, elegant neck. Michael knew precisely who she was. He'd given her the rose necklace on their wedding night. Taking one final look at Zorro, he pulled Margot into a tight embrace. After kissing her, he whispered in her ear. "I have no idea who she is. I only have eyes for you. You are the perfect woman."

ЖХЖ

The storm that had been brewing all day broke just as the bell tower tolled. Eleven piercing chimes rang out simultaneously with the rumbling of thunder. Winds from the Mohave Desert hurled in through open terrace doors, blowing out the cinnamon-scented candelabras in the ballroom. Pellets of cold hard rain pounded helter skelter on the windows. The crystal chandelier swayed back and forth like a pendulum. It flickered once, then twice. And then pandemonium erupted when all went dark.

CHAPTER NINE

"All right, everyone," Michael announced with gusto. "Just settle down and relax. We'll have the candles burning again in no time. Thunder storms in the Mojave Desert are few and far between, but Red Rock Canyon is in for one tonight. All the doors and windows are closed, so no wind or sand can blow in. And we have plenty of food and libations to keep everyone happy, so just relax. In another hour it will be midnight and time to ring in the New Year. So eat, drink, and be merry. I'm sure the power will be back on before long."

Michael hustled off to his office for his cell phone, wanting to call the electric company to see how long power was expected to be out. Of all times for a power outage, just when he wanted to make an impression. His temples throbbed with anxiety. And what the hell was his slut of an ex-wife doing at the ball when he'd told her to never return?

Agitated, he tried the electric company. The line was busy. Frustrated, he snapped the lid of his phone shut and cussed the power company out with names his uncle had taught him in Italian. Feeling as wild and reckless as the storm, a plan began to emerge in his mind. It was time to orchestrate the long over due assassination of Candace. She'd been duly warned.

Ж�Ж

The cinnamon-scented candelabras burned, casting the masqueraders in dim shadows. Zorro sat at the bar, sipping on a bourbon on the rocks. Michael crept up behind her and whispered in her ear. "Nobody makes an entrance like you do, darling Candace. You have every man in the place rock hard."

"Michael," she purred, her smoky voice as smooth as silk. "I knew you'd recognize me." She ran her hand over his masked face. "The role of Valentino suits you. You are still the most handsome man I've ever set eyes on."

"And there were certainly enough of them," his voice came out low and husky. "How many men, Candace? Did you ever keep count of how many lovers you had during our marriage?"

"You were the only one that ever mattered," she rubbed up closer. "We had something real special between us. Being back in the ballroom tonight stirs all those old memories. Like the way you used to hold me in your arms when we glided across the floor. And afterwards," she slid her hand down his chest—and lower still. "We set the sheets on fire, remember, darling?"

"We had our moments," he said. "But I also remember kicking your trashy ass out of Vegas and telling you to never return. And yet here you are, an uninvited guest at my masquerade ball. You know the extent of my wrath better than anyone. Yet you dare to defy me. Why is that, Candace?"

"Because I love you, darling." Sexuality oozed from every pore. "You and only you. Let's sneak up to our old bedroom and see if we can rekindle some old flames. Come on, sugar. Let's get between those satin sheets and set the night on fire."

Michael leaned very close, massaging her leg with his fingers. In a voice raw with sexuality, he whispered, "Darling Candace. How can I resist. Meet me in Uncle Carlos's suite in ten minutes. We'll ring in the New Year together. You have no idea how much I want to be alone with you. Beautiful, beautiful Candace. I promise to make you scream."

ЖҚЖҚ

Quiet as a Ninja assassin, The Hunter crept up the long

and winding staircase leading to the upper wing. Focused on his mission, his senses were as keen as the predators stalking the wood for prey. From nearby woods, a coyote howled, its eerie wail slicing through the night. Visualizing the coming attractions, a sinister smile crossed his lips.

Prowling down the corridor to Carlos DeVeccio's suite, his favorite song played in his head. *A hunting we will go, a hunting we will go. Heigh ho the dairy-o, a hunting we will go. We'll kill a fox and put her in a box. Heigh ho the dairy-o, a hunting we will go.*

Blending into the shadows, he shimmied along the wall until he reached the door. He stopped and listened, his ears strained for even the slightest sound. Adrenaline and testosterone surged through him, the alpha male personified. He fingered the Zorro sword in the pocket of his flowing robe, the one he'd lifted from the shapely thigh of his ex-wife. Grinning, he crossed the threshold, his footsteps prompting music to play.

Boasting a chamber of horrors, the décor consisted of face masks surrounding a satin-lined coffin. Gleaming red eyes glowed in the dark. An Evil Jester leered, his mouth twisted into a wretched grin. Blood oozed from the brain of Frankenstein. The flesh-tearing fangs of a werewolf opened in mid-howl, and every ten seconds, he howled at the moon. Walking across the room to the coffin, an old floorboard creaked. The Hunter stood before his entourage of the living dead and took a bow. "Stay tuned for coming attractions. Coming soon to a theater near you. Get yourselves a big tub of buttered popcorn and get ready to scream. Queen Bitch Slut Dies Tonight."

Ж҉Ж҉Ж

Undulating up the long and winding staircase in her crimson body suit and flowing cape, Candace DeVeccio moved with the legs of a dancer. It didn't matter that the lights were out. She knew every inch of the mansion. This had been her home when she was married to Michael.

Being the wife of the billionaire tycoon had been one sweet ride. Nobody could pour it on like Michael DeVeccio. Mr. Personality himself. He'd charmed her right from the start, making all her fantasies come true. She'd come on to him one night after a show at his club. After one private dance in his office, he had been putty in her hands. A few of her legendary strip teases, and she'd had a ring on her finger the size of a rock.

The same ring Margot Montgomery had on her finger tonight, she chortled. As if that mousy little thing had a clue how to keep a man like Michael DeVeccio happy. But she did and it wouldn't be long before she had his eyeballs rolling to the back of his head. That three carat rock belonged to her, and after tonight, the rose-shaped diamond surrounded by emeralds would be back on the third finger of her left hand.

She hadn't wanted the divorce. It was all Michael's idea. He'd traveled so much she'd gotten lonely and found comfort with other men. Lots of other men. And one of her lovers had been Michael's uncle, Carlos DeVeccio. The horny old coot. But now he was dead and Michael had inherited all his sweet billions.

She recalled the night Michael had come back to the mansion early from one of his business trips and had caught her and one of his dealers going at it—right in their marital bed. He had beaten her within an inch of her life. And as for Sammy, the vultures in the desert had probably feasted on his carcass for a week.

In spite of Michael's golden rule of betrayal, he'd allowed her to live in exchange for a favor. Suspecting her affair with Carlos, he had surveillance equipment installed all over the mansion. Once he showed her the very graphic video of her and his uncle going at it in the satin-lined coffin, he'd used it to his advantage.

Michael suspected his uncle knew more about his parents' accident than he'd let on, but couldn't prove a thing. Desperate to uncover the truth, Michael blackmailed Candace into getting Carlos to confess on tape. If she failed, she'd be killed. Stuck between a rock and a hard spot, Candace had done things to the old coot that disgusted even her. But those things had made the old man sing like a canary and the taped confession had saved her life. After her mission was a done deal, Michael kicked her out of Vegas and told her if she ever returned, he would rip her lungs out.

Reaching Carlos DeVeccio's bedroom, she got a little thrill as old memories surfaced. Just a few more seconds and she'd fall into the arms of her lover. She smiled to herself.

She had returned to Vegas for a reason. She was flat broke. But after tonight, Michael would be her ticket back into the world of luxury. Then she'd be mistress of the manor once more. And more to the point, she'd have access to his billion dollar bank roll.

With a devious smile, she pushed her way through the heavy mahogany door. Crossing the threshold, she entered the house of horrors. Carlos DeVeccio had been a real nut, one straight out of the books. But with her fetish for face masks, she loved his collection and had often come into his wing just to admire them. What a thrill it had been to have sex in the coffin, howling along with the werewolf. Some might think it a bit kinky, but they didn't know what they were missing. Calling out to her lover, her pulse quickened a beat. "Michael? Are you here yet, darling?"

That's when she heard it, manic laughter from the final circle of hell. A slither of fear trickled down her spine, releasing a wild rush of adrenaline. Carlos?

She thought about the death of Lacy Diamond. Two Ninja assassinations were no coincidence. Sensing danger, she felt for her sword. It was gone. Panic soared through her. Where the hell was it?

The laughter got louder and louder, moving in closer and closer. It seemed to be bouncing off the walls. She couldn't tell from which direction it was coming. Just then, the bell in the tower gonged, thundering off the walls like canon balls. Instinctively, she covered her ears with her hands. Where the hell was Michael?

Evil eyes from the face masks followed her every move. She had to escape this hell before it was too late. She couldn't think over the gonging of the bell. Every few seconds, the werewolf howled at the moon. She screamed, even though she knew no one would ever hear her. Floundering in wild disarray, disoriented by the darkness and relentless gonging, she searched in vain for the door. Her arms swam in mid-air, like a person drowning, desperate for an anchor, something to hold onto. She reached out and grabbed at nothing. She had to find a way out of this mausoleum of the living dead before it was too late. Where the hell was Michael?

The laughter got closer. Perspiration drenched her skin. The chilling laughter echoed in her ears, louder and louder, closer and closer. The bell in the bell tower broke through the thin filament of sanity she had left. The werewolf open his mouth and howled at the moon. Where was Michael? He'd know what to do. He was a master swordsman. His fencing skills were extraordinary. He could wield a Ninja star with his eyes closed and hit the mark. Where was he?

Blood thundered in her ears, but not loud enough to block out the manic laughter. It was close but she couldn't see a thing. She wished she had her sword. She turned to run; it was too late. She heard a distinct click. The killer had just depressed the button on her Zorro sword, releasing the thirty-seven inch blade. His psychotic laughter reached an ear-splitting crescendo just as the bell in the tower gonged out its last chime. From the dark shadows, Valentino pounced, her Zorro sword gleaming in the moonlight.

"Surprise!" he thrust the sword into her heart. "I promised to make you scream, darling Candace. Let me hear you scream."

CHAPTER TEN

The bell in the bell tower chimed twelve times, ringing in the midnight hour. Its piercing gong echoed through the grand ballroom along with the blasting of party horns and shouts. To add to the excitement, the electricity came back on, illuminating the ballroom in brilliant white light. The Voodoo doll started a celebratory dance around the ballroom, and before long, a parade of happy masqueraders joined in, singing their hearts out to *Auld Lang Syne*. The party was back in full swing, bigger and better than ever.

"Margot," Michael kissed her passionately. "Happy New Year."

"Where were you?" she pushed him away. "You've been gone for the past hour. Midnight came and went...fifteen minutes ago. People have been asking about you. Where have you been?"

His eyes narrowed to stone cold slits. "Hold on, hold on. Dare you question me? Do you have any idea what kind of damage a desert storm can do if even one window or terrace door is left open? Desert storms can do irreparable damage. I went to my office to call the staff at the carriage house. Then I called the electric company to see how long they expected power to be out. Why do you think the lights came back at precisely midnight, just in time to ring in the New Year? Allow me to fill you in. Because Michael Alan DeVeccio has connections, that's why. And if you ever doubt me or my whereabouts again, you'll be very sorry. Now, come on. I want to dance with my fiancé."

ЖЖЖ

Jack the Ripper was smashed. He'd been slugging back Rum Runners all night long and needed to find a bathroom. Tripping over his own two feet, he staggered around the mansion in circles. If he didn't find one soon, he would have an accident. Just as he circled the same area again, he spotted the staircase. His vision blurred and he saw double. If that winding staircase didn't get him on the way up, it sure would on the way down. Throwing caution to the wind, off he went.

He charged through the upper wing, trying one door after the next. *Come on*, he urged himself. *Hurry up*. Spying a door at the end of the hallway, he hoofed it at a brisk pace and barged through the door and came to a dead halt.

Wretched face masks hung on the wall, their gleaming red eyes shrouding the casket in an eerie glow. And sitting upright in the satin-lined coffin was Zorro, her sword pierced straight through her heart. Just as he went to flee, a werewolf with flesh-tearing fangs howled at the moon.

Stunned out of his drunken stupor, Jack the Ripper tripped over something and landed face down in a puddle of blood. Propping himself up on his elbows, he stared up at Zorro. A latex skull mask distorted her face, her beautiful face. Gagging and gasping for breath, Jack the Ripper lost the contents of his stomach. Then he pissed his pants.

Running down the corridor like the hounds of hell were on his heels, he ran straight into the butler. "It was you! You killed her!"

The butler backed up when he saw the Ripper's blood-stained hands. Pressing the alarm, he called security.

Within seconds of the alarm going off all over the mansion, Michael came charging, Margot and several guests trailing behind. "What the hell's going on?" he demanded, staring the two men down. "Someone better start talking."

Jack the Ripper pointed a bloody finger. "He did it. He killed Zorro. I came up here looking for a bathroom and stumbled into that chamber of horrors," he gestured toward

Carlos DeVeccio's suite. "Right down there. He killed Zorro with her own sword and laid her out in a coffin. The butler did it."

"Settle down," Michael commanded, doing his best to commandeer the crowd.

But they'd been drinking heavy all night long and were determined to see the corpse. Like a wild stampede, they tore down the hallway to the crime scene. Utter chaos erupted once they crossed the threshold. Chilling organ music pumped out followed by blood-curdling screams as they poured in.

"What the hell?" the Mysterious Stranger screamed. "What kind of a sick joke is this, some grand finale to the masquerade?" Overcome with morbid curiosity, the Veiled Lady moved in for a closer look. "Oh my God! It's Zorro! Someone killed her with her own sword!"

The guests, fueled by the consumption of alcohol, gathered around the coffin to view the corpse. The Voodoo Doll peeled the mask off Zorro and shrieked, "Look at her mouth, all twisted. Does anyone know who she is?"

"I know who she is," Michael stepped forward. "That's my ex-wife. That's Candace DeVeccio."

Just then the werewolf opened his mouth and howled at the moon. Masqueraders took off in all directions, their piercing screams echoing through the barrel-shaped corridor. Utter pandemonium broke out as they traipsed down the hall, tracking blood on the rug. But they didn't get too far.

"Hold it right there," a policeman flashed his badge. "Las Vegas Metro PD Homicide. Nobody's going anywhere."

ЖѺЖѺЖ

Crime Scene Investigators filed into the suite to investigate the homicide. The victim sat upright in a coffin, a sword skewered straight through her heart. Her red feather mask and a rolled-up latex skull mask lay askew next to her.

Detective Diego Santiago did the initial walk through, checking the corpse and crime scene for trace evidence. The air bristled with his don't-mess-with-me attitude.

The victim, a thirty-one year old Caucasian female, identified as Candace DeVeccio, ex-wife of Michael DeVeccio, had been one of the guests at the masquerade. Her long platinum wig, partially off her head, was tinged with blood.

"Looks like the killer left the signature calling card," Santiago gestured to the skull mask in the coffin. "And if those drunken masqueraders hadn't screwed up the crime scene, we might have gotten some fingerprints. Because of them, the killer may have just slipped through our fingers once more. Oughta haul all their asses downtown for tampering with a crime scene. Nonetheless, scrape the fingernails for any possible DNA. Sweep for body hairs and fibers, check for semen. Swab the inside of the mouth."

Blood and gore seeped out of the stab wound, the acrid smell permeating the air, strong and pungent. Dark clumps of coagulated blood seeped into the white satin lining of the coffin.

Santiago stared at the corpse. The murder had the billionaire's name written all over it. Before the body had been tampered with, the familiar morbid skull mask had covered her face, DeVeccio's personal calling card. But instead of using a Ninja star, he'd used the victim's own sword as a murder weapon. He had to be demented to do something so barbaric, slaughtering a guest while hosting a masquerade, the ex-wife no less. But they were dealing with a lunatic, a man with no conscience or soul. Shutting off his emotions, he worked the scene. "Let's do it."

"Talk about bringing in the New Year with a bang," Officer Stevenson said. She noted the time for the record. "Medical team responded to nine-one-one, arriving at 12:31 a.m. Pronounced victim, identified as DeVeccio, Candace, at 12:36 a.m."

CSI took photos, drew sketches, and documented the scene. Forensics evidence was processed for the lab. The feather mask, the skull mask, wig, murder weapon, and scabbard were labeled and processed. The team dusted for prints, both latent and visible. Clad in dust masks and gloves, they knelt on knee pads as they developed 2-D footwear impressions.

Even after a solid decade with homicide, Santiago never got used to the finality of death. But he had the uncanny ability of getting into the mind of a killer, and the team had come to rely on his incredible instincts. Hard bodied and lean, he had attitude personified. "Who identified the body?"

Detective Stevenson eyed the werewolf before looking

down at the mutilated corpse. "Her ex-husband. Michael De-
Veccio."

"Did he identify himself as the killer? Cause there's not a
doubt in my mind who offed the victim. I just have to prove
it. And when I do, the billionaire's going down hard. Who
found the body?"

"Russel Harrison, dressed as Jack the Ripper. Now there's
a chilling thought. Claims he was upstairs looking for the
John. Guess he found a hell of a lot more than a pot to piss
in."

"Where is he now?"

"Down in the living room, chugging back enough motor
oil to gag a horse. Strong coffee for these drunks all around.
Not a sober one in the bunch. Except for Brooke O'Toole.
Nothing stronger than water passed her lips since she's
pregnant."

The medical examiner had just finished up when Santiago
joined him. After a brief pause, he asked, "What have you
got?"

"Massive internal hemorrhaging, external bleeding kept
to a minimum. Victim took a single stab wound in the lateral
aspect of the left ventricle. Blood collected in the pericardial
sac. Heart stopped tickin', all that excess fluid. No rigor mortis. Body was definitely moved post mortem. No visible sign
of semen or rape."

Santiago recalled how pretty Candace DeVeccio had
been. Looking at her mouth twisted in a silent scream, it was
hard to imagine she'd been such a striking beauty.

The medical examiner gathered his things and left. CSI
place the corpse in a body bag and zipped it closed. Santiago
thought about the victims. What was the link? A fiancé and
an ex-wife.

And how were these two murders connected to the billionaire's uncle?

CHAPTER ELEVEN

Officers worked the living room of the DeVeccio estate, questioning guests about the homicide. Unmasked faces revealed stunned expressions as news of the gruesome murder registered. The alcohol's effect wore off and in its wake left the cold, hard reality of death. The DeVeccio living room was as large and spacious as a mausoleum. And just as cold.

Santiago sat with Brooke and Jimmy O'Toole. Since Brooke was the only guest at the party who hadn't been drinking, he was more apt to take her seriously.

"Mrs. O'Toole, Candace DeVeccio was married to your husband's cousin. Did you know that was her tonight, dressed as Zorro?"

"No way," Brooke sipped on her bottled water. "No one knew who she was, but everyone noticed her the minute she came in, especially the men. I guess you could say an aura of mystery surrounded her."

"And when the victim was married to Michael DeVeccio, did she masquerade with this aura of mystery?"

"Oh my, yes. Candace loved to fool everyone at these parties and made a hobby of collecting Mardi Gras masks. She'd never reveal her identity until long after midnight."

"What kind of relationship did she have with her ex-husband?"

"Turbulent."

"How so?"

"It went from red hot to ice cold on a weekly basis. I'd describe it as a love-hate relationship. Candace challenged Michael and he fed on those challenges. Just between us, I think she got off on getting kicked around. She liked it. She wore battle scars like badges of honor. She thrived on making Michael insanely jealous. She taunted him by flaunting her affairs all over the Strip. And there's one more thing, detective. You'll notice it the minute you talk to Margot Montgomery, Michael's latest fiancé. The engagement ring on her finger is the same ring he gave to Lacy and Candace. And they're both dead."

"Interesting," Santiago said. "But back to DeVeccio and his ex-wife. How did the marriage end?"

"Badly. Michael told Candace if she ever showed her face in Vegas again he'd rip her lungs out."

ЖЖЖ

A female officer questioned Russel Harrison, the man portraying Jack the Ripper. "So you danced with Zorro an hour before finding her body in the upstairs wing?"

"Oh yeah."

"What did you talk about?"

"Our bodies did the talking. She was Zorro, the sex goddess. What a body. I wanted her. Every man in the place wanted her, would have killed for her. Poor choice of words, all things considered."

"So you were all hard for her," the officer said. "Try thinking with your brain instead of your dick. Did Zorro have her sword strapped to her leg when you danced?"

Russel Harrison ran his hand through his crop of short sandy hair. Torment haunted his bloodshot eyes. He frowned slightly, as if trying to call up a memory. "I held her in my arms, spun her across the floor. And yeah, I held her so close I felt her sword strapped to her leg, her left thigh. Now that I think about it, I asked her if I could flick it out. We both chuckled over the sexual innuendo. But you know how the Zorro sword works. A button unleashes a thirty-seven inch blade. Oh yeah, Zorro was definitely armed with her sword when we danced. And now she's dead." His hands trembled. He reached for his coffee that had gone cold. He brought the fragile china cup up to his lips. The dark brown fluid swished in the cup before sloshing over the edge and spilling onto his black satin pants. And then something jogged his memory.

"Wait. Even though I was smashed and all the lights were out, I know what I saw. I was stumbling around in the dark, looking for a bathroom. And I remember passing Zorro at the bar. She was rubbing up to her ex-husband, real sexy like. And then he slid his hand up and down her thigh, right over her sword."

ЖЖЖ

On the other side of the room, Santiago questioned Michael. "Did you invite your ex-wife to the masquerade?"

"Indeed not." Michael reached into his pocket and fished out a Marlboro. He tapped it three times before he lit it. He waited for the rush of nicotine to filter through his brain. Then he slowly exhaled. "Candace and I have been divorced for over ten years and the marriage ended badly."

"How so?"

"My ex-wife was a slut."

"And was infidelity the grounds for your divorce?"

"Absolutely. A man in my position can not afford to have a wife who sleeps around. You see, detective, if a man can't control his own wife, he can't be expected to handle billion dollar contracts. And for the record, I had the marriage annulled. Even though I am a Catholic and vowed to stay married forever, I draw the line when my wife flaunts her affairs all over town, and in our marital bed."

"Did you know that was your ex-wife tonight at the masquerade? Did you know Zorro was none other than Candace DeVeccio?"

"Of course I did." Michael took a drag of his cigarette and looked out the window. The sun was rising to meet the horizon. Mountain bluebirds chirped cheerfully from nearby ponderosa pines. Then he turned to the cop. "No woman could ever compete with Candace. She had it all. The way she entered a room on a whisper of silk, the exotic scent of her skin, and her voluptuous body. You see, detective. No man could be married to a woman like Candace and not know the precise moment she entered a room."

"And did you talk to your ex-wife tonight?"

"Certainly."

"About what?"

"She said she couldn't stay out of Vegas, even though I told her never to return."

"Why was that?"

"She wanted to rekindle old flames."

"Did you ask her to leave your party?"

"On the contrary. I invited her to ring in the New Year."

"Did you see her go up to the upper wing?"

"No. After our brief conversation, I went to my office to get my cell phone. I called my staff at the carriage house and then I called the electric company to see how long they expected power to be out in the canyon."

"Just a few more questions. What were the last words you spoke to your ex-wife when your marriage ended?"

With meticulous precision, Michael flicked the ash of his cigarette into an ashtray. Then he looked Santiago directly in the eye. "I told Candace if she ever showed her face in Vegas again I'd rip her lungs out."

"And did you? How about it, DeVeccio? Payback for all that screwing around she did when she was your wife? Did you murder Candace DeVeccio? Did you set up a lover's tryst in your uncle's bedroom, pierce her through her lying cheating heart, and then lay her out in a coffin?"

"Absolutely not."

ЖѺЖѺЖ

After the Crime Scene Investigators and guests had gone, Margot and Michael sat on the teakwood patio. With the desert breeze stirring through the ponderosa pines, the beauty of the Red Rock Mountains all around them, and the cheerful chirping of mountain bluebirds, it was hard to believe a gruesome murder had taken place inside. But it had and everyone was on edge. The early morning sun was already hot, but Margot felt a chill as cold as Lucifer's black soul.

So many questions. Who killed Candace and why? Why was Michael's ex-wife at the masquerade ball in the first place? And why had Michael lied to her about knowing the identity of Zorro when he knew exactly who she was from the moment she'd entered the ballroom? Something else throbbed at her subconscious like a nervous tick. What was all this about Michael telling Candace if she showed up in Vegas, he'd rip her lungs out? Just an idle threat? Not likely.

So who did it? One of the masked guests? Everyone was drinking heavy, and with the entire mansion as dark as a tomb, it was impossible to keep tract of anyone. Minutes before the clock struck midnight, someone murdered Michael's ex-wife in his uncle's chamber of horrors. Carlos DeVeccio must have been completely nuts because only a raving lunatic would sleep in a room with a coffin surrounded by faces from the living dead.

And those evil eyes, watching, following. Who could sleep there other than a demented soul? The morbid happenings of the night before sent shivers skittering down her spine. But nothing was more chilling than the sight of Zorro, laid out in a blood-stained casket with a stake pierced straight through her heart.

Margot watched Michael pluck a glossy purple grape from the fruit bowl. Licking the juice from his fingers, he winked at her before going back to his paper. How could he be so nonchalant when a grisly murder had taken place in his home? And something else bothered her. When all the guests had been commandeered into the living room to be questioned by the police, their eyes were tormented with shock and horror. Michael's, on the other hand, blazed with unnatural brightness, like a child who was on an all day sugar high. While others mourned in the aftermath of death, Michael seemed to bask in it.

An icy chill snaked through her, settling in her stomach. Even though a murder had been committed at the masquerade, even though the victim had been none other than his ex-wife, and even though the mutilated corpse of Candace DeVeccio had rendered everyone else speechless, Michael worked the room like a king entertaining guests at a banquet.

Margot took off her rose-colored glasses and took a long, hard look at Michael. For the first time since she'd met the billionaire business tycoon, she saw the shrewd and ruthless man who ruled one of the largest business conglomerates in the world. Her heart sank.

Not only had he fallen off the pedestal she'd placed him

on, but something simmered at a low burn in the back of her brain. No one could account for Michael's whereabouts during the time his ex-wife had been murdered. Feeling the intense heat of his gaze, she turned her head to face him. From behind the paper he was reading, she watched his eyes slowly peruse her body from head to toe. Then he grinned at her.

ЖЖЖ

Yawning, Michael folded the Wall Street Journal and placed it on the table, a handsome teakwood with a chic mosaic inset. Stretching, he rested his hand across the back of Margot's chaise lounge, playing with a strand of her blonde hair. The sun teased out the coppery highlights, giving it the sheen of a new penny. "Hope you're hungry. I've had cook prepare a gourmet breakfast. Eggs Benedict with hollandaise sauce, hash browns, breakfast meats, and fresh blueberry muffins. Just wait until you sink your teeth into cook's culinary delights. He's been with the family for years. Your taste buds will explode with ecstasy."

Margot stared at him. "Michael, how can you even think about gorging on food when your ex-wife was murdered last night? Doesn't it make you sick what someone did to that woman? The media is calling it the work of the Red Rock Slasher. Doesn't that bother you? Because the image of her mutilated corpse in that coffin will give me nightmares for the rest of my life. And you sit there basking in the sun, casually sipping on coffee while thinking about food?"

Michael stared at her long and hard, as if she were a petulant child trying his patience. "Margot, my slut of an ex-wife is none of my concern. I had enough of her trashy behavior when I was married to her. If someone chose to stab her in the heart, no doubt she deserved it. Hat's off to her slayer."

"How can you be so calloused, so removed? Whoever butchered Candace up like a carved turkey couldn't be human. Her body was savagely mutilated, and seeing that didn't faze you?"

Michael refilled his coffee. Then he looked at her, his eyes empty and hollow. "Not in the least."

Dumbfounded, Margot watched him go about his business as if finding the slain corpse of an ex-wife in his home was an every day thing. Who was he? Did he have ice in his veins? Her mouth went bone dry. Lightheaded, she reached for some bottled water and drained it. Once hydrated, she continued. "When I asked you if you knew who Zorro was last night, you told me you didn't. Then I overheard you telling Detective Santiago you knew precisely who she was the minute she entered the ballroom. Why did you lie to me?"

Michael placed his coffee down on the table and took her hand in his. "Margot," he traced the diamond he'd given her. He stared into her eyes. "Because I didn't want to upset you. The truth of the matter is, Candace came to the masquerade ball to try and get me into bed. She came on strong, rubbing up to me. She went so far as to snake her hand around me to see if she could arouse me. She whispered crude suggestions in my ear, wanting to rekindle old flames between the sheets. Don't you see? Candace came to the party last night to seduce me. Being the gentlemen that I am, I was trying to spare you the embarrassment of knowing any of that. So, did I lie to you? Yes. I lied to you because there was no reason for my beautiful fiancé to know the sleazy tactics my slut of an ex-wife would stoop to in order to get me back."

A little shocked and a little amused, Margot raised an eyebrow. "While I appreciate your chivalry, you don't need to protect me from such things. I'm well aware of what women do to get a man, especially one as rich and powerful as you. It doesn't surprise me Candace wanted you back. She had it all and she threw it all away. But that's all hearsay in light of her death. What we need to focus on is this murder. The killer got into your home last night, the home I'm moving into once we're married. If someone was able to slip in here so easily and kill one of the guests, who's to say it won't happen again? And the police have no leads or suspects. This cold blooded killer, whoever it is, is some demented psychopath. I'm scared, Michael. The killer seems to be stalking all the women in your life. What if I'm next?"

"Margot," he soothed. "I promise the killer won't get you."

As usual, his buttery soft voice settled her. Feeling somewhat better, she went over and sat on the edge of his chaise lounge. With no sleep and her over stimulated nerves, more caffeine was the last thing she needed. But it was there and the rich aroma smelled like heaven. Pouring herself a cup, she inhaled the mocha blend. It tasted as good as it smelled. After taking a few sips, she looked up toward Carlos DeVeccio's suite. "How could your uncle sleep in that haunted house with all those masks on the wall? And what would possess him to have a coffin in his room? Was he insane? Suffering from some mental illness?"

"My uncle was as sly as a fox. Those masks are from some of the most primitive islands in the world. Uncle Carlos started collecting them shortly after I moved in. It was his hobby, his passion. Those masks are worth a small fortune. And the coffin adds the perfect atmosphere to the room. It's custom made. With the contour mattress and pillow, it's great for getting a good night's sleep. When I'm stressed out over a business deal, I sleep in it, and always wake up feeling refreshed. Mental illness indeed. Don't be ridiculous. Carlos DeVeccio was every bit as sane as I am."

Cook shuffled toward them, pushing an antique trolley filled with all the makings of the promised gourmet breakfast. The mingled aromas filled the air. The smell was insatiable. In spite of herself, Margot's stomach growled. When had she last eaten?

"Where would you like this, Mr. DeVeccio?"

"Set it up on the umbrella table. We'll serve ourselves. And for future reference, Ms. Montgomery prefers hazelnut coffee, black and strong."

"Duly noted."

Michael touched Margot's knee. "Once we're married, this will all be yours. And that will give you full access to the staff, the limousine, and so much more. All you need do is say the word." As if to demonstrate, he snapped his fingers to get the attention of the man stocking shelves behind the half moon bar. "Robert, a couple of Bloody Marys."

"Coming right up, Mr. DeVeccio." Robert mixed up the ingredients, adding just the right amount of vodka and Tabasco sauce. He grabbed two glasses from the bar, scooped several cubes from the ice chest, and poured the spicy concoction over them. Whistling, he topped each drink with a lemon wedge and a crisp celery tree, and presented them with a smile. "Here we go then, a nice round of Bloody Marys."

Sipping on her cocktail, Margot took in the patio fanning out in front of her. It was a Garden of Paradise. It had everything she could want: a geometric sunken pool with a cascading waterfall, a tropical fish pond, aquatic plants, and an English rock garden.

With its teakwood furniture and complementing accents, the patio boasted an atmosphere of comfort and luxury. Chaise lounges with splashy colorful cushions encompassed the pool. Just beyond the rock garden, lush, thriving eucalyptus trees landscaped the arbor. Shrouded by ponderosa pines, a Javanese bench offered a shady respite from the heat. Then she looked at Michael, so handsome and debonair. But was he? Or was his charm as phony as the garden of paradise masking this house of horrors?

CHAPTER TWELVE

While Margot showered, Michael listened to the media coverage of the murder of Candace DeVeccio. Little did they know. Turning off the television, he walked toward the great room, strutting down the corridor with an air of supreme confidence. The queen bitch slut was finally dead. Betraying their wedding vows all those years ago with his uncle had been a big mistake. He should have killed her when he discovered their lovers' tryst. But rather than kill her, he'd used her to his own advantage.

Something about the way Uncle Carlos had raised him as his own son to take over the family business had always bothered him, a case of more than meets the eye. If anyone could make a man spill his guts in the throws of passion, Candace could. After doing things with her body that would make a contortionist proud, she'd gotten dear old Uncle Carlos to come clean with his dirty little secret. And since Michael was a man of his word, he'd granted her a reprieve and allowed her to live. With the videoed confession proving his uncle was the ultimate betrayer, he'd put an end to Carlos DeVeccio's miserable life. Permanently.

Tapping a cigarette three times on the bar before lighting it, he reminisced about the night before. It had been the perfect way to start off the New Year. With the theatrics of Mother Nature, it could have been a stage show. Murder in a

Blackout. Plunging the sword into her cheating heart the precise moment the bell in the tower gonged out the midnight hour had been the grand finale.

Candace had it coming, after all. She loved to taunt and tease men with her feminine wiles, promising a night of seduction with a bat of her sultry green eyes. And oh how she loved to make an entrance, gliding in on a whisper of red silk and White Diamonds. Nobody could tease and taunt better than his ex-wife. How well he knew. But he'd lost his infatuation with her the minute she started messing around on him behind his back. The Goddamn whore! She thought she was so clever, cheating on him every chance she got.

Candace was yesterday's news. Now it was time to focus on his cousins, the brothers O'Toole. He couldn't wait to hunt them down, one by one, along with their mother, sweet Aunt Monica.

As Michael passed the sabre swords on the wall, he envisioned fencing with his uncle. Such secrets were harbored in these walls. Carlos DeVeccio had brainwashed Michael from the time he was twelve years old. In order to undo the morals his parents had instilled in him, the hunting song played from hidden wall speakers. *A hunting we will go, a hunting we will go. Heigh ho the dairy-o, a hunting we will go. We'll catch a fox and put him in a box. High ho the dairy-o, a hunting we will go.*

And once the hunting song got in his blood and he started thinking of himself as an action figure in an action movie, killing became a sport.

Digging into the pocket of his beige wool trousers, Michael retrieved his cell phone. Despite his betrayal, Uncle Carlos had achieved his goal. Under his tutelage, Michael had become the master manipulator. It was time to do a little manipulating right now. Punching in the numbers, he got Eve Carlton on the first ring.

"Hello, Eve. Listen, about your little problem we discussed last night during our spin around the dance floor. It's all taken care of. I paid off all your debts, interest free. Now about that favor. I need you to contact the police and convince Detective Santiago you saw Jack the Ripper plunge the sword into my ex-wife last night at the party. I don't care how you do it. Make it happen and make it believable."

With a devious smile, Michael reached up and reverently

removed his saber sword from the wall. Assuming the position, he placed his right foot in front of the left, bent his knees, and raised his sword.

"One more thing, Eve. If it isn't on the evening news tonight that Russel Harrison's been arrested for the murder of Candace DeVeccio, you just might be the next victim."

ЖЖЖ

Pouring two fingers of bourbon, Michael walked out to the balcony and stared into the foothills surrounding his home. Memories he'd buried in the back of his mind for the past thirty years resurrected, good memories of his cousins when they'd been the best of friends. A part of him longed for those days, a time in his life when he had been free and not tethered to responsibilities.

After his parents died and he moved in with his uncle, loneliness consumed him. He was only twelve and didn't have any friends. His uncle traveled; he was busy building his empire. Monica O'Toole, his mother's sister, lived nearby with her three sons. That first summer, she insisted that he spend time with her and her boys. Aunt Monica looked so much like his mother, he often fantasized that they were all one big happy family. She treated him like a son, showering him with love and affection. Hanging out with Johnny, Ricky, and Jimmy, hiking the trails of Red Rock, fishing on the lake, and camping under the stars while discussing their futures had filled a void in him.

The day they took an oath to be blood brothers stood out as his all time favorite. The four of them were at Keystone Thrust, hiking through a petrified forest, looking for stone logs that had washed down to the base of the cliffs. They had found themselves separated, and Johnny was the first to stumble across a fossilized log. Michael could still hear the excitement in his voice as it echoed across the canyon.

"Rickyyyyy! Jimmyyyyy! Michaellllll! Down here, quick come see. Hurry!"

Following the sound of his voice, they found Johnny deep in the underbrush of an ancient forest, pointing to a tree limb that had turned to stone. "Told ya guys I'd be first to spot one, and check it out. Looks like the head of some sea creature. See the outline? Must have got stuck in there and calcified a few million years back. We gotta get a shot of it."

"Cool," Michael said, tracing the imprint of the sea urchin with his finger. "Uncle Carlos said the petrified logs were used as weapons of the wolf gods and are omens of good luck."

"Only a chump would buy that one," Ricky chortled. "Sounds like something the old coot would dream up, just to see how gullible you are. Here's the real deal, Mikey boy, so listen up. Billions of years back, Red Rock Canyon was under water. Once the sea receded, all the creatures died and the calcium mixed with minerals to form limestone studded with fossils. And when tree limbs and stumps washed down from the highlands all those centuries ago, they calcified into petrified logs."

"Knock it off, Rick," Jimmy chided his younger brother. "Nobody wants to hear one of your long-winded geography lessons. Besides, there's something to be said for that old legend about the wolf gods. Take a listen some night when we're out here campin'. You'll hear it, sounds like some weird chanting ritual."

"Hey, I know," Johnny grinned, snapping a few more pictures. "How bout we take an oath to be blood brothers, the four of us? Since me and Rick and Jim are birth brothers, we'll make Michael our blood brother. Come on, what do ya say? Mingle our blood right here on this sacred stump. How bout it, kid?"

Michael grinned. For the first time since the death of his parents, he felt a family connection. "I say let's do it. Hold on, Gotta pen knife in my pocket."

As the sun set over the Red Rock Cliffs of the Mojave Desert, the four cousins took part in the ancient ritual, mingling their blood on the sacred log in the forest. One by one, Johnny, Ricky, Jimmy, and Michael each made a small cut between his thumb and forefinger before shaking hands and swearing lifetime loyalty. A breeze blew through the ponderosa pines, sounding like the wise old whispers of the Paiute Indians buried thousands of feet below in the windblown sand.

"All for one, and one for all. Blood brothers now and forever. Until the end of time."

Ж◇Ж◇Ж

Fishing a Marlboro from the pack, Michael tapped it three times on the railing before lighting it. So much for family loyalty, he mused, a far away expression clouding his clear blue eyes. Taking that oath all those years ago on one of the sacred logs in the forest had meant something to him. It filled a void in him after the loss of his parents. The four of them had vowed to be there through thick and thin. One for all and all for one.

But the O'Toole brothers had betrayed the vow when they turned on him. Also, there was that little matter of stealing his birthright, the ultimate sin.

Just as he killed Uncle Carlos for his betrayal, he would kill his cousins. One by one, Johnny, Ricky, and Jimmy would die by the sword, along with their mother. And after the death rattle had spewed from the throat of each sinner, he would place the mask of the betrayer on each corpse. Then, and only then, would vengeance be served.

CHAPTER THIRTEEN

Santiago tore down Charleston Boulevard, heading toward the DeVeccio estate. He had more questions for the billionaire. But first things first, he needed a cup of strong coffee to give him a second wind. It had been a long, grueling night at the crime scene, and today hadn't been much better. Pulling into Starbucks, he hopped out of his vehicle and hustled through the crowd and ordered a jumbo mug to go.

After the rush of caffeine had him wired enough to do a marathon, he felt human again. Almost. As he drove down the road, he thought about the DeVeccio murder the night before.

The homicide had the billionaire's signature all over it, but as usual, he hadn't left so much as a trace of DNA. If not for all those drunks parading through the crime scene, some key evidence might have been left behind. What a scene it had been, all those gruesome masks surrounding a coffin with a corpse. Michael DeVeccio had to be certifiable to do something so heinous. But was it any wonder the billionaire had become a demented sociopath after being raised by one? Just a glance into Carlos DeVeccio's chamber of horrors gave a very disturbing glimpse into the old man's head. Some role model.

Stopping at the light, Santiago thought back to the Carlos

DeVeccio murder ten years earlier. It had been a hell of an eye opener for his first day on homicide. He remembered every detail as if it were yesterday. A naked corpse with a Ninja star in the throat and a skull mask on the face. The nephew called it in after finding his uncle in the bathroom. Santiago's first reaction was to think that Michael DeVeccio was guilty as sin. He had said all the right things, he gave the same story word for word when questioned about his whereabouts, and he had an iron-clad alibi. With nothing to convict him on other than a gut instinct, Michael DeVeccio had gotten away with murder.

Now, ten years later, the crime that was never solved was being reenacted.

So what was the link connecting all three murders? The choice of weapon was always a blade, twice with a Ninja star and once with a sword. And all three victims had a skull mask covering their face. Why would DeVeccio leave such a bizarre calling card? What was the motive? If it was betrayal, why would he kill his ex-wife ten years after the marriage had ended? Frustrated, he dug into his pocket for a stick of gum, craving a cigarette. What was he missing? Once he figured the link connecting all three victims, he'd have a motive.

Santiago drove his unmarked vehicle up the long driveway to the estate, his mind still on the investigation. The billionaire had chosen specific body parts for a reason. A definite pattern. Throats were usually cut to symbolize betrayal. Since the old man's throat had been slashed open and diced with poison, he'd apparently done something his nephew considered to be the ultimate betrayal. While Lacy Diamond had not been poisoned, her voice box had been severed, indicating the killer didn't want her talking. The ex-wife was a give in. DeVeccio drove a stake through her cheating heart to brand her as a slut.

As Santiago walked toward the house, he got inside the mind of the killer. Michael Alan DeVeccio reminded him of a robot, programmed to say and do the right thing, devoid of all emotion. He was a man with no conscience or soul. Being raised by a man who ordered hits on a daily basis would make killing seem like a recreational sport. Michael would have grown up believing he was above the law.

In the world of organized crime, good deeds were rewarded and enemies were snuffed off the face of the earth like bad rubbish.

Santiago rang the bell, still thinking about the murders. The butler appeared, looking as stiff and rigid as a figure in a wax museum. With his stone cold eyes and bald head, he reminded Santiago of someone who'd had a lobotomy.

ЖѺЖѺЖ

The billionaire sat lounging in front of a roaring fire, smoking a Marlboro and sipping on a bourbon on the rocks. He looked up. "Back so soon?"

"Excuse the hell out of me for interrupting cocktail hour." Santiago strutted in. "Got a few more questions about the murder."

DeVeccio yawned, flicked the ash of his cigarette in the ashtray, and crossed one leg over the other. "Detective Santiago, as far as I'm concerned, I told you everything you need to know about my slut of an ex-wife last night. If someone chose to kill her, thrust a sword through her heart, no doubt she deserved it. I applaud the killer's fine marks-manship."

"Well, get this, DeVeccio, I'm not through with you. This case is far from over. Someone killed your ex-wife at your highfalutin cocktail party during a blackout. Any ideas who might want her dead?"

"Now there's a loaded question," DeVeccio guffawed. "My ex-wife screwed half the men in Vegas, and teased the rest. It wouldn't surprise me if an entire stadium of men wanted to get even with Candace. She was a real cock teaser, and she got off on it. So your guess is as good as mine, detec-tive. Apparently my ex-wife pissed off the wrong guy and he got his revenge."

The psychological profile fit, Santiago summed up the bil-lionaire in a heartbeat. Definite sociopath, no remorse or re-gret, justifies murder in his mind. Lies rolling off his tongue as slick as the devil himself. Santiago stuffed a fresh stick of Juicy Fruit in his mouth. "What was your relationship like with your uncle before he was murdered?"

"Uncle Carlos?"

"Yeah. What was it like being raised by a gangster? Did he teach you how to kill, be a trained assassin? I can almost feel sorry for you, DeVeccio. Must have been rough, being told by your father figure that it was perfectly all right to kill, going against everything you believed in, all those high standards. I bet you had to dissociate from yourself in order to slash someone's throat. I know I would. Is that what your uncle taught you, to kill the enemy with a sword, and then cover the corpse with a mask?"

Michael raised his glass. "You watch too many movies. Rather than teach me to be a trained killer, my uncle taught me how to run one of the most powerful construction companies in the world, the one he built from scratch. I owe a lot to Uncle Carlos. Without him, where would I have been after my parents' death? And as far as teaching me how to kill with the sword, you have it ass backwards. Uncle Carlos taught me how to fence, just down the hall in the great room. My uncle was a master swordsman and passed that honor onto me.

"To answer your question, my relationship with my uncle was that of a father and son. I idolized him and had nothing but the utmost respect for him. I hope I made him proud. Finding his corpse in the bathroom rendered me speechless. But, just as I told you ten years ago, it was the work of one of his enemies."

"So if you're such a master swordsman, what do you know about the Zorro sword?"

Michael walked over to the bar and refilled his drink, pouring a generous amount of bourbon. He turned to Santiago. "I know a hell of a lot about the sword. A button unleashes a thirty-seven inch blade, sharp and deadly."

"A fan yourself?" Santiago chewed on his gum. "Got one in your collection?"

Michael took a sip of bourbon and set his glass down. Sweat trickled down the sides of the heavy crystal, forming a ring on the dark mahogany bar. "The reason I know so much about the Zorro sword is simple. I bought it for Candace, as a birthday gift for her twenty-first birthday."

CHAPTER
FOURTEEN

"You gave your ex-wife the Zorro sword for her birthday?"

"She was my wife then, ten years ago. Candace had some bizarre obsession with Zorro, she was her biggest fan. So naturally, she'd want her sword. My ex-wife took lessons in martial arts, and for a woman, she wasn't bad. Not that she was in my league, far from it. During our marriage, we often fenced a bit before dinner in the great room. We preferred fencing opposed to working out with weights. It's great for the cardiovascular system, really gets the heart pumping, good for over all muscle tone. You ought to try it, Santiago. It wouldn't hurt you to lose a few extra pounds around your middle, get rid of that beer gut that's starting. Middle age spread can be a real problem."

"So when did you get your hands on her sword? When she was rubbing up to you real sexy at the bar? When the lights were out and no one could see you run your hand up her leg and slip the sword out of its scabbard with such slick fingers she never caught on? Is that how you did it, DeVeccio? Whisper crude come-ons in her ear and make plans to go at it in your uncle's room for old time's sake? But instead of stabbing her with Cupid's arrow, you stabbed her with her Zorro sword, straight through her lying cheating heart?"

Just as Michael was about to answer, Margot entered the

room, catching the end of the conversation. "Detective Santiago, you can't be serious. You think Michael killed his ex-wife? With her own sword? You're accusing him of committing that heinous crime?"

"Margot," Michael came to her side. "This is all hearsay, pure speculation on the detective's part. Nothing for you to go getting all upset about. Don't you see what he's doing? He's looking for someone to pin the murder on."

Margot's face turned as white as her angora sweater. Her eyes darted nervously from Michael to the homicide cop. Her voice cracked. "Detective Santiago. Surely after questioning all the guests until the wee hours, you have some substantial evidence to arrest someone? Please don't tell me this killer has once again slipped away without a trace?"

Santiago studied Margot Montgomery. Although she was pretty, she was nothing flashy. Not the trophy type he'd expect the billionaire to flaunt on his arms for show. No comparison whatsoever to either Candace DeVeccio or Lacy Diamond. They were showgirls, exotic dancers. With a royal-like grace, she struck him as high-class and sophisticated, and all wrong for the billionaire.

Dark circles haunted her green eyes, giving them a look as stormy as the sea. With the last of the setting sun teasing out the coppery highlights in her hair, he had the urge to run his fingers through it. He cleared his throat. "Unfortunately, Ms. Montgomery, at this time, we have very little to go on." He looked at her ring, the rock that had been on the stiffened hand of Lacy Diamond minutes before they carted her off in a body bag. His stomach rolled at the memory. "That's some ring you're wearing. How long have you been engaged?"

Margot glanced at her finger. "Michael proposed to me last week, on Christmas Eve."

With an abrupt turn, Santiago faced Michael. "You were about to tell me about the little rendezvous you set up last night with your ex-wife in your uncle's bedroom?"

"Santiago, despite the sleazy attempts my ex-wife made last night to set up a midnight rendezvous, I declined her offer. I told her she was more than welcome to stay and ring in the New Year, but I had no interest in rekindling old flames. That was the end of our brief conversation, and the last time I ever saw her alive. I rang in the New Year with my fiancé."

"And you can verify this, Ms. Montgomery? You were with Michael DeVeccio at midnight?"

Margot licked her parched lips. She couldn't account for Michael's whereabouts for the better part of an hour before midnight. And when he finally materialize, it was quarter past the hour. Wasn't it only a few hours ago she'd wondered if he'd killed Candace? Was Michael a killer? Could Michael have killed his ex-wife? She didn't know. She felt faint. Santiago's penetrating gaze burned a hole in her. She stumbled over her own words, "Ah, let me think…"

Michael jumped in, putting an arm around her shoulders. "Detective Santiago, as you are aware, we had a hell of an electrical storm last night that wiped out power all over Red Rock Canyon. Other than a few candles, the entire mansion was completely dark. It was impossible for anyone to keep track of one another. As I've told you, I went to my office to get my cell phone. I made several calls, one of which was to my staff at the carriage house to make sure all the windows and doors were closed. The other call I made was to the electric company to see if they could give me an idea of how long power would be out. And miraculously, the power came back on at midnight, just in time for the celebration. So by the time I joined Ms. Montgomery, it was probably a few minutes after midnight."

"I'll need to verify the date and time of those calls, so I'll need your cell phone. And when I get the pathologist's report confirming the exact time of death for your ex-wife, you might want to contact your attorney."

"Do I need an attorney, detective?"

Santiago's brown eyes glinted like molten glass. "You threatened to kill your ex-wife. You openly admitted it. Others can testify. You told your ex-wife if she ever returned to Vegas, you'd rip her lungs out. And what do you know? Candace DeVeccio rolled into town last night, dressed for seduction in a crimson body suit, comes on to you real strong, and is stabbed to death minutes after an eye witness sees you run your hand up her leg and finger her sword. You want to know if you need an attorney? What do you think?"

Michael fished a Marlboro from the pack and tapped it three times before lighting it. He crossed one long leg over the other. His burgundy Wing Tips gleamed in the sun. After blowing a perfect smoke ring into the air, he put his thoughts into words. "I'll tell you what I think, detective. I think a man's innocent until proven guilty. I think your homicide team is taking a lot of heat from your superiors because you have allowed the killer to slip through your fingers three times. I think Red Rock is in an uproar over these murders. I think you want these murders solved so badly you are willing to pin them on the first sap that comes along. Well hear this. Michael Alan DeVeccio is no sap. Be warned. Mess with me and you'll regret it. You have no idea how miserable I can and will make your life. Just so we understand each other."

"Well, hear this," Diego sneered. "Don't fuck with me. Mess with me and you'll live to regret it. Just so we understand each other."

Michael smiled, his eyes gleaming. "I'd say we've set our boundaries."

Santiago turned on his heels to leave. He stopped in front of Margot and stared at her ring. "Are you aware of that ring's history?"

"What do you mean?"

"CSI peeled that ring off Lacy Diamond's finger when we dragged her corpse out of a bathtub, the finger that was stiff with rigor mortis. Not a pretty sight. Picture it the next time you take a gander at that gaudy rock. And for the record, Candace DeVeccio wore it when she was married to your boyfriend. So unless you have a death wish, Ms. Montgomery, you might want to think twice about wearing that oversized bauble."

ЖЖЖ

With a heavy heart, Margot watched the homicide cop drive away, turning onto the sloping hills of Red Rock Canyon. The sun slowly set over the Mojave Desert, the tranquil merging of crimson and lavender blue skies in complete contrast to the turmoil in her heart. She turned to Michael. "I don't know quite where to begin."

Michael went to the bar and freshened his drink. "Can I get you a cocktail?"

"I don't want a drink. What I want is answers. Santiago is hell-bent on pinning these murders on you, or at the very least, the murder of your ex-wife. And in all honesty, he has a pretty good case pending: a threat, a corpse, and the murder weapon, a sword you could handle with your eyes closed, a sword you gave her. Add to that, the fact you're going around bragging about being a master swordsman, how you're the best and no one can compete. It's like you're taunting the police, daring them to pin the murders on you.

"And yet you sit there, all self-righteous when you're being questioned, like you're above the law. Your lack of emotions disturbs me, Michael. That gruesome murder last night didn't even move you. Everyone else will have nightmares. So, is it any wonder you're the prime suspect in your ex-wife's murder?

"Furthermore, can you imagine my shock to learn my engagement ring was pried off the corpse of your fiancé and worn by your ex-wife, another dead body? Call me naïve, but I thought you chose that ring for me and only me. You sure had me fooled. But, no more. I have no intention of sinking any deeper into your cesspool of lies." Margot removed the ring and tossed it at his feet. "FYI. You know how men don't want to marry a woman who's been around the track a few times? Well, this woman doesn't want a ring that's been worn by a couple of stiffs. I don't have a death wish. I have no intention of being the next woman with a pierced body part."

"Bravo!" Michael applauded with great theatrics. "You ought to be in the movies." He slammed his drink on the bar with a resounding thud and closed in on her. "Darling Margot. I do believe you've missed your calling. You could win an award. Perhaps they could use you on CSI. You have the case all figured out and are ready to convict me without as much as a trial. You disappoint me. I expect my fiancé to stand by my side, no matter what. Yet you dare and defy me?" His icy fingers caressed her neck. "Feel these hands, these loving caring hands. Then you tell me, are they the hands of a killer?"

Shocked and horrified, Margot watched his eyes glaze over with something so cold and empty it sent an icy chill snaking through her. He looked like a man on the edge. His brilliant blue eyes had lost all their zest, all their sparkle. They had the stone cold glaze of a killer. She backed up, but his grip tightened.

"Margot?" his fingers squeezed around her neck like a garrote. "Did you not hear my question? Allow me to repeat it. I asked you if these hands feel like the hands of a killer. Answer me!"

Her heart skipped a beat. She feared she might black out. Was Michael the killer? Did he kill his ex-wife at his own party? Lacy Diamond? His uncle? She didn't know. She couldn't be sure. But if he was some nut, she was on the next flight out of Dodge. For the moment, she needed to think, find a way to get his hands off her neck before he throttled her to death. She touched his fingers, his ice cold fingers, and gave the performance of her life.

"Of course I don't think your hands are the hands of a killer, Michael. Don't be ridiculous. Do you really think I'd be here right now if I thought that? Now, let's just relax. I think I'd like that drink now if you don't mind, how about a shot of whiskey, straight up?" She let out her breath as his hands dropped to his side. Choosing her words carefully, she talked as he poured her a drink. "I've reached a decision. I'm leaving for Chicago in the morning. I need time to digest all that's happened. We got engaged far too soon. I'm seeing a different side of you, and frankly, this other side of you frightens me."

His penetrating gaze seared straight to her soul. He shoved the drink in her hand, the amber fluid sloshing over the rim of the led crystal. "You'll regret this, Margot. I was willing to give you the world on a silver platter and spend the rest of my life treating you like a queen. And the ring you so carelessly tossed at my feet, allow me to fill you in on its history. That beautiful ring is a family heirloom. It belonged to my mother. Mama told me to give it to the girl of my dreams. Candace let me down with all her screwing around. Lacy was only interested in my money. Even though I'd hoped three would be the charm, it looks like you're not the girl of my dreams either.

"You stand there, hurling accusations at me, running away when the going gets tough. Well, hear this. I'm seeing another side of your personality as well. And frankly, Margot, I don't like what I see. What happened to that woman I placed so high upon a pedestal? You take some time to decide if a future with me is truly what you want." The air bristled as he bent down and snatched up the ring. A venomous smile curled his lips as he traced the hollow of her throat with the tip of the diamond. "Don't mess with me, darling Margot.

Betray me and you'll live to regret it. Betrayal in my world is unforgivable. Doubting my innocence has caused you to fall from grace. My marriage proposal still stands, but don't take too long to make up your mind. You know what they say. Wait too long—and the offer expires."

Just as Margot turned to leave, breaking headlines flashed across the television screen. "Arrest made in the Candace DeVeccio murder. Channel 2 News is first to report. Eyewitness comes forward. Eve Carlton, a guest at the masquerade held in the DeVeccio Estate last night, named Russel Harrison as Candace DeVeccio's killer. With the blood of the victim on his hands, Harrison was one of the suspects. Russel Harrison, CEO of the Vegas National Bank, arrested and waiting bail. We'll report more on this story as it unfolds."

Margot stared in disbelief. A whirlwind of emotions stormed through her: relief, shame, humiliation, regret, and overwhelming joy. The killer had been caught. It wasn't Michael. How could she have doubted his innocence even for a second? It wasn't Michael. They could have their life together and live happily ever after. She ran to him and flung her arms around him. "Oh, Michael. I am so sorry for ever doubting you. Can you forgive me, darling?"

"Margot," he placed the ring back on her finger. "Of course I can. We'll have a Valentine wedding and live happily ever after."

A smile coiled his lips. Eve had pulled it off. Three cheers for Cleopatra. It was perfect. Russel Harrison, poor sap, had been framed for murder. And The Hunter reigned.

CHAPTER
FIFTEEN

To the accompaniment of heather harps, flutes, and violins, the *Ave Maria* drifted sweetly through the rose garden of Colony House Estate. The sun cast its warm amber glow on the lavishly manicured grounds. A gentle breeze rustled through the trees, stirring the delicate scent of the roses. Under sun-drenched skies, guests gathered in the *Gone with the Wind* setting for the Valentine wedding of Margot and Michael.

Looking very suave in a black Oleg Cassini tuxedo, the groom stood beneath the oval-shaped trellis. With a subtle tinkling of bells, the maid of honor sauntered up the path of crushed rose petals. In a chic one strap red beaded illusion, Sophia looked like a doll from Camelot. And when the bride strolled up the path of roses on her father's arm, cameras zoomed in for a close up to capture the moment.

Like a vision on a cloud of white silk, Margot sashayed up the path of roses to Michael, her green eyes sparkling with love. Donned in a strapless silk organza gown with diamante, pearl gems, and Swarovski crystals, she shimmered in the late afternoon sun. A stole of roses on organza completed her wedding ensemble. A headpiece of rhinestones and crystals complemented her gown.

"You are simply flawless," Michael whispered in her ear. "I've never seen you look lovelier."

"And you've never looked more handsome." A tear glistened on her cheek. "I can't wait to become your wife."

Surrounded by clusters of red roses, the couple exchanged their wedding vows beneath the beautifully trimmed trellis, making promises of love and fidelity.

"Darling Margot," Michael placed the ring on her finger, "to the perfect woman."

"Always and forever," Margot slid the ring on his finger. "I promise to love you until death do us part."

ЖЖЖ

The Scarlett Room invited guests into Tara with its captivating setting. Whimsical figures portraying Scarlett and Rhett looked so real that the walls seemed to vibrate with their presence. Marble floors gleamed under the brilliancy of a Baccarat chandelier, and a spiraling staircase led to upper balconies. Guests sat on plush sofas enjoying cocktails while being entertained by classical music.

"Oh, Michael," Margot whispered, emotion caught in her throat. "This is what I've always fantasized about, a *Gone With the Wind* wedding."

"Margot," he kissed her. "This is only the beginning."

Silver candelabras graced either side of the appetizer table, and red roses in Waterford vases lined the mirrored wall. The scent of lemon-crusted medallions of beef, spicy shrimp, and Jonah crab claws wafted through the air. Michael picked up a long stemmed double dipped strawberry and traced the tip of it on Margot's lips. Then, he tasted those lips and whispered in her ear, "I can't wait to be alone with you."

With the gentle strum of a violin, the Viennese Waltz began and the bride and groom glided across the ballroom floor. On a romantic lilt, Michael ended the dance by placing his left thigh under Margot's right thigh. To applause and whistles, he lifted her high into the air before bringing her back down to earth with the greatest of ease.

With eyes only for her husband, Margot slid down the length of his body, her hands locked around his neck. When her feet touched the ground, she was so close to him it was as if they were one. His arms tightened around her waist, pulling her even closer. He was incredible, so sexy. Staring into his eyes, blue eyes that had grown dark with passion, she knew that she had found her destiny.

Ж◇Ж◇Ж

"Some bridal dance," Sophia joined Margot up at the bar. "Man, oh man, thought you two were gonna set the place on fire, all that body heat. I'm telling you, girlfriend, the room was smoking. Sure wish I had met a dude like Casanova when I was single. He treats you like a queen, better hang on to him."

"I intend to." Margot accepted a glass of champagne from a server dressed like a soldier from the Civil War. "I still think I'm dreaming; this all seems too good to be true. I'm sure gonna miss you, though. What will I do without you, Sophie? And I'll miss working in the museum. After I get back from my honeymoon, I'll go downtown to the cultural district and check out the galleries. Hopefully someone will need a curator."

"Ah, man," Sophia took a healthy slug of her Mint Julep. "Some girls have all the fun, an entire month in Tuscany. I don't know what I'd do first—try out all that Italian food, get my fair share of the wines, or have wild sex in one of those sweet Tuscan vineyards amidst all the grapes. But all kidding aside, I'm just glad they caught the killer, the Red Rock Slasher. Cause I gotta tell you, girl, I was pretty worried about you when I caught it on the news, another of Casanova's corpses. And this one, sitting straight up in a coffin, with a sword pierced straight through the heart. Man, oh man, wish I could have been at the masquerade to see that chilling scene. Betcha Hollywood's already in the throws of a thriller. Hey, I know, you can write the book."

"Something to think about," Margot laughed. "Listen, Sophia, enjoy yourself and mingle, have another Mint Julep and some food. I'm gonna go chat with some guests. Catch up with you later."

"You bet. Hey, who are those hot lookers up at the bar with Michael? Man, sure wish I was single. So, who are they? They look like some real hell raisers. Bet they really know how to tear the place up, eh?"

"Those are Michael's cousins, the O'Toole brothers. They grew up together and were really close when they were younger."

ЖОЖОЖ

"Hey, kid," Johnny grinned, lifting his Samuel Adams, his fat cigar stump between his lips. "To my cousin, sure hope this bride doesn't end up a stiff. Here, here."

Michael raised his glass to his cousin. Then he looked across the bar to his wife. Catching her eye, he winked at her. "No way. Margot is the perfect woman."

The Scarlett Room featured a vaulted ceiling and stained glass windows. The crystal chandelier cast a warm glow on guests, creating a romantic ambiance. A mirrored wall with gold leaf edging enclosed a solid oak bar, and the life-sized sculpture of Scarlett looked so real it was easy to imagine her charming every man in the South.

"Man, this place is laid out," Ricky reached into the sterling silver cigar box and chose one, rubbing it between his fingers. "Check out the architecture, Spanish Renaissance blended with Victorian. Think maybe I'll draw up some blueprints, come up with something similar for our next O'Toole resort. Could be our best yet."

"Go for it, bro," Jimmy did his shot and chased it down with a Miller. "Draw some up and we'll take a look. Tough part will be getting Ma to okay them."

"Just like the old days, huh kid?" Johnny said from the corner of his mouth. "To old times and old memories."

"Here, here," Michael raised his glass. "To the Four Musketeers."

"Ah, man. Remember when the movie came out? Bet we caught the flick a dozen times that summer, maybe more. Thought we were tough shit, acting out every scene from the movie. Those were the days, right, kid?"

"Or, how about the time we all hiked up to Red Rock." Michael tapped his cigar three times on the bar before lighting it. "You remember, up to Keystone Thrust, looking for petrified logs in the forest. You were first to find one, Johnny. Can still hear your voice booming across the canyon, all full of yourself cause you won the bet."

"Ah, forgot all about that. Must be goin' back some thirty years, right? Can't remember what the log looked like for shit, though."

"It was a log with some iron rich red running through it,

looked like blood. You remember...it had some sea creature embedded in it. You decided right then and there, we'd all take an oath to become blood brothers, the four of us. So we did, on the sacred log, vowing friendship and loyalty for life."

"That's right," Ricky chimed in, peering at Michael through his trendy glasses. "Ya start shootin' off some crap about the petrified logs being omens of good luck, weapons of the wolf gods."

"Damn straight," Jimmy held up his glass to the bartender. "I remember the ceremony, mingling our blood on the old stump. Imagine doing that now, might all catch AIDS. But hey, three decades back, who knew?"

"That's right," Michael said. "That petrified log in the forest in the canyon still has our blood on it."

"Come on," Johnny chortled. "Who the hell's gonna remember that? We were just kids playing stupid games. It didn't mean anything. It was worth a few laughs, though."

A stone cold glaze came into Michael's eyes. He raised his glass to his cousins, his blood brothers. "To forgotten oaths and forgotten promises." He took a deep drag of his cigar and studied his cousins.

Johnny, grinning that shit-eating grin, fat cigar stump stuck between his lips, so full of hot air and excitement it was a miracle he didn't self-inflate. Smooth and suave in an old gangster kind of way, a guy's guy and a ladies' man. He served as financial adviser for all of the O'Toole dynasty, but not for long.

Then there was Jimmy, subdued and laid back, a family man, married with twins on the way. Too bad he wouldn't live long enough to see them.

And the worst of the lot was Ricky, the anal retentive prick, peering through rose-colored glasses. Damn jerk always got on Michael's last nerve.

Michael smiled to himself, thinking of the coming attractions. Massacre of the Musketeers. And like Uncle Carlos, Lacy, and Candace, his cousins would soon come face to face with The Hunter.

"I still can't figure out why Russel Harrison killed your ex-wife," Jimmy did a shot. "I mean, what was his motive?"

"Half the men in Vegas had one," Michael guffawed. "She could get a guy hard with a bat of her sultry greens. She broke up marriages as fast as Elvis performed them in his chapel of love."

"So what the hell was Cleopatra doing in the old man's wing when she supposedly witnessed the stabbing?" Johnny snickered. "Wanna know what I think? I think good old Russ Harrison was framed."

"Yeah, but he had blood all over his hands, Candace's blood," Jimmy added. "If that ain't evidence, I dunno what is. Good ol' Jack the Ripper makes a comeback."

Michael flicked the ash of his cigar. "Well I'm damn glad he put my slut of an ex-wife out of her misery. You know what they say: you never know when it's your last day on earth."

Michael DeVeccio had the right to decide who would die and when. He would even the score for his blood brothers' betrayal. When The Hunter came a calling, dressed like the grim reaper, wielding a death sword into the throat of each sinner, it would indeed be sweet revenge. And Ricky would be first to die.

And if betraying the oath wasn't enough, he'd learned their dirty little secret. Oh, yes. He knew precisely where sweet Aunt Monica got all those millions to start her empire. His aunt and cousins had betrayed him in the worst possible way. The money that had been used to build the O'Toole Dynasty into the major competitor of the DeVeccio Dynasty had been his stolen birthright.

Smiling at the brothers O'Toole, he said, "One more round for old times? Here, here! To my cousins, my blood brothers."

CHAPTER SIXTEEN

A romantic ambiance awaited Margot as Michael carried her across the threshold and into their candlelit bedroom. Soft classical music drifted from hidden wall speakers, and a scattered array of sweet rose petals led a seductive path to the Casablanca bed. A single red rose lay across the satin pillow. Champagne chilled on ice next to a platter of succulent strawberries, and a sensual desert breeze blew in from open balcony doors.

"This is perfect," Margot touched her husband's cheek, "and so are you."

"I've dreamed of this night," Michael's voice was low and husky. Kissing her, he carried her to the bed and placed her down in front of it. Gazing into her eyes, he ran his fingers through her long coppery hair, losing himself in its silky essence.

How he wanted her. He needed her more than his next breath. For as long as he lived, he would never get enough of her. She was his undoing, the perfect woman. Staring into her eyes, he would drown in pools of liquid jade. She unraveled him. He needed her in a way he'd never needed anyone before. "Margot," he kissed her with a tenderness he had no idea he possessed. "You are so perfect."

His words washed over her like a sweet summer rain. He had to be the most romantic man God had ever created, and he was all hers. She wanted him. Now she would finally have him. Her heart pounded in eager anticipation. All those un-spoken promises would at last be fulfilled.

Drawing her close in his arms, he kissed her lips, brand-ing them. The need to possess stormed through him. She was his. His mouth came down on hers hard and rough, his tongue teasing and taunting, delving deeper and deeper. Their tongues mingled together in a feverish rush, faster and faster until the kiss softened into a feathery brush of lips.

"What you do to me," his eyes darkened with raw sexual-ity. His hands tightened around her waist, slowly moving up and down her body, exploring, teasing, toying with the lace-up buttons, and expertly undoing them one by one. Her dress slid down her body, shrouding her feet in a cloud of white silk. She stood before him in a lace teddy looking sexy and vulnerable and completely his.

His sinewy muscles tightened. With nimble fingers, his hands caressed her while his gaze swept over every inch of her body. He peeled off her lingerie, his fingertips throbbing with need. How he wanted to rip the garment to shreds and plunge into her like a wild stallion, but he didn't. Instead, he gingerly slid the lacy apparel down her body until she stood before him, flawless and beautiful in her nakedness.

His eyes grew dark and heavy with passion. The over-whelming desire to take her roughly pushed him to the brink of madness. His voice trembled, "You are simply flawless."

Picking her up, he placed her on the bed of satin sheets, devouring her lips, her throat, her breasts, rearing back only long enough to undress. His smoldering gaze seared into hers as they made love until the last of the burning embers cooled.

ЖҲЖ

A feeling of peace and tranquility lingered in the air the following morning as the newlyweds basked in the after glow of their lovemaking. Sitting on the garden terrace of their bedroom with the Red Rock Mountains engulfing them, they enjoyed a continental breakfast. With a satisfied smile, Margot plucked a raspberry from the bowl, dipped it in cream, and savored the moment. She gazed at the mansion that was now home, a private enclave deep in the foothills.

The cheerful chirping of the bluebirds echoed the joy in her heart.

Brushing the crumbs from his trousers, Michael stood up and sighed. "As much as I hate to leave my beautiful bride, I need to go to the office for a few hours, or we won't be going in the morning for our honeymoon." Winking, he added, "And there's nothing in the world I'd rather do than spend an entire month with you in the Tuscan countryside."

"I can't wait," Margot smiled, thinking of all the romantic nights ahead. "Hurry back."

"Nothing in this world could keep me from coming back to you," his gaze lingered on her well-toned body, all golden bronze from the sun. "Did I mention how much I like that satin negligee?"

Margot smiled seductively.

Michael stared at her for a long time, filled with the memory of the night before. "If I don't leave now, I never will." Kissing her, he added, "Get some rest. Our flight leaves for Tuscany bright and early in the morning."

Settling back in the teakwood chair, Margot longed for nothing at all. She was Mrs. Michael Alan DeVeccio. Yesterday had been the most perfect day of her life. She held up her ring to admire it, a striking diamond on a band of gold. A little thrill went through her. She was married.

Savoring the sweetness of another raspberry, she watched a butterfly land on her arm, its wings beautifully arched. Butterflies were a symbol of change, she mused as it soared away with a flutter of wings. And her life had just undergone a complete metamorphosis. She' had married a billionaire tycoon, moved into his luxurious estate, had an entire staff at her disposal, and was about to embark on a romantic Tuscan honeymoon for an entire month. She had married the most wonderful man in the world. Michael made all her dreams come true—and nothing would ever make her stop loving him. Nothing.

CHAPTER SEVENTEEN

From the cypress-lined cobblestone streets to the umbrella tables in the courtyard, Tuscany offered a taste of old-world Italy. Garlic, basil, and oregano spilled out of colorful window boxes, and flower carts and bistros lined the corner sidewalks. Keeping with the age old traditions of long leisurely lunches, quiet strolls, and afternoon siestas, Tuscans maintained a little of yesterday in today's modern world.

"Look at all those vineyards," Margot snapped pictures as their car careened down the mountainside. Deep purple, brilliant crimson, and glossy amber covered the landscape with a plethora of colorful vineyards. Wild roses and honeysuckle bloomed abundantly on a hillside bordered by fragrant lemon trees. An age-old olive tree sat on top of the hill, its gnarled branches reaching upward as if in prayer. Capturing the moment, Margot sighed. "No wonder Italy had some of the most legendary artists. With all these Tuscan treasures, it's a painter's dream."

Michael turned, his eyes filled with nostalgia. "There's the fishing port where my father fished every day for sardines. Everything is exactly the same. Look how happy they are."

Under sun-drenched skies, fishermen lowered their nets into the sea, retrieving heavy loads of sardines, sea bass, oysters, and mussels. Amidst the squawking of seagulls and harbor bells, colorful fishing boats bobbed in the water.

"Papa loved fishing, and I loved spending time with him. Look over there; see how the fishermen all take their catches to those stands. That's how Papa made his living, selling the sardines at the fishermen's market. Then there were his vineyards. Papa had the richest soil in the land. He grew red grapes the color of rubies. During the fall harvest, his grapes produced a full-bodied wine, rich and robust, bottled and labeled under the DeVeccio private collection. If only I could taste his wine one more time."

"This is like slipping back into another century," Margot watched a woman in a stained apron wrap fresh fish in newspaper. "The sights and sounds of the harbor could entertain me for hours."

"This part of Tuscany is an inland harbor, just a tiny fishing port where people prefer a simple life. You won't find them using cell phones or computers around here. And look off to the left." Rolling meadows blooming with roses, blue bells, yellow buttons, and dandelions ran free. "See that hillside over there," he pointed. "That's where I used to pick flowers for Mama. In my mind's eye, I can still see her face, all lit up with joy when I presented her with a bouquet of wild flowers."

Margot had never seen Michael so animated, so full of life. He had let his guard down, rambling ninety miles a minute, not weighing his words with his usual caution. Whatever popped into his head rolled out in an excited gush.

She saw the boy in him, an innocent child reliving precious memories of fishing with his father on the sea and picking wild flowers for his mother. His eyes were big and blue, filled with the innocence of youth. As she watched memories he'd harbored for the better part of thirty years resurrect, emotions tugged at her heart.

"Look over there." He gestured to a lush countryside. "Those fields are full of porcini mushrooms, fresh greens, and garden vegetables. And see the chickens and all those fat pigs, ready for slaughter. This is *Montalcino*, most famous for the tradition of *la cucina povera*."

"*La cucina povera?*"

"That's right," he laughed robustly. "Peasant cooking based on food that's home grown or gathered in the wild. You haven't lived until you've had a meal prepared with farm grown meats and fresh greens and vegetables from the good earth. On top of that, these Italian women add an extra ingredient: love. Mama certainly did. We had pigs and chickens in our villa, and nobody in the land grew sweeter or plumper tomatoes than Mama. And her spaghetti sauce," he kissed his fingertips. "Mama made the best."

Most of the restaurants resided on beaten paths or back alleys, making them serene refuges. Eateries varied from the simple *trattoria* to the wood-burning pizzerias to the more upscale. Every block had at least one sidewalk cafe, inviting strollers in for a glass of wine and a sample of their meats and cheeses.

"Let's stop in here for a glass of wine," Michael suggested. A man doing charcoal drawings in the street looked up from his easel as they approached. Michael turned to Margot. "Maybe you can sit for a portrait. I'd love a keepsake of our honeymoon to put on my desk."

With the warm sun on their backs, Margot and Michael sat on a stone bench surrounded by olive trees, sharing a bottle of Chianti and warm, gooey pizza. The tantalizing aroma of garlic and basil drifted through the air.

"See that mountain over there," Michael's eyes grew misty. "That's the mountain my parents' car went over that early May morning. It's a day I'll never forget as long as I live. Their car crashed over the mountainside and burst into flames before it ever hit the ground. Mama and Papa were killed instantly. It was the day my life in this fishing port came to a screeching halt."

Margot placed her hand on her husband's arm, her heart full of compassion. "I'm sorry, Michael. I can even imagine what you must have gone through. You were only twelve, a young boy on the verge of becoming a teenager. As if those years aren't turbulent enough. You must have been devastated."

Michael swiped at a tear. "I couldn't believe it when they told me. I thought it was some kind of sick joke, someone playing a prank. But Uncle Carlos was visiting that week, and when I saw his face, I knew it was no lie. My parents were dead and my world as I knew it was over. It was such a shock, such a brutal shock. I went into a deep depression and barely remember the funeral."

The emotions on Michael's face tore at Margot. Nobody knew this side of him, the vulnerable part he kept under such tight control. And now she understood why.

After his parents' death, he had built a brick wall around his heart. It touched her deeply, making her want to erase the painful memory from his head. But she couldn't. She felt such sorrow she wanted to weep for the boy in him. Not knowing what else to do, she took his hand. "Thanks for sharing such intimate memories with me, Michael. It can't be easy, reliving that horrible morning all those years ago. You were left all alone with no where to go. You said your uncle was visiting when the accident happened?"

"Yeah," Michael refilled their wine glasses. "I guess I never told you about Luciano, Uncle Carlos's only son."

"No. You mentioned him, but never told me the details. What happened to him?"

"He was killed, a fatal gun shot to his head. It happened in the great room, right in front of my uncle and several guests on New Year's Eve at one of the masquerades. Luciano was my uncle's pride and joy. He was eighteen years old, handsome, intelligent, and a born leader with a savvy sense of business. Uncle Carlos loved flaunting him around at social gatherings, making sure everyone knew the DeVeccio Dynasty would thrive for generations.

"These masquerades were the highlight of the year for my uncle. He got a real kick out of dressing in one of his masks and topping the evening off with a grand finale in front of all the big players of Vegas and several competitors. At the end of the night, Uncle Carlos called everyone into the great room. He chose several people at random and dared them to play a game of Russian roulette. Everyone begged to be chosen because the grand finale was the highlight of the evening, and until this particular party, no one ever got hurt.

"The gun was filled with blanks, my uncle assured every-one. It was just a game, the finale to the masquerade. Here all along, Uncle Carlos had one bullet in his gun, intended for his leading competitor. Uncle Carlos chose his son to take a turn to show it was on the level. So the chosen formed a cir-cle and all took a turn with Uncle Carlos's revolver. Then it was down to two, Luciano and Brady O'Toole. And that's when things got ugly.

"Somehow Luciano took the bullet intended for Brady O'Toole and was killed instantly. Uncle Carlos went ballistic. He snatched one of the sabre swords from the wall and killed

Brady O'Toole. Then he took his skull mask off the wall and put it on his face. He told everyone if they repeated a word of what they saw, they'd regret it. Brady's body was never found and my uncle bought out the O'Toole casino."

Michael gazed out to sea, his mind a million miles away. A gaggle of seagulls swooped down on the water from the jagged cliffs, their tormented squawking echoing over the harbor. The layers of blue and gray skies blended with the puffy white clouds aimlessly drifting. A far off look settled in Michael's eyes as he pitched his pizza crust to the birds.

"Losing Luciano was real hard on my uncle. That's when he came to Tuscany to visit his brother, to catch up with old family ties. And that very weekend, my parents were killed in that car crash. After my parents' funeral, it was decided I would move to Vegas with Uncle Carlos. From that day on, my uncle treated me like his son and trained me to take over the business."

"That's quite a story," Margot said. "I often wondered what happened to your cousins' father. Since this all went down better than thirty years ago, they would have been pretty young, like you. No wonder you were so close when you first moved to Vegas with so much in common. All four of you had just lost a father. That alone would have formed a bond."

"Yeah, we were inseparable," Michael stared at the sloping mountainside where his parents' car had lost control. His eyes glazed over as he relived it. "And if not for my cousins, I would have probably gone nuts. But still, I wanted my life back, my simple life in Tuscany. Summers spent fishing with Papa, catching fresh sea bass and sardines with the sun beating down on my back, and harvesting grapes from the vineyard. The smell of fresh sea air was a part of me, my heritage. The fishing port and all the sounds of the harbor haunted my dreams for a good while, the squawking of seagulls, the ringing of the harbor bell.

"I missed Mama, her sweet smile. She was so proud of me, it showed in her eyes. Nothing can compare to a mother's love, pure and unconditional. I can still see Mama's face light up when I'd pick wild flowers for her in the meadow. She'd get a tear in her eye and tell me I was the best son in the whole wide world. Then one day it all came to an end. It wasn't fair. They were so full of life, so full of love.

They left me all alone, an orphan at the age of twelve. I cried myself to sleep every night for the first year, drenching my pillow with tears.

"You see, Margot, even though Uncle Carlos and Papa were brothers, they were total opposites. Where Papa was a simple man with simple needs, Uncle Carlos craved power and prestige. They lived by an entirely different set of standards. Their morals were like night and day. Where Papa was a God-fearing man and lived by the Bible, Uncle Carlos was a man who instilled fear and lived life by the sword. Instead of turning the other cheek, he believed in getting even. With Uncle Carlos, it was an eye for an eye. Be rewarded or be damned. He gave as good as he got. Betrayal in his world was unforgivable. That was his motto, what he seared into everyone, his family, enemies, and employees. It didn't matter who it was, the message was crystal clear. The power of his wrath was unspeakable. That took some getting used to.

"My uncle raised me with an iron fist and defying him would have been a big mistake. I had it all at my fingertips—a mansion in Red Rock, money, power, and prestige. Uncle Carlos gave me the best education—from schools in the Swiss Alps to Ivy League colleges. I had the world by the tail. But it didn't come without a price. You see, Margot, nothing comes cheap or easy. It all boils down to money and self esteem and how much of yourself you are willing to sell."

"So, you eventually got used to all that power?"

"After a while," Michael topped off their glasses with the last of the Chianti. "Once I adjusted to the fact I was being trained to take over the business, everything fell into place. It became a growing addiction; the more I had, the more I wanted. I saw what Uncle Carlos was: a Vegas icon. He was respected all over the Vegas Strip. My uncle was a legend and was giving me the keys to his kingdom. How could I not be seduced by all that power?"

"And your Aunt Monica and your mother were sisters, right?"

"That's right," Michael said. "Two sisters with totally different goals. Mama was a country girl with dreams of marrying a fisherman and never leaving the harbor, while Monica wanted nothing more than to get out. Mama loved Tuscany, the home of her heart. How she loved planting her flowers and vegetables in the countryside, digging her hands in the rich fertile earth. She married Papa, a poor fisherman and they made their life on the sea.

"But Aunt Monica was different. Everything about Tuscany repulsed her, the fishing port, the smell of the sea, you name it. Mostly, she hated being poor. It embarrassed her. From the day Aunt Monica was born, she had dreams of being rich and famous. She was obsessed with marrying a rich man and getting as far away from her dirt poor roots as she possibly could. She told my mother she would marry the first rich man who came along. And when my aunt was eighteen, Brady O'Toole came into her life and took her away to Vegas, the city of bright lights and excitement. That was the beginning of the O'Toole Dynasty."

CHAPTER EIGHTEEN

One evening while Margot and Michael strolled through the villa, they came across a restaurant on a rural path. Authentically European with high ceilings and stucco walls, they fell into one of Tuscany's best kept secrets. Candles in wrought iron holders flickered on scarred wooden tables, and a strolling violinist added to the romantic ambiance.

"Good evening," a waiter greeted them with gusto. "Some wine, of course?"

Michael scanned the impressive wine list before making a selection. "We'll have a bottle of *Brunello Di Montalcino*."

"Excellent choice," the server beamed. "A rich, robust Tuscan Red. You'll love it, just you wait."

The window gave chase to a sweeping view of *Castello Banfi*, a medieval castle towering over rolling forests and lush, fertile vineyards. Peach and olive trees landscaped its hillside.

"That's Tuscany's highest mountain," Michael pointed to where the castle stood. "Rumor has it on warm summer nights, lightning dances all around the castle in a devil-may-care sort of way. They say the mountain shields the castle from getting struck by lightning."

"What a bewitching tale." Margot was still staring when the waiter presented a salad of fresh greens from the hillside. When the tantalizing aroma of warm garlic bread filled her senses, her mouth watered and she forgot all about the castle. The salads, topped with Asiago cheese, shimmered with red ripe cherry tomatoes and green and black olives.

Margot lost herself in Michael's eyes. She reached across the table and ran her finger along his wedding band. "Did you ever wonder how your life would have turned out if your parents' car hadn't gone off the mountain all those years ago? I mean, do you think you would have stayed in Tuscany and made a living on the sea like your father, fishing for sardines? Or, do you think you would have wanted more out of life like your Aunt Monica?"

"Who's to say?" he bit into a piece of warm flaky bread. "I can't change the hands of fate, so why look back and play the 'what if' game. Although it took some adjusting, the life Uncle Carlos gave me was one I came to crave. Once I took control, living at the DeVeccio estate became the life I wanted. And as you know, Aunt Monica and her three sons lived so close to Uncle Carlos, Johnny, Jimmy, and Ricky were like my brothers. So for a while at least, the O'Toole family filled a void in my life. I thought of my cousins as my siblings. Aunt Monica treated me like one of her sons, and she looked so much like Mama, it was easy to pretend we were all one big happy family. I came to adore her, idolize her even. But when her boys got a little older, in their early twenties, everything changed. Or perhaps I should say Aunt Monica changed."

"How so?"

"You remember how I told you that my uncle bought out the O'Toole casino when Brady O'Toole was killed? Aunt Monica focused her attention on raising her boys. But once Johnny, Ricky, and Jimmy were in their early twenties, she decided to go back in the casino business with their help. She became one of the shrewdest businesswomen in Vegas. It wasn't long before her casino business snowballed into building luxury resorts all over the world.

"Aunt Monica taught her sons the trade, and under her tutelage, they formed a powerhouse construction company. Like I said, my cousins and I were all in our early twenties back then; that was about the time our friendship ended. Before long, the two families became fierce business competitors. It wasn't until recently I found out just how money hungry dear Aunt Monica was. You see, Margot, she betrayed

Mama, and I've recently learned her dirty little secret. Now that I know, everything makes sense.

"A few months ago, I found out where Monica O'Toole got the money to build her empire. You remember I told you my aunt wanted to marry a rich man so she could leave Tuscany and never look back? Well, it turns out Brady O'Toole didn't have so much as a pot to piss in."

"But," Margot frowned. "So if Brady O'Toole was so poor, where did they get the money to start their casino business?"

"Unbeknownst to anyone, my grandfather was a very wealthy man. But he preferred a simple life and never left Tuscany. Like my father, he was a fisherman and fished for sardines in the harbor. My grandparents had two children, Monica and Angelica. Monica was older than Mama by two years. So when my grandfather died and the will was read, it all came out. My grandfather left several million dollars to the oldest sibling, Monica. But it was with the understanding she'd give half of that inheritance to Mama when she turned eighteen.

"Rather than lose so much as one penny of her precious inheritance, Monica took the money and ran to Vegas with Brady O'Toole. So between my aunt's money and Brady's sharp mind for business, they made quite a team. But that wasn't what upset Mama. She didn't care about money, far from it. What hurt her was that her sister never bothered with her again. Aunt Monica had a one track mind. Getting rich and building an empire. So there you have it—the roots of the O'Toole Dynasty. You see, Margot, half of that dynasty is my birthright."

"How incredibly selfish," Margot said. "Your aunt is no better than a criminal, a common thief. You'd think it would bother her conscience. I know doing something like that to someone in my family would sure haunt me. I couldn't live with myself. Basking in the glory of all that dirty money is a sin."

"Precisely," Michael agreed. "And my cousins were no better. Once each of them turned twenty-five, he received a handsome inheritance, a provision in the will for each grand-child."

"I'm so sorry," Margot let the unfolding drama of Michael's life settle. "But you never did say how you found out your aunt's dirty little secret? How did you stumble upon it just a few months ago?"

"Lacy Diamond told me."

"Lacy Diamond? Your fiancé before me?"

"That's right. She told me the night we got engaged, in Venice."

"How would Lacy Diamond know anything about how your Aunt Monica got the money to build the O'Toole Dynasty?"

"Uncle Carlos told her one night. Even though he never let any company secrets slip the whole time he built his empire from the ground up, Lacy was his Achilles heel. He confided in her and trusted her implicitly. Nothing went on in Vegas that Uncle Carlos wasn't aware of. He knew how the O'Tooles got their hands on the investment money. They were our number one competitor in business after all, and Uncle Carlos knew everything about the competition. Just like an election. Secrets have a way of coming out and money talks."

"But I still don't understand why your uncle would have told Lacy. You said she was his confidant? How so?"

"Pillow talk, Margot. Uncle Carlos and Lacy Diamond were lovers."

CHAPTER NINETEEN

Ricky O'Toole stood on the deck of his ranch in the Red Rock Mountains, drinking a cup of coffee. A raven flew overhead, casting a shadow on the landscape spanning the length of the parapet. Tucked away deep in the foothills, his ranch lie nestled in a wealth of wildlife. Surrounded by red rocks and cliffs punctuated by waterfalls and shallow streams, he couldn't imagine living anywhere else in the world

Finishing the last of his coffee, he placed the Indian mug on the railing and stared at the beauty around him. The late afternoon sun shimmered like a jewel amidst the lavender blue sky. A slight breeze rustled through the Joshua trees, stirring the air with their sweet scent. On an impulse, he decided it would be the perfect day for hiking the trails. Or maybe some rock climbing. Hearing tires on the gravel driveway, his thoughts were interrupted. His large German Shepherd darted across the yard, snarling and barking as he trampled through a patch of purple sage.

Turning around, Ricky watched his brother leap out of his Jeep Wrangler and slam the door. "Easy there, Sampson," he held out his hand to let the dog sniff it. "It's me, Johnny. There's a good boy." With the dog yipping at his feet, he popped the lid of his trunk and pulled out a cooler and lugged it up to the deck. Spotting his brother, a slow easy grin spread across his face. "Hey, kid, hope you're hungry. Brought enough food to feed a horse."

Ricky jogged down the steps and took the cooler from his brother. "Holy hell, what's in this thing, bricks?"

"Ah, man," Johnny took off his sunglasses and wiped the sweat from his brow. "What can I say, kid, the wife loaded it up, packed it full of leftovers. Chicken, roast beef, potato salad, you name it. Her family came in and she cooked food like it was goin' out of style."

Ricky gripped the handle tight. "I'll go fetch us a couple a cold ones."

Johnny watched the dog run off to a shady respite beneath a Yucca tree. Fumbling in his pocket for a match, he lit his cigar. Gazing out into the foothills, memories of hiking, fishing, and camping with his brothers and cousin skittered across his brain.

"Some view, huh?" Ricky joined him, tossing him an ice cold long neck. "This is God's country out here in the wilderness, far away from civilization. Wouldn't trade it in for the world."

Johnny took the cigar stump from his mouth long enough to slug back half the beer. "Dunno, kid. Kind of lonely out here. Ya know me, gotta be around all the lights and excitement, where all the action is. Besides, me and the wife are kinda worried about cha livin' out here on the range, in the middle of nowhere. Lacy Diamond's place isn't so far from here and some nut slashed her throat. Maybe it's time you move back to the city, closer to home. Or at least come stay with us, just till the killer's caught. It's no good livin' all alone out here in the middle of nowhere. We have Mama almost convinced to move in with us till this killer's caught. Like I said at Michael's wedding, no way do I think Russ Harrison is guilty of murdering Candace. Know what I think? I think whoever slashed Lacy's throat did Candace, too. And God only knows where the freak'll strike next. So come on, what do ya say?"

Ricky brushed the cigar ashes littering his railing. Then he glared at his brother. "Man, Johnny. Get over it, stop watchin' all those crime shows. No way am I leavin' my home, getting' scared off just cause someone broke into Lacy Diamond's place and slashed her throat. She was a whore, our cousin's very expensive whore. Rumor on the street has it she was a user, messin' with some pretty strong stuff. Drinkin' too. If you think some psychopath's stalkin' the foothills, you're nuts, man. Get over it. Besides, if someone did break in here, Sampson would rip 'em apart, limb by limb. Got my guns, too. A semi-automatic and my rifle. Ya need to come out on the trails with me, just like when we were kids. You've been sayin' ya will, so how about right now? How about I pack a cooler, some of that chicken and a few cold ones? I was just about to head on out, before it gets dark."

Johnny glanced at his watch. "I'd like to, Rick. But I can't do it today. Gotta meeting in about an hour. Then I promised Anna and the kids we'd go to dinner and a show, catch the new action flick playin' at the mall. Some other time, huh?"

"Yeah, all right. I'll let ya off the hook this time, but soon, Johnny. Now I wanna shove off before it gets dark. Gets pretty cold up in the mountains this time of year. Tell Anna me and the mutt'll be eatin' good for a week."

"Yeah, I'll do that. Hey, maybe it's time you got yourself married, settle down and have a family. Somethin' to think about, bro. Speakin' of marriage, did I mention Michael's back from his honeymoon? Saw him struttin' into his club earlier."

Ricky snorted. "Wonder how long it will be before he gets bored with the new bride? Ya know what a Casanova our cousin is. He'll find a new one, sooner or later. He always does."

Johnny jogged down the path to his jeep, the easy going grin back on his face. "All right. How about we get together Friday night, you and me and Jimmy. We'll do the town, tear the place up, what do ya say?"

"Sounds like a plan."

"All right, Ricky. See ya around, kid."

ЖЖЖ

From the deep shadows of the woods, The Hunter watched his cousin from a pair of close range binoculars. Totally oblivious, Ricky tossed a knapsack, plenty of bottled water, and a denim jacket into the trunk of his Ford Explorer. The Hunter scoffed. The anal prick was always prepared, just like a boy scout. Crouched down behind a petrified log, he continued his surveillance.

Ricky made one final trip into the ranch, then closed the door. The Hunter waited, sweating beneath his black hooded jacket, the smell of dank air and pungent rot filling his senses. A gaggle of ravens swooped overhead, their throaty cries echoing through the woods. The Hunter traced his finger over the log where the cousins had taken their oath all those years ago, a slow rage fueling him for the kill.

He watched Ricky get into his truck, back down his gravel driveway, plow down the road leading to the highway. The rumble of low gears and heavy engine reverberated through the forest. With the hunting song playing in his head, The Hunter shimmied through the thicket, crushing dry twigs and pinecones beneath his booted feet. From deep in the woods, an owl hooted, followed by the mournful wail of a coyote. The cry of the wild aroused him.

Charged with an overload of adrenaline, he sprinted up the adobe steps. From inside, the German shepherd snarled and barked, giving a ferocious warning. The Hunter smiled. Through latex gloves, he fingered the Ninja star, the one laced with a drug to put the dog to sleep for a few hours. Then he fingered the death star in his other pocket, the one that would put his cousin to sleep. Permanently. He opened the door a crack and wield the throwing star into the canine. It didn't take long for the drug to have its soporific effect. Within a few seconds, the dog grew lethargic, stumbled back and forth on shaky legs, and collapsed in a heap on the terra cotta floor. Humming, The Hunter stepped over the sleeping mutt. He had work to do.

Helping himself to a bourbon on the rocks, The Hunter envisioned his cousin strutting through the door, totally oblivious. Ricky would rush in, not a hair out of place, wondering why Sampson wasn't barking. Then he'd see him, slumped in the corner of the foyer. That's when he'd let his guard down, nothing on his mind but the sick mutt. The Hunter fingered the Ninja death star, a grin forming on his lips. Ricky would sense his presence, feel that first prickle of fear skitter down his spine. Then he'd look up and see him, but it would be too late. His fate would be sealed. Looking around, he spotted the photo of the four cousins posing as the Musketeers for the masquerade. The Hunter scoffed derisively. All for one and one for all, indeed. Pulling out a nogahyde chair at the bar, he made himself comfortable while he waited.

ЖЖЖ

Hearing tires on the gravel driveway, The Hunter slipped on his latex skull mask and fingered the Ninja star in his pocket. This was the best part, catching the traitor off guard, then watching the fear when realization dawned. He couldn't wait to wield the death star into his throat, cut off his voice box, prevent him from ever lying again. Power soared through him as he got into Ninja attack mode.

From outside, Ricky stood at his front door, his ears keenly alert. Something was off, not quite right. A niggle of fear raced down his spine, making the hair on the back of his neck stand straight up. Shit. It was all Johnny's fault, all that talk about some nut stalking the foothills. He was never afraid before and wasn't going to start looking over his shoulder every time the wind blew. But then he realized what was wrong. Sampson wasn't barking. Why? He always yipped like a pup when he heard the truck pull in the drive-way. Why wasn't he barking?

From deep in the woods, a coyote howled, its keening wail chilling. Come on, get a grip, he told himself. But some-thing was off. He fingered his cell phone in the pocket of his denim jacket, wishing it was his gun, his semi automatic. Should he call the cops? And tell them what? His dog wasn't barking at him. Yeah, right. He'd sound like some paranoid schizophrenic. No way. Sampson was probably sleeping, tak-ing a snooze. He was just being ridiculous, all because of Johnny. Then he remembered he hadn't locked his door. Why not? Because he never did and wasn't about to start now just because Johnny had him spooked, just like when they were kids. Heaving a sigh, he shoved his way through the door, calling out to his dog. "Sampson, here boy."

And that's when he saw him, all sprawled in the entry-way, limp and lethargic. "Sampson! What's wrong, boy?" he leaned down to check his pulse, relief storming through him when he felt one. Faint, but it was there. Just as he was about to pick him up and take him to the vet, he sensed a presence looming above him. Whipping his head around, he saw the masked man. Then he saw the glint of a Ninja star whizz across the room, straight for his throat. He tried to duck, but it was too late. He slumped to the hardwood floor in a crumpled heap. The last thing he saw was Michael's face when he peeled off the mask and grinned at him.

CHAPTER TWENTY

Cruising down Las Vegas Boulevard, Diego Santiago passed DeVeccio Plaza just as Michael DeVeccio was strutting through the beveled glass doors of his palace, looking as pompous and arrogant as ever. How his fist itched to wipe that smug expression off his face, knock him flat out on his billion dollar ass. So, he had returned from his Tuscan honeymoon, had he? The homicide cop scoffed. He might think he was off the hook for the killings in Red Rock Canyon, but Santiago knew better.

From the moment Eve Carlton waltzed into police headquarters claiming to be an eyewitness to the murder of Candace DeVeccio, it was all wrong. The charges were trumped up and he knew it. He just didn't know why. Yet. Somehow DeVeccio had manipulated Eve Carlton into framing Russell Harrison. And since Harrison was spotted fleeing the crime scene with the victim's blood all over his hands, homicide had no choice but to arrest him.

DeVeccio probably danced on his ex-wife's grave when that breaking news aired. Santiago feared for the new bride, the trusting Margot DeVeccio. Wasn't she smart enough to realize she was married to a pathological liar? A master manipulator? Could she be that blind? Maybe it was time the new Mrs. Michael Alan DeVeccio took off her rose-colored glasses and took a hard look at the man she slept with before she became the next victim.

Try as he might to prevent it, Santiago saw Margot De-Veccio everywhere. Like it or not, she'd gotten under his skin. Something about her tormented green eyes had touched a primal instinct in him that made him want to protect her. She stirred his blood. He felt something for her he had no right feeling. She was married to the prime suspect in a murder investigation. He should know better, and he did.

How he had hated telling her about the other women who had worn her engagement ring, but what choice did he have? She had been crestfallen, and he had been the one responsible for putting that hurt look in those bewitching green eyes. The news had devastated her. Yet she needed to be told. Not that it had done a lick of good, he hissed between clenched teeth, reaching for a stick of gum, wishing it was a cigarette.

Just as Santiago drove past the Bellagio Fountain, the dancing water show got underway with its lively rendition of *Hey Big Spender*, its brilliant jets undulating a rippling effect on the lake. Smiling, Santiago's fingers tapped rhythmically on his steering wheel. No matter how drained or emotionally strung out he felt, the light show on the water always lifted his spirit like a fountain of youth. He let out a long sigh, releasing some of his pent-up tension. For a brief few seconds, the water show offered a break from homicide

But his thoughts wandered back to Margot DeVeccio. What would it be like to go on a date with her, to bring her here to a show on the lake? He envisioned her jade green eyes dancing with a flirtatious, come hither look. Then she would turn to him, and her eyes would be filled with passion. Passion for him. Damn. Flicking on his turn signal, he shot into the next lane. Why did she have to fall for the billionaire?

He needed something incriminating on DeVeccio, something to prove he had killed his ex-wife, fiancé, and uncle. But what? DeVeccio was as cold as ice and just as slippery. There was no doubt that Michael Alan DeVeccio was a trained assassin, a man without a conscience or soul. And didn't his initials suit him all the way down to his billion dollar balls: MAD.

With the desert breeze smacking him in the face, Santiago whizzed past another block of glittering lights. Many of the magnificent resorts and casinos on Las Vegas Boulevard had been built by gangsters, Carlos DeVeccio among the biggest. And the old man had raised his nephew into his likeness. With the pulsating beat of the night life all around him, Santiago could only imagine the psychological scars of being raised by a man with such twisted morals.

Tapping his foot to the gyrating beat of the song blasting on his radio, Santiago thought about some of the serial killers he had investigated over the years. The psychosis seemed to always stem from a childhood trauma, either sexual or emotional. Being raised by the head of one of the biggest crime families in Vegas would have definitely traumatized a young and impressionable kid.

He pictured Michael DeVeccio as a boy, a kid living in a remote Tuscan fishing port. His parents would have showered their only son with love. Michael would have been a happy, well-adjusted boy, content to become a fisherman like his father. He would have believed that the world was a good place and bad things only happened to bad people. His parents would have taught him the difference between right and wrong, given him a good moral upbringing. Michael would have been taught to honor and obey. His life as he knew it would have been perfect. Until the kid turned twelve and his world as he knew it tumbled down around him like the great Wall Street Crash.

How could a kid as sheltered as that handle such a drastic shock? One day fishing on an inland sea harbor with loving parents, the next being thrust into the manipulative, controlling hands of a gangster, a man who trained him to kill. Santiago wondered what went through his mind after a murder. Did he ever think about those morals his parents had instilled in him all those decades back? If his mother were alive, could she reach him? Make him stop? Make him feel remorse or regret for his crimes? What would Michael DeVeccio do if he thought his mother had witnessed him doing these heinous things to a human being? After being deprogrammed and brainwashed by his uncle for decades, would it be too late to reach the part of him which was once decent?

ЖЖЖ

When Santiago finally pulled into his neighborhood, he was beat, dead tired. It had been a long and grueling day.

Thinking about the cold beer in his refrigerator, he was damn glad to put the day behind him. Maybe he would grill that steak he had wanted to cook for the past few nights. His mouth watered at the thought of a fat, juicy steak with all the trimmings, grilled medium rare with onions and mushrooms. Maybe topped off with his favorite hot sauce. He could smell it, smoking on the grill. No gas drill either. He preferred char grilling, the good old fashioned charcoal taste. Then, after taking a hot shower to massage his aching muscles, he'd roll into bed and drop off before his head hit the pillow. Just as he turned up his driveway, his cell phone rang. Damn. It was downtown. He flipped the lid of his phone back and barked, "Yeah?"

"The Red Rock Slasher struck again."

"Shit," Santiago snarled, all thoughts of his grilled steak forgotten. "Who is it?"

"Ricky O'Toole. His brother called it in, found him with a Ninja star in his throat and the skull mask on his face. Body was still warm. Another corpse all dressed up for the morgue. And one more thing, Santiago. This one was found with his glasses on, post mortem."

CHAPTER TWENTY-ONE

With the hunting song echoing in his head, Michael crossed the threshold to the great room, his blood tingling with the aftermath of the kill. His fist held high in the air, he charged across the hall to his uncle's portrait, mocking the man in the mural. "You would have been proud of my hunting skills tonight, Uncle Carlos. Another stellar performance. You trained me well. Under your expert tutelage, I learned how to hunt like a Ninja soldier, silent and deadly, just like an action figure in an action movie. Vengeance was served tonight in true DeVeccio style."

Breaking into fits of manic laughter, Michael danced around in circles like the Joker. Cackling like a wild hyena, he thrust his fist in the air and howled at the moon. "Long live the king! No one in this world can outwit, out play, or out maneuver Michael DeVeccio. Long live the king!"

ЖꝎЖꝎЖ

With a sudden jolt, Margot bolted upright in bed, jarred from sleep by manic laughter. Her heart galloped at a wild rhythm. Some nightmare, she thought, scooping Zeus up in her arms. The cat looked as frightened as she did, his tail thumping, his hair on edge. Holding the fat tabby in her arms, her heartbeat slowly tapered down to a normal rhythm. The dream terrified her, hysterical laughter so real it made her shudder. It was like something in some horror movie, leaving her completely unnerved. Yet, it seemed to be coming from downstairs, right below her. Flicking on the Tiffany lamp on the night stand, she peered at the clock. Two in the morning and no sign of Michael.

Warm air blew in from open terrace doors, rustling the silken drapes. Chills danced up and down her spine, her backbone as tight as piano keys. The cat leaped from her arms, hissing as he scampered off for shelter beneath the bed. Reaching for her robe, she went out on the balcony. The cool desert air rippled through her hair like invisible fingers, making her skin tingle. A hunter's moon hung low in the dark sky. The eerie stillness of the night unsettled her, taking her back to the night of the masquerade. A coyote howled in the distance, its keening slicing through her raw nerves. Goose bumps prickled her skin. A sense of uneasiness crawled through her as she gazed into the deepest part of the thicket. She sensed evil lurking in the deep dark woods. She couldn't shake the feeling that something was wrong, dead wrong.

Something about Russel Harrison killing Candace didn't sit right with her. What would make a prominent bank owner commit such a gruesome murder at a masquerade party? And why would he do it with such morbid theatrics? The pieces didn't fit. Her back went rigid. Was the real killer still out there, watching and waiting for just the right moment to pounce out of the shadows and—

"Looking for the boogie man?" Michael's arms tightened around her waist. He whispered in her ear, his breath hot and slurred with whiskey. "What have I told you a million times? The safest place you can be is in my arms. Now, come to bed. You have no idea how much I want you."

ЖОЖОЖ

Streaming sunshine poured in through the terrace doors of the master suite. From the ponderosa pines, bluebirds chirped merrily, the dawning of a new day. Michael toyed with a lock of Margot's long, coppery hair. Strands of it fanned out over the satin covered pillow of their Casablanca bed. She reminded him of an angel. He traced his finger along the contour of her slender neck, thinking what a shame it would be to wield a death star into all that soft, fragrant skin. And, oh, what a waste it would be to cover her angelic face with the skull mask, the death mask. But if she betrayed him, he would do it in a heartbeat and never look back. Absolute power would always reign.

The DeVeccio Dynasty would rule the world. But in order for that to happen, the legacy had to continue for generations to come. The only way to ensure that was to propagate the DeVeccio bloodline by having sons. And it was high time Margot played her part. Kissing her, he watched her sleepy green eyes open; then he took great pleasure in watching them grow hot with passion.

"Michael," she reached for him. "Come to me."

ЖЖЖ

Sitting on the terrace enjoying coffee and Danish, Margot and Michael bathed in the warm aftermath of their lovemaking. Margot felt totally at peace and more in love with Michael than ever. The insecurities she had felt last night had been put to rest the minute she fell into her husband's arms. The perfect husband and the perfect lover. Sighing, she stared out into the cliffs of Red Rock Canyon. A large raven soared into the thicket of the deep underbrush, its harsh call echoing across the mountains.

With the sun just rising to meet the horizon, it had the promise of a gorgeous day. Like layers lifting and disappearing into thin air, the murky skies transformed from a dull slate gray to a clear azure blue. Like her husband's eyes, she thought, thinking how they changed color with his mood. Every time she stared into those pools of icy blue, she drowned a little deeper. She looked into those eyes now, and got weak in the knees. The way he made her feel when he looked at her stole her breath. Reaching for his hand, she linked her fingers with his. Nothing could ever come between them or make her stop loving him.

"I almost forgot," Michael went into the bedroom. "I bought a gift for the perfect woman." He returned with a jeweler's box and presented it to her with a beguiling smile. "For you."

Shimmering in the early morning sun, a blue diamond on

a white gold chain sparkled. Margot held it up to admire it. The diamond captured sunbeams, exploding into a rainbow of colors. "Oh, Michael," she touched the stone, a Princess cut in a flawless setting. "It is simply awesome. The diamond reminds me of your eyes, such a pretty color, so brilliant."

"I'm glad you like it," Michael said. "It was designed for a queen, and that's just what you are, my queen." He removed it from her fingers and hooked it around her neck. "There, now it's befitting." Staring into her serene green eyes, he said, "I was hoping you had some news for me by now, Margot. You look so radiant this morning. Are you pregnant with my son?"

Stunned, Margot stared at her husband. "Pregnant? No. We've only been married for a few short months. Surely we want to wait a while before having children. We've barely returned from our honeymoon, and there's still so much adjusting to do. Not only that, but I was thinking of going downtown later on this week to see if one of the art museums needs a curator. I miss working, hosting galas. Being a curator is in my blood. Planning the shows and hosting them fulfill me. Being around all those antiques in an art gallery excites..."

"Hold on, hold on," Michael's blue eyes narrowed into steely slits. "Let's get something straight right here and now. Mrs. Michael Alan DeVeccio will not work like some commoner. You are married to one of the richest men in the world. And the most powerful. There is no need for you to bring in an income. Over my dead body will you work. Your only job is to keep me happy and have my sons. Do I make myself perfectly clear, darling Margot?"

"What?" her mouth dropped open. "Could I be hearing right, Michael? Are you ordering me around like some wife from medieval times, demanding that I produce an heir to your kingdom? Is that what I'm hearing?"

"Precisely," he took a step closer, fingering the diamond around her neck. "I've given you the world. You live in a mansion filled with the priceless antiques you seem to crave; you have gowns cut from the finest of silk; your diamonds out dazzle the neon lights of Vegas; and I've given you a Porsche which far outshines any other car on the Strip. All I ask in return is for you to carry an heir to my kingdom. Is that really so much to ask? I think not. It's high time you gave something back in this marriage. Otherwise, I just might have to revoke some of your privileges. Perhaps I've been too lenient with you, allowed you too much luxury."

"Too much luxury?" anger glinted in her eyes. "How dare you insult me. I never once asked for the gifts you shower me with. They're not important to me, Michael. All the luxuries in the world can't buy happiness. It isn't the diamonds and cars and gowns I love, it's you. I love the gifts because they're from you, my husband. But standing there demanding I have a son is downright barbaric. It's something I won't stand for. If this is the way our marriage is going to be, then maybe we'd better discuss a divorce rather than a child."

An uncomfortable silence hung between them as thick as a hot desert night. Lines pinched the corners of Michael's mouth, drawing his lips into a thin hard line. "There will be no talk of divorce, Margot. Are you forgetting you promised to love me until death?" His fingers caressed her neck. "If you ever utter such nonsense again, you will be very sorry. Mark my words. As I've told you before, I can and will make your life very unpleasant—should you defy me in any way.

"Now that we have that settled, allow me to fill you in on your duties as my wife. The golden rule in my kingdom is loyalty. Never lie to me, Margot. It would be a big mistake. Betrayal in my world is unforgivable. Uncle Carlos raised me as his son to take over the DeVeccio Dynasty. We are one of the most powerful construction conglomerates in the world, building luxury resorts in every continent. And just as my uncle has passed his legacy on to me, I will pass it on to my son. First and foremost, that is your number one priority, getting pregnant. Your other duties as my wife will be to shimmer and shine at the galas I host in the ballroom. But not just as a trophy wife. I demand that my wife be cultured, worldly, and sophisticated in the arts and current events. Why do you think I chose you for the role of Mrs. Michael Alan DeVeccio? Because you fit the bill. Do I make myself perfectly clear, darling Margot? And about my son. You will get pregnant—and soon."

CHAPTER TWENTY-TWO

"Just a minute," Margot countered, her temper rising to full boil. "First you order me to get pregnant on command, then to add insult to injury, you demand that I give birth to a son? What world are you living in? When the time is right for us to have a baby, we'll discuss it together, rationally. What do I look like, a machine you can pump full of change and hand pick your selection? Well, hear this, Michael. I'm not a machine and I won't be treated like some brainless dimwit. If and when I do become pregnant, neither one of us will have any say so in the sex of our child. There's a fifty-fifty chance of either, boy or girl. And what would be so wrong with a girl? Wouldn't that make you proud? Daddy's little girl?"

"Absolutely not. A girl would be a waste, totally useless in the business world. The DeVeccio Dynasty will thrive for generations to come, and that can only be achieved through a son."

"I can't believe my ears," Margot stared, just as Zeus pounced onto the railing and hissed, his eyes focused on Michael. "What generation are you living in? Women today run major corporations, raise families, and do it all with a sense of harmony and balance to boot. How dare you stand there all high and mighty, stating that men are better than women simply because you have penises. That's downright..."

"Watch your mouth," Michael warned, his blue eyes blazing with heat. "You'd better quit while you're ahead. What did I tell you about defying me? The next time you get the urge to shoot off your mouth, you'd better think twice. If I were you, I'd weigh my words very carefully. As far as having a son, make it happen. Because if you don't, you'll be very shocked at the consequences. And that, Margot, is no threat. It's a promise."

Horrified, Margot opened her mouth to speak. But one look at Michael changed her mind. His eyes had glazed over with the same iciness she had seen the night she tossed his engagement ring at his feet. It terrified her.

Nervously, she fingered the blue diamond around her neck. It suddenly weighed her down, feeling more like a ball and chain than a precious gem. She felt trapped. Who was this man? This Michael standing in front of her doling out duties was a far cry from the man who'd shared so much of himself on their honeymoon. That man was sweet and vulnerable, nothing like this controlling and domineering madman standing in front of her.

The sound of tire tracks in the driveway interrupted Margot's thoughts. Diego Santiago emerged from his unmarked vehicle. Her heart skipped a beat. She didn't know what he wanted, but a visit from a homicide cop couldn't be good.

"Detective Santiago," Michael called out. "What brings you calling so early in the morning? Out for a leisurely cruise around the neighborhood? Or perhaps you've come to extend your congratulations to the newlyweds?"

"Cut the bull, DeVeccio," Santiago barked. "There's been another murder in the foothills, and guess whose corpse I just sent down to the morgue?"

"I have no idea. Do I look clairvoyant? Why don't you fill me in on the mystery corpse? Otherwise, we could be here all day guessing whose body is on a slab. As intriguing as that sounds, I have a meeting in an hour."

"If you could drag yourself away from your gourmet breakfast," Santiago bellowed, his voice echoing through the surrounding Red Rock Mountains. "How about coming down here and answering a few questions. And FYI, DeVeccio, it looks like the Red Rock Slasher is back in business. But that shouldn't surprise you since you knew Russel Harrison didn't kill your ex-wife. You framed him for the murder and we both know who the real killer is. Take a look at yourself in the mirror on the way down. He'll be staring right back at you."

"My wife and I will join you in the parlor in a few minutes, detective," Michael put an arm around Margot. Kissing her, he added, "We're still on our honeymoon. Perhaps while you're waiting, cook can scrounge up some leftovers from our gourmet breakfast."

ЖҲҲ

Santiago was staring out the window when Michael and Margot came into the parlor. He turned to face them, his penetrating brown eyes watching the billionaire closely. He scratched the stubble on his chin, his jawline tight, his lips thin and stretched in a hard line. He stood with his legs apart, his tattered jeans riding low on his hips. He tapped the toe of his scuffed up cowboy boot. "Where were you last night, DeVeccio?"

"At my office," Michael pressed a button on the wall. "Bring some coffee and a nice cool pitcher of ice water." He met the gaze of the homicide cop. "Now, where were we? Oh, that's right. You were about to tell me whose corpse you took to the morgue, unless you intend to keep me in suspense for another fifteen minutes." He yawned. "And, dare I say, it's no wonder you can't solve a case. You need to speed things up a bit, quit dragging your feet. Well come on. Inquiry minds want to know. Who's the mystery corpse?"

"Your cousin, Ricky O'Toole."

Margot gasped, "Ricky's dead?" She covered her mouth. All the color drained from her face. "He can't be dead, not Ricky. He was just at our wedding." She reached for Michael's hand. "He was so full of life, so outgoing..."

"Sit down, Margot," Michael guided her to the sofa. "Have a seat and you'll feel better." He glared at Santiago. "Who killed Ricky?"

"You did, of course, DeVeccio. How about coming clean and clearing your conscience, you heartless bastard."

"Santiago," Michael poured a cup of coffee. Bringing it up to his lips, he stared at the cop over the rim. "As far as killing my cousin, don't be ridiculous. I'd no more harm a hair on his head than I would my beautiful new bride."

"Is that so?" Santiago looked at Margot. "And if the beautiful new bride knew what was good for her, she'd run for her life. Otherwise, she might be the next corpse belly up in the county morgue."

"Watch your step, Santiago," DeVeccio warned. Reaching into his pocket, he fished a Marlboro from the pack and tapped it three times before lighting it. "Don't forget who you're dealing with. I've given you ample time to find this killer stalking the foothills. I'm not in the habit of dealing with such incompetence. All these unsolved homicides must be so frustrating for you. And if I might be so bold to add, all these black marks on your record would not make for a glowing review. Oops. Not the cock of the walk you thought you were. Just a few words to the wise, detective. Since you're obviously having so much trouble solving all these crimes, allow me to give you a few pointers."

Setting his empty coffee cup on the sideboard, Michael strutted across the parlor to the chess board. Picking up a sleek, ebony king, he rubbed it between his fingers, a smile twisting his lips into a sneer. Meeting Santiago's gaze, he grinned at him.

"You see, Santiago. Your serial killer is very clever. He's taunting you, playing you for the fool you are. Whoever killed my uncle, my fiancé, my ex-wife, and more than likely my cousin, is one and the same. And I'd be willing to bet my reputation that Russel Harrison, your alleged Jack the Ripper, is innocent as the day is long. So if it isn't me and it isn't Russ Harrison, I'd say you better get out there and start searching for clues. Your serial killer is playing to win, much like a game of chess. Now, as much as I'd like to stick around and give you more pointers, I need to get to work. Some of us do excel at our jobs. I think you've worn out your welcome. If you have any more questions, contact my attorney."

"Just one more thing," Santiago hissed. He reached into his case and withdrew some photos, up close and personals of the corpse. "Take a long, hard look at your cousin. Pretty morbid, huh? Made me sick when I saw it. Go on, take a good look."

Michael flipped through the plastic encased photos of his cousin, totally unmoved. After viewing each one, he handed them back and smiled. "You know what I think? I think your serial killer, your Red Rock Slasher, is a master wielder. And you know what else? This has professional assassin written all over it. You'll never catch him. Whoever he is has been getting away with murder for years. Hat's off to his sense of humor. Putting my cousin's glasses back on his corpse was brilliant. I'd love to meet him."

"Michael!" Margot had slipped behind her husband to view the forensic photos of the crime scene. Gasping, her strangled cry caught in her throat. "Only a raving lunatic could be capable of doing something so chilling."

CHAPTER TWENTY-THREE

The following morning, the police arrived at the DeVeccio estate with a search warrant, going over every inch of the mansion and grounds with a fine-tooth comb. The whole while, the billionaire sat there, leisurely sipping on a cup of coffee while going over his stock reports on his laptop. Margot, on the other hand, nervously paced the floors like a woman waiting for the jury to return with a verdict.

Santiago jogged down the spiraling staircase, his penetrating gaze focused on the new bride. Her heels clicked on the marble corridor as she paced. She looked at him, her green eyes huge with fright. The minute he looked into them, he saw the truth. She knew she was in way over her head. And she felt trapped. He could smell her fear, her skin reeked of it. Turmoil haunted her eyes. She was a woman pinned between duty and desire. If push came to shove, would she come forward with incriminating evidence, do the right thing, her civic duty? Santiago didn't think so. Not if the billionaire threatened her.

Scare tactics would work like a charm on someone as gullible as Margot, a woman who was totally sheltered from the corrupt world of Michael DeVeccio. The billionaire would play on her by filling her head with sweet nothings one minute—and death threats the next. Pissed off for not finding anything, he stomped across the threshold to the great room and joined his partner. Stevenson stood staring up at the imposing portrait of Carlos DeVeccio.

"Now that's what I call modest," Santiago studied the mural of the Vegas icon. With his fist held high in the air, the sense of Carlos DeVeccio's power emanated throughout the room.

Santiago chortled, "Look at that face. Now there's a mug only a mother could love."

"Hell of an icon," Stevenson commented. "So he's the man who raised Michael DeVeccio. No wonder the dude's got one twisted mind."

"Yeah," Santiago agreed. "Too bad Carlos DeVeccio chose a life of crime. Homicide could have used a ball breaker like him on the force. Picture being in lock-up with him for twenty minutes. With that unblinking stare, he'd make hard core criminals sing like canaries. And as hard as it is to imagine a ruthless icon as a father figure, that's exactly what he was to Michael DeVeccio from the time he was twelve. Since dear old Uncle Carlos ran one of the biggest numbers rackets, drug rings, and God only knows what other illicit doings, he would have passed the secrets of his trade onto his nephew."

"Yeah," Samantha Stevenson said, looking around the large room. She envisioned the colorful personalities of all those old time gangsters. "You can bet there's a skeleton or two buried behind those walls. I can just picture all them sitting around drinking the best of whisky and smoking premium cigars. And the whole while, Carlos DeVeccio would be ordering the next hit. Hell of a thing to picture. It says a lot about the old coot's psychological profile, doesn't it?

"It's obvious he thrived on control and manipulation. He must have really gotten off on crushing the little piss ants under him like bugs. Those sabre swords would have sent an unspoken warning to the members of his organization. How much do you want to bet those menacing blades were used to deal with traitors? I can feel the evil in this room. If I were clairvoyant, I'd see bloodshed in this hall, and plenty of it. And you wanna know what's creepy? Even though Carlos DeVeccio's been dead for ten years, not one damn thing in this room's been touched. The legendary Carlos DeVeccio still reigns here in the great room, his private domain."

Santiago nodded, scratching his chin. "Got that right. And that's the reason why the billionaire is as nutty as a loon. His uncle brainwashed him for so many years, molding him into his likeness, somewhere along the way, Michael DeVeccio lost his identity. I'd bet my left nut, even though he's a grown man, he still lets dear old Uncle Carlos run his life. Just one look at the portrait of the legendary icon says it all. Hell, he scares the crap out of me, so just think what fear like that would do to a kid of twelve. Somewhere in his twisted mind, Michael DeVeccio still feels obligated to honor and obey."

"Hit the nail on the head, I'd say. Kind of sad, though. If not for the billionaire killing off people in his family left and right, I might even choke out a tear or two. Carlos DeVeccio ruined the life of his nephew by stealing his identity. Makes you wonder how he would have turned out if he stayed in Tuscany. He might be a decent guy instead of a demented killer. But there's something that bothers me about this profile we've sketched on Michael. If his uncle trained him to kill the competition, that would explain why he killed his fiancé, his ex, and his cousin. The fiancé and the ex no doubt cheated on him or betrayed him in some way, and the cousin is an O'Toole, the DeVeccio's number one competitor. But what would his motive have been for killing his uncle? Inheriting all those billions is a give in, but I have a hunch there's something more to it. Something to do with the ultimate betrayal. So, what did Carlos DeVeccio do to betray his nephew enough to make him hurl a death star into his throat, one laced with poison, guaranteed to dole out a painful death?"

"That's the billion dollar question," Santiago said. And once we get it all figured out, we'll be able to piece together the rest of the puzzle, make the psychological profile fit. The uncle intimidated the kid into cheating, lying, and no doubt killing. Carlos DeVeccio had to be the master of control and manipulation, the very traits he drilled into his nephew. If he wasn't so pathetic, I'd salute the bastard. Carlos DeVeccio accomplished his goal with flying colors. He made his nephew, Michael Alan DeVeccio, into his clone."

"So," Stevenson ran her fingers through her hair, feathering her bangs all askew. "How the hell do we prove the nephew is the serial killer?"

"Wish I knew." Santiago looked up at the portrait of the Vegas icon. Then his gaze went to the sabre swords on the wall. "Carlos DeVeccio taught Michael how to get away with murder, and so far, he has. But the billionaire's mind is as twisted as a tornado. Sooner or later, it's bound to blow out of control. It's all about power with him. He wants to control the world and everyone in it. But I've seen the way he looks at his new bride. I think Margot DeVeccio is the only woman he's ever come close to loving. He idolizes her. Michael sees her as the perfect wife, and she probably touches the one brain cell in him that's still decent. But the way I see things, if the new bride ever falls from grace, the billionaire will go berserk. If that happens, there is no predicting his wrath."

"Think DeVeccio will be at Ricky O'Toole's funeral tomorrow?" Stevenson wondered. "After all, he was his cousin."

"Bet your ass," Santiago chomped hard on a stick of gum that had long since lost its flavor. "He wouldn't miss it for the world. And for that matter, neither would I."

CHAPTER TWENTY-FOUR

Gleaming sunshine streamed through a cloudless horizon as mourners filed up the steps of St. Paul's Cathedral for Ricky O'Toole's funeral. Organ music from the balcony filtered out the stained-glass windows and onto the street. From the bell tower, eleven chimes rang out, their piercing peels ringing across the canyon as the funeral mass commenced.

Santiago quietly slipped into the back pew and took a seat. Every pew in the massive cathedral was filled. He recognized several mourners—entrepreneurs, celebrities, and politicians—all coming to bid a final farewell to Ricky O'Toole, one of their own. Monica O'Toole sat in the front row with her family: Johnny, his wife and their three sons, along with Jimmy and his pregnant wife. Just across the aisle, looking properly bereaved, sat the billionaire and his wife.

Diego Santiago observed DeVeccio. Somber faced and dry-eyed, he presented a handsome man in the prime of his life. All decked out in one of his billion dollar custom-made suit, designed for a tall man with broad shoulders and narrow hips. He wore his raven hair slicked straight back, his posture erect as a soldier standing in an inspection line.

Margot stood at his side, playing the part of the perfect wife. She wore a dark charcoal gray suit with a black velvet collar. The form-fitting jacket nipped in at the waist and flared out over her hips, giving her a vintage 1920 look. She had her hair drawn back at the nape of her neck with a jeweled comb. The gems picked up the sunbeams streaming through the stained-glass windows, causing a rainbow of colors to sprinkle down her back. She reminded Santiago of an actress who'd just stepped off the set of an old movie.

The closed casket lay at the front of the cathedral, solid mahogany with brass handles. A huge bouquet of white roses decorated its lid. Father James O'Malley offered words of comfort to the family, stating Ricky had gone to his eternal reward. As the mass concluded with the singing of Amazing Grace, the bereaved openly wept.

The pall bearers brought the casket down the aisle, a slow-moving procession of six. Michael served as one, along with Jimmy, Johnny, and three other men Santiago did not know. Monica O'Toole walked ahead of the casket, hanging onto the arm of her escort. Her brown eyes shimmered with unshed tears and had the dazed look of someone who had been sedated. Diego Santiago's heart went out to her, a woman hanging on by the skin of her teeth. Jimmy and Johnny clutched the brass railing of the casket, red-eyed and shaken. Brooke O'Toole openly wept. Santiago couldn't help but wonder how long it would be before the billionaire decided to kill off his other two cousins.

As the pall bearers reached the end of the aisle, Santiago watched Michael DeVeccio. With a firm grip on the coffin handle, he sang the lyrics to Amazing Grace as though he were a contestant for American Idol. For a man once close as a brother to Ricky O'Toole, Michael DeVeccio didn't shed a tear. When he passed Santiago, his lips coiled up like a demented circus clown. His eyes gleamed with smug satisfaction. The billionaire was playing a game of cat and mouse, daring the cop to catch him. Michael Alan DeVeccio had to be the coldest and most cunning sociopath of his generation, plucking off the members of his family one by one.

ЖꙶЖꙶЖ

Flowering Joshua trees landscaped the grounds of Our Savior's Cemetery, their fragrant scent mingling with the smell of the freshly dug earth. As the family and loved ones gathered around the casket, Father James O'Malley prayed over the deceased. "Because God has chosen to call our brother Ricky from this life to himself, we commit his body to the earth, its resting place, for we are dust and unto dust we shall return."

In the distance, the cheerful chirping of mountain blue-birds drifted through the cemetery, creating a sense of peace and harmony. Mourners tossed a single white rose on the casket as they left. A bronze headstone marked a grave for Ricky O'Toole, right next to his father, Brady O'Toole, where they would rest together in the deep, quiet earth. When the DeVeccio couple passed the casket, Michael's charismatic voice transcended through the crowd.

"I shall miss you, Ricky. Even though we weren't close for some time now, growing up with you and your brothers was the best time of my life. You and me and Johnny and Jimmy were blood brothers, the Four Musketeers. Goodbye, my cousin, my friend. Rest in peace."

ЖОЖОЖ

Later on that afternoon, Margot sat at the pool, idly watching the breeze ripple through the clear blue water. She'd never felt more helpless or more trapped in her life. If she had any doubts before, she didn't any longer. She was married to the Red Rock Slasher. She licked her dry lips, reaching for her bottled water. How could hands that caressed her with such tenderness be the same hands that killed with such violence? It frightened her. Her husband, the man who whispered sweet nothings in her ear was the same man who killed without remorse. It sickened her. Seeing one of the photos from the crime scene had repulsed her. If Michael could do something that morbid to his own cousin, his own flesh and blood, what would he be capable of doing to her?

"What a beautiful addition you are to the pool," Michael appeared at her side. "But as sexy as you look in that little bikini, I much prefer you with no clothes on at all."

Margot stared at Michael, wishing he would go away. He'd just gotten out of the shower. She could smell his soap, his shampoo, his cologne. She used to love the smell of him, but not anymore. What used to fill her with erogenous thoughts now made her gag.

Michael ran his hand along her stomach. "Are you sure you're not pregnant with my son, Margot? I just find it hard to believe as much as we make love, you haven't conceived."

"No. I'm definitely not pregnant."

"You do want to have my son, don't you?" he ran his hand along her cheek. "Allow me to repeat the question. You do want my son, don't you?"

Appalled by his touch, chills prickled her flesh. "Well, actually, we never discussed children before we were married. I take partial responsibility for that. We got married before getting to know each other, and I think I confused love with infatuation. We are from totally different backgrounds; our morals are worlds apart. And this obsession you have about having a son bothers me, Michael. It makes me wonder what you'd do if I had a girl. And another murder of someone close to you disturbs me. There are just so many unanswered questions in my head and... I want out of the marriage. I made a horrible mistake and want a divorce. Please, Michael, try to understand."

"Understand?" His long fingers coiled around her throat. "I understand perfectly well. Over my dead body will I grant you a divorce. We will stay married until death do us part. You will have my son, an heir to my kingdom. Do I make myself clear, darling Margot? Because if you ever dare to bring up the subject of divorce again, the next jewelry around your neck will be a gold star."

Margot gasped. Who was this stranger about to throttle her?

More frightened than she had ever been in her life, she let out the breath she had been holding as his fingers slowly uncoiled. Badly shaken, she watched him turn on his heels and leave. Within seconds, she heard the squealing of tires as he tore down the driveway in his Jaguar.

Stunned, she stared into the serene pool water, her head spinning. Reaching out to pet Zeus, she stroked his back, wondering who she could turn to. She watched a beautiful butterfly skim the surface of the water before fluttering away. The stillness of nature was in complete contrast to the wild beat of her heart.

Tears threatened and her temples throbbed. She had to get away from Michael before his threat became a reality. She traced the ligatures of her windpipe, his chilling words reverberating in her head.

Looking up at Carlos's suite, she pictured the mutilated corpse of Michael's ex-wife, propped up in a coffin with a stake driven through her heart. A shiver went through her. Then another image flashed through her brain. Michael standing over her in a grim reaper mask.

She felt weak, dizzy with fright. She recalled the nightmare she'd had a few nights ago. All that manic laughter sounding as if it were coming from the final circle of hell. Was it a dream? Or was it Michael? For all she knew, it could have been coming from Carlos's suite, just down the hall. Who could she turn to? She couldn't trust anyone. Then it hit her. Diego Santiago, the homicide cop.

Margot stared up into the azure blue sky. Not a cloud in the horizon. Then she gazed into the foothills of Red Rock Canyon where all those murders had been. And in all probability, she was married to the man responsible for doing all those heinous crimes. How could Michael slaughter people like animals? His uncle? His fiancé? His ex-wife? And his cousin? The very thought of him killing them and covering their faces in masks was so horrifying it made her want to scream. It sickened her, repulsed her. Her stomach rolled.

Who was Michael DeVeccio? She thought of the Frida Kahlo self-portrait, The Two Fridas, depicting a mirrored image of one's self. Then she thought of Michael. That's exactly what he was, two personalities in one body. It all stemmed from his tumultuous childhood with his uncle, the man who had single-handedly corrupted him after the death of his parents. And after reliving such loving childhood memories with him on their Tuscan honeymoon, it all made sense.

Margot could only imagine the nightmare of living with a man like Carlos DeVeccio. Just one step into the great room characterized his demented personality. She'd felt a hushed undertone of pure evil the first time she'd crossed the threshold. Then there were those deadly swords. And what kind of a freak would keep a collection of grisly face masks in the room where he slept? Not to mention that morbid coffin for a bed. No wonder Michael had such a twisted mind.

Margot's heart raced, her pulse fast and unsteady. Her temples throbbed with pain. Everything around her rotated out of control. It was coming. It had been years since she'd had one, but she was having one now. A full-blown panic attack.

From deep within, a keening wail erupted until it crescendoed into an ear-splitting screech. The world around her stopped revolving. Everything was focused on the wild beat of her heart. She couldn't hear the birds chirping. She couldn't feel the sun bathing her body. All she could hear was the sound of blood thundering in her ears from the overload of adrenaline raging through her system. Every pulse throbbed beneath her flesh until she wanted to jump out of her skin.

Everything was all wrong. Her world crashed down around her and she couldn't stop it. She was married to a killer, a cold-blooded serial killer. He'd murdered his cousin, his ex-wife, his fiancé, and his uncle. Was she the next victim? Michael had threatened her, hadn't he?

Images of Michael stabbing her in the heart flashed through her mind like a movie in fast forward. He stood above her, laughing, bubbling over with fits of dark psychotic laughter. He dressed her up in one of those horrifying masks from his uncle's wall. It was the werewolf with the flesh-tearing fangs. His eyes gleamed with an unnatural brightness. A psychotic grin formed on his lips as he kissed her corpse and whispered in her ear, "Darling Margot. Until death do us part."

"Noooooooooo!" she ran up the spiral steps leading to the mansion. Her heart galloped wildly in her chest. She couldn't catch her breath. She didn't know what to do. Unsteady on her feet, she hurried to the sink and thrust on the cold water tap, splashing her face again and again. Gasping for breath, she sat down at the breakfast nook and threw her head in her hands and sobbed her heart out.

Doing her best to compose herself, Margot tried to focus on something other than Michael killing her. But it didn't work. Needing to stop the freight train raging through her head, she yanked a chocolate cake from the refrigerator, digging into it with both hands. For the past decade, her bulimia had been a thing of the past, but her life was spiraling out of control, and her binging and purging stemmed from stress. Disgusted with herself—but unable to stop, she pulled out a carton of butter pecan ice cream and dug in with a spoon, gorging until she scraped bottom.

Grateful it was the staff's day off, she fled to the bathroom and resumed old habits, puking her guts out until there was nothing left but the dry heaves. Then like a robot programmed to perform, she splashed toilet cleaner into the bowl, brushed with vigor and flushed. Mortified that her life was slipping away from her, she called Santiago and made arrangements to meet him in the park.

CHAPTER TWENTY-FIVE

The Willow Springs picnic area sat amidst red sandstone cliffs and cottonwood trees. A slight breeze swooshed lazily through the ponderosa pines, peaceful and serene. Looking around for Santiago, Margot took a seat on the picnic table and sipped her bottled water. Casually dressed in a t-shirt, cut off shorts, and a pair of running shoes, she waited, brushing a fallen twig from her leg. The Lost Creek Trail led to a thicket, a waterfall, and a babbling brook snaking through a canyon. Blue jays bickered from forest pines.

A rustling in the sagebrush interrupted the quiet. Detective Santiago cycled toward Margot on a mountain bike, his ponytail flapping in the breeze. Yanking off his helmet, he leaped off his bike in a smooth jump. "Mrs. DeVeccio, what a shock to hear from you. What's going on? Has your husband done something the police should know about?"

Suddenly Margot went rigid. What was she doing in the middle of the wilderness of Red Rock Canyon with a homicide detective? If Michael found out she was meeting with the cop hellbent on pinning the serial killings on him, he'd be outraged. But she was here and might as well start talking. Still, she hesitated. Licking her dry lips nervously, she looked over her shoulder, half expecting to spy a death star whizzing her way.

"There's no one here," Diego Santiago said, sensing her

apprehension. He spread his arms in a wide birth. "Just you and me and the birds. Tell ya what. How about we take a little walk along the trails under the cottonwood trees. It's a nice hiking trail. Maybe we'll spot a rare bird. Come on, let's relax and maybe you'll tell me what's on your mind."

The thicket proved to be a bird lover's haven, nesting grounds for many different species. Santiago pointed out a few as they walked. "Look up in that pinyon tree, way up on top. See it, a Western Scrub Jay. There's nothing like spotting a rare bird. And there isn't a bird I don't recognize by its color, shape, or mating call."

"Lincoln Park in Chicago has its fair share," Margot volunteered as they strolled along the trail. "The park in the fall is so awesome, brilliant leaves blazing in the sunlight. It's like the woods are on fire. You'd be surprised how many bird-watchers are out early in the morning with binoculars glued to their eyes. When I had time before work, I'd get a cup of coffee and sit on the bench and just take it all in. I guess I'm a little homesick, my family and friends are there."

"What did you do in Chicago?"

"I was a curator for a Mexican art museum for ten years," Margot said. "I hosted galas and shows, organized all the themes, and did a lot of traveling. I wanted to check out the galleries in downtown Summerlin, but apparently that's not an option."

"Which is the reason for this little meeting," Santiago smoothly shifted gears. "What's on your mind, Margot? Tell me what's bothering you."

Margot looked into Diego Santiago's brooding brown eyes, so trusting, so sincere. "It's my husband. I think he has some kind of mental illness, a dissociate identity disorder. He fits the profile, has all the signs. You see, I learned a lot about Michael while we were in Tuscany on our honeymoon. He was like a different person, pointing out the fishing port where he fished with his father and the hillside where he picked wild flowers for his mother. He let his guard down completely. There was a sparkle in his eyes I'd never seen before. He got this expression on his face when he relived fond memories, one of an innocent young boy. It was obvious how much he adored his parents and how much their accident traumatized him. If you could have seen him, Santiago. He was so different, so vulnerable. The way he rambled on without weighing his words, the joy in his eyes when he relived memories of his youth, and the special bond he had with his parents on that fishing port, you'd know what I mean.

"Apparently, they had a very good relationship, full of harmony and balance. But everything changed when they were killed. He pointed out the mountain where their car went off the cliff, and the look in his eyes broke my heart. It was as if he was reliving that day thirty years ago. He was only twelve at the time. He went from a simple life with loving parents—to a life with a ruthless uncle. I'm sure the morals he instilled in Michael were as down and dirty as they get. I think whatever went on in the great room was so shocking and morally disturbing to Michael, he completely dissociated. I never met Michael's uncle, but one look at his portrait is all it takes to see how domineering he was.

"It seems he was very powerful and very connected. He must have intimidated Michael into doing things totally against what his parents taught him. You can imagine the stuff that went on in the great room with all those old time gangsters. Those swords on the wall were put there for a reason. What kind of a nut would wear a skull mask when holding meetings? Carlos DeVeccio corrupted Michael and damaged him for life. I believe with all my heart he ordered Michael to kill anyone who got in the way of the DeVeccio Dynasty.

"There's a connection between Carlos DeVeccio, the swords, those grisly face masks, and all the serial killings. It all has to do with betrayal. I can't tell you how many times Michael has told me not to dare and betray him or else. That's why I'm here, Santiago. I'm afraid Michael is going to kill me. I think I'll be the next victim. He has this obsession I give him a son, an heir to his kingdom. A daughter would never cut it. He made it very clear he wants a son to propagate the DeVeccio bloodline. Can you believe he actually used that word? Propagate? Who talks like that?

"I was so disturbed by his behavior at the cemetery and all these unanswered questions about the murders I asked him for a divorce. He told me it would never happen and if I ever brought it up again, I'd be wearing a gold star. Don't you get it? I'm married to the Red Rock Slasher, and unless I stay in the marriage and produce an heir to his kingdom, I'll be the next corpse carted out of the mansion in a body bag."

Diego stared at her for a long time before saying anything. He picked a pinecone from the ground and crushed it in his hand. Then he looked directly into her haunted green eyes. "We need proof. Would you be willing to work with us to help us get that proof, Margot? You'll never be in danger. I'll make sure you have undercover protection at all times. What are your plans for the next few days?"

Margot stared at him in disbelief. Was he nuts? Work with the police to trap a demented psychopath? A master manipulator? A cold-blooded killer who got away with murder every other week? How many times had police protection been promised to a woman with round the clock surveillance? Yet the killer still managed to slip past the undercover cops and get in. And the next day the woman was carted off in a body bag after she had been brutally raped and murdered. Was she willing to out manipulate Michael DeVeccio, with his psychotic grin and stone cold eyes? Not in this lifetime.

"I can't. Michael's been getting away with murder for years. He was taught by the master manipulator, and he'd be onto me in a New York second. I'm not the type to hide things, certainly not from someone as cunning as my husband. Actually, there's more to the story, the reason I wanted to meet with you in private. It's about a vendetta Michael has with his cousins, the O'Toole family. I don't think he would have ever told me about it, but like I said, he was different when we were in Tuscany. He told me things about the O'Tooles which could shed some light on these killings. It all goes back to his mother and Monica O'Toole. They were sisters, you know, but very different. Monica wanted the world and went for the brass ring. When their father died, he left several million dollars to his oldest daughter, Monica. She was supposed to give half to her sister, Michael's mother, when she turned eighteen.

"To make a long story short, Monica married Brady O'Toole, took the money and ran, using those millions to start their dynasty. Michael's mother never got a penny of the inheritance. A clause in the will provided for each grandchild to receive a substantial inheritance on his or her twenty-fifth birthday. While Johnny, Ricky, and Jimmy O'Toole each got his, Michael never got a dime. That was about the time they dissociated from Michael. Michael only learned of this a few months back, and he is out for blood, literally. Don't you see? The way Michael sees things, the O'Tooles stole his birthright. That has to be why he killed Ricky, as a personal vendetta. And if I'm right, Jimmy, Johnny, and Monica are next."

A flock of blue jays bickered as they swooped across the sky, casting long shadows on the gravel-lined grove. Santiago watched them as he fished out a piece of gum from his shirt pocket. After offering Margot a peppermint stick, he stuffed it into his mouth, chewing on it methodically.

"Here's the plan," he said. "First of all, I agree with everything you said. I've suspected for some time that Michael was brainwashed by his uncle. No doubt the old coot taught his nephew to lie, cheat, and kill. Carlos DeVeccio stole Michael's identity by molding him into his own clone. Your husband has no conscience or soul and believes he has every right to kill anyone who gets in his way. He is the master manipulator, just like his uncle. I've done my homework where Michael Alan DeVeccio is concerned, and he has a birthday next week. Plan a big splashy party for him with all the big players of Vegas. That will put you in his good graces and keep you safe for the time being. I'll be working undercover as one of the caterers. I'll plant a surveillance camera and some other equipment in the mansion. We'll get him, Margot. It's just a matter of time."

CHAPTER TWENTY-SIX

Balcony doors opened to a Mediterranean-inspired terrace overlooking the foothills of Red Rock Canyon. A warm desert breeze stirred through the trees as the sun set behind the mountains, casting the sky into shades of peach and lavender blue.

A smoky glass table had been set with Bone china in a lilac pattern, a DeVeccio family heirloom. White orchids in a cut glass vase graced the center. Soft music drifted from hidden speakers, setting the scene for seduction. The mingled aromas of garlic and tangy spices wafted through the mansion.

"Have a seat," Margot kissed her husband when he entered the dining room. "Cook will pour the wine I chose. And doesn't the lobster fettuccine smell delicious? Come to think of it, I haven't eaten all day. But after all that eating we did in Tuscany, all that rich food, skipping a meal or two won't hurt me."

Michael smiled. "You are perfect just the way you are, Margot. It pleases me to see you adjusting to your role as Mrs. Michael DeVeccio. I can't tell you how happy it makes me to come home to my beautiful wife who has had cook prepare one of my favorite meals."

"Just doing my part," Margot broke off a piece of the warm crusty garlic bread. "Which reminds me, Michael. You have a birthday coming up next Saturday. I was thinking of throwing you a party, a big splashy affair in the grand ball-room. What do you think of that? We could do it up in style, invite all the movers and shakers of Vegas. A grand affair fit for a king. What do you say?"

Michael's lips curved into a wide grin. "What a splendid idea, Margot. A celebration is just what we need after all these funerals. I think it's time to start entertaining again, reopen the gates to my palace. I want to throw parties that will outshine and out glitter all other parties on the Vegas Strip. I intend to host nothing but the best from splashy is-land patio parties to galas in the ballroom. My parties will be-come legendary all over The Strip, just like the ones Uncle Carlos hosted in his day. Only the rich and famous of Vegas will be permitted to enter the gates of my kingdom. I can see it now, big players from the most dazzling casinos, celebrities and politicians, all hoping for an invitation. And what better time to start these parties than my birthday?" he forked up a generous mouthful of pasta and licked his lips.

"Indeed yes. I'll have the best of champagne, exotic floral arrangements, and the jazziest band this side of the Big Easy. Everyone will know Michael Alan DeVeccio can match the legendary parties of Carlos DeVeccio. And when you pro-duce my heir, it will be up to my son to match my parties when I grant him the keys to my kingdom."

"It will be a night to remember," Margot raised her wine. "I mean it, Michael. Saturday night can't come soon enough."

"Ah," Michael patted his belly. "That dinner was delicious. But I've saved room for coffee and dessert. There's nothing like chocolate mousse and a cup of rich Swiss Mocha. And I want a chocolate cake for my birthday, totally decadent and fit for a king."

"Oh, Michael," Margot patted his hand. "I'll see to it that you get everything you deserve. You just leave it all up to me. It will be a party to end all parties."

ЖЖЖ

Classical music drifted out of hidden wall speakers as Margot and Michael dressed for the white tie gala. In spite of her feelings, she couldn't help but notice how suave and debonair her husband looked. From his tails and white bow tie to his patent leather shoes, he resembled a Hollywood actor from a bygone era. For a fleeting second, she saw the man she'd fallen in love with, a Vegas icon who'd stolen her heart. But that was before she knew his dark side, his dark rapture.

Admiring his reflection in the mirror, Michael combed his raven hair straight back. The look flattered his finely chiseled features. His hypnotic blue eyes glittered as bright as his diamond cufflinks. Turning to Margot, he smiled. "I do believe we're donned for elegance. And you, darling Margot, are definitely dressed to the nines."

Margot applied a coat of cherry red lipstick, followed by a smudge of gloss to add shimmer and shine. Picking up the pearl handled mirror, she checked her back. The red silk tube dress hugged her like a second skin. To complement the backless gown, her hair was swept up with jeweled combs. She watched in the mirror as Michael came up behind her and bestowed a diamond necklace around her neck. She cringed as his teeth gently grazed her ear, whispering seductive promises of things to come. She felt the beginnings of his erection as his hands slowly groped her. Stepping away, she said, "I never did understand that expression, dressed to the nines."

Michael watched her move away, his eyes slowly perusing every inch of her. "Allow me to explain. The nine muses, daughters of Zeus, were goddesses of the water. According to legend, they soared up to the celestial heavens on the wing of a poet, vowing to preside over the nine arts. So, if someone describes you as being dressed for the nines, it means you are dressed to impress one of the muses. And you, Margot, will impress everyone at my birthday party tonight."

Margot applied perfume to her throat and wrists. The scent was sweetly subtle, Sachet of Roses. Satisfied with her look, she slipped on her elbow-length white silk gloves. The fingertip gloves complemented her ruby red nails and her diamond wedding ring. Michael placed his top hat on his head and extended his arm. "Ready to make our grand entrance? My guests await."

ЖΟЖΟЖ

Margot and Michael descended the grand staircase leading to the foyer. From the west wing, the jazzy sound of the

Big Easy drifted out of the Ballroom and through the entire mansion. The spicy aroma of baby back ribs wafted out, Cajon style. When Mr. And Mrs. Michael Alan DeVeccio made their grand entrance, laborious applause thundered through the hall, followed by robust singing of Happy Birthday. Michael beamed, riding high on the tails of the extravaganza.

The grand ballroom had been lavishly decorated for Michael's birthday party. Helium balloons shaped like crowns floated through the room, and the hardwood floors gleamed beneath the amber glow of the crystal chandelier. Tables draped with flowing white tablecloths and red roses centered the hall. Jasmine-scented candelabras burned brightly on either side of the dessert table. In the center, a seven-tier decadent chocolate cake fit for a king sat on a cut glass pedestal. Caterers bustled around with appetizers and trays of champagne, while bartenders busied themselves behind the bar, preparing libations of the house.

Michael made his rounds, basking in the celebration of his forty-second birthday. Strutting around the ballroom looking like the Great Gatsby, he shook hands with several politicians and celebrities. The charm rolled off his tongue in spades. He enchanted guests with talk of the latest DeVeccio Plaza being built in the heart of San Diego Bay, just adjacent to Coronado Island.

"It will be the biggest and best of the DeVeccio resorts to date," Michael's charismatic voice boomed across the ballroom. "An extravaganza. You'll be there for the grand opening, of course?"

Margot scanned the room for Santiago. He was supposed to be working undercover as one of the caterers, but she didn't see him. While Michael was engaged in conversation with the governor about supporting his upcoming campaign, Margot studied the servers. Several men and women in starched white uniforms worked the room, bustling back and forth from the kitchen with steaming platters of hot hors d'oeuvres. A procession of caterers filed in, pushing chrome plated serving trolleys with enough pizzazz to entertain the King of England.

Margot watched as they set platters of salmon puffs between perfectly chiseled ice sculptures. She scanned the room, but Santiago wasn't among them. A bit uneasy, she turned to leave. She better mingle with the guests before

Michael noticed her staring at the help. Motioning to one of the servers for a glass of champagne, she grabbed a flute of the bubbly and headed into the crowd.

Just as she took her first sip, a caterer approached her. He had snow white hair, blue eyes, a white mustache, and spoke with a thick Spanish accent. "But, excuse me, Senora DeVeccio. I apologize for my rudeness, but there is a problem in the kitchen requiring your immediate attention."

Margot stared at him in bewilderment. "Everything seems to be running smoothly," she frowned, a bit perplexed. Then the light went off in her head. It was Santiago, looking old enough to be her grandfather. She felt a little thrill, as if she were playing out a character in a play. Setting her champagne down on the side board, she nodded. "Of course. Just give me five minutes to tell my husband. He wants to introduce me to several guests I haven't met yet."

Santiago watched her sachet across the Grand Ballroom, looking drop dead gorgeous in her red silk gown. When she had made her grand entrance into the ballroom, his reaction to her had been all male and very primal. He ached with desire for her and had been so distracted he had nearly dropped the tray of champagne flutes. Margot Montgomery DeVeccio had to be the most beautiful woman he had ever laid eyes on. But as gorgeous as she looked in her red silk gown and dazzling jewels, she presented an untouchable aura as cold as the diamond around her neck. Chic and elegant, but he much preferred the Margot he had been with at Willow Springs; the down to earth woman in the t-shirt and cut off jeans.

When Margot reached the kitchen, Diego had just pulled a tray of stuffed mushrooms from the oven, fussing over them like a gourmet chef. Armed with his cooking thermometer, he announced, "The crab meat has to be just the perfect temperature before it explodes with flavor." With the greatest of finesse, he gently placed them back in the oven and set the timer for two more minutes. Turning to Margot, he said, "Now, Senora DeVeccio, about that problem with the shrimp. I can meet with you after checking with our supplier. Would ten tomorrow morning be good for you, where we met to discuss the menu?"

Taking the cue, Margot nodded, "Yes, that will work for me. Now about those crab meat mushrooms. Please be sure to serve them while they're piping hot." Giving Santiago a departing nod, she turned on her heels and walked down the marble corridor to the Ballroom.

Shadowed by her insecurities, Margot thought about the plan. It worried her. What if Michael caught on and figured out she was working with homicide to nail him as the serial killer? She wouldn't stand a chance. What was she thinking? Santiago would be gone as soon as the party ended, leaving her in the manipulative hands of a madman.

Who was she kidding? Trying to out play Michael DeVeccio had to be insane. If he discovered the birthday bash for him had been planned so Santiago could plant surveillance equipment in the mansion and in his vehicles, she would not leave the mansion alive. And she would never see Diego Santiago again. Her heart fluttered as she anticipated their little rendezvous in the morning in the park. Not that this was the time to be thinking about romance with a killer hot on her heels, but sometimes Cupid had a mind of its own. On a wistful sigh, she entered the ballroom.

Under soft lighting, couples danced in the orchid-scented hall to the old time classic *As Time Goes By.* Music floated in the sultry summer air as soft as a gentle breeze.

Just as Margot reached for a drink, Michael took her hand and led her out to the middle of the floor. Using fancy footsteps that would give Fred Astaire a run for his money, Michael glided Margot along the floor as smooth as swans gliding across a lake. Holding her gaze, he sang the words of the song in her ear. *"You must remember this...a kiss is just a kiss...a sigh is just a sigh...as time goes by..."*

Margot followed his footsteps beat for beat, holding his gaze the whole while. The seductive lyrics seemed to crawl inside her skin, stirring memories of the first time Michael had sung the song to her. Thinking back, she'd felt so cherished and so loved. Now his love had turned to an ugly obsession. Michael owned her the same way he owned his worldly possessions. And he would no sooner give her up than he would one of his priceless heirlooms. If she gave birth to a son, the heir to his throne, God help them both.

From across the room, feigning interest in a fruit salad, Diego Santiago watched the billionaire. DeVeccio had to be the most arrogant bastard on the face of this earth. All smiles, basking in the glow of the red carpet treatment. What a jerk. The billionaire wouldn't be so self-righteous when he was locked up in a padded cell, in a nut house where he belonged. Now that Santiago had planted surveillance cameras, it wouldn't be long. The way Santiago figured, after so many years of being brainwashed by a domineering uncle, Michael was still allowing him to run his life. And with a little luck, the billionaire might let something slip in the sanctuary of the Great Room. Somehow Santiago could envision it. He pictured Michael standing in front of the imposing portrait of his uncle, assuring him he would obey his orders to kill.

When DeVeccio twirled Margot around in an impressive spin, Santiago wanted to punch something. What an egomaniac. He looked like the Great Gatsby himself, all decked out in that formal getup, his coat tails flapping this way and that as he danced around the floor, all foot loose and fancy free. And those shoes. Only a royal asshole would prance around in a pair of white patent leathers with enough shine on them to glow in the dark. That top hat, come on. But, all in all, the billionaire could cut the rug without breaking a sweat, the same way he slashed his victims.

Picking up a tray of appetizers, the detective worked the room. Watching DeVeccio entertain with such pizzazz the week after murdering his cousin in cold blood was downright chilling. Santiago had no doubt DeVeccio had killed his cousin, his fiancé, his ex-wife, and his uncle. He looked across the floor at the gorgeous Margot DeVeccio. She stirred his blood. After spending a day in the woods with her, getting to know her, he wanted her more and more. Not just sexually, either. He could fall in love with her, and the thought of the smug billionaire harming one hair on her head filled him with the rage of a warrior. If DeVeccio ever placed one of his bizarre face masks on the corpse of Margot, Santiago knew he would kill DeVeccio with his bare hands.

Red hot fury bubbled through Santiago when DeVeccio folded Margot into a tight embrace and kissed her sweet lips. It sickened him. As predicted, she was in the good graces of her husband now that she had thrown him a royal birthday bash. But what would happen if she failed to get pregnant with his son? Would she become the next victim? Over his dead body. If there was one thing Diego Santiago would do in this life, it would be to catch the billionaire off guard, put him away for life, and then make a move on Margot, the sweet Margarita.

CHAPTER TWENTY-SEVEN

Michael played with a lock of Margot's long golden hair while she slept. After throwing him such a smashing birthday party, he was more convinced than ever she really was the perfect woman. Memories of the night before filtered into his brain. How fortunate to have such a beautiful and thoughtful wife. Throwing such a gala had put her back in his good graces, and once she presented him with a son, an heir to his throne, he would give her the world. He smiled when she opened her sleepy eyes.

"And how does my gorgeous wife feel this morning after hosting such a wonderful birthday party for me? It was fit for a king, a grand affair. It did my heart good to see the doors of the DeVeccio home open once more, just like the old days. The way everyone kicked up their heels on the dance floor, I dare say the foxtrot and the waltz are about to make a major comeback. And wasn't everyone pleased when I made that generous donation for the children's wing at the hospital? Now that I'm backing the governor for this year's election, he'll be putty in my hands."

"I had an interesting conversation with the owner of Hastings Art Gallery," Margot yawned, stretching to wake up. "She throws all these splashy parties when she introduces new artists. She was quite impressed when I told her I was head curator for an art museum in Chicago for ten years. Actually, she offered me a job in her gallery. I really would like to meet with her later on this afternoon, Michael. It would mean the world to me, please. I hadn't realized how much I missed hosting galas until last night."

"Hold on, hold on," Michael glared at his wife. "Since you obviously suffer from short-term memory, allow me to re-fresh it for you. Mrs. Michael Alan DeVeccio will not work. You have no need to bring in an income. Need I remind you I am one of the richest men in the world? So you can just get that crazy notion of working out of your head. I forbid it. As I've told you, the only job you have is keeping me happy and bringing my son into this world. I've given you ample time to get pregnant and my patience with you has worn thin. I think it's time to turn up the heat a little, move things along."

Margot watched his eyes glaze over with such an iciness it chilled her to the bone. A ripple of fear skittered down her spine. He stared at her with such intensity she backed up before he throttled her. She bolted from the bed but was stopped short when his steely arm locked around her waist.

"I'll tell you when you can leave our bedroom, sit still. We aren't finished with our conversation. Pay attention to what I'm about to say because I have no intention of repeating myself. If you're not pregnant by this time next month, you will have an encounter with the Red Rock Slasher."

Margot went completely numb. Could she be hearing right? Michael had once again alluded to being the serial kil-ler, the Red Rock Slasher. Even though she had suspected her husband for some time, hearing it from his own lips terri-fied her. He glowered at her, daring her to prove he was the killer. She stared into his eyes and went ice cold. Why did she marry him when that little voice in her head screamed for her to run for her life?

Tears threatened to fall, but she refused to succumb to them. If she let her guard down, Michael would have the up-per hand more than ever. She had to fight back, use reverse psychology on his psychosis. She would play up to Michael and convince him he was right. But how in the hell she was going to convince a madman everything in his twisted mind was lucid, she had no idea. Her hands trembled but she reached for her husband and charmed him with a smile wor-thy of an Academy Award.

"You're right, Michael. I agree with everything you've said. With all the love making we do, it's shocking I'm not yet pregnant with your son. But by this time next month, there's not a doubt in my mind I will be. And of course it will be a son. A girl in the DeVeccio bloodline would be useless. Only a son can carry on the legacy."

ЖЖЖ

Margot watched Michael tear down the driveway in his signature red Dodge Viper. How the car suited him. After his venomous words, she envisioned him as a poisonous snake with hollow fangs in his upper jaw, waiting in the deep underbrush to slither out and attack. She gazed into the foothills, searching for an answer to a no-win situation. She had thirty days to get pregnant or die by the sword, like some barbaric ritual. She stared at her wedding ring, a symbol of love and fidelity. Then she thought of the whispers in the night, the whispers of her husband, the whispers of a killer, and she turned to stone.

"Your breakfast, Mrs. DeVeccio," cook placed a tray in front of her. "Two poached eggs on whole wheat toast and a fresh fruit cup. Your hazelnut coffee will be done brewing in a minute."

The smell of the food made her queasy. Her stomach rolled and she shoved it away. How she detested Michael, the man she had vowed to love and honor for the rest of her life. She had precisely thirty days to get pregnant—or she'd be the next corpse in the morgue. The clock ticked away the minutes of her life—and the noose around her neck tightened. She bit her lip until the coppery taste of her own blood mingled with her saliva. She still had two hours before she met with Santiago. She took in her surroundings and never felt more trapped. What had intrigued her only weeks ago now resembled a mausoleum.

Falling back on old habits when it came to stress, she grabbed a blueberry muffin from the table, slathered it with butter, and ate every morsel. Not caring that cook was giving her the evil eye from the kitchen, she snatched a few more and repeated the ritual. Then she ate the breakfast cook had prepared and made a quick dodge for the bathroom. Locking the door, she shoved the rug away from the toilet, tossed back the lid and proceeded to stick her middle finger down her throat until the last of her food had been vitiated.

Ashamed and disgusted for falling prey to her bulimic

ways, she hopped on her mountain bike and pedaled toward the park with a vengeance. Her heartbeat accelerated until it was running on full overdrive. With the warm desert breeze in her face and her hair all askew, she came to a screeching halt when she got a stitch in her calf.

ЖЖЖ

Sitting in the picnic area of Willow Springs, she tried to compose herself, both physically and mentally. Her mouth felt as dry as the Mojave Desert. Reaching into her backpack, she pulled out her bottled water and drained it in three seconds flat. Once hydrated, she felt only somewhat better. She had a bad taste in her mouth from forcing herself to vomit. How could she possibly protect herself from her lunatic husband? More to the point, how was she supposed to get pregnant within thirty days? The bickering blue jays from the surrounding tree tops echoed the turmoil in her heart. By the time Santiago got there, she was so worked up she hurled herself into his arms.

"Diego," she blurted, rambling on and on ninety miles a minute, wrapping her arms around his neck. "He threatened me; he threatened to kill me if I'm not pregnant with his son in thirty days! I'm so scared I don't know what to do. How can I get—"

"I know, Margot. I know." he said, holding her close, stroking her hair. "We taped the conversation. Last night in between playing chef, I managed to hook up some surveillance equipment. We heard every word he said to you, but even though he alluded to being the Red Rock Slasher, he never once admitted it. Your husband knows how to play the game, telling lies and taunting the police is second nature to him. He's been doing it his entire life. He wants you to know who he is and he wants you to know you can't prove it. He has us all right where he wants us, under his thumb."

"You heard him?" Margot asked, her cheeks a fiery shade of red. "Just how much did you hear or see?"

"Margot," Santiago looked at her, a bit flustered. "Ah, Mrs. DeVeccio. Believe me, we're not perverts; we just want proof that your husband is the Red Rock Slasher so we can use it in court. Even though there's no doubt he's our man, we just can't arrest him without solid evidence, either DNA or by his own confession."

"I'm afraid," Margot stared into Diego Santiago's brooding brown eyes. "I can't live with a man who's killed so many people, the last one being his own cousin, his own flesh and blood. He's mad, completely nuts. But if I leave him, he'll find me and I'll be the next body with one of those Ninja stars in my throat. I'm ready to crack under the pressure. Can't you do something? You're the homicide cop. I can't live like this, not knowing what he'll do from minute to minute."

Diego wanted to take her away and shield her from her nut of a husband. He wanted to throw her down on the ground and make wild, passionate love to her. But he couldn't. He cursed himself for becoming emotionally involved with the wife of the alleged serial killer. He ought to know better.

Diego Santiago knew he had to keep a distance, draw the line between duty and desire. If he didn't, he would lose focus on tracking the killer and let his guard down. Drawing a hard line, he stepped back a few paces and fixed Margot with a cold hard stare. "Do you own a gun, Mrs. DeVeccio?"

"What?"

"I want you to learn how to shoot, learn how to protect yourself. If you're free for the next hour or so, we can go out to the shooting range down on Cactus Road. If not today, soon. With a nutcase like your husband, having a handgun in your possession would be a wise move. The psychological profile we've sketched of the Red Rock Slasher describes your husband down to the last trait."

"You're right. But a gun? I don't think I could shoot a human being, even someone as sick as Michael. I'll think about it, really. But not today. I need to get back before I'm missed. I can't risk any more time away from the mansion. He could be watching me, spying on me. I don't know, Santiago. I'm no psychologist, but from the things he told me in Tuscany, it all adds up. Don't you think?"

"Without a doubt. Your husband's mind is so twisted he has delusions of grandeur. He fancies himself king of the world, and once he has an heir to his kingdom, he envisions the DeVeccio Dynasty ruling the universe. Michael DeVeccio believes he can have whatever he wants with the snap of his fingers. In his mind, he's above the law and above reproach. And it all stems from years of being brainwashed by his uncle, another nut without a conscience or soul. He probably drilled it into his nephew's head over and over again to kill anyone who got in the way of the DeVeccio Dynasty."

Margot sighed. "He sees himself as judge and jury, deciding who has the right to live and who deserves a death sentence. I think it's all about revenge and personal vendettas with Michael. In his demented mind, he probably felt he had every right to kill his ex-wife for her betrayal during their marriage. And from what he told me while we were in Tuscany, the reason his cousins and aunt deserve to die is because they stole his birthright from him. Michael doesn't kill without reason. From what I can gather, he kills any and all who betray him or the DeVeccio Dynasty. And now I'm on his hit list. What should I do, Diego?"

"I wish I could arrest him right this minute, Margot. But I can't. We need proof. And with the surveillance equipment planted in the estate and the tracking devices in his vehicles, we'll get him. I have a pretty good idea of why he covers the corpse with a skull mask, but is there any reason you can think of? Something that could shed some light? Any ideas, anything at all? Something about the parties at the mansion, the masquerade balls? Did your husband ever mention anything specific about those parties?"

"Yeah," Margot felt a little chill at the memory. "One night in Tuscany, Michael told me about his uncle's son, Luciano. He was Carlos DeVeccio's only son. He was the heir to the DeVeccio throne. But Luciano died in a horrible accident at one of the masquerade parties. This was years ago, more than thirty. Something did strike me as odd, but it's probably nothing, not even worth mentioning."

"What is it?" Diego's ears perked up, knowing from previous cases the smallest thing often was key evidence in solving the case. "Tell me what it is."

"Like I said," Margot shrugged. "It happened more than thirty years ago, before Michael lived at the estate. But it might shed some light on things. You see, Carlos DeVeccio killed Luciano. He didn't pull the trigger, but he planted the bullet in the gun that fatally shot his only son. The bullet was intended for his competitor, a guest at the masquerade. When it killed his son instead, Carlos went nuts. He grabbed one of the swords from the wall and killed the competitor. Then he covered his face with the skull mask on the wall. The competitor was Brady O'Toole."

CHAPTER TWENTY-EIGHT

Santiago drove through the foothills toward the home of Monica O'Toole. The time had come to pay the family matriarch a visit. Dark secrets had been brewing between the two families for generations and it was time to get to the bottom of this ongoing rivalry.

As he drove deeper into the foothills, the temperature dropped considerably. He spotted her mansion in the distance. Arabian knights guarded the gate. A rose arbor enclosed the mansion, and trailing vines of Bougainvillea blew in the breeze like lace curtains. Lemon and orange trees bordered the manicured lawn. Designed with Moroccan architecture, copper finials and downspouts adorned the barrel-tile roof. Hopping out of his vehicle, he jogged up the shady cloistered walk and rapped three times, using the star door knocker.

Expecting a butler or maid, it surprised him when Monica O'Toole answered the door, pale and misty-eyed. Dressed in a pair of raspberry capris, a white blouse tied around her waist, and a colorful silk scarf, she looked lovely. She offered him a faint smile.

"Detective Santiago. Please come in. I was just packing to go to stay with my son for a while. Have a seat"

Capturing the flavor of Morocco, geometric tiles, arched doorways, and blue undertones added warmth and character to the spacious rooms. Plush gold sofas with a scattering of throw pillows enclosed a sitting area. Elaborate wall sconces flanked either side of the mirror above the stone fireplace. A sandalwood candle burned, scenting the air with its rustic fragrance. Santiago sat down on an oversized goat skin chair, sinking into its cushiony fullness.

"Before you ask, Mrs. O'Toole, there's nothing new in the case. No arrest has been made in the murder of your son."

Tears glistened in her golden brown eyes as she padded barefoot across the tapestry rug to the bar. "Can I get you a drink?"

"An ice water would go down easy."

Monica wordlessly removed a bottled water and then poured herself a glass of Merlot. "Here you go. Now, why don't we get to the point of your visit. Why are you here if you don't have anything new to report in my son's murder?"

Santiago unscrewed the lid of his water and took a sip and recapped it. "What was Michael DeVeccio like when he first moved to Vegas?"

"Sweet. My nephew was a Darling boy who'd just lost his parents. My heart went out to him. He was my sister's only child and I wanted nothing more than to nurture him, keep him from the clutches of that monster, Carlos DeVeccio."

"Why was that?"

"Because he was no good, filthy rotten to the core. Carlos DeVeccio was as low down as they come and had every intention of corrupting my nephew with his indecent morals. I didn't want him raising my sister's kid."

Santiago stared at her, this beautiful woman with the olive colored skin, tormented golden brown eyes, and long, ebony hair. Then he looked a bit deeper into those haunted eyes and saw secrets, dark secrets that were tearing her up. If he had to stay all night long and well into the morning, he would get the truth out of her. He met her gaze.

"Start talking. Let it all out and don't hold back. You know something, something big."

Biting her bottom lip, her shoulders hunched, she looked him square in the eye. "I don't know where to begin. But I'll do my best. As you know, Michael's mother and I grew up in the Tuscan countryside where Papa fished for a living. My sister Angelica was perfectly happy living on a fishing port, content to be poor. Not me.

"From the time I was a little girl, I wanted out of that stinking fishing port so bad I could taste it. My sister always encouraged me to follow my dreams. Instead of making fun of me, she cheered me on, my biggest fan. She told me if I wished hard enough on a star, all my dreams would come true. Angelica gave me this on my eighteenth birthday." She reached in her blouse and gingerly fingered a trinket on a chain, a tarnished gold star. "This was the last gift my sister ever gave me. Every night I wished on it. And two weeks after I turned eighteen, Brady O'Toole came into the harbor to sell his fish. It was love at first sight. Brady was the man for me, but he was dirt poor. It didn't matter, though. One look and I fell hard. Money no longer mattered, as long as I could be with Brady.

"But around that time, my father drowned in a fishing accident, and when the will was read, we learned he was a millionaire. Since I was the oldest sibling, my father left the entire inheritance to me with the understanding I'd give my sister Angelica her share when she turned eighteen. I knew my sister didn't care about money, but I did and it made me selfish. I got stars in my eyes and ideas of building an empire bloomed. Brady was business savvy, and between us, we opened our first casino on the Vegas Strip."

"You're not telling me anything I don't already know," Santiago interrupted, checking his watch. "So unless you can tell me something new, we'll be here all night."

"I'm getting to that." Monica O'Toole sipped her wine. "My father provided for each grandchild on his or her twenty-fifth birthday. I had three sons, Johnny, Ricky and Jimmy. Michael was the only child born to my sister. I got to feeling guilty about the way I'd taken off with the money, forgetting all about my sister. So when Michael was born, I knew I couldn't cheat him out of his rightful inheritance. So when he turned twelve, I returned to Tuscany and made up with my sister. I begged her forgiveness and told her about Michael's birthright."

"You returned to Tuscany?" Santiago asked. "And your sister never told Michael? She allowed him to go on believing you never made amends with her about stealing her money?"

"This is so hard," tears streamed down her face. "The reason my sister never told Michael was because she was killed before she had a chance."

"What?"

"That's right. My sister didn't drive, so her husband, Michael's father, dropped her off at the café on top of the mountain where we met for lunch. While we made up, Michael's father went off to the village to do some marketing. I felt like the weight of the world had been lifted from my shoulders. My sister forgave me, drew me into such a tight embrace I can still feel her arms around me. She didn't care about the money, just about me running away and losing touch with her. Knowing Michael would be provided for thrilled her. She couldn't wait to tell her husband and her son. But she never got the chance to tell Michael. Their car crashed over the mountainside right in front of me."

"You saw it happen? You were on that mountain when Angelica and Joseph DeVeccio's car plunged over and exploded in a ball of flames? You were an eyewitness?"

Noticing the room had grown dark, Monica flicked on a lamp. Then she picked up a king from a chess board, a smoothly carved piece made from camel bone. She idly fingered it as her mind drifted back in time. "Yeah, I was an eyewitness to the accident. I still have nightmares about it. The first thing I thought about was Michael, how to tell my nephew his parents had been killed. Then I remembered Carlos DeVeccio was at the villa with him, visiting.

"He'd come to Tuscany that particular week, on the pretense of mourning the death of his only son Luciano. Carlos DeVeccio never did anything without a reason. He had the whole thing planned, the horrible accident that killed my sister and her husband. You're a detective, figure it out. Don't you get it? Carlos DeVeccio was the master manipulator. With no other sons to take over his dynasty, he decided Michael would be the next best thing. Once Carlos DeVeccio decided he wanted something, nothing got in his way. Unfortunately, he wanted Michael. Carlos DeVeccio came to Tuscany to kill his brother and his wife in order to gain custody of his nephew."

CHAPTER TWENTY-NINE

Santiago's blood tingled with excitement. He had hit pay-dirt. At long last, he had the motive, the reason the nephew killed his uncle. Wishing he had a cigarette, he reached for a stick of gum and stuffed it into his mouth. His mind raced. "And how did you find this out? Certainly Carlos DeVeccio didn't confide in you, make you a part of his master plan."

"Far from it. I figured it out, put two and two together. I knew better than anyone how low the snake would crawl to get what he wanted, and he wanted Michael. Nothing was more important to Carlos DeVeccio than building his empire. He'd do anything to make it thrive for generations. But he couldn't very well do that since his only son was dead, and after his bout with prostate cancer, there wasn't a chance in hell that he'd produce another heir. So this presented a prob-lem for the old man, one he quickly remedied. The minute I looked into his beady brown eyes at the funeral, I knew he had arranged the accident for his own gain.

"He had dreams of ruling the world, owning the most powerful construction company ever built. And he came up with the master plan, seeing Michael as the golden opportu-nity. So the bastard went for it, grabbed the brass ring by killing his own brother and my sister in order to gain custody of Michael. You see, other than a difference in age, Luciano being older than Michael by six years, the resemblance between them was striking. So he got what he wanted, an heir to his kingdom, someone to mold into his clone, someone he could count on to keep the DeVeccio Dynasty thriving for generations, someone whose heart was as cold and black as his own. Michael fit the bill and a new monster was created in his likeness.

"I fought it, did everything in my power to stop it. No way did I want Carlos raising my nephew, my sister's only child. I tried to get custody, but the cold-hearted bastard laughed in my face, reminding me how he killed my husband." Walking to the end table, she picked up a photo of a handsome man with brown hair and laughing eyes. A tear slid from her eye as she traced his cheek with her fingertip. Setting it down, she turned to Santiago. "The bullet that killed Carlos's son in an accident was meant for my husband, Brady O'Toole.

"Thirty years ago, before the DeVeccio Dynasty or the O'Toole Dynasty existed, it was just the DeVeccio Plaza and The Bradley. Our club, The Bradley, started getting more business than Carlos's club. He fixed that by arranging a hit on my husband. He decided to get rid of the competition by killing Brady at one of his masquerades. And to keep me in line, he threatened to murder my three sons unless I sold him my club. What choice did I have? I knew that monster wouldn't think twice about carrying out his threat. So Carlos DeVeccio got my club, full custody of Michael, and slowly but surely corrupted his mind with his unscrupulous ways."

"Even though you didn't get custody of your nephew, you still tried to influence him? Isn't that right, Mrs. O'Toole? It's a well-known fact Michael DeVeccio and your sons were very close when they were young. Wasn't he at your house quite a bit, especially during the summers?"

"That's right. When Michael first moved in with that creep, I insisted on spending time with him, doing my best to keep the good in him alive. For a while, it worked. Johnny, Ricky, and Jimmy took to Michael at once, treated him like a brother. They hiked the trails, camped in the forest, fished on the lake, all the things kids that age do. If I couldn't raise my sister's boy, at least I could give him a sense of family. But the older Michael got, the more influenced he became by Carlos DeVeccio, and the more like him he became.

"It broke my heart to watch Carlos DeVeccio steal his

identity away, brainwash him into believing it was all right to lie, cheat and kill. All the good morals my sister and her husband had instilled in Michael were slowly replaced by the low-down morals of his uncle. My boys noticed it, too. Michael became very competitive, challenging, even. No matter what it was, swimming, fishing, rock climbing, Michael had to be the best. He had to win—and it was all because of Carlos De-Veccio, drumming it into his head over and over again he had to be better than everyone else. It saddened me to watch his pretty blue eyes turn cold and distant.

"He started picking fights with my sons, just to prove he could win. Then one summer his uncle decided it was time for him to learn how to fence and become a master swordsman, just like him. That's when I saw something in his eyes die, go cold. He scared me. I watched him fence once, and his eyes were devoid of all emotion, like someone who had snapped, someone I didn't want my kids around. They were in their early twenties then and I did everything in my power to turn cousin against cousin.

"It wasn't hard. My sons no longer enjoyed Michael's company. He'd changed. He was all full of himself and ideas of ruling the world. And what's more, I believe Michael was smart enough to figure out what his uncle had done, how he'd arranged his parents' accident in order to get custody. Once he knew for certain, he did exactly what his uncle had trained him to do, kill. I can't prove it, but I know the truth in my gut. My nephew, Michael DeVeccio, killed his uncle ten years ago. And since Carlos DeVeccio believed in covering the corpse of his enemies with the death mask, that's precisely what Michael did. In Michael's eyes, Carlos DeVeccio deserved to die for his betrayal."

Monica sauntered over to the bar and refreshed her wine, tears spilling down her face. Then she walked to the window and gazed into the foothills.

"After Carlos's death, I decided to rebuild my casino business with the help of my sons. Each of them started a casino on the Strip after they turned twenty-five, and together, over the past decade, we turned our business into a dynasty, building luxury resorts all over the world. Now we're the DeVeccio's number one competitor.

"I've been keeping a very close eye on my nephew and these recent killings in Red Rock. Michael suffers from delusions of grandeur, believing he can do whatever he wants simply because he can. How it would destroy my sister to see her boy now, what he's become, a serial killer. He's been getting away with murder for years. There's no doubt in my mind he killed his uncle, fiancé, ex-wife...and...my son. He killed my Ricky, his own cousin, with a Ninja star, just the way his uncle taught him to do, and then he covered his face with a skull mask. He knows, somehow he found out about the money. That's the only thing that makes sense."

"Is there any way you can prove this, Mrs. O'Toole? Anything you can think of that will give us the proof we need to convict him? Get your nephew the help he needs?"

"Nothing. He's a cold-blooded killer, taught by the master. Like I said, somehow, Michael found out about the inheritance. He is well aware that I cheated his mother out of her fair share all those years ago, and no doubt he knows about the inheritance each grandchild was to be given on his twenty-fifth birthday. Like a sixth sense, I feel it in my bones. My nephew plans to kill his cousins, one by one. And I'm certain I'm on his hit list as well."

"We'll get him." Santiago stood up, restless. He had to get something on the billionaire before he killed again. "Don't you worry. I'll put surveillance on your home immediately. And you're right. We're dealing with someone deeply disturbed. There's no predicting when he'll strike again. But he will. You shouldn't be out here all alone. You said you're going to your son's?"

"Yes. I'm going to Johnny's, first thing in the morning."

CHAPTER THIRTY

Monica O'Toole locked the door after Santiago left and double bolted it. Then she punched in the security code. She felt restless and uneasy, memories of her son filling her head. How could Ricky be dead? Her son, her baby? A slight breeze blew in through the open window, stirring the scent of sandalwood across the room. Sadness washed over her, filling her heart with pain. The candle was the last present Ricky had given her, and the image of him lighting it and singing Happy Birthday pulled at her heartstrings. Burying her face in her hands, she quietly wept.

After daintily blowing her nose, she walked to the bookcase. A wistful sigh escaped her lips. She studied family photos of the boys playing football in the yard with their dad, the five of them around the Christmas tree, and one of Ricky playing tennis. Then she picked up the silver framed picture of her three sons and their cousin Michael, camping at the lake, one big happy family.

"Why, Michael?" wretched sobs spewed from her very soul. "How could you kill your own cousin, your own flesh and blood? How could you do it?"

"I'll be glad to tell you, Aunt Monica."

Whipping her head around, Monica O'Toole watched her nephew slither out of the shadows from behind the bar. He was dressed in a black hooded jacket, his face shrouded in a latex skull mask. Glinting in the moonlight spilling in through the open window, a Ninja star gleamed in his hand.

"I can't tell you how much I've been looking forward to this long, over due conversation, Aunt Monica. Now it's your turn to fess up. You know what they say. Confession's good for the soul. You have precisely five minutes before I slit your throat for betraying Mama, stealing her share of the inheritance and my birthright. Well, come on, the clock's ticking away the minutes of your life. Tick tock, goes the clock. Four and a half minutes till show time."

"Michael," Monica took a step closer, her heart racing with adrenaline. Panic soared through her but she had to keep her cool. She'd talk him out of this death wish, get him the help he needed. She licked her lips. "Please put that thing away, no more killings. Just give me a minute and I'll explain. My father provided for each grandchild on his or her twenty-fifth birthday. I felt so guilty about what I did, stealing the money, forgetting all about your mother. So when you were born, I knew I couldn't possibly cheat you out of your inheritance. When you were twelve years old, I returned to Tuscany and made up with your mother and told her how sorry I was."

"Liar!" Michael's pulse throbbed in his throat. "How dare you lie about Mama. You never came to visit her in Tuscany and you never made amends with her about stealing her money. She would have told me. How dare you lie about Mama, my sweet, sweet mother."

"I'm sorry, Michael," tears streamed down her face. "Listen to me. The reason she never told you was because she was killed before she had a chance."

"What?"

"That's right. Your mother didn't drive, so your father dropped her off at the summit café on the top of the mountain where we agreed to meet and talk. While we were making up over coffee and pastries, your father did some shopping at the market. Everything was fine. Your mother forgave me with open arms. We even laughed about the old days. All was forgiven. And she couldn't wait to tell you about your birthright. But she never got the chance. Much to my horror, I saw your parents' car crash over the mountainside."

"No way. You got it all wrong. Uncle Carlos was there that week and would have mentioned it. The old man knew everything about everyone at all times."

Monica stared at her sister's only child, the child that had grown up to become a serial killer. His latest victim had been her son, the son she had just laid to rest. Now he had come for her. She had to stop the madness and get him the help he so desperately needed. She tried to reach him.

"You're right, Michael. Nothing ever got past Carlos De-Veccio, and he never did anything without a reason. As you probably figured out, with no other sons to take over his dynasty, he decided it would be you. He didn't come to Tuscany that week to mourn Luciano. He came to arrange an accident. Carlos DeVeccio came to Tuscany to kill your parents in order to get full custody of you."

"News flash," Michael's fingertips squeezed around the Ninja star, ready to wield it. "Tell me something I don't know. I figured that out ten years ago. Why do you think I killed the sorry son of a bitch? Dear old Uncle Carlos turned out to be the master betrayer. He deserved what he got, death by the sword and the mask of death on his shriveled up corpse. It was indeed sweet revenge. Did he think he could train me to be a killer, mold me into his likeness, and not have me figure him out? The idiot got what he deserved. But we're getting off track. We're here to discuss Mama and your betrayal. So come on. Tick tock goes the clock. Three minutes before I slit your throat."

"Listen to me, Michael," Monica prayed for guidance. "I had every intention of giving your mother the money I owed her, along with your inheritance, honest."

"Lying bitch!" Michael took a step closer. "I never got a penny of Mama's inheritance. You gave it all to your three sons, my cousins, my blood brothers who turned on me. You're all traitors and will all die by the sword. Two minutes, Aunt Monica."

"Please, Michael. Let me explain how things were back then. I wanted to make things right with you after your mother and father were killed. I tried to get custody of you because I didn't want my sister's boy being raised by that domineering monster. But Carlos DeVeccio laughed in my face. Not only that, but he demanded I give him your share of the inheritance. He said he earned that money for taking you in. Don't you see? I didn't cheat you out of your inheritance. Your uncle did. He used it for his own gain, his own selfish needs. He told me if I ever told you what had become of your inheritance, he'd make sure my sons suffered in unspeakable ways. And after seeing what he did to my husband, I believed him.

"I did everything in my power to have you close to me. That's the reason I had you over so much when you were a boy. I wanted my sister's son to have a sense of family and a good moral upbringing, traits you'd never get from that low down gangster. I was so afraid of what would happen to you living with such a nut. I knew the more time you were under your uncle's thumb, the more like him you'd become. Can't you see what he did? He brainwashed you early on, filling your head with grandiose ideas of ruling the world. He taught you how to lie and cheat, and how to kill. Can't you see how wrong that is, Michael?"

Michael puffed out his chest and cackled. The sound of his dark laughter made Monica's skin crawl. What a pathetic monster her sister's sweet little boy had become. A part of her wept for him. But she had to do something and soon. He'd been trained by the best and could wield a sword with his eyes closed and hit the mark. She prayed for guidance.

"Michael, listen to me. You killed your mother's nephew. She's probably turning in her grave. Please, Michael. Let me help you. For the sake of my sister, let me take you to a doctor who specializes in mental illness. Let me help you before you..."

"Hold on, hold on!" Michael tossed the Ninja star from hand to hand, furious. "Could I be hearing you correctly? Mental illness indeed. Michael Alan DeVeccio is as sane as they come. And as far as that bull you tried to shove down my throat about handing my inheritance over to my uncle, you're the one who's as crazy as a loon. You're no better than your sons!"

Ranting and raving like a man possessed, Michael growled like an animal and wielded the death star at his aunt, bellowing at the top of his lungs, "Guilty as charged!"

Bleary-eyed with shock, Monica O'Toole slumped to the floor in a crumpled heap. With the candle flickering in her unfocused gaze, she muttered the words, "God help you."

Jumping up and down on the balls of his feet like the Joker, Michael pointed his finger at his aunt. Dark laughter erupted from the back of his throat as he watched her body go limp and lethargic. Crouching down as she slipped away, he peered into her shocked eyes and hissed, "Give my regards to Ricky."

But with a sudden jolt, Michael's euphoria turned dark. His aunt reminded him of his mother, the way she looked when she was sleeping. He heard voices in his head, growing louder and louder like a swarm of bees. He covered his ears to stop the chaos. But the voices screamed in his head until they reached an ear-splitting crescendo. Then all was quiet as he heard the sweet voice of his mother. *"Michael. What have you done? How could you kill my sister, your aunt? What happened to my sweet little boy, my blue-eyed boy that used to pick wild flowers for me? Don't you remember? You made me so proud, and now look at you. You're a killer, a no good killer. Stabbing your aunt was like stabbing me. You hurt me. You broke my heart. My heart weeps for you. Killing is wrong. You are evil. Evil. Evil. Evil. Evil."*

"Mama, come back! I'm sorry, Mama. Don't leave. Come back. Mama! Mama! Don't leave me! Not again! Mama! Please come back to me! Mamaaaaaaa!"

And as Monica O'Toole drew her last breath, Michael thrust himself on her body and wept like a little boy.

CHAPTER THIRTY-ONE

Under the tutelage of Diego Santiago, Margot learned how to handle and shoot a gun. The shocking news of Monica O'Toole's death on the wake of Ricky's funeral convinced Margot to take action. Her deranged husband was the serial killer, and unless she stayed with him on the pretense of loving him and wanting to give him a son, she would be the next victim.

She'd given her word to Santiago to do everything in her power to set Michael up, trick him into saying something incriminating so they could get it on the surveillance equipment. She had been at the shooting range every day for the past week, but today was her final day. She just couldn't risk Michael finding out how she'd been spending her afternoons. For all she knew, he'd been having her followed, or spying on her himself. So far her luck had been good. But that luck could change. A cold feeling went through her at the thought of no longer being with Diego. She had been with the homicide cop every day for the past week, and every day she fell a little more in love with him.

Doing her best to keep her emotions at bay, she concentrated on her aim. Positioning her feet in proper pyramidal base, she leaned forward, got a firm grip on the.22 revolver, and hit the Bulls-eye.

From the shadows, Santiago watched her every move.

He admired her spunk. She had obviously struggled with the decision to handle a gun, a deadly weapon, but she realized protecting herself against her deranged husband was a necessary precaution. The haunted look in her bewitching green eyes tore at his heart and soul. And all because of the billionaire, the raving lunatic.

He'd caught everyone off guard when he slipped in and killed Monica O'Toole, barely more than a week after her son's death. The fact DeVeccio had broken in minutes after he had been with her was keeping him up at night. The thought of that happening to Margot made him crazy, filling him with a rage he'd never known.

He wanted her. He thought about her always, making love to her again and again, all through the night. She starred in his fantasies, his very sexually arousing fantasies. His hands itched to touch her. Margot DeVeccio stirred his blood. And if he didn't have her soon, he would go out of his mind.

The thought of Margot going home to the killer tormented him. How could he live with himself if something were to happen to her? He berated himself for not getting the evidence necessary to lock the cold-blooded bastard up. The warrior in him desperately wanted to hunt DeVeccio down and throttle him with his bare hands. From the first time he had laid eyes on Margot, he'd wanted to kill the belligerent billionaire. But he wasn't about to spend the rest of his life in jail. He hadn't spent the past decade on the force just to toss his badge over the cliffs of the foothills.

He needed to get the evidence on DeVeccio to prove he was the serial killer of Red Rock Canyon so he could lock him up where he belonged. He needed proof and he needed it fast. Margot had less than two weeks to get pregnant, or she would be the next corpse with a Ninja star wedged in her throat. The thought of DeVeccio making love to Margot filled him with a jealous rage. The thought of her producing the heir to the DeVeccio Dynasty alarmed him. If Michael Alan DeVeccio had a son, the boy would grow up with the same grandeurs of delusions as his father. With two nut cases believing they controlled the world, God help them all. Walking toward Margot, he wondered where it would all end.

ЖЖЖ

"Nice shot," he said. "But another week would perfect your aim; it would give you a better sense of balance."

"I can't risk it," Margot said. "If Michael knew how I've been spending my afternoons, my life would be over. I can't go on with this façade much longer, Diego. Living with Michael is like being entombed in a mausoleum with a madman, knowing sooner or later, he'll catch me. I feel trapped and scared out of my wits. He's nuts, all that talk about him and his son ruling the world. That must be what his uncle did to him, brainwashed him with delusions of grandeur until he went crazy."

"Got that right," Santiago took a step closer, the scent of her skin getting to him. How he wanted her. He inhaled deeply, searching her eyes. "You know I've been giving some thought to the Monica O'Toole case. The pattern changed. She had the Ninja star in her throat, but there was no death mask on her face. And I think I know why. I sat around talking with her for a good while, minutes before your husband slit her throat. I kept thinking how much she resembled her sister, Michael's mother. Judging from all the pictures I've seen, the two sisters could have been twins. Maybe it's just a hunch, but my hunches usually pay off. I'm thinking the reason Michael couldn't bring himself to shroud his aunt's corpse in a morbid death mask was because of the striking resemblance to his mother."

"That makes sense," Margot said. "And I agree. I've seen pictures of Michael's mother. Outside of being a few pounds heavier than Monica O'Toole, they could have passed for twins. I can't tell you how many times Michael told me how much he was drawn to his aunt because she looked so much like his mother. He even said when he was with his cousins and his aunt, the resemblance was so similar it was easy to pretend they were all one big happy family."

"Still, one thing bothers me, though," Santiago stated, a frown creasing his brow. "How did your husband find out about the inheritance? Sure as hell wasn't his uncle who told him, or his aunt. Monica O'Toole kept quiet to protect her sons. So who let it slip?"

"I thought I told you," Margot fired a bullet that ricocheted through the mountains. "Lacy Diamond told Michael."

"Lacy Diamond?"

"Yeah. Apparently she was Carlos DeVeccio's lover. And

according to Michael, she was his uncle's Achilles heel. He confided in her, spilled a lot of family secrets. The inheritance was one of them."

Santiago reached into his pocket for a stick of gum and let this settle. "So, DeVeccio and his uncle shared the same woman. Why doesn't that surprise me? But this new information sheds some light on why Michael killed Lacy. Don't you see? Carlos DeVeccio must a let a lot of old skeletons slip out of the closet. Lacy Diamond must have had enough dirty laundry on the DeVeccio Dynasty to bring it crashing down like dominos."

"That would certainly explain a lot." Margot accepted the peppermint stick Diego offered.

Santiago ran his hand through his hair. "I got a real clear picture of Carlos DeVeccio all those years back. Gives me a pretty good psychological profile of the nephew. The uncle taught his nephew to be a trained assassin from the time he was a young teenager. He brainwashed him into believing killing the enemy with a sword and covering the corpse with the death mask was justifiable. So he kills his aunt but doesn't cover her corpse with a mask. This change in pattern bothers me. If my hunch is right, this last kill would have got to Michael. Not because he killed his aunt, but because he killed his mother's likeness. It makes him one step closer to losing the tight control he's had on his life."

Staring into Santiago's liquid brown eyes, Margot put the safety release on her handgun and tucked it away in her purse. This was it. A tear fell from her eye. The thought of never seeing Santiago again filled her with despair. Just knowing she would see him every afternoon had made living with Michael tolerable. But now that their afternoon rendezvous at the shooting range had ended, working with the police to catch a serial killer seemed downright ludicrous. How could she go home to that mausoleum of a mansion knowing full well she may never come out? A chill slithered down her spine at the thought. But when Diego took her hand in his, a bolt of heat surged through her entire system.

"Be careful, Margot." He stared into her bewitching green eyes for a long time. "Handguns are dangerous and deadly. Make damn sure you keep it hidden from your husband because with a nut like him, there's no telling what would happen if he thought you'd betrayed him. Surveillance equipment's all hooked up, but could be we can't get there fast enough. As much as I hate placing you in harm's way, you're our best chance of getting the evidence on DeVeccio to pin the serial killings on him. Work your womanly wiles on him, whatever it takes. We need something solid on tape. Get him talking about the swords, his uncle, the masquerade balls at the mansion, or the night Luciano was killed. Trip him up. We're counting on you." he touched her cheek. His voice was laced with just a hint of his Spanish heritage. "I'm counting on you, more than you know."

ЖЖЖ

Margot cried all the way home. She had wanted nothing more than to throw herself into Santiago's arms and stay with him. But she couldn't. Provoking Michael at this point would be a deadly game, one she couldn't afford. The police were counting on her to trip Michael up, make him say something incriminating on tape. Diego was counting on her. His touch had sent sparks soaring through her like a bolt of lightning. That man of few words got to her in a way Michael never had.

Because she couldn't seem to help herself, she compared the two men. While they were both intelligent, brilliant even, their integrity was unparalleled. While Diego remained cool under pressure, Michael was as explosive as a volcano. Their virtues were worlds apart. Diego's morals consisted of high ethical standards—Michael's were totally corrupt and morally unethical. While Michael demanded respect, Diego earned it.

Driving through the wrought iron gate leading to the mansion, Margot's head was in a daze. Fate had certainly dealt her a bad hand. If only she had met Diego before falling in love with Michael. At her wedding, she had been so sure Michael was her one true love, her soul mate. Well, wasn't fate having a grand old laugh at her expense? Just when she thought her life couldn't possibly get any worse, she'd gone and fallen head over heels for the homicide cop, Diego Santiago, her destiny.

CHAPTER THIRTY-TWO

A bit shaken, Michael walked to the great room, thinking about his mother. It had been years since he'd heard her voice in his head and it left him reeling. She'd been weeping and he'd been responsible for making his sweet mama cry. How could he forgive himself for that? The only woman in the whole world who had ever been completely honest with him and had treated him with nothing but unconditional love. How he hated himself or hurting her, his beautiful mother. She had scolded him, called him evil. Was he? Was he a bad person? His mother thought so, so he must be. She had seen him kill her sister. She was upset with him. "Mama." He rubbed his throbbing temples. "Mama, don't be mad, please don't be mad at me. I love you, Mama. I did it for you. Mama, come back."

For the first time in thirty years, he felt remorse, shame. Was killing wrong? His parents had taught him the difference between right and wrong. From deep within his subconscious, the Ten Commandments rang in his head. *Honor thy parents. Thou shall not steal. Thou shall not lie. Thou shall not kill.* Michael swiped at a tear, the memory of reciting them to his mother so real it made him tremble. Killing was wrong, a mortal sin. But killing bad people was another story. Killing the betrayer was what he was put on this earth to do, his mission. Isn't that what Uncle Carlos had drummed into his head since he was twelve? Betray me and die by the sword.

The fog clouding his brain slowly lifted, leaving him strong and confident once more. It all made sense. His mother was so good she couldn't see the bad in others. She had never seen the evil side of her sister. But Michael had seen it and had taken care of things, settled an old family vendetta. And he felt better for it. Just like his uncle used to tell him after a hunt, "We are the avengers, son. Executing the offender is a necessary evil. And nothing in life is sweeter than sweet revenge."

Pouring himself a bourbon on the rocks, Michael thought about his mother, his sweet mama. How he wished she were alive to meet Margot, his wife and soon to be mother of his son. Women like Margot didn't come along every day; he cherished the ground she walked on. He had finally found a woman worthy of wearing his mother's ring, and it would stay on her finger until death. Margot was so different from Candace or Lacy. She would no more betray him than his mother would have betrayed his father.

Annoyed with himself for his brief confusion, he planned the next execution. The time had come to take care of things, finish settling the family vendetta. Monica and Ricky had been cast to the demons where they could burn for their sins, and now it was down to Johnny and Jimmy. Hmm. Which brother should be first to die?

But something else needed his attention before he eliminated the two remaining offenders. The money. Mama's money. He had to get it back for her, and that couldn't be achieved after the O'Tooles were all dead and gone. No, it had to be done while Johnny was still living, still keeping the books on the family fortune. Pulling out the picture of his mother he kept in his wallet, he looked into her eyes, so honest and trusting. Running his finger along her cheek, he swore he could smell the wild flowers he used to pick for her. "I'll make things right, Mama. Just leave it all up to me. I'll make you proud."

ЖҖЖ

"Your 9:00 appointment is here, Mr. DeVeccio. Shall I send him in?"

"Yes, Anna. Send Mr. Jones right in."

Michael watched his software engineer come through the

door of his office suite. He held advanced degrees in both mathematics and systems design. With his broad knowledge and experience, he'd been an attractive asset to DeVeccio Construction and had been hired on the spot after completing his internship. With increased emphasis on computer security, he had been an outstanding employee. Until recently.

With a click of his personalized mouse, Michael saved the finance spread sheet he'd been working on, sat back in his ergonomic chair and stared him down. "You disappoint me, Jed."

Jed Jones stuffed his hands into the pockets of his beige Dockers, fumbled with the loose change, and shuffled nervously from foot to foot. Being summoned in for a meeting with the big boss had him on edge. He chided himself for acting like a chump. No way was old money bags gonna make him sweat. He was too cool.

"Have a seat." Reaching over, Michael picked up the king from his chess set and methodically rubbed the smooth, ivory figurine between his fingers. "Strategy is the most fundamental part of chess. In order to win, you need to know precisely when to go in for the kill, wouldn't you agree?"

Jed smirked silently. *Come on. Come on. Keep cool. Don't let Mr. Big Shot see you sweat. He's playing you, toying with that five grand chess piece. You're the king and I'm just the pawn, the weakest and least valuable piss piece on the board.*

"When I honored you with a position at my company after your internship, I saw tremendous potential in you, a major asset to my company. I'm no longer impressed, Jed. You disgust me. Look at yourself. You have a fantastic job at one of the most prestigious firms in Vegas and you're letting it all slip away. And for what? Slumming with drug whores. Need I remind you of your duties as my computer software engineer? Allow me to refresh your memory.

"You are required to have superior problem solving and analytical skills as well as outstanding people skills. And need I remind you of the importance of the special attention to detail? I've been getting bad reports on your performance, your lack of concentration due to your recent drug use. Are you forgetting the golden rule in my company, Mr. Jones? The no drugs policy? I had big plans for you, Jed. Plans of you going far in my company, in my world. The pay would have been phenomenal and you would have climbed the corporate ladder of success. But looking at you now, it would be a mistake, a bad judgment call, and I'm not in the habit of making either."

Jed's brain was scrambled, his thoughts racing helter skelter. He tapped his fingers on the solid desk. *Shit. Mr. Big Shot preaching to me, judge and jury. Who the hell does he think he is? Mr. Money Bags sitting there all righteous in his executive office with all the trimmings. As if his blue balls don't bleed red.*

"How long have you been addicted to heroin?"

"Hey, I don't use…"

"Don't lie to me, Jed. It would be a big mistake. My employees understand from the beginning if they are caught using, they will be dealt with on the spot."

Jed Jones scoffed to himself. And just what was Mr. Big Shot gonna do about it from behind his big shot desk, run him out of Dodge?

"Don't ever try to play me. You'd come up short, every time."

Looking around, Jed noticed a set of swords on the wall, sharp, dangerous, and deadly.

Following his gaze, Michael said. "I'm a master swordsman. I was taught by the best."

Jed had the urge to hurl his fist into old money bags nose. He wouldn't be so high and mighty then. Mr. Big Shot down for the count. Blood all over old money bags big shot suit. What a rush.

"I just may have the answer to your problems," Michael lowered his voice. "Listen and listen carefully."

Jed squirmed in his seat. He wasn't about to let old money bags see his fear. A nervous twitch in his eye told him whatever proposition the big man was about to make was as down and dirty as it got.

"I know all about the trouble you're in, Jed. With your substantial gambling debts, you've managed to make enemies all over town with some pretty shady people. How long do you think it will be before they do more than rough you up? That shiner under your left eye is nothing compared to what they'll do to you if you don't pay up."

"So I'm a little behind the eight ball," Jed confessed. "No big deal. I just need a few more days and I'll come up with the cash."

"Dream on." Michael pressed a button and a smoky glass window separated, revealing a fully stocked bar. Pouring bourbon into two glasses, he handed one to Jed. "Looks like you could use a drink."

Jed took the drink and downed it quick. It went down as smooth as silk. He could get used to the good stuff from the big shot's private collection.

"Here's what I'll do for you." Michael did his shot neat. "I'm going to send you to my private drug clinic in Zurich to get clean. After that, you will be sent to Italy for updating your financial expertise in computer software. When you return, you will be ready to do the O'Toole job for me."

"The O'Toole job?"

"That's right." Michael fished out a Marlboro, tapping it three times on his oak desk before lighting it. "I want you to hack into the O'Toole stock."

"And why would I do that?"

"Ah," Michael picked up another chess piece, placed it down as if planning his next move. "Not for the money. I have more than my cousins will ever hope to have in ten life times. I don't need their fortune, not by a long shot. Let's just say it's a matter of vengeance. Now here's the plan. My cousin Johnny is financial advisor of the O'Toole stock. When you come back from Italy with a new attitude and a new face, you will apply for the position as software engineer at O'Toole Construction. Make yourself invaluable, gain everyone's trust. When you've earned it, go in for the kill. Hack into the stock and transfer all funds into my Swiss bank account. How does that sound to you, Jed? You do this little favor for me—and I'll pay off all your gambling debts, get all those loan sharks off your back. A clean slate shall we say?"

Jed Jones licked his lips, his head shrieking with turmoil. So this was the name of the game, where the little piss pawn piece scampers across the board. Embezzlement. Gotta think, he told himself. If I don't do the job, it will be my ass on the slab in the morgue, just like cousin Ricky. Guess I know who the Red Rock Slasher is now. Gotta think.

"Well, Mr. Jones," Michael smiled. "Do we have a deal?"

Closing the deal with a shake of his hand, Jed felt as if he'd just sold his soul to the devil.

"And Jed, my private jet will take you to Zurich immediately."

CHAPTER THIRTY-THREE

White hot fury bubbled up in Michael. What the hell was wrong with Margot? As much as they made love, she should be pregnant with Michael Junior by now. He wanted a son and it would happen. He ruled it so.

He thought about his own roots into the DeVeccio Dynasty when he first came to live with his uncle at the mansion. Saturday mornings had been spent in The Great Room where the family congregated to discuss business over brandy and cigars. Afterward, cook served steaming platters of veal, hot sausage, and buckets of pasta. Michael had enjoyed learning the family business and couldn't wait to introduce his son to the world of absolute power. Michael Junior would be brought up with the same morals that had been instilled in him. And when the time was right, he'd be expected to honor the DeVeccio code of honor.

Getting a cup of coffee, Michael went over the blueprints for the new luxury resort he was building in the heart of San Diego Bay. It would be an extravaganza. More elaborate than any of his other hotel resorts in either Las Vegas or Italy.

Sipping on his coffee, he envisioned the biggest and brightest of his resorts. The DeVeccio Plaza would overlook Coronado Island, and Ristorantes serving Mediterranean cuisine would give the casual west coast an old-world ambiance.

The DeVeccio Plaza would showcase fine imports from all over the world as French silks, South American art, and Italian leathers, while the resort would have an exotic spa, several gambling casinos, and gift shops. The outdoor patio would invite guests to relax on elegant teakwood lounges either in the cool shade or under the warm rays of the sun. In the center of the turquoise swimming pool would be a waterfall shrouded by coconut trees. And just beyond the pool, cafe tables with umbrellas would surround the bar and grill.

The newest DeVeccio resort wouldn't be just for adults either. With his son in mind, Michael had designed it with an amusement park, putt-putt course, arcades, and several theaters. It would be a child's fantasy land, bigger and better than any that were currently standing.

The marina would offer sailing and a yacht club. Cruise ships would depart both day and night, complete with slot machines, poker tables, and Blackjack. Michael looked forward to taking his wife and son to the resort as soon as it was built.

Checking his appointment book, he was pleased to see he was free for the remainder of the day. Just thinking about the coming attractions for later on that evening made his blood tingle. The brothers O'Toole were in for quite a surprise. But first things first. It was time to go home and create his clone so the DeVeccio empire could rule the world.

ЖФЖ

Sipping on an after dinner brandy, Margot watched the sun disappear behind the Nevada mountains, turning the sky into a serene lavender blue. The thought of tripping Michael into saying something discriminating on tape made her uneasy. How was she supposed to accomplish that when he never missed a beat? Giving Michael a sidelong glance, she watched him press a button on the wall. A smoky blue glass partition opened, revealing a well-stocked wet bar. Humming away, he measured precisely two fingers of bourbon into a shot glass and poured it over the rocks. Going about his business without once looking up, he started his laptop and brought up the DeVeccio stock report. Judging from his expression, the numbers pleased him.

Catching her eye, he winked. "My net worth has jumped $39.5 billion to $49 billion, placing me way at the top of the rich list. It won't be long before I'm the richest man in the world. By the way, did I mention cook and the butler found the surveillance equipment Santiago planted the night he invaded my birthday party, posing as a caterer? Cook and the butler do daily sweeps for tracking devices and caught Detective Santiago doing the dirty deed on our own house camera. He might think he can trip me up, but he ought to know by now that no one in the world can outwit, out play, or outmaneuver Michael Alan DeVeccio."

Margot's heart sank. No more surveillance? How could she trap the madman now that the video and tracking devices had been removed? And worse, far worse, she was alone in this huge mansion with a killer—and no one would be watching. Panic splayed her nerve endings. Just as she was about to jump out of her skin, the doorbell rang. She looked at Michael. "Are you expecting someone?"

"Indeed, yes," Michael closed his financial reports and turned off his computer. "And they're right on time. I invited my cousins over, just like the old days. I thought it might get their minds off the unfortunate demise of their mother and brother."

The butler came in, Jimmy and Johnny on his heels. Thin and drawn, they both looked as if they hadn't slept for a week.

"Welcome," Michael greeted his cousins, a wide grin spreading across his face. "I can't believe it's just the three of us. Who would ever think all those years ago when we fancied ourselves the Four Musketeers, one of us would actually die by the sword. I guess you just never know when it's your time—or how you'll die, isn't that right, cousins?"

Jimmy's blue eyes hardened. "You got that right. There's no telling how or when you might die. And as far as coming down to just the three of us, damn straight. It's just you and me and Johnny."

"Yeah, kid," Johnny sucked on his cigar stump, talking out of the side of his mouth. "And after tonight, might just be down to me and Jimmy."

ЖҢЖҢЖ

Behind the closed doors of the great room, Michael and his cousins gathered in the back of the hall. A semi-circular mahogany bar enclosed pool tables, computers, and inlaid rows of chess, checkers, and backgammon. A vintage House of Staunton chess set featured smooth ebony and ivory pieces. Serving the bourbon straight up, Michael picked up one of the kings and rubbed the figurine between his fingers. "Strategy is everything, wouldn't you agree, cousins? In order to win, you need to know precisely when to go in for the kill."

Jimmy's eyes blazed with anger. "Yeah, I'd say so, Michael. And I'd say you enjoy the game, the thrill of the hunt. Isn't that right, cousin? In that twisted mind of yours, you line up all your opponents in a neat little row and knock out the competition, player by player. How about it? And now it's all come down to a family rivalry, a score to settle. You're hellbent on letting me and Johnny know you're the king—and the two of us are pawns, the least piss ant pieces on the board."

"How very astute you are," Michael beamed. "My hat's off to you both, here, here. To the brothers O'Toole. Capturing the opponent off guard is the name of the game. And, like a game of chess, life is a game of strategy, consisting of setting and achieving long-term goals. Just to set the record straight, Michael Alan DeVeccio plays to win."

"Well, guess what, cousin?" Jimmy got in Michael's face, giving him a hard shove that sent him sailing backward. "James Albert O'Toole plays to win, too. Just look at you all self righteous, thinking you can rule the world with that twisted mind of yours. Don't try to play me, cousin. We know damn well you killed Ricky and Mom. And I guess me and Johnny are the next opponents you plan to wipe off the board, huh? Well, come on. Let's see you try." His eyes darted to the set of swords on the wall. "Ya wanna go at it, head to head, do a little fencing? Let's do it."

"Yeah, kid," Johnny's voice had a steely edge. "If we stab ya in your good for nothin' heart, place a death mask on your corpse, ain't a court in the land that'll convict us. They'd applaud us for layin' rubbish like you curbside."

"You good for nothing son of a bitch," Jimmy rushed in on Michael, slamming his fist into his nose, knuckles popping dense cartilage. Blood gushed out, streaming down the front of Michael's crisp white polo shirt. Before he had time to recover, Jimmy sucker punched him in the jaw, sending both men directly under the swords on the wall. With lightning speed, Johnny jumped in and snatched one, wielding it through the air, challenging Michael to a dual.

"Well, come on, kid, grab a sword, let's do a little fencing, just like the old days. Or aren't' you man enough to go at it head to head? Cause playin' a game of solitaire with a Ninja star ain't fair game in my book. So, come on, let's do a little fencing, practice our swordsmanship, just the way we did back in the day when we played out the Four Musketeers."

"How can I refuse?" For a fleeting second, an eerie quiet hummed through the hall. Then Michael spun on his heels and grabbed a sabre sword, wielding it through the air, its blade hissing through the night like a deadly tornado. "I give you credit, Johnny. I didn't think you had the balls to take me on. You know I'm the master swordsman. No one can beat me. But come on and try. Be my guest. Let the fun begin. By the way, are we fencing with face guards?"

"No way, kid," Johnny's blade swooshed through the air, the tip aimed right at his cousin's throat, missing it by a hair. "I wanna see your face when I kill ya, totally unmasked and piss in your pants scared when you go down."

"You flatter yourself, Johnny," Michael wielded the sword at his cousin, knocking the cigar stump from his mouth. "Next time I'll slice off your lips. You wouldn't be so quick to shoot off your big mouth then, would you, Johnny?"

"Ya sick bastard. Mama was good to ya, treated ya like a son. Ya pay her back by killing her? That's low, even for scum like you. And Ricky adored you when we were kids, idolized ya even. So ya kill them. And for what? Ya make me sick and deserve to die by the sword, and that's just the way I'm taking ya out. Any last words? A confession from your coiled-up lips? Huh, kid?" With lightning speed, Johnny tightened his grip and thrust his sword.

Quick as a wink, Michael reached into his pocket and snatched out a Ninja throwing star and wielded it at Johnny's hand, numbing it. Johnny's fingers lost their tight grip and the sword clanked to the floor. Taking a bow, Michael replaced his sword in its wooden holder, went to the bar and poured a bourbon. "I'd say it's about time to end the game. You know throwing stars were originally used to slow down an opponent. I'd say mission accomplished. You should know by now, cousins, no one can out wit, out play, or outmaneuver Michael DeVeccio. Oh, and cousins, just one more things so you'll be forewarned and forearmed. The next Ninja star might do more than slow down the opponent."

"This'll end tonight," Jimmy charged at Michael like a bull. The air bristled with electricity. Just as he scooped up Johnny's sword, his cell phone rang. It was Brooke's jingle, the one they'd programmed to signal she was going into labor. Snapping to his senses, he flung the weapon at his cousin's feet. "Come on, Johnny. My wife's in labor." He glared at Michael. "This is far from over, cousin."

"Damn straight," Johnny pitched his cigar stump on the floor and stomped on it. Then he spit on it. "Your days are numbered, DeVeccio. Beware."

CHAPTER THIRTY-FOUR

The following morning, Margot felt like a caged tiger. The minute Jimmy and Johnny showed up last night, she had debated whether or not to call Santiago. By the looks in their eyes, they had come to kill Michael. They were onto him. And while they didn't kill him, they had roughed him up pretty good. They broke his nose and got in some pretty good punches to his jaw, by the looks of things. Where would it all end? The days ticked off in her head. If she wasn't pregnant by her next cycle, Michael would kill her without any remorse. How she detested him and his touch. Even if she made the deadline, how could she guarantee him a son?

Mountain bluebird chirped from the ponderosa pines bordering the mansion. Rather than cheer Margot up, the singing played on her last nerve. Hearing a chorus of crickets, she all but jumped out of her skin. Biting her lip, she sighed in disgust. She fought the urge to binge and purge. She had to get control of her life before it was too late.

Even so, in spite of all the turmoil in her life, all she could think about was Diego Santiago. He wasn't movie star handsome like Michael, and he certainly didn't possess the suave and debonair charms of her husband. What he did possess was honor, something none of Michael's billions could buy. And this white knight in shining armor had won her heart.

On an impulse, she jumped into her Porsche and tore

rubber until she reached Ruby Ridge, a rural area where Santiago lived. Rolling down her window, she inhaled the fresh country air and felt more alive than she had in weeks. The sounds of nature exploded all around her. White and blue herons chirped from age-old cottonwood trees, and a magnificent gold eagle soared gracefully over the neighboring hay fields.

As soon as Margot got out of her car, she heard the gentle strumming of a flamenco guitar. The melodious lilt of the Latin music drifted through the air, soft and sweet. Drawn to it, she ran up the steps and peered into the round arched window. Mesmerized by what she saw, she stared in awe.

Bathed in sunlight, Diego sat in front of a fireplace, tenderly holding the small guitar. He strummed the strings with outward flicks of his fingers, producing a rhythmic roll reminiscent of castanets. Silhouetted in partial sunlight and partial shadows, he gently caressed the lustrous neck of the wooden guitar.

When the song ended, Margot quietly knocked at the door, feeling as if she had finally come home.

Even before Diego opened the door, he knew it was her; the beautiful woman with the bewitching green eyes. Even if he hadn't heard the sound of her tires in the driveway, even if he hadn't caught a glimpse of her watching him through the window, he would have sensed her presence. And knowing she was watching him, listening to him play the love song he'd written for her made it all the sweeter. With his heart thumping, he flung the door open and pulled her into his arms.

"I had to come," she said in a breathless voice, feeling his muscles quiver and bunch beneath her fingers. "Oh, Diego. I had no idea you played the guitar. And with such finesse. What a beautiful song, so bitter-sweet."

Diego's broody brown eyes grew dark with passion. "I wrote it for you. I call it my Sweet Margarita."

"Diego," Margot felt butterflies in her stomach. "That's the loveliest thing anyone has ever done for me."

"The words come straight from my heart," he said. "You are always on my mind. I've wanted you since the first time I ever laid eyes on you. Every time we were together, it was more and more difficult to keep my hands off of you. Even though this will complicate things, God help me and God help us both. I've fallen hopelessly in love with you. I want you more than I have ever wanted anything or anyone in my life."

Margot kissed him, her lips hot with desire. The sweet scent of lavender and roses drifted in from the windows. Wind chimes tinkered together in a delicate tango, guardian angels dancing in the rose-scented air. From another room, the bluesy sound of jazz drifted through the house, its suggestive undertone sweetly erotic.

A gentle breeze stirred, mingling the freshly budding freesia with the scent of lavender and roses. Diego's long dark hair billowed around his face, casting his handsome features into shadows. With his lips promising to devour, he had the look of a dark pirate about to show no mercy.

"Margot," he whispered, his lips caressing her neck with smoldering kisses. "My sweet Margarita, how I've wanted you." His hands expertly played her body, his fingers massaging all the pressure points until she gasped in ecstasy. "Just let yourself go. Let me love you, my sweet Margarita."

Closing her eyes, she slipped into a state of utter nirvana. "Never stop, Diego. Never stop."

"I dream of making love to you," his words were potently seductive. "You are in my heart and soul, and all of my fantasies."

Margot shimmied closer, wanting to get so close to him their two hearts beat as one. Wrapping her hands around his neck, she tangled her fingers through his long silky hair. "You are the man I have waited for my entire life. You are the man I will die wanting."

Kissing her, he pushed her down on the oval rug in front of the fireplace. Poised above her, his penetrating gaze seared into hers, watching her eyes dilate when he slid his hands up her tank top and cup her breast.

His fingers swiftly undressed her, taking a moment to admire her coppery body. Her blonde hair with burnished red highlights fanned around her face like a veil. "You are so beautiful, my sweet Margarita."

Her breathing unsteady, she ripped his shirt off. His broad shoulders were bronze and muscular, his chest a mat of dark curly hair. Sleek and powerful, he looked like a wild untamed panther.

Rearing back only long enough to undress, he peeled his

clothes off with lightning speed. His body quivered with want and need. Blatant sexuality darkened his eyes to deep pools of black. He kissed her passionately, their tongues intertwining as one.

Margot was a mass of sensation, her senses keenly alert and ready to snap. How she wanted him, needed him. Her cool hands slid down the length of him, squeezing, stroking, and watching his dark eyes roll to the back of his head. He moaned softly, calling her name.

Diego's hot Latin blood soared through his veins. He wanted her; she was his. With one sleek move, he swept down on her, whispering the words, "My sweet Margarita, you are the one."

Ж Ж Ж

Smiling that evening as she reminisced about her rendezvous with Diego, Margot played the piano, the sweet fluttering of keys in harmony with her heart. How could she live without Diego? The bitter sweet memory of *My Sweet Margarita* played in her head. Nothing could have touched her more than the love song he'd written for her. The gentle weeping of the flamenco guitar pulled at her heart strings like nothing ever had. A tear slid down her cheek. Plucking a red rose from the vase, she toyed with it, wishing with all her heart that Diego, her white knight, would come dashing through the doors of the DeVeccio kingdom to rescue her.

Margot stared out the window into the cliffs of the rugged terrain. Restless, she took a stroll around the grounds. It seemed like only yesterday when her life was so perfect. She recalled the first time she had seen the mansion. She thought it resembled a castle in a fairy tale. With its grand sweeping staircase, elegant ballroom, and terrace balconies, she had been completely drawn in and taken by its *Gone With the Wind* appeal. When she married Michael, she felt like a princess, and Michael was her Prince Charming. But with all its splendor, it paled in comparison to the cozy home of her Latin lover.

A blue dragonfly skimmed the surface of the pool, reminding her of the first time she had lounged on the patio with Michael. She had been completely mesmerized. Looking at it now filled her with sadness. She wanted to be with

Diego, her one true love. Her heart silently wept. She needed to find a way to be with him. Forever. But it just wasn't possible until they proved Michael was the Red Rock Slasher. Margot sighed, her mind on Diego. What that man could do with that flamenco guitar made of Spanish cypress stole her breath. He gently caressed the lustrous neck of the instrument with the same skillful fingers he used to seduce her to heights of ecstasy. She touched her belly and sighed. Looking upward to the soft billowy clouds, she whispered a prayer.

CHAPTER THIRTY-FIVE

A few weeks later, Margot had no doubt she was pregnant. For the last several days, she had been sick to her stomach. What else could it be? Sitting in the bathroom, she waited for the results of her home pregnancy test. Bracing herself for the big moment, she looked at the counter and smiled. Positive. She felt a little thrill, certain the baby she carried had to be Diego's. Now that she'd met the deadline to become pregnant, it would buy her some time until Diego found the evidence to put Michael away for the rest of his life.

Tonight she would tell Michael the good news. And for the sake of her unborn child, she would put on the show of her life when she informed him of his upcoming fatherhood. She envisioned the scene. Soft music and candlelight, and the words he had longed to hear for so long. But it was all wrong. The romantic evening she envisioned should be for Diego, not her husband.

ЖҚҚҚ

Margot studied her reflection in the beveled mirror of their bedroom. Dressed in a chic black cocktail dress and a diamond necklace, she examined herself from every angle. Was it her imagination or did her stomach seemed fuller already. She turned sideways and felt a surge of warmth in her belly, followed by the rush of hormones and odd sensations of pregnancy. Giddy with delight, she traced her fingers along her stomach as new feelings fluttered through her. Lord, how she wished Diego were here so she could tell him about the baby. Her heart skipped a beat at the thought. Turning out the light, she started down the hallway. She heard Michael's footsteps in the foyer. Her pulse quickened.

Standing at the top of the winding staircase, she looked down to see Michael staring up at her. She smiled at him, anticipating his reaction. But suddenly, the room spun in circles and everything around her went dim. Her knees buckled, threatening to give out and she grabbed for the railing.

"Margot," Michael started up the steps, taking them two at a time. "Don't move."

She felt strange, too weak to do anything but grab onto the banister for dear life. Michael charged toward her, his face a distorted blur. The smell of grilled fish wafting through the house nauseated her, causing the coffee she had had earlier to churn in the pit of her stomach, a flaming bundle of acid hurling upward. Michael shook her shoulders, shouted something, but his words sounded muffled, muted by the humming in her ears.

"Margot," he grabbed her around her waist just as she slumped into his arms. "What's wrong?"

Blinking, she brought him into focus, too weak to say anything as he backed her up to the top of the landing

"You scared the hell out of me," he ran his hand along her cheek. "What came over you? Your face is as white as a sheet."

Not that this was where she had planned on telling him of his upcoming fatherhood, but it was as good a place as any. Feeling better once the dizzy spell passed, she regained her footing and smiled. "I planned to tell you over dinner," she took a deep breath. "Michael, I'm pregnant; I just found out today."

Expecting him to whisk her off her feet the second she announced her pregnancy, she waited, the eerie silence sending alarm skittering down her spine. She watched his face twist into an ugly mask of horror. Frightened, she backed up, the spiral staircase far too close—and far too foreboding.

"Who's the father?" he shook her, his hands tightening around her waist. "Tell me, Darling Margot, who's the father?"

Margot stared, horrified. From downstairs, the haunting instrumentals of Moonlight Sonata drifted upward, the chilling lilt of piano keys sending shivers dancing up and down her spine. She licked her lips.

"Answer me. Who's the father?"

"You are... you're the father!"

"Liar!" his hands wrapped around her neck, throttling her. "Tell me, Darling Margot, who's your lover?"

Was he just taunting her? Playing with her? Testing her fidelity? She licked her parched lips, her voice coming out in a hoarse whisper. "You."

"Lying whore!" he slapped her across the face. "Goddamn whore!"

"Michael, please." She begged, blood thundering in her ears. She started down the winding staircase, trying to slip past him, but only made it to the second step before he stopped her with his arm of pure steel. In one swift move, he yanked her against him, her back colliding into a chest of solid muscle.

"Do you want to know how I am certain I'm not the father of your baby?" "Shall I tell you?"

Margot shook her head. He was going to kill her just like he killed the others. Michael was the Red Rock Slasher. If she had any doubts before this minute, she didn't any more. She needed to see Diego before she died; he needed to know about their baby. Michael, the man she had once loved and adored, was going to kill her.

"Cat got your tongue?"

His hand covered her mouth and nose, cutting off her oxygen.

"Allow me to clue you in, my lying, cheating whore of a wife, I'm sterile."

Shock hurled through Margot. Sterile? Michael? He had to be joking. But as his words cut through, so did the impact of what it meant. If Michael wasn't the father, Diego was beyond the shadow of a doubt. Tears gushed from her eyes. She wanted her knight to rush in and rescue her and carry her off into the sunset.

Michael whispered in her ear, his breath laced with bourbon. "Isn't it ironic my doctor should call me to inform me my sperm count is far too low to ever father a child the same day you announce you're pregnant. So if I'm not the father of your baby, someone else planted his seed in you. You betrayed our wedding vows. Infidelity is a sin, and sinners need to be punished. You do remember our wedding vows, the ones where you promised your undying love and fidelity until death do us part, don't you?"

"Michael," she managed to pull his hand from her mouth and nose. She gasped for breath. "Mistakes happen all the time at clinics and labs. They probably mixed up your test results with someone with a similar name. Have the test redone."

"Mixed up with someone with a similar name?" his dark laughter echoed through the mansion. "There is only one Michael Alan DeVeccio, the one and only."

"Please, Michael," Margot tried to reach him. "Mistakes happen all the time, really. Let me go—I beg of you. Please!"

"Bravo!" he clapped theatrically. "What kind of a fool do you take me for? You're no better than my slut of an ex-wife. Candace could never keep her pants on. But you. I thought you were different. I cherished you above all others. I thought of you as the perfect woman, the woman worthy of wearing my mother's ring. You let me down and you will be punished for your betrayal."

Knowing she was about to die, Margot looked into Michael's eyes and saw pure evil. She thought of Diego, the love song he'd written and sung for her, and she fell apart. She needed to see him, tell him she was having his baby. But it would never happen. It was too late. The stages of her life flashed through her mind in rapid concession—childhood memories, her lakefront bungalow, the art museum, and her whirlwind romance with Michael, the Red rock Slasher. But it was the image of Diego that she would carry with her to the sweet hereafter. All she could do was pray. Michael was going to kill her and there was nothing she could do to stop him.

"You whore!" He tossed her down the winding staircase, his eyes blazing with madness. "Over my dead body will you have your bastard child!"

Like a limp rag doll, Margot tumbled down the long and winding staircase, landing at the bottom with a heavy thud. Fading out into a world of unconsciousness, the last sound she heard was the manic laughter coming from Michael, echoing through the halls like demons from the last circle of hell.

CHAPTER THIRTY-SIX

Pacing the floors of St. Hernando's Hospital, Michael waited for news of Margot. She was in surgery for an intracranial hematoma resulting from her fall. Running his hands through his thick raven hair, he relived the scene earlier that evening.

How could she betray him, Margot, the perfect woman, the woman he'd placed so high upon a pedestal? He'd trusted her, believing she was pure like his mother. He'd shoved Margot down the steps for one reason and one reason only. He wanted her to have a miscarriage. The thought of her being pregnant with another man's baby enraged him. And the thought of passing her lover's sperm off as his was unforgivable.

Just the thought of Margot betraying him sent ripples of white hot fury through his entire body. The goddamned whore. How could she betray their wedding vows? How could he have been so wrong about her? She'd fooled him with her naïve innocence, caught him off guard. What a joke. Unable to prevent carnal images of his wife and her lover from popping into his head, he crushed the empty Styrofoam coffee cup between his bare hands—and planned his vengeance.

A blackness wedged its way into Michael's heart, burying whatever love he had felt for Margot. The slut deserved what she got and then some. She would pay for her sins. He would track her lover down, and the punishment he had in mind for him would be merciless. And he wouldn't disguise his identity behind a mask either. Margot's lover would know exactly who was torturing him before he died a slow and painful death.

Michael watched a man in his early thirties with blonde hair and a thinly groomed mustache sit down and pick up a copy of the newspaper. He eyed him with suspicion, wondering if he might be his wife's lover. How long had she been screwing around behind his back? Never in a million years would he have suspected it of Margot. And with all her pathetic wailing she could have starred in a soap opera. But she hadn't fooled him for a second. Indeed not. Did she think she could get away with such betrayal? Betrayal was unforgivable in his world, and the whore would get hers! She needed a good lesson in domestic discipline. He would teach her the meaning of male dominance; he looked forward to it with eager anticipation.

With a lecherous smile, Michael envisioned the coming attractions, the alpha male in him rising high above his anger. He would bide his time; he wasn't heartless after all. As soon as she recovered from her head injury, it would be time for her opening debut. Coming soon to a theater near you. Locked in a House of Horrors.

Michael's thoughts were interrupted by Margot's neurologist. "Your wife is out of surgery, Mr. DeVeccio."

"How is she? How's my wife?"

"Resting comfortably. She was very fortunate. Her intracranial hematoma was small and localized, and we were able to suction it out of her skull with little trauma."

"And our baby?"

"I'm sorry," the doctor placed his hand on Michael's shoulder. "I'm afraid she lost it. The shock of the fall was too much for a fetus so small."

"Can I see her?"

"Only for a few minutes."

"Of course."

"Your wife was very lucky, all things considered. The paramedics reported she took quite a nasty fall on those marble steps. The damage could have been far worse, even fatal."

Michael clucked his tongue. "Damn high heels. And to think minutes earlier we were discussing names for our unborn child, and now..."

The doctor patted Michael's shoulder. "These things are in the hands of God, a higher force. If you will excuse me, I have surgery in ten minutes."

Ж◊Ж◊Ж

Sliding glass doors and partitions around eight beds separated the ICU from the nursing station. A nasal cannula tube delivered oxygen to Margot, and machines monitored her vitals. An automated blood pressure cup inflated around her upper arm, a drain gurgled, and the infusion pump measured another dose of fluid into her IV. As Michael stood watching from the doorway, a nurse wrote information on her chart.

"How is she?" Michael stared at his wife before looking at the nurse.

"Her vitals are stable for the moment," the nurse replied, placing one hand on her ample hip. "You can only stay a few minutes."

He would stay as long as he liked. In the mood he was in, the last thing he needed was some tub of lard nurse giving him shit.

A huge elastic bandage hugged Margot's head. Other than the purple contusions beneath her eyes, her face was as colorless as a corpse. She had cuts and bruises on all visible parts of her body, along with two broken ribs, tightly wrapped with Velcro around her torso.

Michael ran his finger along Margot's cheek. "Has she opened her eyes yet?"

"No," the nurse adjusted the tubing. "She's heavily sedated with morphine and anticonvulsant drugs to prevent a seizure."

"I'll sit with her until she comes out of the anesthesia," Michael patted his wife's hand. "I want to be the first person she sees when she opens her eyes."

Ж◊Ж◊Ж

She ached all over. Not wanting to open her eyes, she preferred the comfort of the surreal place she was floating in, drifting in and out of consciousness. Her head throbbed, and she felt something tight and uncomfortable squeezing her arm. Somewhere in the distance, she heard a faint beeping, its musical rhythm as soft and steady as a summer rain.

Cool fingers snaked around her wrist. Were they feeling for a pulse? This had to be some type of dream, a nightmare where they intended to bury her alive. She needed to tell them she wasn't dead.

She was vaguely aware of murmurs, muted and distant. Someone pried her eyelids open and flicked a bright light in them. She thought she heard her name, far away in the distance, muffled, distorted. She fluttered her eyes.

"She's coming around," Michael said. "Get her doctor."

Margot opened her eyes to see Michael peering down at her.

"Welcome back to the living. I'm so glad you came back to me after your fall. I was so worried."

Why was he looking at her that way? Looming over her? She tried to speak, but her mouth was too dry and she seemed unable to move. Where was she? Every inch of her body ached, and her mind was in a thick fog. Why couldn't she remember anything?

"Hello Mrs. DeVeccio," a doctor materialized in front of her. "You're doing just fine. You're in St. Hernando's Hospital. You just had an operation."

Before she could stop him, he shot that penlight in her eyes again, blinding her with brightness.

"Margot," Michael touched her. "You took quite a nasty tumble down the staircase when you tripped on your heels."

A wild gush of panic hurled through her, drenching her body in perspiration. She went to scream but nothing came out other than a few pitiful wheezes. Her head throbbed terribly, but the touch of Michael's hand brought the chilling memory back with amazing clarity. He tried to kill her and the baby, Diego's baby. He flung her down the steps as if she were bad rubbish, something to get rid of. Her heart sank. Did she lose her baby? She looked into Michael's eyes as she sucked water from the straw in the glass the nurse held to her lips. She sucked hard. And she knew. Her baby was dead; Michael had killed Diego's baby. And she was next on the hit list. Her voice came out in a hoarse rasp, but her hysteria pushed out the words,

"He tried to kill me! He's the Red Rock Slasher!"

"Give her 4 cc of ativan," the doctor ordered. "She needs

to be sedated and restrained before she hurts herself or someone else."

"He did it...he threw me down the steps...he killed his first wife!"

As the drug took its soporific effect, Margot heard one of the nurses say, "Violent episodes are quite common after brain trauma. We see it all the time. Confusion and disorientation are all part of the healing process."

ЖЖЖ

A week later, Margot sat in her hospital room waiting to be released. Red roses surrounded her from every corner. The air was thick with the funereal smell of death. The beautiful red rose she once loved was now her nemesis because, it haunted her; it reminded her of him.

"Ready to go home, Margot?"

It would be a cold day in hell before she ever thought of that mausoleum as home again. His estate no longer held any attraction to her. Instead, she viewed it as hell and thought of Michael as Lucifer. The minute she could, she would go to Diego.

"I wasn't going to upset you with this news," Michael unfolded a copy of the Chicago Tribune. "But it concerns your mother."

At the mention of her mother, Margot felt sick. Grabbing the paper from him, she quickly scanned it, her heart thrashing in her chest. "Entrepreneur, Sara Montgomery, owner of an upscale clothing boutique on Michigan Avenue, robbed at gunpoint in her shop late last night. Although she wasn't hurt, she was badly shaken up. Her assailant escaped on foot and was described as wearing a ski mask and dark gloves."

More frightened than she had ever been in her life, Margot stared at Michael.

"Terrible thing," Michael clucked his tongue. "Did you ever notice bad things happen to good people?"

Chilling images skittered across Margot's mind, images of her mother with a death star in her throat and a ghoulish mask on her corpse. Her crazy husband had just threatened her mother.

"And by the way," Michael kissed her. "Just in case you get any ideas about reporting your little accident as a domestic, leaving me, or displeasing me in any way, the next time there's a break in at your mother's shop, her corpse will be all dressed up for the morgue, compliments of the Red Rock Slasher." His icy fingers caressed her neck. "And wouldn't you feel guilty, Darling Margot, knowing you could have prevented your mother from dying a slow and painful death?"

CHAPTER THIRTY-SEVEN

Diego Santiago paced the hardwood floors of his living room, furious. If only the smug billionaire hadn't disconnected the tracking devices he had planted the night of his birthday party, he would be behind bars by now. Now homicide had no more to go on and were back to square one. No more hidden cameras, GPS tracking devices, Internet tracking, or cell phone chip.

And where in the hell was Margot? A solid week had come and gone and she was no where to be found. Why hadn't she been in touch with him? According to the butler with the stone cold gaze, Mrs. DeVeccio was out. Pissed off and hellbent on finding her, he had obtained a search warrant and had combed every inch of the mausoleum but had come up empty. She was gone without a trace. The only sign of Margot had been the lingering scent of her perfume, sweet, subtle, and totally unforgettable.

His mind raced, his thoughts wandered. Was Margot pregnant? Pregnant with his child? Had their plan worked? Not that they had dared utter the words out loud, but they both knew what they were doing. Oh, yeah. Trying to buy some time until they had the evidence to convict the sick son of a bitch. Because if Margot hadn't met the deadline, that noose around her neck would cut into her throat like a Spanish garrote. Or in this case, a Ninja death star.

Frustrated, he ran his fingers through his mane of long hair. What kind of a demented idiot would put such a unrealistic demand on a woman he supposedly loved so much—get pregnant with a son in thirty days or die by the sword. Damn. He snatched a cigarette from the discarded pack on the mantel and lit up, the rush of nicotine swarming through his brain. After a few drags, he snuffed it out, his heart racing from the addiction he knew he would never kick. Agitated, he picked up his flamenco guitar, tenderly stroking the strings with the same finesse he had used on his woman. Memories of Margot floated across the room, a bittersweet reminder of the afternoon he would never forget.

She consumed him. Everywhere he looked, he saw her face, her bewitching green eyes. How he wanted to free her from the clutches of the madman. She'd gotten under his skin, and the thought of DeVeccio hurting her tore him up inside. She was so beautiful, so sweet. He'd never felt hair so silky soft. The way it looked when the sun teased out the burnished highlights, all ablaze with flames of copper. He remembered how it fanned around her face like spun gold when they made love, so pretty he couldn't take his eyes off her.

And the way she'd whispered his name. Chills grazed his skin at the memory. "Margot," he whispered, grabbing his Glock, fleeing through the door in three seconds flat. Jumping into his Ford Taurus, he tore down the road like a man on a mission, vowing to find Margot if he had to search every corner of the world.

ЖЖЖ

Driving up to the wrought iron gate leading to the DeVeccio estate, Detective Santiago shoved his identification under the security camera. Within a few seconds, the heavy gates lifted with a creaky groan. The guard dogs growled and snarled, bearing their canines. Casting them a sidelong glance, he thought it a damn shame they had never turned on their master.

A fleet of dream machines lined the driveway, the vehicles he had rigged when he posed as a caterer. If the GPS trackers were still under the hood, the police could monitor the billionaire's moves from their computer. But now they were gone. Not that it really surprised him. Knowing DeVeccio, he probably had the entire estate swept for the latest spy techniques twice a day.

The grounds lurked with the eerie stillness of a cemetery, the manicured lawn masking skeletons beneath the deep quiet earth. The curtains had been drawn, barring all sunlight from entering the dreary mausoleum. From deep in the woods, a raven cried out, its throaty call menacing and foreboding. Sensing the evil submerged behind the estate, Diego Santiago's hot Latin blood ran cold. Taking the steps to the mansion two at a time, he rang the bell and waited, tapping the tip of his scuffed-up booted foot impatiently.

"May I help you, detective?" the butler inquired, the tone of his voice crisp and curt.

"Yeah," Diego snarled between clenched teeth. "Quit being such a dick head and step aside. I'm here to see DeVeccio, and unless you want your skinny ass hauled downtown, you'll get out of my way."

"Mr. DeVeccio has been informed of your arrival." The butler glared at Diego through stone-cold eyes. "Follow me, Mr. And Mrs. DeVeccio are in the parlor, waiting for you."

Diego's heart skipped a beat. Wherever Margot had been for the past week, she was back. Relief swarmed through him, his legs going weak. Thank God. He fought the urge to run to her and free her from the clutches of a madman. But he couldn't. Because if DeVeccio picked up on even the slightest spark between him and his wife, her life would be over in a New York second. Scratching the stubble on his chin, he walked through the doors of the parlor. The change in the air was so strong it was palpable.

Margot sat on the sofa next to Michael, far too close for comfort. He had his left arm firmly planted around her left shoulder, and she had her right hand on his knee. Through her carefully applied makeup, he detected faint contusions beneath unfocused eyes. The billionaire's chin jutted out a mile, his eyes gleaming with smug satisfaction. Margot's shoulders were stiff and rigid, her posture far too poised. It was all wrong. They might look for all the world like couple of the year, but he knew better. The picture-perfect portrait the billionaire had painted was as phony as a two dollar bill.

No doubt DeVeccio had set the scene, keeping Margot in line with threats. An icy chill snaked through him when he stared into Margot's eyes. What the hell had DeVeccio done to her? This woman wasn't the same woman he had fallen in love with, his sweet Margarita with the bewitching green eyes. This Margot had been programmed, prompted to say and do exactly what the nut job commanded her to do. Like a robot, he thought. He could tell by her pupils she'd been sedated with just enough drug to take off the edge, but not enough to forget her part in the performance. Damn. What had he done to her?

The DeVeccios were dressed for the masquerade, all spruced up and powdered down. The billionaire sat there in a navy blue pinstripe suit, his chest puffed out in his custom-designed threads. Margot looked the part of the regal queen in a flowing gown of pleated pink silk, the perfect trophy wife for the billionaire to wear on his arm. A Waterford vase spilling over with exotic orchids graced the marble coffee table in front of them.

"Santiago," Michael smiled. "What can we do for you? Surely you didn't come all the way out to our humble home uninvited to dine with us, did you?"

Tamping back his rage, Diego put his temper in check. He had done his share of domestics when he had worked the streets. It was always the same, a woman who chose to be a victim because fear kept her quiet. Time after time, a woman called the police to report a domestic after being beaten within an inch of her life. By the time police arrived at the scene, all was forgiven and the victim refused to press charges. And they all wore the same tight-lipped expression on their faces as Margot, resigned to keep their battle scars to themselves.

Santiago's eyes grew as dark as midnight. He wanted to rip the smug billionaire apart, limb by limb for touching a hair on Margot's head. He wanted to take Margot in his arms, but he couldn't. Instead, he fixed her with the hardened look of a seasoned homicide cop. "What happened to your face, Mrs. DeVeccio? And don't even think about lying to me because I can see the bruises under your makeup. Despite the fact you tried to hide it, I can see the carefully camouflaged bandage in your hairline. Talk to me, Mrs. DeVeccio. How did you get so beat up?"

The pulse in Margot's throat fluttered as tears threatened. She licked her dry lips and opened her mouth to speak but nothing came out. An awkward silence lulled in the air. Gingerly caressing Margot's cheek, Michael took control, his voice so soft it came out in barely more than a whisper. "Allow me, Darling. I think you've been through enough in the past week, and I don't want you being drilled by the good detective." Glaring at Santiago, he said, "My wife has been in St. Hernando's Hospital for the past several days. When she was coming down the stairs to tell me the joyous news of her pregnancy, she tripped in her high heels and took a nasty fall. My wife underwent brain surgery for a localized hematoma, and unfortunately, she lost our baby. I am taking my lovely wife on an extended trip to Tuscany to recuperate. Isn't that right, Darling?"

Margot cleared her throat. She felt Michael's fingers squeeze her shoulders with just enough force to let her know she'd better make every word count. Images of her mother's corpse raced through her mind. Staring at Diego, she gave an impeccable performance worthy of an Oscar. "That's right, Santiago. My husband and I are taking a second honeymoon to Tuscany. We're very sorry about the loss of our baby, but when we return from Italy, I have no doubt I will be pregnant again. A second honeymoon is just what we need to mourn the loss of our first child. I was just telling my handsome husband how much it would mean to me to renew our wedding vows. After all, we will be in one of the most romantic places in the world—and we're more in love than ever. Isn't that right, Darling?"

CHAPTER THIRTY-EIGHT

Images of Margot were displayed on monitors all over Michael's home office. With the sophisticated system installed in the DeVeccio estate, he tracked her every move from his computer. And now that the homicide cop was hell bent on pinning the murders on him, believed they were out of the country, he could complete his work in Red Rock Canyon. Very soon, his master plan would reach fruition. His lips coiled into a snake-like grin. *Everything is right on schedule,* he snickered to himself. *I'll be long gone before Santiago knows what hit him.* With a click of the mouse, he followed Margot through the mansion, tracking her every move.

Nervous and afraid, she peeked outside from behind the heavily draped windows. The sun-drenched rooms were veiled in muted light, the dreary dimness as thick as the sweltering heat of the surrounding Mojave. Her jaw line was rigid, her teeth clenched so tight her mouth looked as if it had been wired shut.

She shifted from foot to foot on a pair of four-inch stiletto heels, fretting over the list of chores that had been doled out to her since cook and the butler had been let go. Her list of things to do included a seven-course gourmet dinner fit for a king, washing and ironing Michael's clothes, and polishing the family heirlooms and marble tables until they gleamed. Scrambling around in a short red leather skirt, a black spandex tank top with a scarlet heart blazing across it, and heels far too high and uncomfortable for all the leg work expected of her, she bit her lip until it bled. Dashing across the kitchen, she snagged her black lace stockings on the chair, cussing when she got a run.

Pleased with the show, Michael watched Margot take one of her tranquilizers for anxiety. "Go on," he urged, a rush of pleasure hurling through him as she downed the pill with a glass of water. "Down the hatch, that's a good girl." He chuckled to himself. "I'm so good I really ought to write thrillers for Hollywood." Dark laughter exploded as he pointed a finger at the screen. "Little do you know I replaced your Valium with hallucinogenic drugs days ago. Every day, Darling Margot, you'll become more unraveled and more undone by the hallucinations invading your mind."

How it satisfied him to watch his wife question her sanity. And this was nothing but a sneak preview of things to come. "Oh yes, boys and girls, grab yourselves a big tub of buttered popcorn and get ready to scream.

ЖЖЖ

Later that evening, feeling miserable in an outfit two sizes too tight and heels far too high, Margot prepared Michael's gourmet dinner. Roses from the garden had been arranged in a vase, and every course of the gourmet meal from appetizers to the black forest cake had been done to perfection.

But something was wrong with her. Her heart galloped and her eyes felt strange, like they were rolling around in her head. She couldn't be certain, but she thought she heard hushed whispers within the walls, coming closer, buzzing louder and louder like a swarm of bees. What was it? Michael was working from home, in his office off their bedroom, and he had fired cook and the butler. The gardeners had left hours ago. Or had they? Then she heard footsteps, slow and heavy, causing the wooden floorboards to moan under their weight.

Creak. The hair on the nape of her neck prickled. The footsteps were coming toward her, slow and steady. Creak. Her heart pumped wildly, her hands slick with sweat. Luciano? Carlos? Candace? Too many ghosts roaming this mansion. But the dead couldn't hurt her, could they? Creak. She fled across the room, tripping over her own two feet in her haste to snatch one of the knives from the cutlery board. Creak. Frightened out of her wits, she hurled around, ready to wield her weapon at the killer. Padding into the room was Zeus, her beloved cat, meowing for his dinner. She let out her breath and put the weapon down, certain it was just her mind playing tricks on her.

Sweating from every pore, she hustled around the kitchen, petrified she had forgotten something. After shoving the coconut shrimp and crab triangle appetizers in the oven, she sautéed the pan-seared tuna in the lemon garlic sauce. The scalloped potatoes were just about done and the chocolate cake was indeed fit for a king. Just as she doused the salad with dressing, pure virgin oil, vinegar, and herbs, topped off with Asiago cheese, she sensed a presence looming behind her. The hair on the back of her neck stood straight up. Certain it was Michael, she spun around and screamed loud enough to wake the dead. Candace stood before her, naked in death, her Zorro sword pierced straight through her bleeding heart.

With her gnarled, bony fingers working to pry the sword loose from her rotted corpse, wretched sobs escaped her throat. Her once beautiful face was ravished with decay. Long ruby fingernails tugged and pulled, tugged and pulled, causing more blood to ooze from her seeping wound.

In a voice as sweet as an angel's, she said, "Run, rabbit, run. Run for your life before he kills you like he killed me. Haven't you figured it out by now? He's the Red Rock Slasher. Run, rabbit, run."

Overwrought with grief and shock, Margot blacked out, the salad forks clanking to the floor with a hollow thud. The clatter reverberated in her ears, until it faded away and everything went quiet. She opened her eyes, weary and afraid, frantically searching the kitchen for the walking dead. Nothing. Had she just imagined it? Dreamed it?

She felt confused and disoriented. Everything in her life was spinning out of control. She took a deep breath and composed herself. But not for long. Manic laughter closed in on her from all directions, the same laughter that had aroused her from sleep all those weeks ago. Then she heard the front door open and slam shut, the lock latching into place. Her heart galloped. Didn't Michael say he was working from home today? Or did he? She couldn't be sure. But wherever he had been all day, ready or not, the madman had just entered the mansion.

"Good evening," Michael addressed Margot with a curt nod, flinging his jacket over her arm. Loosening his tie, he turned to her. "Bring me a bourbon on the rocks and the appetizers I ordered. I can't tell you how much I'm looking forward to the stuffed chicken and all the trimmings I requested for tonight's dinner. You did make stuffed chicken, sweet potatoes, and biscuits, didn't you? And a pumpkin pie for dessert with whipped cream? Because if you didn't, I'll have to punish you by locking you up in the Great Room where all the dead spirits roam."

Ж)Ж)Ж

Behind the doors of the great room, Margot paced the floors like a pirate walking the plank. She heard the skeletal remains of traitors, rattling behind the walls. Voices raw with hysteria begged to be freed from the room.

Margot felt an icy chill as someone resembling a young Michael walked straight through her. Luciano? The curtains swooshed and the lights went out. A woman fluttered about, lighting candles with a Zorro sword. Candace? Margot pounded on the door until her knuckles bled.

"Let me out! Michael, let me out!"

Hearing footsteps behind her, she whipped her head around just as Carlos DeVeccio stepped straight out of his portrait, grabbed one of the swords from the wall and plunge it into Luciano's heart.

"Take that, you traitor."

Margot watched blood puddle at his feet as he slumped over, looking at his father with loving eyes.

"Why, Papa?"

"For betraying me. You know the rules son: Betray me and die by the sword." Dark laughter bubbled out of Carlos DeVeccio as he removed his skull mask from the wall and placed it on his son's corpse. "And you're next" he pointed at Margot. "It's time for your trial."

"Order in the court, order in the court," Carlos slammed his fist on the table with the force of a judge's gavel. "I find the accused, Margot DeVeccio, guilty of betrayal in the first degree. You will die by the sword for your sleazy adultery. I hereby order the Red Rock Slasher to pierce you straight through your lying cheating heart. Death by the sword for the queen bitch slut."

Screaming, Margot ran to the door and pounded on it. Suddenly all laughter ceased and the door swung open, sending her sailing straight into Michael's arms.

"Going somewhere, Darling Margot?" he whispered in her ear. "Don't you know there's no escaping me–until death do us part."

Ж◇Ж◇Ж

As the weeks continued, Margot's life teetered on the brink of sanity. Nervous and afraid, paranoia ruled her world. Images of the walking dead swooned around her, Carlos, Luciano, Candace, hideous laughter rolling out of their twisted mouths. Eyes followed her every move, watching, waiting. Feeling faint, she reached for an apple from the fruit dish. Just as she went to take a bite, a gnarled hand popped out of the wall and split the apple in two with a sword. "It's me, Jack. Jack the Ripper. Remember me? My mission is to wipe out all the whores of the world. This was just to let you know I'm coming for you. Soon. Next time it'll be your head." Loud psychotic laughter echoed from behind the wall as Margot slumped to the floor.

Ж◇Ж◇Ж

Michael chuckled to himself from his office, slapping his hands together with gusto. Bravo! Whoever said they don't make horror shows like they used to never saw a Michael De-Veccio production. Superb. He sipped on his bourbon, fished a Marlboro from the pack and tapped it three times before lighting it. Indeed yes. Thanks to the drugs, he had his wife right where he wanted her. Under his thumb.

Everything was right on schedule. Jed Jones had returned from Italy with a new identity and was working for Johnny O'Toole as his software engineer. Soon Jed would embezzle the family stock and transfer it to a Swiss bank account where it could never be traced. Once that was accomplished, his mother's soul could rest in peace. Then he would take care of his two remaining cousins. And then it would be Margot's turn, his perfect wife. He would save the best for last.

CHAPTER THIRTY-NINE

"Did you see the paper this morning?" Michael sipped coffee at the kitchen table, scanning the headlines. "Looks like I'm an uncle. Seems after weeks of false labor, the O'Toole twins were born late last night, a boy and a girl. Perhaps I'll drop in on my cousin and his wife to congratulate them later on this afternoon. After all, it is my duty as their uncle."

Margot didn't like the sounds of that. What was he up to, she wondered, pouring batter into the waffle iron, hot grease hissing and spewing on her face and arms. She cast a sidelong glance his way; her insides turned to water. He was watching her, his creepy eyes slowly raking every inch of her body from head to toe. How could she have ever loved him, this demented monster with no heart or soul? He folded the newspaper, running his forefinger over the crease three times. His lips curled upward, forming a venomous sneer.

A foreboding chill snaked through her with such force she bit her lip until it cracked open. Someone was about to die. Who? Jimmy? Brooke? Good Lord, not one of the twins! With her uneasiness mounting, she kept an eye on the waffles, making sure they were grilled to a golden brown. Rushing to the other burner where the bacon fried, she turned it, her heart galloping. She checked the clock. Precisely two minutes to get breakfast on the table and she still had to squeeze the oranges for his juice.

Where would it all end? She thought about Diego. Had he forgotten all about her? He couldn't have actually believed her rigged-up story about going to Tuscany with Michael to renew their wedding vows, could he? Telling him that bold face lie had been the hardest thing she had ever done, but if she didn't do as Michael commanded, the madman would kill her mother. Frustrated, she blew her bangs out of her eyes as tears gushed. She thought she might go mad. Her head throbbed and her heart raced. Why wasn't that Valium settling her nerves? It was supposed to lessen stress, not add to it, after all.

"Margot?" Michael snuck up behind her, causing her to drop the spatula. "What the hell are you making?"

An icy chill skittered down the back of her neck where his hot breath had fanned it. Turning off the griddle, she turned to him. His eyes were stone cold, his lips tightly puckered. Her heartbeat tripled. "Your breakfast, Michael. Just what you ordered: waffles and bacon. And if you give me a second, I'll squeeze the oranges for your juice. Just let me..."

"Hold on, hold on," his long fingers clamped around her neck like a vice. "What have I told you about disobeying my orders?"

"I haven't."

"Don't lie to me, Margot. It would be a big mistake. Now answer me. What the hell are you making?"

Tears streamed down her face. She gasped for air as his grip tightened. Her eyes pleaded for mercy. The eerie quiet hovered between them like the calm before the storm.

"Answer me! Don't make me ask you again...or else."

"I'm making your breakfast, waffles and bacon. I..."

He slapped her across the face and glared at her. Turning on his heels, he went to the table and picked up her list of duties for the day. With great ceremony, he unfolded it and handed it to her. "Read it out loud."

Through eyes misty with tears, she read the breakfast menu, gulping in the air that had been suppressed from her lungs. "Mushroom omelet with goat cheese, sausage, Bloody Mary."

"You know what happens when you disobey a direct order from your master, don't you, Darling Margot?" he took a step closer. "A day locked up in Uncle Carlos's suite with all those face masks. And Margot, remember how the crime scene removed my uncle's satin-lined coffin for evidence? Well, guess what? I had it replaced, and that's where you'll be doing your penance. Locked in the casket.

"Need I remind you what happened to my slut of an ex-wife the last time she was in there?" Gales of laughter bubbled from the back of his throat. "She came out in a body bag. The slut got precisely what she deserved for screwing around on me. So you just think about that while you're locked up in your coffin. You know what they say, sooner or later, we all have to die." he grinned as he reached into his pocket and pulled out her pills. "And just because I loved you the best, I'll subdue you with two tranquilizers." he poured her a glass of tap water. "Take your medicine, down the hatch like a good wife."

ЖЖЖ

"Michael!" Margot screamed from the satin-lined coffin, scraping her fingernails along the wooden lid. Scratch. Scratch. Scratch. "Let me out of this coffin, please! Don't let me die in this casket, please. I'm sorry. I'll never do it again. Please!"

The hearse-shaped clock on the desk ticked by the minutes of her life, loud and maddening. She stopped screaming long enough to catch her breath, her hands searching every corner for a way out. How long had she been entombed in this coffin, this death trap? It seemed like hours, probably only a few minutes had ticked by. How long before she suffocated? Panic soared through her, her skin drenched with sweat. Then she felt air vents on the sides of the casket.

Hope rose as the panic eased. So she wasn't going to suffocate from lack of oxygen. Michael's intention had been to scare her to death. And it was working. But dammit, she would fight it every step of the way. Margot Marie Montgomery DeVeccio was a survivor. She would just close her eyes and pretend she was in a bed, her bed at her bungalow in Chicago, not this satin-lined coffin. After Michael felt she'd suffered enough, he'd let her out. Or would he?

But just then, the pipe organ began, its bellowing chords raising every hair on her body. The chilling music played on and on and on. Images of a funeral dirge raced through her head. Not just any funeral. Her funeral.

Blood thundered in her ears. The door opened and closed. Creak. Heavy footsteps approached the casket.

Someone cleared his throat. "Dearly beloved. We are gathered today for the funeral of Margot DeVeccio." The preacher said in a reverent voice. "Because God has chosen to call our sister Margot from this life to Himself, we commit her body to the earth, its resting place, for we are dust and unto dust we shall return."

Margot screamed until her throat was raw. She had scraped her fingers to the bone, the tips throbbing as blood seeped out. Didn't they know she was alive? Was she about to be buried alive, somewhere on the grounds with all the other skeletal remains? Panic soared through her. She was going crazy locked in the coffin. She kicked and screamed and yanked strands of her hair out of her head. Michael was insane, a demented psychopath. She didn't want to die. She wanted to live. She wanted Diego. Where was Diego? She prayed he'd rescue her before it was too late. She thought of Candace, Michael's ex-wife who'd been slaughtered to death in the original coffin the night of the masquerade ball.

Woozy and faint, she felt the effects of the Valium kick in. But her anxiety mounted with every beat of her heart. Through the drug-induced haze, a light bulb went off in her head. She hadn't been taking tranquilizers at all. Michael had switched them to mind-altering drugs. No wonder she'd been skitzo for the past several weeks, seeing and hearing things that weren't even there. The bastard had been manipulating her, controlling her with drugs.

It was too late to stop the hallucinatory effects. He had given her two pills, doubled up on the poison. Oh, no. It was too late to stop the nightmare playing in her mind. She clutched the sides of the coffin, bracing herself for the hellish terror as the sounds closed in around her coffin. A sword hissed through the air, hideous laughter echoed in her ears, and every few minutes, the werewolf howled at the moon. Then she felt them, crawling on her, slithering up her body, spiders, big, hairy spiders. And the pipe organ played on and on, her funeral dirge reverberating in her ears.

"Help me!" she screamed as someone unlocked the lid to her coffin, the wooden boards moaning as the lid went up. Creak. Creak. With a sudden heave, the lid popped and she stared into the hollow eyes of a corpse, blood oozing out of its brain. She bolted upright, desperate to escape. The monster transformed into Michael. In the darkened room, the steely blade of a sword gleamed. He shoved her down, harsh laughter pouring from his black soul.

"It's time, Margot. I told you I'd come for you. I've come to thrust the sword through your lying cheating heart for your betrayal. And just because I loved you the best, I'm going to allow you to choose your own face mask from Uncle Carlos's private collection. Go on, pick and choose, time's a wasting. Tick tock goes the clock. Now, pick one so I can place the mask of the betrayer on your corpse."

"Let me go!" She swung at the monster but her hand went right through him. He laughed in her face. "Don't you know by now, Darling Margot? You'll never be free of me. Until death do us part."

Suddenly Michael's face transformed into a werewolf with the flesh-tearing fangs. He grew wings and landed on her, like a vampire. His fangs sunk into her jugular vein with piercing pain. Blood and gore gushed out, staining the satin-lined coffin. "No!" she screamed, staring at the gore drenching her body. Then, the werewolf transformed into Michael.

He glared at her, his red eyes gleaming with fire. "Betrayal in my world is unforgivable. Betray me and die by the sword. Sluts like you deserve to die. Who is your lover? I demand to know? Who is your lover? Whose sperm did you try to pass off as mine? Answer me! Answer the werewolf!"

"Michael, please. Let me go. I'll never tell anyone you are the Red Rock Slasher! Please Michael? If you ever loved me, let me go from this hell!"

"Die by the sword," dark laughter bubbled out of his throat as he plunged a long blade into her heart. "I warned you, and I'm a man of my word."

Then as she closed her eyes to the perpetual darkness, the Evil Jester pounced off the wall and leaped on her, yanking the sword out of her heart. He snickered, a lecherous grin on his twisted mouth. "My turn, slut? Rumor has it you're easy. Well, come on. Give it up for the Evil Jester."

Psychotic laughter closed in on her. The werewolf with the flesh-tearing fangs howled at the moon. All of a sudden, the bell in the bell tower rang, echoing through the mansion like some gong from the medieval days. The resounding echo reverberated in her ears again and again, making her crazy. Just when she didn't think she could take any more, Candace swooned above her, pointing one of her long ruby fingernails at her. Crazy as the rest of them in this nut house, she cackled like a wild hyena, petting a snake slithering out of the gaping hole in her chest.

She glared at Margot and cackled all the louder. "I tried to warn you. But did you listen? You should have run before he locked you in the coffin. There's no escaping now. You can never leave this house of horrors. You're one of us now, one of the living dead. Welcome to the Hotel Carlos DeVeccio."

CHAPTER FORTY

Strutting into the DeVeccio parlor with an air of confidence, Jed Jones looked every bit the highly paid executive.

"Welcome back, Jed," Michael shook his hand. "Have a seat and we'll discuss business."

The clinic in Switzerland and the training in Italy had done wonders for Jed, molding him back into the software engineer he once was. His scruffy appearance was gone, and he'd had a major attitude adjustment. Giving him the once over, Michael was not the least surprised Johnny O'Toole had hired him on the spot. The man standing before him had great potential, and Michael knew he would pull off the job with flying colors.

"Very impressive, Jed," Michael said. "I trust my people in Italy treated you well."

"Yes sir, Mr. DeVeccio. Their technology in corporate software is highly sophisticated."

"Shall we get down to business?" Michael walked over to the bar. "Name your poison."

"Macallan on the rocks."

"Very good," Michael nodded his approval.

As he poured their drinks, he studied the man sitting in his parlor, doubting that his own mother would recognize Jed Jones as her son. The result of the cosmetic surgery to remove his hooded eyelids totally changed his appearance.

Blue contact lenses gave his eyes a look of great intellect. And the well-trimmed goatee along with the three-inch shoe lifts were the perfect addition to Jed's disguise. With his new look and new identity as Andrew McDermott, it was all systems go.

"Here's the plan," Michael handed Jed his drink. "Today's the day I want you to hack into the O'Toole stock and transfer it to my Swiss bank account. Make it happen at noon when the entire office is out to lunch. You've had ample time to break security and it's time to do it. Johnny will be out of the office most of the day, spending time with his brother and newborn twins. Make damn sure you don't make any mistakes. After the job is done, disappear without a trace, getting rid of your identity as Andrew McDermott. Go anywhere in the world, but never come back. This is your one shot at redemption, Jed. Don't make me sorry I put all this time and effort into you. Make it happen."

Jed sipped his drink. He had learned it was a dog-eat-dog world and he had all intentions of staying alive. "I believe that covers the ground work, Mr. DeVeccio. Rest assured I will do the job."

"That concludes our business then," Michael raised his glass. "To Andrew McDermott."

ЖҲЖҲЖ

Sneaking out of the mansion incognito in case Santiago was snooping around, Michael left the mansion disguised as the driver. Hopping into the sleek limousine, he checked his look in the rearview mirror. Not bad, he thought, adjusting his toupee and mustache. Placing a red cap on his head, he careened down the road to O'Toole Construction. He wanted to make damn sure the O'Toole job was done to his satisfaction, see the transfer of funds with his own two eyes. Otherwise, he fingered the death star in his pocket. Jed Jones would never leave the country alive.

ЖҲЖҲЖ

With the clock ticking, Jed Jones (alias Andrew McDermott) booted up his computer and went to work. Cool and confident under pressure, he waited for the screen to illuminate. He typed in a series of complex passwords, and the entire spreadsheet of the O'Toole stock appeared in all its glory. After several clicks of the mouse at precisely twelve noon, Jed embezzled all the family fortune into a Swiss bank account where it could never be traced. His mission a done deal, he closed all documents and spreadsheets, turned off the computer, and was out the door. From his bird's eye view in the closet, Michael grinned. Now for act two, the trip to the maternity ward of St. Hernando Hospital to settle the score with the remaining O'Toole clan.

ЖҞЖ

"Hello, hello," Johnny bust into Brooke's room, his arms filled with helium balloons in pink and blue. "Uncle Johnny came to check out the new niece and nephew. Hey, kid, congratulations." He punched his brother in the arm. Walking to the bed, he planted a big kiss on Brooke's lips. "And how's our little mommy after that rough labor, huh?" he peeked into the bassinet at Nicholas and Monique, both babies sound asleep. "Chips off the ol' block, kid. They both got the O'Toole charm already."

"Oh, yeah," Jimmy beamed, adjusting their blankets. "How's that?"

"They both snore, could hear them down the hall."

"I'll have you know my Darlings do not snore," Brooke laughed, looking tired but happy. "They're perfect. And they both have midnight blue eyes and raven hair. Jimmy and I are both blonde."

"If only Mom were here to see her new grandchildren," Jimmy said, emotion caught in his throat. "And Ricky."

"Damn our cousin," Johnny clenched his fist. "Damn bastard's gonna get what's comin' to him some day."

"Yeah," Jimmy said. "If Brooke didn't have false labor pains a few weeks back, Michael might be six feet under. But his day's coming."

"Well, for today anyway," Brooke held up her hand. "Let's just concentrate on the birth of Nicholas and Monique and celebrate their lives and our good fortune."

"Amen." Jimmy kissed his wife just as a heavy-set nurse came in, wheeling a cart with a bottle of sparkling cider, two glasses, and a red rose.

"Compliments of our hospital," she smiled, shoving her thick-lensed glasses off her face as she poured the bubbly into the glasses. "Oh, you have company. I only brought two glasses, I'm sorry."

"No problem," Jimmy grabbed a water glass. "Allow me to do the honors. Here we go, toast one up to the newest members of the O'Toole clan."

"Here, here," Johnny gulped his drink and refilled it. "To Nicholas and Monique. Hey, this champagne ain't bad for non-alcoholic stuff. It sure is a hot one out in the desert today. Goes down real easy."

"To Nicholas and Monique," Brooke sipped her drink, feeling all was right with the world. Her twins were born and they were perfect. A boy and a girl. "Check on them, Jim. Make sure they're both covered and still breathing."

"Relax, babe," Jimmy smiled, refilling all the glasses. But he snuck a peek into the bassinet and grinned. "Sleeping like angels."

Suddenly, Brooke felt dizzy and disoriented. Too much excitement. She closed her eyes, feeling sick. After finishing the last of the bubbly, Jimmy and Johnny doubled over in pain, convulsing with spasms as they slumped down in their chairs. From the door, the nurse smiled.

Waiting a few minutes for the poison to seep into their systems and do the job, she quietly slipped back in the room, her hands sheathed in latex gloves. Humming, she put a skull mask on each corpse—and just to let Santiago know it was the work of the Red rock Slasher, placed a Ninja star at the base of each throat. Whistling, the nurse went into the bathroom and removed her wig and thick bifocals. Then she peeled off the disgusting uniform and heavy padding which added fifty pounds to her stature.

Michael grinned at his reflection in the mirror. "Who says three's a crowd? Killing three for the price of one saved me a lot of leg work."

Putting his toupee and mustache back on, Michael remade himself into the limousine driver. He tipped his red cap to his mirrored reflection.

"For you, Mama," He said. "I did it all for you. Vengeance was served on the O'Toole family for stealing your inheritance and my birthright."

With the weight of the world lifted from his shoulders, Michael went to the sleeping infants, removed Nicholas from his bed and hugged him tight. "Daddy's here to take you home." He placed him in his large canvas bag, zipping it closed with plenty of air so his son could breathe. Quietly slipping out the door, he cast a final glance at his cousins, the traitors. He clucked is tongue.

"Too bad about you, Brooke. Just a case of being at the wrong place at the wrong time." His work in Red Rock was just about complete. Now for Margot, his perfect wife. He'd thrust the sword into her cheating heart and then whisk his son off to his uncle's ski lodge in the Swiss Alps where they'd rule the universe. Indeed yes. He had a son, Michael Junior looked just like him and he couldn't wait to teach him the ways of absolute power.

Michael walked out of the hospital, swinging his bag back and forth, singing his favorite song to his son. *A hunting we will go, a hunting we will go. Heigh ho the dairy-oh, a hunting we will go.*

ЖЖЖ

"Let me out!" Margot screamed from within the chambers of Carlos DeVeccio's suite. "Somebody help me."

With his Ninja sword in hand, the death mask in his pocket, The Hunter unlocked his uncle's door and went in. The pipe organ was a real turn on, a graveyard smash. How it pleased him to hear the slut beg, frightened out of her wits, knowing sooner or later, she would die by the sword for her betrayal. And it was show time. His heart pumped a wild rhythm, sending a gush of adrenaline hurling through him. He loved the kill, watching his victims' eyes grow wide with horror when they knew it was coming. And The Hunter had come to pay Margot her due. Calling out to his wife, he bellowed, "Ready or not, here I come."

Margot's muffled screams filtered through the air vents, loud and clear. The Hunter grinned. Popping the lid, it flew back and Margot bolted upright, eyes wild with fright, patches of hair ripped out of her head, bloody fingers clutching the sides of the satin-lined coffin.

"Michael, please no!" she wailed, wretched sobs spewing when she spotted the bladed sword. She clutched her heart, trying to prevent the cruel attack she knew was coming any second. Her heart raced, blood thundering in her ears. "No!"

"I have no choice but to kill you," Michael's eyes gleamed with madness. "You betrayed me. You cheated on me, and you tried to trick me into thinking your lover's seed was mine. Tell me who he was and I might reconsider. Tell me, Darling Margot. Who's your lover?"

"No one."

"Liar!"

"It's true, believe me. Let me go and I'll never say a word about you trying to kill me, honest." She held up her left hand. "I'm wearing your mother's ring. Can you kill me knowing that, Michael?"

Hearing his mother's name sliced through some of the evil that had wedged its way into his heart for the past thirty years. He looked around. Then he looked at Margot's ring, his mother's ring, the rose-cut diamond surrounded by emeralds. How could he kill his wife when he was thinking of his mother? Tears flooded his eyes. But then he heard his uncle's voice in his head. "Honor the DeVeccio code: Betray me and die by the sword." With renewed vengeance, he came at Margot with the sword, ready to wield it into her lying, cheating heart for all he was worth.

You're evil. Evil. Evil. His mother's voice screeched in his head. Killing is a sin, a mortal sin. You are evil. Evil. Evil.

"No," Michael dropped the sword, his eyes wild and frantic. "I'm not evil. I'm your good boy, your good son. I'm sorry, Mama, no more killing, I promise. Just please don't be mad, Mama. Mama!"

Margot stared in horror and disbelief as Michael crumpled to the floor and wept like a child. Getting away while the going was good, she quietly slipped out of the casket and left the suite while Michael had his breakdown. Where was her gun? The gun Diego had given her? Then she remembered. It was stuffed in her cedar chest. If she hurried up, she could get it and be safe. Racing down the hallway, she slipped into the master bedroom and listened. She could hear Michael sobbing, talking away to his mother. He was sick, and she almost felt sorry for him.

Rummaging through her clothes, she felt the cold metal of the gun. She took it out and checked. Thank God, it was still loaded. She stood up, searching for her purse and car keys. She turned to leave and spied Michael silhouetted be-

hind the doorjamb. In his hand, a Ninja death star gleamed
in the late afternoon sun.

"Planning the great escape, Darling Margot?" his laughter
chilled her to the bone. "You'll never leave me. Don't you
know I'm the master swordsman. No one in this world can
out wit, out play, or outmaneuver Michael DeVeccio."

Margot licked her parched lips, pointed the .22 revolver at
Michael's heart, Diego's words reverberating in her head. *If
the gun is aimed at the target and the trigger is pressed and
the shot released, the bullet will hit the mark.*

"Goddamn whore!" chaotic rambling spewed from Michael's lips, unparalleled to anything she'd ever heard.
"Honor and obey. Betray me and die by the sword. Me and
my son will rule the world, the universe. Three cheers to the
DeVeccio heir. My son was born today. Michael Alan DeVeccio Junior is the splitting image of me. And now I've come for
you." He aimed the death star at Margot. "Any final last
words, Darling Margot? A last confession before I send you to
hell for your sins? Speak now or forever hold your peace."

Margot fired her gun three times, collapsing in a heavy
heap on the floor, her hand trembling from the after shock of
the gunfire that ricocheted off the walls. What had she done?
She had just killed her husband in cold blood, shot him to
death. How could she live with herself, taking a life, going
against all she'd been taught.

But then some of the haze in her head cleared as she realized Michael was still standing there, laughing at her, pointing. There was no blood spurting from his chest, no guts, no
gore. Had she just imagined shooting him? The lingering effects of the drugs in her system? But then Michael hurled the
Ninja star into her arm and she faded out. The last thing she
heard was his babbling. "You stupid woman. I'm wearing a
bullet proof vest. I found your gun weeks ago and have been
waiting to see if you dared use it on me. Stupid, stupid
woman. No one in this world can out wit, outplay, or outmaneuver Michael DeVeccio. I am the king of the universe."

CHAPTER FORTY-ONE

Detectives Diego Santiago and Samantha Stevenson tore through the gate of the DeVeccio estate. The security camera had been disengaged and the guard dogs were no where in sight. They had just left the crime scene in Brooke O'Toole's hospital room where all hell was breaking loose.

The frantic cries of Monique O'Toole had brought a nurse running, straight into the ghoulish nightmare. And just in the nick of time. Brooke and Jimmy and Johnny O'Toole had been rushed to surgery and had their stomachs pumped. They were expected to make a full recovery. And with the skull masks on their faces and the Ninja stars planted on their throats, Santiago knew it was the work of DeVeccio. He just hoped it wasn't too late for Margot.

They sped up the driveway, jumping out of the car, guns aimed and ready. Racing up the stone steps to the mansion, Santiago tried the door. It opened. Barging into the foyer, he yelled, "Police."

Several other detectives had arrived on the scene and had separated throughout the mansion, searching. Rage and fear battled it out in Santiago's head. DeVeccio had taken Margot somewhere, and he had the O'Toole baby he'd kidnapped. Where the hell would he take them?

"Got something here," Stevenson yelled from the great room. "Better come check it out."

Santiago fled down the corridor, his scuffed up boots hammering the hardwood floors like hail stones. The portrait of Carlos DeVeccio had been shoved aside to reveal a steel-vaulted room. On the wall was another vault, door wide open. "Holy shit," he whistled. "There must be five hundred Ninja stars in there and just as many latex skull masks. Looks like we finally nailed the billionaire, but we might be too late. We gotta find him. That nut's got Margot and the O'Toole baby. God only knows what he'll do with them."

"Upstairs, detective," one of the officers yelled. "Up in the house of horrors. Better come quick."

Fear snaked through every vein in Santiago's body. He pulled out his cell phone and called the forensic team. He wanted them up in Carlos DeVeccio's suite, pronto. If that sick sociopath had done to Margot what he had done to his ex-wife, he couldn't even go there. And when he saw the coffin with blood stains on the satin lining, chunks of coppery blonde hair in the casket, ten pink broken fingernails, and a discarded sword on the floor, Detective Diego Santiago fell to his knees and prayed.

ЖЖЖ

She felt wonderful so wonderful. Her white knight had rescued her from Michael and they drifted through the sky on a billowy cloud of satin and lace. Diego Santiago was all she ever wanted and more. She wanted to make love to him again and again. She reached for him.

"Get up, Bella," Michael loomed above her, a screaming infant in his arms. "What's wrong with ya, woman? Gonna sleep all day or what? My nephew needs fed and changed."

Stunned, Margot bolted upright, her heart pounding. Where had the baby come from? When she saw the identification bracelet dangling from his tiny little wrist, reality dawned.

The newborn was Nicholas O'Toole. Michael's obsession to have a son had apparently driven him to abduct his own nephew. Panic surged through her. She looked around. Where were they? And why had he called her Bella? Bella had been Carlos DeVeccio's wife. She scampered out of bed and raced to the window and gasped. Mountains and glaciers surrounded miles and miles of black forests and steep ravines. Far off in the distance, she recognized the peaks of the mighty Matterhorn towering high above the Swiss Alps.

Overcome with the need to bolt, run for her life and take her chances in the desolate Alps, Nicholas's frantic cries stopped Margot cold. She had to think, had to protect this newborn from the clutches of the madman. She gently took him from Michael. Surely the FBI had been called in on a child abduction to an O'Toole heir. With Diego working the case, they would figure out where Michael had taken them and would come to their rescue. She bit her lip, the baby's panic fueling her own as he wiggled and wailed in her arms.

"Michael, are there supplies up here?"

"Ya crazy woman, what's wrong with ya?" Michael's voice had a sanctimonious edge. "Callin' me Michael. Ya lost your mind or what? It's me, Carlos, your husband. Michael's my nephew, my brother's kid who I'm raisin' to take over the business. Ya crazy old bat, ya just ain't been right since Luciano's death. We're up here at my ski lodge in the Alps, ya know where we used to come for weekends after we were first married. Luciano was conceived here, don't ya remember? Now listen up cause I ain't gonna keep repeatin' myself. Kitchen pantry's stocked full of stuff, formula, bottled water, food. Diapers are in the boy's room, right next to ours. Geez, Bella, gotta wonder boutcha. How bout makin' me some breakfast, bacon and eggs, some strong black coffee. Go on, Bella, whatcha waitin' for, Christmas?"

Frightened out of her wits, Margot stared at Michael, her mouth agape. He had totally snapped, gone off the deep end and had taken on the identity of his uncle. Her mind raced. She desperately tried to tamp down her mounting fear. Did Michael really think he was Carlos DeVeccio and she was his wife Bella? Dear God, no. She rocked the screaming infant in her arms, her head woozy. How could she keep this baby safe from the clutches of a madman, a man who'd totally dissociated from himself?

"Hey, Bella," Michael's voice thundered across the chalet. "Ya see what I do with my cigars? Big Al and the boys'll be comin' over for the meetin' tomorrow night, so make sure we got plenty of booze. Make some pasta and sausage. Me and the boys, we got business. And when my nephew's older, I'm gonna teach 'em the ropes of the family, the ways of absolute power." He shot his fist high in the air. "The DeVeccio

Dynasty will rule the world."

ЖҚЖҚЖҚ

Margot feared for her life and the life of Nicholas. Michael's grandiose delusions became increasingly more and more bizarre with each passing day, and she didn't know what to do. They were in one of the most remote and desolate regions of the Swiss Alps, surrounded by treacherous mountains, forests, and glaciers. There was no power, no cell phones, no vehicles or means of escape. Just plenty of logs and candles.

Where had all the supplies come from, she wondered. And who had brought them here, dumped them off in the middle of nowhere? Michael's pilot? Was he coming back for them? When she opened the bedroom cupboard, it had all her casual clothes in it. Jeans and sweatshirts and hiking boots. She prayed Diego and the FBI would find them because as far as she could see, it had been a one-way ticket.

No sooner had Margot gotten Nicholas settled down in his crib when she heard Michael singing to him. Curious, she crept to his room and peeked in.

Michael towered over the baby, his fist held high in the air, bladed sword in hand, singing.

"*A hunting we will go, a hunting we will go. Heigh ho the dairy-o, a hunting we will go. We'll kill a fox and put him in a box. Heigh ho the dairy-o, a hunting we will go.*"

Something in Margot went ice cold. Nicholas's screams ripped through her like a harsh winter wind. Over her dead body would Michael plunge that blade into that innocent child. His own nephew. Rushing past him, she snatched the baby from the crib and held him tight, cooing to him as her heartbeat tripled. Anger soared and she let him have it.

What's wrong with you?" she hissed between clenched teeth. "Can't you see how scared he is? Were you planning on killing your own nephew? And what could be wrong with you, singing that morbid song to him? Don't do it again, I forbid it."

"Ya what?" Michael cracked her hard across the face. "Who the hell ya think ya are, Bella? Ya know the rules. Honor and obey. No mouthin' off, no givin' me no lip or else. No one tells Carlos DeVeccio what to do and gets away with it. That's the huntin' song, same song my papa taught me. And what's this about killin' my own nephew? Ya crazy or what? Boy's gotta learn to recognize the battle blade so he understands the DeVeccio code of honor. Betray me and die by the sword. Now go on woman, get me a bourbon on the rocks."

Ж҉Ж҉Ж҉

Gales of manic laughter woke Margot up. Disoriented, she sat up in bed and looked around in the room that was as black as midnight. She lit the bedside candle, slowly taking in her surroundings as her mind cleared. She was in the ski lodge in the Alps, where Michael had her and Nicholas captive. But then she heard it again, gales of psychotic laughter. A foreboding chill sliced through her straight to the bone. Nicholas.

Heart thumping, she raced to him. He was sleeping soundly, sucking his thumb. Then she heard voices, laughter, and she detected smoke, cigar smoke. She listened, her ears erect. Definitely more than one voice. Diego? The FBI? Hope soared, but caution ruled. She crept down the corridor to the hall which resembled the great room at the mansion. The door was slightly ajar and she peeked in, feeling like she'd just entered the twilight zone.

Michael sat at the head of a large ebony table surrounded by twelve chairs. In all four corners of the room, standing candelabras flickered in the dark, casting willowy shadows on the walls. Silver ashtrays and drinks sat on the table in front of each empty seat, and on the lip of each ashtray, a burning cigar rested. Above Michael's head, two Ninja swords gleamed in the candlelit hall. Michael sat at the head of the table presiding over twelve empty seats, wearing the skull mask, his fist shot upward. Then with a sudden jolt, he slammed his fist on the table with the force of a judge's gable.

"Order in the court, order in the court. This meetin' will now come to order. The honorable Carlos DeVeccio presiding." Michael sucked on his cigar through a gaping hole in the mouth of the mask. "Now ya boys all know the rules. Betray me and die by the sword. And one of ya double-crossed me, thinkin' ya could rob me blind. Now who's gonna own up to bein' a traitor?" his voice thundered across the hall. "Ya boys should know by now, no one in the world can out wit, out play, or outmaneuver Carlos DeVeccio." He pointed to the empty seat next to him. "Pay close attention, Michael. I'm gonna teach ya how to take care of traitors, show ya how to be a good hunter. Pretty soon, son, you'll be expected to hunt, face up to your responsibilities and be a real man. There's gonna be an execution tonight and you're gonna learn how to be an assassin. The traitor's right here at the table, drinkin' my booze and smokin' my best cigars. Someone sittin' here ain't gonna leave these Alps alive, ain't gonna be nothin' left but a corpse. So watch and learn, Michael. Watch the master at work."

"No, Uncle Carlos," Michael pleaded in the voice of a boy. "Please don't kill him. Killing's wrong, a big mortal sin. Mama and Papa taught me the Ten Commandments. Killing is wrong. Please, Uncle Carlos, no."

"Shut up, wimp. You're nothin' but a sissy, a mama's boy. Grow up. You're a disgrace to the family, a freak of nature. No more mouthin' off or I'll give ya somethin' to cry about, in front of the boys. Ya only got one commandment under my roof: honor and obey. Betray me and die by the sword. Remember that rule, son."

Sobs poured from Michael as he went back in time to his childhood. He threw his head on the table, his voice trembling. "I won't kill. It's a sin, Uncle Carlos, a big sin. No!"

"Dare ya defy me, Michael?" he swiped at the air. Then he stood up and grabbed a sword from the wall. "I'm gonna teach ya how to kill, be a hunter. Killin' the betrayer's all for the sake of absolute power. Control and manipulation's the name of the game. The DeVeccio Dynasty will rule the world, the universe. And how do ya think I built my snazzy casino on Las Vegas Boulevard, right next to the Flamingo? By knockin' off the competition and traitors. And you're gonna be The Hunter, startin' tonight. Ya gotta prove your manhood. Why do ya think I programmed the hunting song in every room, in the cars, the limo? So killin' would get into your blood. Think of it as a game, a sport, like an action figure in an action movie. You'll learn to like it, son, I promise. Now take the sword and show me what you're made of. Plunge it into Big Al's heart for rippin' us off. Honor and obey. Don't disappoint me or else. Honor and obey. Take the sword. Do it now, Michael."

And then Margot watched Michael take the sword and stab the air three times before collapsing in a heap on the floor, wretched sobs coming out of him as he got to his knees and looked upwards, begging forgiveness. "Forgive me, Father, for I have sinned."

CHAPTER
FORTY-TWO

Diego starred in Margot's dreams from that night on. Bow and arrow in hand, he let out a warrior's cry of battle as he leaped out of the forest and into the clearing to rescue her from Michael. If only it were true, she mused, feeding a bottle to Nicholas. After what she'd witnessed last night, she almost felt sorry for Michael. No wonder his mind was so twisted, all those conflicting battles raging through him. Watching Michael relive his first kill at the command of his uncle made her weep for the boy in him. Carlos DeVeccio had brainwashed his nephew for so many years part of him lived on in Michael's demented mind. How could she escape the madman and free herself and Nicholas before he turned on them? Tears rolled down her cheeks as she prayed. "Please God, help us all."

"Good morning, Darling Margot." Michael came in on a gust of brisk pine air. He smelled of the wood he'd been chopping. "And how's my beautiful wife and our son today?" he kissed them both and smiled. "So how do you like it up here in the wilderness, far away from civilization. No cell phones, televisions, computers, or any of the modern amenities we've come to depend on in today's society. Just all this beauty of the Swiss Alps. Uncle Carlos used to bring me up here to his ski lodge when I was a boy, when Aunt Bella was still alive, after Luciano was killed. He taught me how to hunt in these very woods. So how about some breakfast? Bacon and eggs? I'll make them since you're busy with our son. You're so gorgeous, Margot. Motherhood really agrees with you."

Margot stared at Michael. How could he dissociate from himself, take on the identity of Carlos DeVeccio one minute and then be in his own mind the next? A time lapse of better than thirty years? He was far more sick than she realized. After what she'd seen last night, she understood. It all made sense. Michael had been psychologically abused by a monster, a gangster without a heart or soul. Carlos DeVeccio had stolen Michael's identity.

Margot watched Michael fry eggs and bacon over the fireplace, remembering the time he'd made breakfast for her and Sophia. If she knew then what she knew now she would have never married him. She bit her lip, nervous and afraid. How long before he killed her?

"Here you go, Margot," he placed a platter of steaming food on the table. "Allow me to pour your coffee. Why don't we go for a walk in the woods later, a little family hike. I want to show Michael Junior the sights and sounds of nature. He'll love all the birds out there, woodpeckers, larks, all kinds of songbirds. You'll enjoy it too. I can't tell you how much it pleases me that you have given birth to my heir. I'll spend the rest of my life treating you like the queen you are." He took her hand and kissed his mother's ring. "Margot, what happened to your fingers and your fingernails? They're all skinned up and your nails are a mess. When we get back to Vegas, I'll treat you to a day at the spa so you can be pampered. And despite what you say, I'm hiring a nanny. Look at you, working your fingers to the bone. Don't worry about those bald patches where your hair fell out. It's strictly hormones from giving birth. I remember Mama talking about hair loss after my birth. You'll drop those extra pounds and your hair will grow back in no time at all. Not to worry. Now finish your breakfast so we can take our little hike."

Ж◇Ж◇Ж

Under the sun-drenched skies of the mighty Alps, Michael took them for a hike in the forest. With the crisp, clean air, alpine scent, and alluring sights and sounds of nature, Margot nearly forgot they weren't just an ordinary family exploring the beauty of the Swiss Alps.

Woodlarks and mountain songbirds chirped noisily from their habitats, and an abundance of fresh water fish swam in the mirror-still waters of the surrounding lakes. With a swooping of wings, a bearded vulture soared down from the azure blue sky and ducked into the thicket. In the heart of the forest, a crimson-crowned black woodpecker drilled into the bark of an alpine.

Margot wished she were here with Diego, birdwatching just as they had in Willow Park all those months ago. How she missed him. She wondered if she would ever see him again. She had no idea how long they had been in the Alps. But judging by the cooling temperatures and the ever-changing foliage, they had reached autumn's end. And once winter set in up in these mountains, no one would ever find them. She searched the woods for a hiker, someone to rescue them. But other than the natural habitat of the woodland pines and the call of the nightingale's echo through the thick black forest, all was quiet.

"Michael," she watched him carefully. "How long are we staying up here at your uncle's cabin?"

"Forever," he kissed her, tweaking the baby's cheek. "Until the end of time. I've transferred all my money up here to a Swiss bank account, and once my son grows up, we'll rule the universe from up here in the Alps. Isn't this great, away from all those pressures back in Vegas? We'll live happily ever after, just the three of us."

"But sooner or later, we'll run out of supplies," Margot's voice caught in her throat. "And how can you get to the bank with no car? We're up here all alone with no power, no transportation, and the baby needs things. We can't just stay here forever, that's insane. How..."

"Margot," he soothed. "Don't you worry your pretty little head. Look over there by the cabin, see it? That's my truck. How do you think we got here from the airport? Did you forget? And what do you mean, no power. Didn't you hear the music playing this morning when the alarm went off? You saw me make breakfast on the electric stove with your own two eyes. I think a walk in the clean crisp air is just what you need to clear your mind, get the fog out."

If not for the baby, Margot would have lost her mind right then and there. But someone had to stay sane, keep the baby safe. Horrified, she watched Michael point out several other things which were only visible in his demented mind. Good God, she just didn't have the expertise to handle a person with such a twisted sense of reality. She didn't want to trigger him off, send him on a killing spree. So she had no choice but to agree to seeing and hearing things which only existed in Michael's mind.

Nicholas suddenly became very animated, pointing wildly, gurgling away. An elegant white swan swooped onto the mirror still waters of the crystal blue lake, barely skimmed the surface, and emerged with a salmon dangling from its beak. The still waters rippled slightly like the calm before the storm.

"Lying whore!" Michael sprinted onto a mount of rocks, his eyes burning with an unnatural brightness. He pointed his finger. "Lying whore! Whose baby is that? Did you really think you could fool me into thinking your bastard was my son? You betrayed our wedding vows. What ever happened to honor and obey, Darling Margot? Lying whore! Betray me and die by the sword. I adored you, allowed you to wear my mother's ring. Take it off! Take it off, slut. You aren't worthy to wear Mama's ring. Give it to me."

Margot spun on her heels and ran for her life, hysterical infant in arms.

Michael bellowed from his makeshift pulpit, ranting and raving like a man possessed. "Die by the sword. He's coming. The Hunter's coming for you and when he catches you, he'll pierce you straight through your lying, cheating heart. Then he'll place the death mask on your corpse and feed you to the vultures. You can run, but you can't hide. The Hunter is coming. He's coming for you. The Hunter is coming to catch you. Catch a fox and put her in a box. The Hunter is coming tonight at midnight!"

Disturbed by the mayhem breaking out in the quiet serenity, the nightingale sang out in protest, taking flight through the thicket as Michael's thundering voice shook the entire forest. With Nicholas clutched close to her heart, Margot tore through the woods of the black forest toward the chalet. If she got there first, she could lock out the madman. "God, help me," she risked a look over her shoulder just as he pounced high in the air, landed on his feet, and gave chase through the forest, gaining speed rapidly.

With the sprint of a marathon runner, Margot ran over

the thick underbrush, slipping on wet pine needles, the smell of the dank earth filling her senses. She couldn't breathe, her heart pumped out blood like a fuel tank. She couldn't fall, couldn't drop the baby. Then she tripped on a gnarled stump, went down on one knee, and regained her footing, her breathing labored. Michael stormed through the forest toward her, twigs and branches snapping beneath his feet, his booming voice alarming a cuckoo bird. "Cuckoo! Cuckoo! Cuckoo!"

"He is coming. Tonight at midnight. The Hunter will catch you. Catch a fox and put her in a box. The Hunter will catch you." his laughter rang through the woods of the black forest.

The frantic cries of the birds reverberated through the thicket. "Cuckoo! Cuckoo! Cuckoo!"

Just as Margot reached the door to the chalet, Michael caught up, snatching the baby from her arms. "Hand 'em over, ya crazy woman. What's wrong with ya, Bella? Racin' through the woods like that with Michael, huh? Even the damn birds think ya gone cuckoo. Didn't ya hear them, cryin' out to ya back there. Ya aroused a whole family of cuckoo birds and nutcrackers. They all sense how looney ya are. When we get back to Vegas, I'm gonna get ya a shrink. Ya just ain't been right since our boy got killed. Come on, Bella, I miss Luciano too, but we gotta move on, here with my brother's kid. Michael's our son now. Forget Luciano, he's dead and buried."

He peered into Nicholas's eyes. "And what's wrong with ya, huh, kid? Cryin' like some sissy, a mama's boy. Don't be such a girl. How ya gonna grow up to be a hunter when a flock of birds gotcha all shook up, huh? Got a grow up to be a man, a real man. A hunter." Michael shot his fist high in the air. "The DeVeccio Dynasty will rule the world. Now listen up, Michael. Your Uncle Carlos's gonna sing ya a song, one I wanna program into your head so ya can grow up with the thrill of the hunt in your blood. Listen up. *A hunting we will go, a hunting we will go. Heigh ho the dairy-o, a hunting we will go. We'll kill a fox and put him in a box. Heigh ho the dairy-o, a hunting we will go.*"

CHAPTER FORTY-THREE

It took Margot forever to settle Nicholas down. After feeding him, she placed him in the cradle and covered him, hoping he'd be warm enough. Kissing him good night, she sang to him, gently rocking him until he fell asleep.

Walking to the window, she looked up to the heavens, wished upon a star, and fell to her knees and prayed. "Please God, please send help."

Realistically, she knew it was impossible, but in her heart, she hoped for Diego to come to her rescue like a white knight. Were the police still looking for her and Nicholas or had they given up searching? How could they find her in this desolate area of the Swiss Alps, so far from civilization? Her family probably had her funeral, knowing Michael had abducted her. She wondered if she'd ever see Diego or her family and friends again.

Who was responsible for dropping them off here in the middle of nowhere? Had it been Michael's pilot? Maybe it was that weird butler or the cook who spoke so little English. Since she had been drugged, she was clueless. She didn't know how anyone with a conscience could do such a thing, knowing that an infant's life would be severely compromised. How could this person sleep at night, thinking about a baby stranded in the mountains? And surely the pilot was aware that the baby had been abducted.

That was the trump card Margot was betting on, even though it was a chance in a million. She was hoping against all odds the pilot would have a guilty conscience and go to the police. But too much time had gone by, and in her heart of hearts, she knew the chances of ever being rescued were dwindling as quickly as the last of the autumn leaves.

The chalet, although warm and comfortable with all the wood fire for burning, was a far cry from the comforts of home. How she missed her bubble baths and showers. She had never been one for roughing it. It was dark now, and the alpine winds had kicked up in the last hour or so, causing the massive trees in front of the balcony to rock and roll above the Rhine River. They made Margot nervous. The thought of being held captive with a madman in the middle of a blizzard in the Swiss Alps was something she couldn't think about. Sighing, she lit the candles just as Michael entered the room, wondering which identity had current control of his mind. When he shot his fist high in the air, she knew—and her body went limp with fear.

But his eyes were different, cold and hard. Other than the time he had struck her when he had thought she was Bella, telling him what to do, he had never looked at her with such hatred. She nervously licked her lips as he glared at her. The change in the air was palpable, sending goose bumps skating down her neck and back.

"Tonight's your hearing. Come with me to the great room where the boys are waitin to cast their votes. Watcha waitin' for? Come with me. I am Carlos DeVeccio and it's judgment day."

This couldn't be happening. Margot stared in shocked hor-ror as Michael placed handcuffs around her wrist and dragged her down the hall to the great room, kicking and screaming. Good God, how could she get out of this alive? And the baby? Her body drenched with sweat, she tripped over her own two feet as Michael shoved her into one of the twelve seats around the ebony table. She watched as he placed his skull mask on his face and slammed his fists down with a jarring thud. All empty seats had been set with cocktails and ashtrays, a burn-ing cigar in each one. In all four corners of the hall, standing candelabras flickered in the darkened room. Michael lit a cigar, letting it hang out of a gaping hole in his mask. With a punch that rocked the whole table, the trial began.

"Order in the court. Order in the court. The honorable Carlos DeVeccio presiding'. We're here tonight to judge Margot DeVeccio for the attempted murder of my nephew, Michael Alan DeVeccio. She shot him three times in the heart, thinkin' she could do him in. But I trained Michael well. My nephew ain't no idiot. He was wearin' a bullet proof vest, got wise to her plan. And before that, she cheated on him, tried to pass off her bastard kid as his. How do ya plead, traitor? Answer me."

Margot stared in horror. What was she supposed to say? She didn't know what answer might get her death by the sword. She prayed to God for the wisdom and courage to handle Michael's psychosis.

"Answer me, traitor!" Michael beat his fist on the table again and again. "How do ya plead?"

What should she do? Her flannel robe was drenched with sweat. She thought her head would explode as Michael's pounding got louder and louder. Not knowing what else to do, she broke down and sobbed.

"Ya had your chance. Now we're gonna vote on your fate, my boys sittin' here. So what'll it be boys?"

"Guilty," Michael announced in twelve different voices. "Death by the sword for her betrayal."

"Seems the boys are all in agreement."

Lord almighty, what should she do? Licking her dry lips, Margot tried to reach Michael, the man buried beneath all those layers of psychosis. "Please, Michael. Come back to me. I promise to get you the help you need. I love you, remember? I'm your Darling Margot. Please come back. You're not your uncle. Your uncle's dead. He did this to you, made you sick with all his brainwashing. You were just an innocent boy. Remember our Tuscan honeymoon? When you showed me the hills you used to pick wild flowers for your Mama? Michael?"

"Death by the sword for the queen bitch slut!" Michael beat the table. "Death by the sword for the queen bitch slut!"

His ranting had awakened Nicholas. His hysterical screams pierced straight through Margot's heart.

"The Hunter will execute you tomorrow at midnight. Take her away, boys. Lock her up and throw away the key."

CHAPTER FORTY-FOUR

Buck Chandler's mind was not on business. He had been messing up major deals for the past three months, and even though he was the CEO of the finance company founded by his granddaddy close to a century ago, he just didn't give a good damn. Nothing mattered. He was drinking heavy, losing weight, and his ulcer was kicking up with all the fury of a bucking bronco.

Staring at her husband that night, Babs Chandler had enough of his odd behavior. Hand on her hip, she demanded, "What in the hell is goin' on with you, Buck?" she wagged her finger. "And don't even think about fibbin' to me cause I'll whup your sorry ass from here to Texas."

"Dear God," Buck ran his hands through his thin crop of salt and pepper hair. "If I don't get this off my chest pretty soon, I swear I'll bust a gut."

"Well," Babs towered above him. "Start talkin'."

Pouring himself three fingers of bourbon, Buck walked over to the portrait of his prized Thoroughbred and stared at the horse for a moment, a tear rolling down his cheek.

"Michael DeVeccio never does anything without a price. Back at his masquerade ball, it came up in conversation I had a pilot's license. Then we got around to talking about Thoroughbred racing, and I told him how someone had poisoned Big Red an hour before last year's race. I asked him for help. I wanted those sons of bitches to pay for hurtin' our top Thoroughbred, so I had DeVeccio hunt them down. He found them and took care of the problem. I knew the day would come when he'd collect, and he called the debt in when he abducted the O'Toole boy and had me fly his family to some ski lodge deep in the Swiss Alps where no one would ever find them. I swear, DeVeccio's lower than a snake's belly, and I'm lower than pond scum for doin' it. I only agreed cause he said if I didn't, he'd kill ya." Walking over to the phone, Buck said, "I'll call the police and turn myself in."

"Ask for Detective Santiago," Babs commanded. "He's workin' the homicide case and he's a personal friend of mine. Diego Santiago is part Navajo Indian. Believe me, DeVeccio will never see or hear him comin'. You and Diego will fly up to the Swiss Alps soon as it can be arranged, and Diego Santiago will take care of Michael DeVeccio."

ЖЖЖ

The plan was set. Santiago and Buck joined forces to organize a rescue mission for Margot and the O'Toole baby. Between Buck's expert piloting skills and Santiago's capability of orchestrating a sneak attack on the enemy, they would get DeVeccio. Santiago prayed they wouldn't be too late.

Even though his first instinct had been to kill Buck for being a part of such a self-serving act, he understood how he had been manipulated by DeVeccio. DeVeccio was a sociopath. Deciding finger pointing at this point would be a waste of energy, they united as a team.

Buck informed the rescue team the chalet lay nestled in one of the most remote parts of the Alps, and with the fierce wind and snow storm heading toward the northern and southern region of the mountain range, the rescue mission couldn't happen at a worse possible time.

Santiago wasn't about to let anything stop him from getting to Margot. The Swiss Air Rescue Helicopter had been advised of the situation and was close behind with a full crew of doctors and paramedics. The Swiss authorities had been informed of an armed and dangerous man, holding a woman and infant and were sending backup. Santiago had his International cell phone in his pocket, ready for whatever lay ahead. Bound and determined to bring Margot and the baby home safely, Santiago and Buck made the journey across the Alps.

ЖЖЖ

High winds and wet blowing snow rocked the fuselage of the twin-engine helicopter as it neared the Alps. Although visibility was poor, Buck managed to maneuver the small aircraft with amazing skill over the high altitude of the rough terrain. As they hurdled through the worst of the squalling snow storm, visibility cleared, and the jagged peaks of the mighty Matterhorn came into view. Symmetrical and spellbinding, the pyramidal summit between Switzerland and Italy was as beckoning as it was foreboding.

Shrouded in brightness by the helicopter lights, the glaciers glistened like diamonds. As the chopper made its final descent, Buck extinguished all exterior lights of the aircraft.

"Just like my military days in the army," he said, masterfully navigating the helicopter through the darkened sky. "Can't alert the enemy we're comin' in." Rolling the throttle to the off position, he hovered briefly before the skid wheels touched the snow covered ground at the foot of the hill leading to the chalet.

"Nice job," Santiago said as they jumped out of the cockpit, landing in a drift of knee-deep snow.

Buck let out a low whistle after the daunting flight, packed a huge wad of tobacco into his cheek, pulled his ski cap securely over his ears, and said, "Hell of a storm."

Surrounded by glaciers, avalanches, and bitter terrain, the uphill journey began. Ferocious winds whipped through the pines, making an eerie, foreshadowing whistle. Banks of snow and fallen trees made walking difficult as well as hazardous. They trudged through the snow in silence. Armed with Glocks and semi-automatics, they concentrated on the mission ahead.

With the aid of light from powerful penlights, the chalet came into view. As they neared their destination, Buck tumbled head first into a deep snowdrift, causing a huge crevasse to form beneath his weight. Thrusting his arm out to assist him, Santiago yanked him to his feet, and they proceeded.

Just as Santiago was about to ask Buck how much farther, he came to a dead halt when his flashlight brought the balcony into focus. A massive pine tree had crashed clean through the middle of the ledge, ripping it off in huge, jagged pieces. The broken ledge hung above the icy and merciless currents of the Rhine River, black and wicked underneath the mighty Alps.

"Good Lord," Santiago whistled, slowly letting out the air in his lungs. "We gotta get in there, pronto." he looked up at the sky, reaching for his International cell phone. "Where the hell's the rescue helicopter with those paramedics? God only knows what we're walking into. Let's go."

Climbing the steps to the balcony, they walked in dead silence, snow and ice crunching beneath their booted feet. Keeping close to the wall of the chalet, away from the ruptured ledge, they inched closer to the glass door of the balcony. Margot's screams pierced through the Alps. Motioning for Buck to get down, Santiago silhouetted himself in the dark shadows of the mighty pines and peeked in the glass door. And his heart stopped beating.

"Catch a fox and put her in a box!" Michael chased Margot and the baby through the chalet with a Ninja sword, a latex skull mask on his face. His bellowing voice rocked the cabin. *"Heigh ho the dairy-o, a hunting we will go."*

"No, Michael," Margot wailed over the baby's hysterical cries, panting in between screams. "Please, no."

"Gotcha." Dark laughter bubbled from deep in his throat as his arm clamped around her waist, the tip of the blade pressed into her throat. *"Catch a fox and put her in a box. Heigh ho the dairy-o, a hunting we will go."*

As many times as Santiago had imagined DeVeccio in action, nothing could compare to seeing it unfold before his very eyes. He aimed his gun at DeVeccio's head, but didn't fire. Too close, too damn close to Margot and the baby's head. DeVeccio was practically on top of them, whispering in Margot's ear. Santiago tightened his grip on the Glock, his hands slick with sweat.

Then suddenly DeVeccio snatched the baby from Margot's arms, his cackles wild and inhuman. Santiago tracked DeVeccio with his aim, not daring to shoot. If he did, the baby would fall out of his grip and get hurt...or worse. Margot fled after him, begging, "Please, Michael. Don't hurt him. Give him back to me, please. He's just a baby."

Still cackling, Michael tossed the baby on the sofa and tore after Margot, "Catcha fox and put her in a box. The Hunter is hot on your heels. Run, rabbit, run!"

Wild with hysteria, Margot raced to the balcony door, flung it open and ran out into the harsh winds, stopping when she got to the edge of the slippery ledge. The ferocious wind howled through the mighty Alps, snow-blanketed branches swaying back and forth. She stared down into the depths of the Rhine River, ice glistening on its rippling currents. Tossing her hands in the air, she screamed, "Help me!"

But it was too late for help. Michael's steely arms snaked around her like a cobra, pressing the tip of the blade in her throat. He whispered in her ear, "Gotcha."

"Police," Santiago came out of the shadows. "Drop your sword, DeVeccio. It's all over."

Michael spun on his heels, freeing Margot. "Detective Santiago. Welcome to the execution of my wife, the traitorous whore. But you'd know all about that, wouldn't you? I had my suspicions but now I'm convinced. You're the one who planted his seed in my wife. It was your bastard she carried in her womb. And you'll suffer. Death by the sword for both of you, a double execution shall we say. Two shows for the price of one." With his Jack-be-nimble fingers, Michael wielded his sword through the air, nicking Santiago's shoulder. Santiago fired his gun, hitting Michael in the chest, sending him skating backwards to the slippery edge of the balcony.

Steadying himself on the balls of his feet, Michael howled like a coyote, his eerie wailing echoing across the mountains. The bitter wind whistled, blowing snow all askew. With his skull mask still on, the laughter grew more and more psychotic. Michael shot his fist high in the air, blood spurting from his wound. "The DeVeccio Dynasty will rule the world. Long live the king!" Then he puffed out his chest, his voice deep and gruff. "Shut up, ya wimp. Quit bein' such a girl. When are ya gonna face up to your responsibilities and be a man, a real man? You're a disgrace to the family, a freak of nature. You are The Hunter, the assassin. Now when I tell ya to kill someone, ya do it, no questions asked. And I'm tellin' ya to plunge the sword into Big Al for rippin' us off. Honor and obey. Do as I say or else. Do it, Michael."

"No, Uncle Carlos," his voice changed into that of a young boy's. "Killing is a sin, a mortal sin. Mama and Papa taught me the Ten Commandments. Thou shall not kill. Killing is wrong."

"Ya big sissy," his voice was deep and gruff. "Get a backbone, kid. Grow up and do as I say. The only commandment you gotta follow now is this one—honor and obey or else. I'm trainin' ya to take over the business some day. Control and manipulation are the driving forces to absolute power. Can't let the competition get in our way. We will rule the world. Kill him, do it now."

Sobbing like a little boy, Michael stabbed the air three times and fell to his knees. "Forgive me, Father, for I have sinned. I'm sorry, Mama. Don't be mad. He made me do it. Uncle Carlos made me kill. Mama, come back. I'm still your good little boy. I'm not evil. I promise I'll never kill anyone again. Mama!"

Then with lightning speed, his fingers snaked out and snatched his sword from the ground. He stood up and bellowed, "I'm The Hunter. *Heigh ho the dairy-oh, a hunting we will go.* Catch a fox and put him in a box. The Hunter is coming." He wield his sword straight at Santiago's heart, laughing hysterically. "Gotcha."

Dodging the sword, Santiago fired his Glock at Michael's chest twice, sending him floundering over the edge of the ruptured balcony. Over the hissing winds hurling through the mighty Alps, the Swiss Air Rescue Helicopter hovering above the chalet, and the baby's wailing, Michael's haunting words reverberated through the mountains as he tumbled to his death.

"Die by the sword!"

EPILOGUE

The Swiss Rescue Team began the search for the missing skier in what was reported to be the worst blizzard in ten years. Blistering wind howled through the Alps as the team trudged onward, listening for transmitter signals.

"Keep an eye out for a yellow knapsack," the leader's voice echoed through the mighty Alps. "She's twenty-five years old and is wearing a red parka."

The rescue helicopter circled above, shedding light on the pure white snow. A snowmobile released a team of rescue dogs. The German shepherds took off, dashing through the deep snow and avalanches, barking and yipping.

"Temperature's been dropping all day," the leader said, listening for muffled sounds coming from the banks of snow. "If we don't find this missing skier in the next thirty minutes, she'll freeze to death. I think it's time to form a probe line."

The twenty volunteers silently formed a line and began probing the snow with their poles as they climbed up the slope. In unison, they probed to the left, middle and then to the right. Once certain no body was beneath them, they moved a few feet and repeated the ritual in silence, listening for any muffled cries.

Suddenly the dogs began barking frantically. The rescue team jumped on the snowmobile and tore through the snow in the direction of the yips. When they arrived, the dogs were digging, barking excitedly.

The helicopter idled above, coming down for a landing. Using flashlights, the rescue team got closer. Dark crimson blood soiled the clean white snow. The dogs barking echoed over the howling wind swooshing through the pines. Then the body was uncovered, the dogs licking and panting.

"Holy shit," the team leader was the first to speak. "What the hell is that? Is it human? It's wearing a green skull mask and a black hooded coat."

"It's a man and he's alive," the paramedics reported, whipping off the mask. "Barely. He's lost a hell of a lot of blood. Let's get him to a clinic. I doubt he'll live, though."

Dear Reader:

I hope you enjoyed Book one in the sequel series. Mask of the Betrayer is my debut thriller, and I thoroughly enjoyed the research. The mind has always fascinated me. It can bend. It can break. It can snap. As I learned in my psychology classes, the majority of mental illnesses stem from a childhood trauma, either sexual or mental abuse. Would Michael DeVeccio have turned out differently if he hadn't been brainwashed by his controlling uncle? While it was pretty alarming to get inside the mind of a killer, Mask of the Betrayer sketches a very prolific picture of the man behind the mask.

Just like the old nighttime soaps, Mask of the Betrayer ends with a cliffhanger. Book two opens two years later with the wedding of Margot and Diego. But will their happiness last? I guess you'll have to find out in the sequel. Coming soon to bookstores near you: Vendetta. Until then, thanks for reading my books. Happy reading!

ABOUT THE AUTHOR

Sharon Donovan lives in Pittsburgh, Pennsylvania with her family. Prior to the loss of her vision, she was a legal secretary for the Court of Common Pleas where she prepared cases for judges in Domestic Relations. Painting was her passion. When she could no longer paint, she began attending creative writing classes and memoir workshops. After a long and winding road, a new dream resurrected. Today, instead of painting her pictures on canvas, Sharon paints her pictures with words.

Sharon is a published author with The Wild Rose Press,

White Rose Publishing and Chicken Soup for the Soul, Tough Times, Tough People. Echo of a Raven is a Recommended Read from the reviewers of Coffee Time Romance & More.

To read more about Sharon, her other books of inspiration and suspense and to sign up for her newsletter, visit her at: www.sharonadonovan.com

Blog: http://sharondonovan.blogspot.com

or Contact her at sharonad@comcast.net. She loves to hear from readers!

Breinigsville, PA USA
30 April 2010
237147BV00001B/3/P

9 781936 167067